"I demand that you stop this, Damien de Ashby, until you explain what you are doing and why."

"What I am doing," he answered, his voice hoarse with what he was suppressing, "is attempting to disrobe you, Alissende. With your permission, of course."

He made the effort to sound far more normal than he felt.

"I do believe that I promised to extract triple payment from you for the tender torments you played upon me in this very tent."

"That you did," she agreed.

"And you admitted to trembling with dread at the prospect of it."

"Aye, I do recall."

"You are trembling now, are you not?" he asked.

Alissende met his gaze.

"Aye," she said. "But no more than you are, I think, my lord."

MARY REED McCALL

"captures your heart."
Samantha James

"[is] dazzling!"
Teresa Medeiros

Other **AVON ROMANCES**

MARY REED McCALL

Sinful Pleasures

THE TEMPLAR KNIGHTS

AVON BOOKS
An Imprint of HarperCollinsPublishers

AVON BOOKS
An Imprint of HarperCollins*Publishers*
10 East 53rd Street
New York, New York 10022-5299

Copyright © 2006 by Mary Reed McCall
ISBN-13: 978-0-06-059374-2
ISBN-10: 0-06-059374-1
www.avonromance.com

First Avon Books paperback printing: June 2006

Avon Trademark Reg. U.S. Pat. Off. and in Other Countries, Marca Registrada, Hecho en U.S.A.
HarperCollins® is a registered trademark of HarperCollins Publishers Inc.

Printed in the U.S.A.

10 9 8 7 6 5 4 3 2 1

Acknowledgments

My sincere gratitude to:

John, Megan, and Rebecca, who make every day a present just waiting to be opened . . .

David and Marion Reed, for their page-by-page critiquing, love, and unfailing support, especially when I'm tearing my hair out with a stubborn character, plot point, or scene . . .

The artists who made my work on this book so much easier with their music, including Josh Groban, Sarah McLachlan, Enya, and Patrick Doyle, whose score of "Non Nobis Domine" from the sound track of *Henry V* plays in the background every time I write a Templar scene . . .

Annelise Robey and Meg Ruley, for generously sharing their immense talents with me . . .

And Lyssa Keusch, for her phenomenal ability to cut through the rock in search of the tiny gem beneath—and her encouragement in helping me polish that until it shines . . .

Thank you all.

Non nobis, Domine, non nobis,
sed Nomini, Tuo da gloriam . . .
(*Not for us, Lord, not for us
but to Thy Name give glory . . .*)

MOTTO OF THE KNIGHTS TEMPLAR

Hell is not only for the dead. I understood this truth when they handed me over for interrogation by the French Inquisition—I and thousands of my Templar brethren, all accused of heresy.

If any were guilty, I knew it not.

As for me, I had never been aught but devoted to the glory of God. That truth did not seem to move my inquisitors. If anything, my protestations of innocence only spurred them on to greater cruelties in their zeal to obtain my confession, until I could no longer utter a word for the agonies they inflicted upon me.

Aye, it was torment so relentless, it is a wonder I survived at all . . .

The letters of Sir Damien de Ashby
The year of our Lord, 1315

Prologue

Château du Étoile, outside Montivilliers, France
March 1308

Darkness fast approached; there could be no further delay.

Shadowy tendrils stabbed through the crimson light creeping in at the shutters of the turret, but Lady Alissende of Surrey remained motionless, her fingers clenched and her heart rebellious under the weight of this decision she was being asked to accept. Breathing deeply, she lifted her troubled gaze first to her widowed mother, the still beautiful Lady Blanche, then to her recently ordained second cousin and adored companion of childhood, Father Michael, seeking some berth from the emotions churning inside her.

There was naught but bleak acceptance in their expressions. That and perhaps the expectation that she

1

should concede to the necessity of what they had placed before her.

Another burst of defiance flared in Alissende's breast, fueled by her desperation. She shook her head, almost choking on the words. "I cannot do this, Michael! Please . . . there must be another way—"

"There is not, *amie*," he broke in, his voice heavy with regret. He lifted his gentle gaze to hers, his brow furrowed. "There is no time to seek another. You know my brother. Hugh will not be content to relinquish his claim to you unless he is compelled by law to it. We were fortunate to gain these few days by fleeing to your mother's holding here, but it is a temporary sanctuary at best." Father Michael lowered his chin, his gaze fixing her, resolute. "You must marry again, Alissende, and now, before we return to England—before Hugh has another opportunity to act again in his pursuit of you. Taking Sir Damien in proxy marriage is the only plausible solution."

Damien.

Alissende closed her eyes briefly as his name stabbed through her, the sweetness and sting of it blending together. It washed over her, along with the image of one still and hot summer afternoon long ago, of sun caressing golden skin . . . of his face above hers, strong and handsome, his expression intense with the agony of pleasure.

Swallowing back the bittersweet memory, she opened her eyes.

"And what of *his* wishes?" she asked huskily, incapable even now of saying his name aloud. "You can be sure that he would not relish the thought of binding himself to me in any way after all that passed between us those many years ago."

"Sir Damien de Ashby is in the hands of the Inquisition and has been for nearly half a year. Believe me when I tell you that such matters mean little to him at the moment," Michael answered, his voice laced with some dark emotion.

Unwilling—unable for her own sanity—to think too deeply on the true meaning behind her cousin's ominous words, Alissende glanced once more to her mother, who looked as though she would gladly take on the burden of her daughter's pain if she could. But no one could help her now. No one, it seemed, but the one man on earth she could not bear the thought of seeing again, much less marrying.

"*Mon Dieu,* but I would as soon take the veil as go forward with this," she murmured.

"That cannot be," Michael countered. "The king would never allow it. As it is, His Majesty will be angered that you fled to France and remarried without his consent. But praise be to God, he is a much softer man than was his sire, and he is more like to forgive an act of disobedience if the reason behind it seems to be one of the heart. The public history of youthful love you shared with Sir Damien makes him the perfect choice for a union undertaken with such haste. He is here in France and in no position to decline. You need the protection to be gained by a marriage with him. It is the only way."

A reason of the heart. Alissende's thoughts fixed on the phrase; if she could have called forth her voice at that moment, it would have sounded strangled at best.

"And yet even if the king's reaction were not a concern," Michael went on, clearly intent on persuading her, "my brother continues to remain so. You are too rich a prize for him to concede. Should we attempt to seclude you in a convent either here or in England, Hugh would take you by force, as he tried to do at your own holding at Glenheim but a month past."

"Of that I have little doubt," Lady Blanche murmured, her elegant mouth frowning.

"It will not come to such if we accept this boon that has been laid at our feet," Michael reminded them. "It has been years, it is true, but Damien is one of the few men I have seen who might be capable of defeating Hugh in combat; I have been told that after leaving England, he served as a Templar Knight within the Brotherhood's most elite circle of warriors, and his skill with the blade is nearly unmatched. However, the danger that he will be lost to us mounts with each hour he remains in the hands of the Inquisition. A choice must be made." He fixed Alissende with his gaze once more. "Only you can decide, Cousin, for it is your welfare that rests in the balance."

Nausea filled Alissende. That Hugh would not rest until something, or *someone,* made him cease his pursuit of her was indisputable. She had known him all her life, and though he and Michael were brothers, they were as alike as innocence was to decadence. Hugh was possessed of a violent and grasping nature, and it was clear that his ascension to the Earldom of Harwick vacated by his late father had made him bold enough to believe that he could simply take her at his will, removing all obstacles, it seemed . . . including even Godfrey Claremont, Earl of Denton—the difficult man who had been her lawfully wedded husband for four years. It frightened her beyond measure.

And yet the alternative was no less frightening in its own way.

"Perhaps I am mistaken in your feelings, Alissende," Michael murmured in response to her long silence. "If accepting Hugh has become more agreeable to you, then—"

"Nay!" she interrupted, sure in that, at least.

Michael nodded, a knowing expression in his kind eyes. "Then you must consider Sir Damien. Through my office as a priest, I could more swiftly arrange the proxy documents. It would not be without risk, of course, but I could see them drawn up along with what will pass, pray God, for a Writ of Absolution from the Inquisition so that Sir Damien will be protected from re-arrest once he arrives in England. We would need to send word to the king, declaring the marriage legitimate, and then prepare to move among your estates here and in England to avoid Hugh until Damien can take his position at your side."

As he said the last, Alissende knew, though she was not looking directly at him, that Michael glanced away for an uncomfortable moment.

Finally raising her gaze from her clenched fingers once more, Alissende locked her stare with her cousin's, heat burning the backs of her eyes and her heart pounding with dread at the enormity of what taking this unorthodox step would mean.

She only need give her consent and it would be done. The proxy documents would be drawn up, the Writ of Absolution would be forged, and a sum of her prodigious fortune would be set aside to pay the men who would steal Damien away from his captivity. Eventually, he would take his place at her side as her husband. As her *husband*, God help her. It would be so easy to say yes, and yet . . .

Michael must have sensed her wavering, for his gaze flooded with understanding before his mouth tightened as he offered the final statement that he had to know could not help but seal her doom.

"I had hoped to spare you the fullness of this, Cousin, but I can see that it must be said to aid you in making your decision," he said, his voice low. "You must consider that the Inquisition in France has never been known for compassion in its methods of extracting confession from accused heretics—and with King Philip the Fair's call to prove the entire Templar Brotherhood guilty of such sins, the French inquisitors seem to have exceeded all previous bounds of cruelty."

Alissende's breath caught, and a sickening sensation twisted in her belly. "I did not realize . . ." She shook her head, anguish filling her. "I—I had thought talk of the inquisitors' brutality to be naught but rumor, spread by those unfaithful to the Church."

"I only wish it were so. But I have seen the results of their interrogations with my own eyes," Michael continued, his words raking at her without mercy, "and the difficult truth is that Damien is suffering, Alissende. More than many a man could bear and still live; he has been tortured ruthlessly by his captors. Even if we are successful in freeing him, he may not survive his rescue."

A bubble of shock seemed to fill Alissende's chest, blocking out all but the gasp that escaped her as she pressed her trembling fingers to her lips.

"But if he dies, then where will that leave Alissende?" Lady Blanche asked, her eyes filled with concern.

Michael frowned. "No worse than she fares right now. At the very least, creating this proxy marriage will gain us valuable time in finding another suitable protector who will be willing to stand up to Hugh and his aggressions."

He must have realized how calculating his statement sounded, for he glanced to Alissende and added more gently, "But pray heaven it will not come to that, and we can liberate Damien in time to restore him to his former strength and vitality."

Alissende's eyes closed again, this time of their own accord, against the hot swell of liquid that came forth unbidden at the mere thought of the kind of torment Michael had described being applied to Damien. *Oh, God.*

She possessed means of stopping his pain; it was irrefutable. That Damien himself would surely despise the very thought of her mattered little in the face of that awful reality. Aye, it had to be done. When the time came, she would bear up under his scorn the best she could. *If he survived. . . .*

With a jerking nod of her chin and a sharp intake of breath, Alissende opened her eyes once more and murmured her agreement in a voice almost inaudible for the tightness constricting her throat. "So be it, Michael. I give my consent to your proposition. Undertake what must be done."

The sensation of coolness swept over Damien's face, accompanied by the curling embrace of blessed fresh air around his body. He struggled to open his eyes even as he felt strong hands gripping him, bearing him up. Dimly, his mind locked onto the knowledge that he was being carried somewhere. Somewhere away from the stench and darkness and pain of his cell. *But where? And why?*

That his captors saw fit to move him now after all this time spent in fetid misery could mean nothing good. Any brief respite he'd been granted before had always been followed by infliction of even greater pain.

Aye, at the other end of this little journey waited naught but more wicked cruelty, worse than what had come before. That thought twisted through him, stealing his breath. He could not imagine any agony more intense than that he had already known. He wouldn't, lest he go mad from thinking on it.

But he need not go quietly to it, either.

And so with whatever strength he still possessed, he fought back against his oppressors' progress. He heard a grunt of reaction and knew the satisfaction of having imposed some discomfort on one of them. Then he braced himself for the retribution that was sure to come, hoping that this time it would be strong enough to release him from this everlasting hell.

But nothing happened other than the same gently rocking movement as before.

Damn them.

Determined to force them to action, Damien sucked in a heady breath of air and coiled the last of his energy into one final act of defiance, lashing out with his arms and legs—demanding reprisal. When his power was spent, he went still. But instead of gut-wrenching punishment, he was shocked to feel the brush of warm breath against his cheek.

"Peace, man," a low male voice murmured, close to his ear. "Cease your struggles. There will be no further harm to you with us."

No further harm?

The phrase echoed through Damien's brain, mocking, surely false.

He wanted to ask why . . . to question those who carried him away from the torment he'd lived in for so long. But he could not find means to utter the words—had not even the ability to open his eyes to look at those who bore him on through the unending night.

Perhaps he was near death, then. The thought lanced through him, bittersweet. Aye, perhaps it was time, and they knew it, having witnessed it so oft in the plying of their wicked trade. He wished he had the ability still to mock the sickening pride they took in such matters. But at least he could go to his end knowing that he had never cowered to them. Death could do naught but force him to finally lay down the burden of this once powerful body, now little more than a vessel of agony.

Someone stumbled, the movement jarring Damien painfully and reminding him that he should try to rest during this temporary reprieve he'd been granted. Taking another breath of air into his lungs, he savored its sweetness before gradually exhaling, his heart slowing and his head feeling heavier.

The rocking motion of his travel continued as they carried him onward, always onward. Making himself remain still, Damien concentrated on conserving his ebbing strength. For no matter what awaited him at the end of this journey, he knew he would not surrender to them. He would resist their unholy torments no matter how they tried to break him. . . .

Aye, he vowed, he would fight them unto his final breath.

Chapter 1

A cottage along the coast of England
Three weeks later

Heat pressed down, the sun glinting through the branches of trees to caress Damien's skin. He was hot. Exhausted, too, but in a pleasing way. He rested on his back, replete, one muscled forearm shielding his eyes from the brightness . . . though not from the sight of her, just visible through that slit of space between his brow and arm.

Alissende . . .

She was so beautiful sitting beside him, with her long, dark hair curling over her breast, her hands busy with something.

"What are you doing?" he asked with a lazy smile, amazed that she could do aught after what had just *passed between them. He shifted his shoulder a bit to see her better.*

She offered that impish look of hers before glancing to him with an expression in her violet-blue eyes that set a new blaze of heat uncoiling through him. But she did not speak, only opening her palms to reveal handfuls of bruised, pale green leaves.

The scent of mint teased his senses an instant before she brushed her hands over his naked chest, and he made a low sound of pleasure at the cooling sensation left in the wake of her touch on his sun-heated skin. So good, that feeling . . . so good . . . and after a moment he reached up to her to pull her close, rolling her beneath him again to take her mouth with his, fully and deeply. . . .

Light stabbed into Damien's eyelids, jerking him away from the sweetness of his dream. He frowned, his lids aching with the effort of forcing them open. Through the hard-won crack of vision, he noted the blurry outline of a long-robed form pushing open a shutter of some kind. Even brighter sunlight flooded the room, then, blinding him, and he made a noise in his throat, turning his head away, trying to lift his arm to block the glare. He could not. His wrists were bound to the frame of padded platform upon which he lay.

Nausea swept through him. Dark, impotent sickness at the memory of such bonds on him before. So many times before, with so much pain that followed . . .

With a strangled growl, he wrenched at the straps that held him, needing to break free, determined to keep from suffering under their diabolical hands and fiendish instruments again. In his struggle, his only covering—a length of cloth or blanket that had been thrown across the lower half of his body—began to slide away, but it was of no matter, for he must free himself . . . he had to break free this time or die in the trying. . . .

"Be still, Sir Damien, or you will tear the stitches I labored so long to put in for you."

The low voice penetrated Damien's mind, along with the sliding, welcome sensation of the cloth being draped over his legs and groin once more. Something about that voice triggered a memory. It was the same one from before, from the night he'd been carried away from his cell. *Peace, man, there will be no further harm to you with us. . . .*

The voice echoed in his thoughts again, and, ignoring the renewed hurts that seemed to sweep through his body with the effort, he raised his head as much as he could, squinting anew to make out the owner of those soothing tones. Slowly, the chamber came into focus. It was a roughly hewn cottage, from the looks of the wattle-and-daub walls and bare window holes; the raw-cut square openings were protected by naught but the shutters that had only recently been pushed open.

Finally, he could see the chamber's other occupant. It was a man, though somewhat older than he'd expected from the youthful lilt of his voice. He looked to be twoscore or a little more perhaps, tall but not overly slender; in fact, he was built like one who handled weaponry, though with short-cut reddish hair and a smooth-shaven face that precluded him from being among the ranks of the Templar Order.

So it was not his former brothers-in-arms who had liberated him, then.

"Where—?" Damien tried to rasp past tongue and throat that felt as if he'd eaten a handful of sand. He swallowed, shaking his head before lifting it up again to demand hoarsely, "Where am I—and why bound?"

"Easy, man, you have just awakened at long last . . . one question at a time. They will be answered before long," the stranger said, taking a seat next to Damien and helping him to a sip of cool water from a beaker that stood near a pitcher on the table. It felt like heaven, that coolness sliding down his parched throat, and Damien gulped at it, until his caretaker tipped it away and set it back on the table with a clicking sound of his tongue.

"Too much so quickly will make you ill. You will have more soon," he added with a reassuring nod in response to the avidity he apparently saw in Damien's eyes. "First, let us dispense with these bindings, shall we?" he murmured, leaning over to untie Damien's wrists from the pallet's sturdy frame. "You have been thrashing about in your fever these many days, and so I was forced to secure you like this to keep you from tearing your stitches, or from dislodging the poultices I'd applied to your burns."

Rubbing his wrists once he was free of the ties, Damien deliberately kept his mind from traveling to the place of memory at how and when those still-throbbing injuries had been inflicted upon him. He remained silent, watching the man beside him shake his head and make that clicking sound with his tongue again while he leaned over and prodded with gentle fingertips, checking some of the stitching he'd just mentioned.

"It was all I could do to bring you back to the land of the living, I do confess it," the man murmured. "When

I first examined the extent of your injuries after your deliverance, I feared your inquisitors had done their worst."

"They had."

Damien's barely audible assertion echoed with such dark finality that the man's gaze jerked up to meet his, a look of surprise passing over his face before it dissolved into a sympathetic smile. "Ah, it is good to hear you respond to my ramblings. It has been so long with no other voice but my own ringing in my ears that I am grateful for the sound."

"How long."

Damien's words came out more as a demand than a question, but his companion did not seem to mind.

"Not quite a month. We are in England, just inland from the Dover coast."

Damien's mind was swimming, but weariness also plagued him with ever-increasing weight, forcing him to direct all his concentration toward forming the remaining two questions it was most important for him to ask before exhaustion claimed him again.

"Who are you . . . and how— Why did you free me from the Inquisition?"

His caretaker paused in the act of getting up, turning back toward Damien and giving him a kind look as he pressed his palm atop the back of Damien's hand.

"I am Fra Benedictus—though my brethren are usually content in calling me Ben."

Damien's body tensed in response to hearing the man's religious title, his reaction almost involuntary, but Fra Benedictus simply nodded in understanding, compassion blooming anew in his gaze. "You need fear nothing with me, Sir Damien. There are many of us in God's service within the Holy Church who decry the methods employed by the Inquisition in France."

Before Damien could say aught in reply, Fra Benedictus brought the cup to him again, encouraging him to drink. "Praise be to heaven that you were spared your inquisitors' final cruelty. The work will be challenging, but God has been merciful in assuring that no permanent damage was done to you. You will regain all the powers you wielded as a Templar Knight of great renown, Sir Damien. It will not take long; you will see."

Damien did not respond at first, for the priest's words had unleashed a flood of black, seething anger he did not know he possessed; the root of these emotions was dangerous to feel, no less voice, in any Christian land . . . but his sufferings had made him reckless. Let this man who had dragged him back from the door of hell know the full extent of the darkness that lived in his soul, if indeed he had one at all.

Meeting his gaze head-on, Damien rasped, "I have no use for the Templar Brotherhood any longer, Cleric—or for God, either. Both are dead to me."

Fra Benedictus seemed taken aback, his face paling before it flushed once again. "That is of no matter, Sir Damien, for I can assure you, God has use for *you*— else you would not be here, capable of drawing the breath necessary to speak such blasphemy."

In the next moment, though, his expression softened and his brow wrinkled with worry. "And yet while I may grant you latitude in uttering such sacrilege in view of the ordeal you have recently endured, others will not. A Writ of Absolution has been obtained for you that will provide some protection from rearrest by the Inquisition in any land, but I advise you to use caution in voicing your disdain for God's grace in the future, Sir Damien, else you will likely find yourself confined to a cell again, even here in England."

"I will . . . consider your counsel, priest," Damien said, grimacing again at the raw burning that commenced in his throat with speaking. "But you still have not answered all."

"What is that? . . ." Fra Benedictus's brows knitted together for a moment before his face bloomed in happy understanding. "Ah, yes . . . you also asked why I freed you from the Inquisition and brought you out of France."

Feeling his grasp on awareness ebbing under the rising tide of a bone-numbing fatigue, Damien only managed a jerky nod. Yet just before he slipped into the abyss of sleep, Fra Benedictus's soothing voice echoed into his ears, as if from afar . . .

"The answer to your question is this, Sir Damien: it was not I who freed you from France—it was a lady. Aye, she paid for your rescue, and in doing so gained the protection she sought . . . that of your name in proxy marriage."

Alissende paced from the solar into the corridor, then down the stairs of the small, fortified manor home where she'd taken refuge for the past week and a half. Opening the door into the courtyard, her gaze fixed on the stable, where she sought the dark-robed form of her cousin Michael, who had ridden up through the gates a few moments past. He bore news for her; she was sure of it. News of what, remained to be seen.

"Is something amiss, Alissende?"

Lady Blanche's voice sounded close behind her, her tone gentle, though Alissende ˙knew her mother had been worn to near collapse these past six weeks. They had traveled from her estate in Montivilliers to the family's second residence in Le Havre, then to Alissende's dowry home here in Fécamp, and the constant upheaval had taken a heavy toll on her.

"Nay, *Mère,* all is well. It is only that Michael has returned."

Lady Blanche only nodded, her mouth tightening. Alissende reached for her mother's hand and squeezed it. A lance of anger stabbed through her at the thought of her mother's suffering like this, and all for the sake of overweening masculine pride and greed. Pray heaven that Hugh had grown tired at last of sending his men in pursuit of them.

"I will go and see what news he bears," Alissende murmured, giving Lady Blanche's hand a final clasp before she tightened her cloak against the cool April breeze and crossed the courtyard. But before she reached the stable door, Michael strode out, his dark hair windblown and his cheeks ruddy from the chill. His face lit when he saw her, and he covered the remaining distance between them in a few running steps.

"I see that you witnessed my return, Cousin," he said, pulling her into a hug that was uncharacteristic for the fierce joy it conveyed, even before he swung her around in a circle.

Smothering her laugh, Alissende clutched at the sleeves of his dark robes until he set her down. "You are in a fine mood, Michael. I hope it is because you have learned something favorable about our resistance against Hugh, for I do not know how much more of this fleeing and watching my mother will be able to bear."

"Ah—well, there may indeed be good news in that quarter, for our ruse to lead him to believe us returned to England appears to have been successful. But that is not what I have come to tell you."

"What, then?"

Alissende slipped her hand into the crook of Michael's arm as they began to walk back to the manor house. She was trying to keep her expression bland and to slow the way her pulse had jumped with his words—knowing, somehow, what he was readying to say.

"It is about Sir Damien."

Alissende's heart did leap into her throat, then, and she swallowed hard. "Aye?" she managed to ask.

"I have received word from my friend Fra Benedictus. Damien's fever has broken. He has much to do on the way to recovery, but he will survive." He pulled a folded parchment from his cloak and thrust it at her, his smile reaching to light his brown eyes. "Here, read for yourself. Is it not wonderful news?"

She stopped walking, half-turning to Michael. As she took the letter, her fingers trembled. Inside this parchment was news of Damien . . . the Damien of here and now, not just the phantom man of all her regrets, longings, and dreams. The Damien who would live, it seemed, to take his place beside her as her husband. She looked away to maintain her composure, reminding herself to breathe. "Has he been told—of me, I mean?" Her voice sounded small and thin in the crisp air, the words hanging on a thread of hope she could not keep herself from feeling.

Some of the light went out of his expression. "Nay,

amie. I thought it best to keep your identity hidden for now." He tucked her hand back under his elbow, trying to look encouraging for her sake, she knew, as they continued the rest of the way back to the house. "But he was told of the proxy marriage," Michael added, "and, according to Fra Benedictus's missive, he did not seem unduly upset by the information. In time I am sure Damien will feel grateful to the person who arranged for his release from the Inquisition's torment— even if that person is you, Alissende."

"We shall see," she murmured, not nearly as certain about Damien's reaction once he learned that she was the bride to whom he was bound. She had known him far better than Michael had—had tasted the single-minded passion he could give in love and had felt the aching absence left behind when he forsook all tender emotion.

"Aye, we shall see," she repeated more softly, trying to still the wishful, desperate voices inside of her with the cold reality she faced. Her fears and yearnings mattered naught, she knew, for either way it was done. Damien was going to live. He would learn that she was his proxy bride.

And there was no going back from that now.

Chapter 2

Glenheim Castle, Surrey, England
June 1308

Damien reined in his gelding behind Ben, pausing outside the gates of what looked to be a very prosperous holding. It belonged to *her,* he had been told, the unknown woman who had purchased his freedom for the price of bondage in marriage. As they waited for the sentry to give them permission to enter, he forced himself to lift his gaze, taking in the fine stone turrets and the scarlet pennants flapping against the blue of the sky—struggling as he did to keep the bitterness from rising into his throat.

At last the gates creaked open. With a click of his tongue, Ben set his mare to a lumbering walk, and Damien gritted his teeth as he rode after him. He had vowed to see through this morn's events, knowing that he owed Ben at least that. For though he was feeling anything but charitable at the moment, he could not deny that during these past three months the friar had become more a friend to him than a caretaker; he had used his herbs and poultices to restore Damien's body to its full strength again and had worked with him through all forms of weaponry, sparring with him out in the field to aid him in regaining his notable combat skills.

He had even tried with great diligence—though to no avail—to restore the spiritual faith Damien had forsaken. Aye, Ben had dragged him unwillingly back to this world, coaxing him, pushing him, until Damien had been able to feel the driving force of life pumping through his veins for himself.

But for all that, Ben had pled ignorance about any but the barest details concerning the matter they were riding to confront here today. He claimed to have been told only that the woman in question was a young and wealthy widow who had needed to remarry swiftly, and to a man of imposing physical stature and superior training in sword-fighting and battle.

The whys of it—why she sought a skilled warrior, why such a hasty union . . . why him of all men, when he had been tainted by the charge of heresy and half in the grave already from torture—he had been unable to learn.

And so it was that as he rode through the gates of the lady's estate, he reviewed everything that he planned to say to the stranger who was his proxy bride, the most important being that he could not accept the role of husband she had thrust upon him.

He would not.

Nay, when he met with her for the first time he would demand release from this union, which needed only the utterance of public vow and consummation to make it lasting. Marriage was not for one such as him. He had learned that hard truth long ago, when he'd been a newly knighted youth, still pure of heart and innocent to the darker side of love.

All that remained was to inform the lady awaiting him of it, and to establish what kind of payment he could offer in exchange for the union she expected.

It did not take long for the sentry to escort him and Ben into the large, cool hall, down a series of corridors, and through several chambers. All who met them along the way stared with open curiosity, and Damien's back tensed. After the time he'd spent isolated from human comfort in the inquisitors' dungeon and then with none but Ben for company during his recovery, it was almost painful to be surrounded by so many people—especially people who gaped at him so frankly. And yet in all logic, he could not hold them to blame, for they knew him only as the former Templar Knight their lady had bought for a husband . . . a curiosity to behold, even if the kingdom wasn't embroiled in the mounting call for the Brotherhood's dissolution. That he had asked for none of this rankled, and it was all he could do to keep from scowling as he strode onward, following the sentry.

At last they approached an elegantly carved door, which, he suspected, would open to the castle's solar. If the opulent rooms he had seen thus far were any indication, this chamber would prove to be as spacious and welcoming as the others had been, free of dust, and richly scented by the costly beeswax tapers he had seen in staggering abundance throughout the keep.

Ben seemed to have been accurate in his depiction of the woman as wealthy: She must be, to afford the kind of luxuries that surrounded them. Jaw aching with tension, Damien fixed his gaze on his friend, who was just now turning to face him. Ben's expression was kind, and for some reason it caused the lance of resentment to stab deeper.

"Are you ready?" Ben asked.

"Nay. And yet I would wager that matters not at all."

Ben looked surprised before irritation flashed in his eyes. "As unfortunate as that is, there is no need to be belligerent about it."

"You would be, were you in my damnable position."

Lips tight at Damien's use of the curse he had asked him on numerous occasions to forbear, Ben retorted, "Were I you, Damien, I would endeavor to sweeten my voice and my tongue. You will recall that the bee flies more readily to the honey than it does to the vinegar."

Damien was readying a rejoinder detailing his thoughts on that sentiment, when the sentry's scratching for entrance at last resulted in the door creaking open. Still clenching his jaw, he flashed Ben a final, dark look before striding past him into the chamber. He'd as soon turn and flee as be led into this room like some sort of prize for the lady's inspection.

The chamber was large, as he'd imagined it would be, but he hadn't been prepared for the sumptuous effect of the light that filled it. The room fairly glittered with the sun streaming in through an astonishing array of glazed, diamond-pane mullions on both sides. However, as he approached the center, his steps slowed and finally stopped altogether. There was no lady present.

There seemed to be no one at all, in fact, aside from the serving boy who had pulled open the door.

In the next instant he realized he had been mistaken. A young man stood in silence at the far end of the chamber, within the shadows near the empty hearth. He had escaped Damien's notice at first because of his dark clothing. *The garb of a priest.* That realization sent a ripple of discomfort through Damien. Unlike Ben, who dressed in the simple gray robes and corded belt of a Franciscan friar, this man wore a floor-length black cassock buttoned down the front; it was cinched at the waist with a matching strip of finely woven faille cloth, the entire ensemble complimented by a rosary of glossy, obsidian beads.

The crucifix that dangled from that string of beads drew Damien's attention, and without warning a wave of nausea engulfed him. He broke out into a sweat, his eyes closing for an instant at the image that flashed into his mind of another, similar crucifix swinging into view as his inquisitor moved in to question him. He'd been stretched upon the rack, almost senseless from the agony of it as he'd watched the dull gold pendant sway before his eyes, to and fro, to and fro. . . .

Breathing in deeply to dispel the memory, Damien clenched his fists and strode forward, closing the distance between himself and the dark-robed cleric. This man had no connection to the zealots who had tortured him. In fact, most of the inquisitors had been Franciscans, like Ben; he could not forget that. Right now all that mattered was that this man likely possessed the answers that Damien needed concerning the lady who had arranged the proxy marriage, and he intended to hear them.

But the nearer he came, the more something about the priest niggled at the back of his memory, like a whisper not fully audible. When at last he reached the end of the chamber, the man nodded his greeting, and Damien nodded back, narrowing his eyes to study him and trying to place where he had seen him before.

Yet before they could exchange any words, the man's face brightened, and Damien realized that he'd caught sight of Ben, who swept past Damien to clasp him in a hearty embrace. The two gave each other a few resounding thumps on the back before they pulled apart, grinning.

"Ah, Father Michael," Ben said with a laugh, "by the blessed saints, but it has been too long!"

"Aye, friend, that it has . . . that it has. You're looking well, though. The ocean air must have agreed with you."

Michael. Damien turned the name over in his mind, the whispers growing louder as the images began to converge in his mind.

Michael . . . aye . . . young Michael de Valles, third son to the Earl of Harwick—that was who this was. Little Michael, grown into manhood . . .

The priest's identity crashed upon Damien in the same moment that the man himself directed a more searching look to him again, asking, "Do you recognize me then, Sir Damien? I was hardly more than a lad when last I saw you, and it has been nearly six years."

"Aye, I know who you are," Damien said quietly, his discomfort and the prickling awareness of what this all might mean increasing with each breath.

"You have done well, Ben," Michael said, shifting

his gaze once more to the friar. He smiled. "I do not recall if I've told you before, but I once yearned to become a knight because of Sir Damien; when I was a boy at court, he was a nearly matchless champion, consumed with righteous fury when battling an opponent, but at the same time so pure of heart that those who knew him dubbed him Archangel."

Michael glanced back to Damien, then, the smile of fond memory still warming his eyes as he added, "Time has been kind to you, sir. You look much the same as you did then."

Damien didn't respond right away; the dangerous emotions that had been at play as the pieces here began to fall into place prevented him from speaking at first. Instead he met Michael's gaze head-on, feeling a surge of dark satisfaction as the young cleric seemed to recoil, his cheerful expression fading in response to the warning he clearly read there.

"I may look much the same, *Father Michael*," Damien at last answered in a deceptively mild tone, "but you will soon discover how deeply I have changed if you do not cease with these niceties and tell me who is behind this proxy union that has been foisted upon me."

Michael paled even further and Ben looked taken aback, yet before either man could do or say anything, Damien heard a whispering of silk behind him. He stiffened, his gaze shifting just slightly away from them. Yet he could not bring himself to turn around and face the person who was approaching them. He would not.

Holding himself as still as he might, Damien braced himself. He struggled to maintain some semblance of control, aware even as he did so that it wouldn't be enough. Nay, not for what he realized, now, was coming.

The light tread of footsteps came closer, closer . . . and then the delicate scent reached him, a subtle, enthralling blend of sweet woodruff and ambergris sweeping up to fill his senses. He closed his eyes, the power of the memories it unleashed twitching through him, tender and aching to the point of pain. Sweet Jesu . . .

He did not need to turn around to know it was her.

"Please, Damien, you must not threaten Michael. You will learn all that you wish to know."

Please, Damien . . .

Alissende's melodic voice echoed, strumming his soul as it had in the thousand dreams he'd endured in the years since last he'd seen her. He opened his eyes, and stiffly he turned his head, trying to call up a stronger blaze of anger to combat the tide of feelings he knew would stab deep when he looked upon her once more. But it did no good.

He met her gaze, and his breath stilled with the intensity of what swept through him. Alissende, who had been both his lover and his curse . . . the woman who had made him want her with a fierceness that had nearly killed him, standing before him now in a seeming mockery of all that had come before.

Damien grasped at the threads of his bitterness and disillusioned anger, subduing the hurt by dint of pure will as he forced a sardonic smile to his lips, embellishing it with a slight nod. He noted that her mother stood just behind her, but he made himself continue gazing upon Alissende in the same way he might constrain himself to keep still through the agony of cauterizing a bloody wound. She was as exquisite as ever, with her skin of cream and roses and that rich, dark hair, the sheer veiling she wore over it powerless to conceal its luster in the wash of sun spilling through the chamber.

But it was her eyes that plucked most at the wounded shreds of his heart. Her gaze pulled him in, drowning him in violet-blue depths that were full of anguish, longing, and something more that he would not allow himself to contemplate if he was to remain strong, as he must.

As he must, heaven help him . . .

"I am the one to whom you are bound in proxy marriage," Alissende murmured, her expression open and vulnerable.

"Why?"

Damien rasped the question before he could stop himself. But she knew what he was asking . . . she knew better than anyone. What had happened between them at court five years ago made this circumstance nigh on impossible to comprehend, and yet here he was, reeling with the truth she had just offered: *She* was his proxy bride. She, Lady Alissende de Montague, who had shown him what it was to feel love beyond all reason and then left him bleeding and broken in the aftermath.

"The reasons are . . . complicated." She frowned slightly, he noticed, and struggled not to break her gaze with him.

He could not find his voice to respond, found himself paralyzed by it all, even though he had once allowed himself countless reveries about what he might do and say—about how he might feel—if he chanced to meet her again. His spine felt stiff and his neck ached as he finally managed to say, "Do not concern yourself with expounding upon them, lady, for in truth, I do not need to hear them. I cannot be bound in marriage to anyone, and I had already resolved to tell the one responsible as much. That the person in question is you makes no difference."

His mouth tightened with the lie, but he pushed on. "This proxy union cannot proceed without my participation in the remaining steps that would sanctify it. And as I must decline," he nodded once more, managing to execute a gallant, if rigid, bow in the style of the charm he'd once possessed, "you will allow me to bid you *adieu*."

He straightened and had half-turned toward the door, intending to escape the chamber before his memories and Alissende's wounded gaze froze him like ice to the smooth wooden floor, when Michael called in challenge, "What, sir—will you allow your pride to govern you and flee before you hear the full truth of what brought you here?"

Damien stiffened at the barb. Every muscle in him screamed for the release to be found in dealing out a satisfying dose of bone-crunching violence to anyone misguided enough to continue trying to stop him, but somehow he found means to restrain himself. For the time being, at least.

The leashed anger radiating from him, however, was apparently sufficient to make the young priest's voice crack as he finished, "If nothing else, my cousin's actions on your behalf have earned her the right to be heard in full this day. You owe her that, at least."

"He is right, Damien," Ben echoed. "You should

hear what brought this all about before you make any final decisions."

"You knew more about this than you let on, I see." Damien shifted a stony glare to the man he had considered his friend.

"Only a little," Ben admitted, "but I remained silent for fear of the very reaction you have shown here today."

"Oh, enough," Lady Blanche broke in, waving her hand at them all imperiously. "Let us simply admit that what we face here is unsavory for everyone involved, and be done with it."

Wonderful . . . now her mother was stepping into the fray as well.

Damien realized that he felt like a cornered animal as he looked round at the three conspirators hemming him in: Ben, Lady Blanche, and Father Michael. But not Alissende. Nay, she remained in the background looking restrained and somber.

Though it was almost painful to do so, he allowed his gaze to linger on her again a bit longer than was necessary, noting that her face was pale and that she was keeping her gaze trained to her hands, now clasped tightly in front of her. If he didn't know better, he might be deceived into thinking she was as uncomfortable with this little reunion as he was.

"You should know, Sir Damien, that my daughter resisted our efforts to initiate this proxy with you," Lady Blanche continued, both startling him and pulling his attention back to her again. "In fact, until Michael made it clear that you might well perish under the questioning of your inquisitors, she would not hear of it."

Damien paused as the import of that information sank in. When he made his response, his jaw felt tight. "Michael was correct in what he told you, lady. However, I do not recall asking to be saved from it."

"And yet you *were* saved, Sir Damien. Because Alissende needs you."

That last comment slammed like a fist into his gut, the irony of it coming now—after all this time—almost too much to bear. He raised his brow and found himself grounding out the one word that from the moment he had laid eyes on Alissende again he had vowed he would not utter . . . the tiny opening he knew he should not grant them and yet could not stop himself from offering anyway.

"Explain."

Lady Blanche proceeded to do just that, while Alissende stood a few steps distant, watching Damien with a kind of painful awareness flooding her; she studied the rigidity of his powerful back, the twitching cords of muscle along his cheek, and the battle-honed contours of his arms that led to fisted hands. Along with him she heard once more the litany of Hugh's crimes against her—of his aggressions and evil deeds, the whole of it punctuated by her cousin's assurance that his brother, Hugh de Valles, the new Earl of Harwick, was an unstoppable, dark force, protected in part by his carefully cultivated position of favor within the royal household—but she said nothing herself.

She could not. Nay, not a word. All that she was feeling had risen up, thick and hot, to fill her throat, keeping her mute.

She had been readying herself for this meeting for weeks, ever since Michael had received word that

Damien would survive. She had rehearsed over and over again how she might feel, what she would say, the memories she would need to subdue when she looked into the stunning blue eyes that had once burned with love for her.

But she had been beyond foolish, she realized, for nothing could have prepared her for the reality of this. This was Damien standing before her, as magnificent as he had been the first time she had noticed him when she'd been but a young maiden and he a hot-blooded new knight at court . . . gentle, sweet Damien—the breathtaking warrior of velvet and steel, tenderness and fire, who had loved her with such devotion that she had become intoxicated with constant longing for him. Being near him had filled her with joy, and she had believed with every fiber of her being when he had gazed into her eyes and vowed that even death itself would have no power to come between them.

But she had changed that. God help her, she had changed it.

She had thought time would mend the gaping wound she had dealt to both their hearts the day she had cast him away . . . had hoped against hope that he might heal, even if he could not forgive.

But he had not healed, any more than she had. She could see that now. The bitter truth of it had been there like a blade in her heart as soon as their gazes had met but a few moments past. She had been swept up in the storms raging in his eyes, knowing she would have to make peace with that if her mother and cousin managed to convince him to stay.

Aye, that and much more.

Silence settled over the chamber, and Alissende

realized that the explanations were finished at last. Damien stood, silent and motionless as before, except for the shallow, even breaths he took. When at last he spoke, it was in a voice that sounded hoarse from restrained emotion.

"Thwarting Lord Harwick seems to be a necessary action, if all you have told me is true, but I still fail to understand why I must be the one to undertake it." He made a sound of disbelief. "There are skillful warriors aplenty throughout England, and many titled noblemen besides who would consider themselves blessed beyond measure to wed a young, widowed heiress such as—" He stopped short, inclining his head slightly as he finished, "—such as your daughter. Why did you not seek out one of them?"

Alissende felt the jab, not only of his carefully worded insult but also of his deliberate omission of her name. He had not uttered it even once this day, she realized of a sudden, and it cut her to the quick.

"Because we were in France when it became clear that extreme measures must be taken to prevent Hugh from seizing Alissende by force," Lady Blanche said, not unkindly. "And so were *you,* in dire circumstances of your own. It seemed an honorable exchange: your life for Alissende's safety. More importantly, you are not a stranger to us. What we knew of you was in your favor, and so the proxy was created to make you Alissende's husband."

"You must have been truly desperate, then," Damien answered darkly, "for it is no secret that I was judged to be deficient for that role five years ago. Naught about me has changed since that time, except for the worse— for now in addition to being a poor and landless knight,

I am also a tarnished former Templar and an accused heretic to boot. If the feigned Writ of Absolution you have procured for me is discovered, then I and anyone connected to me will be subject to arrest and interrogation."

He laughed again, a joyless, sharp sound. "Nay, I am not the man for this duty. Seek another, for I intend to serve no master but myself and am bound for the freedom of Scotland to sell my skills to the highest bidder as a mercenary knight. I have naught to offer anyone as a husband."

He seemed as if he might glance to Alissende then, but he appeared to stiffen in the act, preventing himself at the last moment. "If there is no more to this than what you have told me, then," he continued, "I will needs—"

"If you must know the full truth of it," Alissende interrupted, forcing his gaze to her at last, "you were chosen of all men, Damien, because you are the one man of all who once loved me." Heat filled her cheeks with the admission, but she was bolstered by the steadying dose of irritation that had finally begun to seep through her embarrassment and despondency; it allowed her to tip her chin enough so that she could meet his stare head-on as she said, "That is no secret either, is it?"

The shadowy array of emotions that swept across his face in the charged silence that followed might have made any other woman sink to the floor at his feet, begging forgiveness. But Alissende had lived through far too much of her own pain and disappointment to indulge that kind of visible weakness. She kept her back stiff, never taking her gaze from his.

His eyes glittered down at her in the wash of sunlight, cool blue and filled with a stunning blend of anger and pain; then that sardonic tilt lifted the corner of his sinfully handsome mouth again, sending a stab of desire through her as he murmured at last, "I do not think you wish to explore the fullness of that question now, lady, and in front of this company."

"And yet it is the true reason my family urged me to accept this proxy," she allowed, her voice husky with all she was holding back. "That you and I share a public . . . *history* together," she felt herself flushing again, "presents a better appearance to the rest of the world, permitting the possibility that our match was undertaken in sincerity rather than for simple expedience."

"My brother was training in France when you served at court, Sir Damien," Michael murmured from off to the side, though Alissende noted that Damien did not shift his gaze away from her to look at him, "so you know aught of him from your own experience. But you must understand something about Hugh's grasping nature to fully comprehend the gravity of this."

"And what would that be?" Damien uttered the question, still keeping his attention only on her, the force of his stare unleashing unwelcome ripples of emotion she would not—could not—allow herself to feel again.

"Hugh has spent considerable energy cultivating a position of favor with our new king," Michael continued, "and it was well known at court that he intended to make Alissende his own, once the official mourning period for her late husband ended. That my brother might have been complicit in the hunting accident that took Lord Denton from this world seemed of little consequence within the royal circle, for Hugh applied his influence to smooth over any concerns."

Damien scowled, looking at Michael at last. "One of my Templar brethren, Sir Richard de Cantor, served the king as a weapons trainer many years ago. He confided concern that the new sovereign's judgment might prove weak in matters of friendship."

Michael nodded. "King Edward has not shown himself as shrewd as many would wish in the time he has held the throne, preferring to honor his favorites at the cost of the kingdom's barons and lords. My brother has ingratiated himself to the king in this fashion and had all but persuaded His Majesty to support his marriage to Alissende at the time we fled with her to France. That was why we needed to act immediately, before my brother's increasingly violent attempts to claim our cousin for himself became a royal decree."

Michael walked over and took Alissende's hand in his own, trying to comfort her, and Alissende squeezed gently back, grateful for his concern. "As it stands," he finished, "the king is not pleased with what he perceives as Alissende's impetuous action with this proxy, but he has come to accept it in the belief that it was made out of a love long denied by time and circumstance."

"The proxy has been declared officially at court already?" Damien grated, looking to her and then back to Michael. "By God, but you assume much. You did not even take into account the possibility that I would refuse your plan."

"Oh, but we did, Sir Damien," Lady Blanche broke in once more. "And yet we trusted that you would be moved by the justice of this and agree to aid us. Alissende has freed you from your tormentors, and now we ask that you do the same for her."

Damien's fists clenched again. *As if preparing to ward off a blow . . . as if he yearned with everything in him to reject outright any obligation to her.* The phrase slipped into Alissende's thoughts, but before she could attempt to come to terms with it, Lady Blanche continued to argue her position, undaunted.

"That Hugh will attempt to lay claim to Alissende again, proxy or nay, is a certainty, and there is no other who would be able or perhaps even willing to undertake the charge of her safety in this. You have much to gain, not only in the life that has been restored to you but also in the lands, wealth, and power that are tied to this union. For the sake of what you once felt for each other, will you not consider it?"

Once felt. Nay . . .

The words echoed mockingly through Alissende's heart, underscoring the heart-wrenching truth that for her, at least, the feelings had not truly changed. She had never stopped loving Damien. And no matter how much it hurt, she knew that she likely never would.

She watched him wage his internal struggle, feeling all the while the renewed stabs of misery shooting through her. This was exactly what she had feared would happen . . . what she had wanted to avoid at all costs. This outcome was not unexpected, but she could not suppress the flare of resentment that rose in her nonetheless, reminding her why she had yearned for the peace of a nunnery, where she could know blessed protection from all the intrigues, decisions, and whims of men.

Damien would reject her now, coldly and in front of

these witnesses—an action that she could not refute was but a shadow of the public humiliation she had dealt him five years ago. It did not matter that she had regretted that decision through every moment of the endless time that had followed; what was done was done, and she had little right to blame him for seeking his retribution now that the chance presented itself.

And so it was that when he pushed his hand through his hair and let out his breath, looking from Ben, to Michael, to her mother, and finally to her, she was stunned to see that something else had replaced the acrimony in his expression. He wasn't content by any means, but it seemed that he had come to a decision. It only remained to hear what it was—and he did not leave her waiting long.

"I cannot deny that, whether asked for or nay, your efforts to liberate me from France deserve some kind of recompense. What little honor I still possess compels me to try to meet that obligation in some way."

"It does?" Michael sounded surprised, and Alissende glanced at him, wondering how he had managed to sound so convinced of this plan all along when he'd clearly harbored such serious doubts.

"Aye," Damien said evenly, also glancing to him, "and so I will consent to do my part in this proxy, provided you permit certain additional terms that I wish to set forth."

Michael's expression seemed both hopeful and cautious. "Name them."

Alissende's heart slowed to a deep, heavy cadence in preparation for what Damien might say next, her emotions in turmoil at the thought that he had agreed to aid her at all.

He stood there, tall and powerful, no longer a man besieged but rather a warrior who knew full well his worth in the matter before him. "The first of these terms is the most important one," he answered, "for if it cannot be agreed upon, then naught else can follow."

He shifted his gaze back to Alissende then, pausing anew and making her breath catch at the expression burning in his eyes. And when he spoke, each word landed like a tiny hammer on her wounded heart.

"I will take on the role of your husband, Alissende—but for the space of no more than six months. After that time I demand to be released of it, without penalty or tie, to live as I choose for the rest of my days."

Chapter 3

Damien kept his gaze fixed to Alissende in the wake of his pronouncement, experiencing a kind of clutching sensation in his gut at the wave of vulnerability he saw sweep over her exquisite face. It followed hard upon his very visceral awareness of the way she'd reacted to his speaking her name aloud. He'd had the foreknowledge to brace himself for the moment, conscious of the fact that he had not uttered it yet this day—that in truth it was the first time the sound of it had passed his lips in five years.

Yet she said nothing in response.

"Six months?" It was her mother who broke the silence, her tone indicating how insulting she found his stipulation.

"Aye." He readied himself for the challenges he knew would come now, not only from Lady Blanche but also from Father Michael, and perhaps even from

Ben. Whether or not Alissende would protest remained to be seen. "Six months will provide time enough for you to find a more suitable and lasting spouse. One to whom Alissende can be married as soon as an annulment between us becomes official."

"How can you be so sure that the Church will grant you an annulment, Damien, after a full half year of a marriage lived openly at court?" Ben argued. "Rescinding a sanctioned union is a complicated and holy process, and not as simple as wishing it so."

"Arranging a proxy is normally complex as well, and yet it seems to have been expedited quite smoothly in this case." Damien gave Father Michael a pointed look, drawing an answering flush into the young man's cheeks. "But if Alissende's cousin is not able to exert his influence again, my second requirement should take care of any difficulty. It is this: I will not perform the public oath and ceremony that is necessary to make me a husband in truth. We will need to attest to society at large that vows *were* said, but that they were not in actuality will aid our cause to extricate ourselves from the union when the six months have passed."

He paused for a beat before adding quietly but definitively, "Also, I will not call Alissende by the title of 'wife' in public or in private, though I will do my best to ensure by my demeanor that none have doubt in considering her as such."

Michael made a sound in his throat. "You cannot be serious about such a small matter," he reproached, and it was clear that he thought the portion of Damien's condition had sprung from spite, in retribution for the pain Alissende had dealt to him in their past.

But it wasn't. Referring to her by that title atop the pretense of all else would simply be more than Damien could bear, and he knew it. He leveled his stare at Michael. "I assure you that I am in earnest about it."

A stunned silence settled over the chamber again; it was so still, in fact, that Damien could hear the songbirds outside the castle walls. Alissende remained quiet, turning slightly away from him to avoid his gaze. That was just as well, he decided, for this was difficult enough without the complication of those old emotions—vestiges of long ago that had no bearing now, he reminded himself—pulling at him.

It was Lady Blanche who finally bridged the gap once more, exhaling with a sound of irritation and crossing with brusque steps to one of the mullioned windows. She gazed out of it for a moment until she was seemingly able to bring herself into some semblance of control again, then she twisted her face to him, her expression sharp. "You have quite glibly offered up countered terms, Sir Damien, but you have overlooked one key aspect that neither your best intentions nor the Holy Mother Church has the power to undo."

He raised his brow, inviting her to continue.

"You have made no mention of the babe that might result from your six-month union."

Alissende's flinch in response to that sent a tingle of warning through him, but he had no time to contemplate its import as her mother finished, "Will you be able to as easily walk away from your own flesh and blood should Alissende find herself with child when the allotted time is up?"

Damien thrust that bittersweet image from his mind, subduing the twisting sensation it set off inside him. He had known from the moment he'd decided to stay that he would need to address this, but the reality of doing so suddenly seemed far more difficult than he had anticipated.

"Scoundrel that I am, my lady, even I am not so reprehensible," he managed to say, somehow keeping his true feelings tightly reined. "There will be no child—because the marriage will remain unconsummated."

That finally managed to draw Alissende's gaze back to him, punctuated by her soft gasp, but he did not look fully at her until he had finished saying, "That is my fourth term of agreement, and as such it will provide even more compelling grounds for annulment when the time comes."

Then he did allow himself to look at her, forcing himself not to react to the emotions he saw shadowing her eyes. Disbelief had brushed her cheeks an enchanting pink, and her mouth was slightly open, inviting thoughts he could not allow himself to indulge. She was angry now—and stricken too, unable to shield her expression from him before he saw the depths of her hurt.

And why wouldn't she be? You know the truth as well as she. This term is a moot one, for your union with her was consummated long ago—sweetly, tenderly . . . and, ah yes, passionately too—many, many times over. . . .

The mocking voice taunted him, pushing those delicious memories to the forefront of his mind. He tried to hold them back, but they came flooding through his resistance, making his gut clench anew and almost preventing him from standing firm before her.

He kept his gaze fixed to Alissende, to see what, if anything, she had revealed to her mother or the rest of the world about just how much they had shared during that sultry, enchanted summer. But except for the delicate flush on her face, she remained stoic. In fact, in the next instant, she seemed to undergo a transformation of sorts. Her expression tightened—hardened, even— and the tumult in her eyes cooled; it might have almost made him feel a twinge of shame at what he'd just done.

Almost, but not quite.

He dragged his gaze away from her long enough to note the others in the chamber. Ben and Michael both seemed somewhat abashed at this latest of his terms, while Lady Blanche looked nothing less than relieved.

Alissende had not told any of them the full truth about his intimacy with her, then.

That realization sank like a fist in his belly; he couldn't decide whether he felt annoyed or thankful that she'd kept silent. It did not matter, of course, for her discretion in the matter was what was allowing him to proceed now with this damnable plan into which he had become so deeply embroiled. He would learn more about the whys of her silence later, when they spoke in private.

Right now, everyone seemed to be waiting for her to make clear her decision about the terms he had imposed upon their potential alliance.

She did not disappoint. Just moments ago, her demeanor had shifted from that of the vulnerable, somber beauty she had seemed upon her arrival in this chamber to a woman of composure and cool detachment, even more breathtaking for the strength that seemed to radiate from deep within her.

Now she spoke with all the self-assurance of the noblewoman that she was, standing slender and elegant before him. "You have stated four terms, sir. Are there others?"

"Nay." Damien met the challenge of her stare with the heat of his own. "They comprise all."

"Very well, then. I accept your offer." Her chin tilted a hair's breadth—enough, he realized with amazement, for the regal impression she had cast moments ago to suddenly increase tenfold. "For the space of six months you will act as my husband and protector against Lord Harwick or any other who may seek to coerce me. If you fulfill that duty with competence, then at the end of that term you will be released from all ties to me."

He never broke his stare as he tipped his head mockingly, his voice resonating with dark promise as he answered, "Never fear, lady. When I have done with my part of this bargain, no man, knight, or lord will dare even to think upon you improperly without fear of the consequences. You will be well protected with me, I vow it."

He thought he caught a flicker of something in her eyes once more as he spoke those last words, and he saw with certainty the way her lips tightened. Yet she did naught but offer him a clipped nod in response.

Father Michael, Ben, and Lady Blanche remained quiet, but it was impossible not to feel the almost palpable ebbing of tension that spread in the wake of this resolution. Still, before another easy breath was taken, Alissende stepped brusquely toward the door, turning her head to call to him, as she reached the portal, "A servant will be sent to inform you when I am finished readying the lord's chamber that is yours now by right. Until then, there is time enough to call for some refreshment if you wish."

And then she was gone, slipping into the corridor and leaving him to do as she'd bid or not, as he pleased.

If he hadn't been so conflicted about all that had just transpired here, he might have smiled in grudging admiration. She was remarkable, turning the tables on him just now in what seemed little more than the blink of an eye. With her calm, matter-of-fact manner, she had somehow shifted the power in their developing struggle for control firmly back into her own graceful hands.

For now, anyway.

Encouraging that twinge of irritation to drive out the softer and far more dangerous feelings that had crept in, Damien remained in place for but a moment more before he turned and nodded his leave-taking to the others in the room. Then he trained his gaze on the door through which Alissende had gone, clenching his jaw as he set off to follow her.

He was no lord, but he was no serving lad, either, and she had just dismissed him as if he was, taking it upon herself to conclude their meeting without a by-your-leave. It was the kind of treatment he'd vowed never to accept willingly from anyone, from the time he'd been old enough to use a blade or even his fists in commanding respect; it was one of the reasons he'd sweated and bled, driving himself to be the best in everything he did.

He had scratched his way up from almost nothing—he and his brother Alex, both of them becoming swordsmen of great skill and, eventually, both Templar Knights of the most elite inner circle of the Brotherhood. Yet it did not change the fact that common blood ran in his veins, and he was well aware of just how much that had cost him in his past.

Having to endure snubs and rejection for lack of family pedigree was a truth of this world; he could not alter that any more than he could make himself into a noble lord of a castle, despite the farce of this proxy arrangement.

That didn't mean he had to like it.

The thought burned deeper with every step he took down the darkened corridor. It underscored his resolve to do whatever was necessary to reclaim his integrity, his honor—and his masculine pride as well, the precepts of the Templar Brotherhood be damned. He would begin that process with the woman he had just promised to champion for the next six months . . . for apparently the cool and imperial Lady Alissende didn't understand that he wasn't finished with her yet. Nay, not by half.

But she was about to find out.

Somehow, Alissende managed to maintain her composure in the moments after leaving Damien in the solar, but a jumble of feelings still roiled inside her. Chief among them was indignation. It gave her a kind of strength, though, and so she clung to it.

Her heart ached with what had just happened—with the realization that the man she'd met today was no longer the man she had once loved. This Damien was callous and unfeeling. By heaven, he had looked straight at her and pretended that the tender, magnificent lovemaking they'd once known with each other had never happened. Her own pride had prevented her from refuting him, but she had felt the pain of it nonetheless.

Brushing her hand across her eyes, Alissende finally approached her destination; pushing open the door, she entered the chamber that had formerly been the private domain of her late husband, Godfrey Claremont, Earl of Denton. The windows were shuttered, still, as they had been since his death. Surrounded by the gray atmosphere inside the chamber, she pressed her back against the wall and tried to slow her racing thoughts.

As she allowed her eyes to adjust in the paucity of light, her attention settled on the vast and ornate contours of the bed. It sent a pang through her, and she drew in a shaky breath, glad that she was alone now, as she confronted the old ghosts here. It was her first time in this chamber in nearly a year, and though she had hoped for time to have erased them, she could not deny that this place still brimmed with memories of Godfrey. The thorough cleaning and changing of all the linens, draperies, and bed hangings she'd ordered a few weeks ago before her return to Glenheim had helped, but the images in her mind refused to fade.

Pursing her lips, Alissende crossed the chamber and pulled away the lengths of cloth covering one of the mullion panes Godfrey had ordered fitted into the arched window holes. The glass had been an extravagant expense, but Godfrey had never favored denying himself anything he'd desired; in that respect he had been very similar to Hugh. It was one of the traits, Alissende imagined, that had drawn the two men to each other as friends . . . and one of the shared qualities that might well have led to Godfrey's demise on the hunting excursion they'd taken together that fateful day last summer.

Stepping back from the window and the brighter light filtering through the milky panes, Alissende surveyed the chamber. As opulently furnished as it was, she hated this room more than any other in the castle, and since Godfrey's death, she had taken to sleeping in one of the guest chambers just down the corridor. This was the chamber where she had spent her first night with Godfrey after the marriage her sire had arranged for them . . . where she had endured the painful consummation of their union—made more so by her own fear and by his careless, drunken groping.

She'd been relieved, afterward, that he'd been too deeply into his cups to notice much beyond the fulfillment of his own pleasure. The smear of blood she'd produced on the sheet by poking the tips of two fingers with her tapestry needle had satisfied him in regard to her virginity, come morn.

But it hadn't changed the reality, for her at least.

For the bitter truth was that more than a year prior to her disastrous wedding night, Damien had made love to her for the first time. Over the course of the weeks that had followed, he had awakened her to unimagined bliss. In those secret, stolen moments, she had learned of seduction, of the give and take of sensual pleasure along with him; she had reveled in the breathtaking intimacies they'd shared, savoring the way Damien had played her body with all the skill and sacred concentration of an artist stroking free a masterpiece from his blank canvas.

Aye, Damien had learned to make her rise to the mere whisper of her name on his breath. What she had known with Godfrey could not help but pale by comparison.

That state of affairs had never improved throughout the four years of their marriage. Nay, if anything, much had declined with each month that had passed without the signs of a babe growing within her. Godfrey had become increasingly resentful and sometimes cruel, for it was common knowledge that childlessness was the fault of the woman—another curse to be traced back to the sins of Eve.

She could still see her husband's face, red with disappointment and anger, as he'd accused her of her failings in the matter. If only she desired him more, if only she would remove all other thought but the hope of blessed fruitfulness each time they coupled, then a babe could not help but grow within her. God was punishing her for her shortcomings by giving her a barren womb.

And so Godfrey had taken matters into his own hands, during that last year of his life, insisting that she couple with him nightly; she'd only been released of that duty through the week of her courses each month, regardless of how her body had hurt from such constant and uninvited use.

It had been awful, demeaning, and painful. But as

much as she'd come to resent the man she had married willingly and with her family's blessing, she'd known that she couldn't truly blame him.

He had been right.

She had not enjoyed the fumbled rutting that had comprised the lovemaking in their marriage bed. She had not desired him. Oh, at the beginning she had felt a kind of affection for Godfrey, and certainly she had tried to do her duty to him as his wife. But there had never been any passion. She hadn't been *able* to love him, for the bitter truth was that she'd still loved Damien de Ashby; she always had and likely always would.

Now Damien was back in her life, despising her as much if not more than Godfrey had, though for very different reasons—and she wanted none of it, ever again. She was sick unto death of men, with their demands, their needs, and their arrogant pride. It was why she had yearned to enter a nunnery. She wanted to live the rest of her life as *she* saw fit, not answering any longer to the will of those, like Hugh or the other lords at court, who prized her for naught but her wealth or her cursed beauty.

Her mouth tightened, and she subdued the last of her disturbing memories as she moved to another set of windows. Pulling down their cloth coverings with a snap, she wiped away from the glass the fine layer of dust before crossing to the hearth to lay the makings of a fire. The hearth appeared to be fairly clean, but from a certain angle she could see what looked to be an old piece of charred wood near the back wall; it was just visible in the slant of shadow, and she paused, trying to decide if it would be wise, dressed as she was, to attempt to remove it herself as should be done before laying the new fire.

The alternative, of course, was to wait and call for one of the servants. It seemed unnecessary, though; if she was careful not to touch her hands to her gown when she was done, then completing the task should be simple enough.

Resolved to the action, Alissende threw down one of the window cloths to kneel upon and had just bent over, reaching into the recess of the sooty fireplace, when she felt a sneeze coming on. But she was interrupted by a noise at the doorway, followed by a low, masculine voice that, despite her best intentions, sent a not entirely unpleasant shiver through her.

"I did not realize you were so desperate to escape my company."

Rocking back onto her heels, Alissende scrambled to stand, at the same time pinching her nose in an effort to make the tickling sensation go away. Then she turned to face Damien.

Leveling what she hoped was an unperturbed gaze at him, she said, "As I told you in the solar, I only wished to ready your chamber. There is no cause to think otherwise."

"I was referring to what I saw when I came in here." He nodded toward the hearth, his expression an enigmatic combination of jesting and bemusement.

Alissende bit back another retort when she realized what he meant, and how she must have looked from his perspective behind her, bent over as she was with her bottom in the air and with the top half of her hidden from view in the fireplace. To cover her discomfiture, she glanced at the hearth and coughed slightly, resisting the impulse to rub her nose again. Good heavens, but if she couldn't find a way to stop feeling so—

"I cannot say that I found your position . . . unattractive, however."

Alissende snapped her gaze forward, realizing too late that Damien had crossed the few steps between them while she'd been looking away. He stood less than an arm's length from her now, and her breath caught with a choking sound in her throat. She forced herself to lift her face to meet his gaze, so that he would not think her intimidated by his nearness.

Sweet Jesu, but he was staring down at her in such solemn silence. All but for the heat in his eyes. There was no mistaking the intensity she saw there, and it caused her stomach to do a pleasurable little flip. He was so close that she could sense his warmth, and she could not help but breathe in his scent—a sensual blend of pure male and warm leather, along with the hint of clove and lemongrass from the herbs she knew he favored in his bath. It played havoc with her senses, sweeping her up again into memories so powerful that her knees might have buckled had she not reached a hand out to the small table beside the hearth to steady herself.

More than anything, she wanted to avoid the humiliation of sputtering incoherently, of letting him know just how much his physical presence affected her. And so she found herself pausing until she felt more confident that she could string words together in a reasonable way.

She had just mastered herself enough to form a suitable retort when he suddenly lifted his right hand to her cheek, freezing her into shocked silence once more. His long, elegant fingers slid up along her jaw, while his thumb brushed in a gentle stroke just above the corner of her mouth. And still he said nothing.

The delicious sensation of his touch nearly made her gasp, but against all instinct she forced herself to pull away after a moment of that guilt-ridden bliss. At the same time she issued a command that somehow ended up sounding more like a husky plea. "Pray tell, what do you think you're doing?"

His mouth quirked up in that seductive half smile again, sending a new wave of curling warmth through her. It was followed, however, by mortification, as he lifted the hand that had touched her so gently to reveal the smudge of soot he had removed from her cheek with his thumb.

"Oh . . ."

Any ash that might have remained on her face was surely obscured by the flaming red that filled it, if the heat she felt rising was any indication of the hue of her skin.

"You should be more careful." Damien's voice sounded slightly hoarse, and Alissende knew a flare of satisfaction in thinking that perhaps he wasn't quite as unaffected as he seemed to be. "You are not dressed properly for the task of setting a fire, and soot cannot easily be removed once it invades the fine texture of silk."

"I did not realize that you were so knowledgeable regarding women's fashion," she answered flippantly, in a desperate attempt to distance herself from him in some way.

Damien's reaction was almost imperceptible, but she saw nevertheless that her tiny barb had sunk home. She couldn't help feeling a bit repentant at having taunted him so, though when he replied, any lingering remorse vanished.

"I learned much of various fabrics, their qualities and worth when I lived and traveled through the Holy Land and later, Cyprus," he murmured, his expression sharper now. "But anything I know about the intricacies of a woman's clothing—the feel of a silk gown when one is unfastening it, for example—I learned directly from you, lady."

The comment stung at the same time that it unleashed a powerful swell of something else, something that bound her to him in a way that she knew she would never feel with another man. But it did not matter. They were here by reason of a cold, practical arrangement, and there was no room for sugary sentiment in the mix.

Alissende cast him a dark look and tried to step around him, intending to leave before she said anything to make this situation worse. But he shifted his body, blocking her passage and causing her to speak with him again, this time in vexation.

"Come, sir, and let me pass."

"Nay. We must discuss something before you flee again."

"I am *not* fleeing—and I can think of naught else that needs to be said. You made yourself quite clear in the solar," she replied, still smarting from all that had transpired this day.

"Ah, but this is in regards to what you said only a

few moments ago, when you told me that you came here to ready 'my' chamber."

"Aye." Alissende frowned. "And I spoke the truth. Now that I have accomplished that task, I intend to call a serving lad to complete the last minor preparations. You may settle your belongings here and be secure by nightfall."

He made a sound of exasperation in his throat. "There—you have just done it again."

"Done what?"

"You keep speaking as if I will occupy this chamber alone. I trust you are aware that such an arrangement will not suit."

That set off a wild jangling inside her, and she studied him, readying herself for battle. "Of course it will suit. I am accustomed to sleeping in one of the guest chambers, and I intend to continue doing so for the term of our agreement."

He stood there before her, unmoved; a golden warrior, tall, powerful, and stunningly handsome in his stubbornness. Another tingle of warning slipped up her spine, along with the fear that she might not find means to resist him if he demanded this of her. It compelled her to add, "You cannot expect otherwise, Damien, for it is you who insisted upon celibacy within the bounds of this temporary union."

"I did—and that shall be honored," he answered roughly, keeping her trapped in the intense blue currents of his gaze. "However, we must occupy the same chamber to uphold the appearance of being husband and wife, regardless of it."

Alissende felt a sense of terror grip her, and the

barely controlled passions that had been roiling in her breast flared to life again. Oh, God, he was being cruel to insist upon this. Cruel to demand that she share a chamber with him after all they had been to each other so long ago. She would not allow it. "Why?" she demanded, almost choking on the word.

Damien exhaled sharply and glanced away for a moment before he swung his gaze back to her. "You have been at court far more recently than I, Alissende. Has it changed that much then, in the years I was away?"

"It is as it has always been," she answered reluctantly.

"Then you know as well as I that gossip is like life's blood to them."

"Perhaps. But I do not see what that has to do with where I choose to sleep of an evening."

"You cannot overlook that we will be journeying to King Edward's court before long," Damien contended, "and so will those of your servants who accompany us. Do you think for a moment that even the *hint* of any scandal that occurs between us here will not reach the ears of the noble lords and ladies there—including Hugh de Valles or even the king himself?"

She could not refute what he was saying, yet each word rang like a death knell on her heart. The aching inside her swelled until it was almost unbearable, and she found herself needing to look away from him as he continued his very logically stated argument. "If I am to properly protect you, lady, none must suspect that there is aught between us but the usual familiarity of a newly married man and his wife."

Still she could not bring herself to speak in reply or to look at him.

He grabbed her hand then, startling her as he called

her gaze back to him, and she saw that his eyes burned with emotion. "By God, Alissende, if you will lead me into sin with this agreement we have struck, then you must be willing to do what is necessary to see it through! We must occupy the same chamber at night, whether here, at court, or anywhere else we may need to travel. We have no other choice."

His voice sounded hoarse as he spoke the last part, and Alissende realized, suddenly, that he must dread the idea of this as much as she did—that sharing a chamber with her, of all people, would prove to be a curse for him far more than a long-awaited chance to wound her.

Aye, he wanted none of it.

Yet at the core she knew that Damien was a principled man. He had made a promise to protect her as a husband for six months, and he was bound to keep his word, no matter what it took.

In all honor, she could do no less.

The fight seemed to go out of her with that awareness, leaving her feeling more empty and exhausted than ever. She gently pulled her hand away, glancing down for a moment before lifting her gaze, trying to remain strong. "Very well, Damien. I concede your point and will arrange for my belongings to be secured here before nightfall."

He nodded in a gesture that was as stiff as the strain showing on his face.

"Is that all, then?" she asked, finding it more difficult than ever to maintain her composure in the wake of this intimate conversation with him.

"Aye, Alissende, that is all. For now."

She felt that little catch in her belly again. It disconcerted her even more than it had the first time, for now she felt the weight of what she had just agreed to pressing down on her. After a final, tense pause, she nodded. "I will return in an hour, then, with details of the pledging ceremony we must feign this afternoon."

Then she stepped past and strode purposefully from the chamber—knowing that if she did not leave at that very moment, she might well do something in front of him for which she would never forgive herself.

For right now she wanted nothing so much as to bury her face in her hands and weep.

Damien watched the door click softly shut behind her before he allowed himself to exhale his first full breath since coming in here. If there had been aught left in the hollow, dark place where his faith in God used to reside, he would have fallen to his knees, praying for the strength to see this through. As it stood, there was nothing there to aid him but emptiness and a bone-deep hurt in his awareness of God's absence from him. He was conscious of it more than ever, realizing that, as with the torments dealt him by the Inquisition, he would be alone in facing this ordeal.

And what an ordeal it was. His arrangement with Alissende was a trial the likes of which he had never known. A tender trap ensnaring him on all sides. He was bound by his word to protect her, which meant that his command for a shared chamber must be upheld. Yet he was also bound by his own tortured yearnings—taunted by desires that no longer had a place in his life, and which warned him to stay as far away from her as was physically possible.

They are naught but the carnal wants of a man who has been too long without the comforts of a woman. That phrase repeated itself over and over in his mind. He simply had to master his needs, as he had done during the years he served in celibacy with the Brotherhood of Templars, and all would be well.

But sweet heaven, he would be sharing a chamber—sharing a *bed*—with Alissende . . . with the very woman who was his own personal temptation. He could not risk that she would compare the scarred, tortured shell of a man that he was today with the accomplished lover and noble knight he had once been.

He could not risk creating a babe with her.

And as sure as hell burned for the wicked, he would not risk his heart.

Nay, never again with anyone—but most especially not with her, who had held his love in her palms and then so blithely crushed it to nothingness five years ago.

He let loose a muted groan as he took the few steps to sink into the ornate chair in the corner of the chamber. He tried to cool the raging in his brain. But even with all the warnings abounding in his mind, his thoughts were already awhirl with tormenting images and relentless fantasies. He managed to shake his head ruefully, a rusty-sounding laugh escaping the tightness of his throat.

Only time would tell how foolish he had been to insist upon sharing this chamber with Alissende, and how long he would find means to resist touching her . . . how long he could go on playing at lovers with her, without making her his own in truth again.

He decided that he had to be the most ill-advised, daft, and reckless man in all of Christendom.

What in the devil's name have I gotten myself into? The mocking voice kept up the challenge until Damien shook his head once more, closing his eyes and tipping his face into his hands.

For the sad truth was that he had no blessed idea.

No idea at all.

Chapter 4

Alissende paced the great hall nearly three hours later, trying to appear interested in the activity around her as servants set up and readied nearly two dozen tables for the feast that would take place after the feigned wedding ceremony. A serving lad unfolded a long, rectangular cloth to lay atop the wooden table nearest her, snapping it to remove any lingering wrinkles, before letting it waft down, releasing as he did the clean scent of the lavender sprigs that had been packed between the folds of fabric.

She watched his and the other servants' progress, focusing on their efforts so that she could avoid thinking about what she and Damien were about to do . . . trying to forget that she would need take his arm soon and walk publicly with him from the castle to the stone church in the village; there, although it was customary to perform such vows on the steps, before the eyes of villagers and castle servants alike, they would retreat inside and shut the doors, presumably to pledge their troth in private. It was being done so, her cousin Michael had assured any to whom he spoke, out of deference to Damien, who after years of serving in the Templar Brotherhood, felt the need for personal reflection and confession prior to speaking marriage vows.

The excuse seemed to have been accepted, and so Alissende had retreated to what had formerly been her chamber in the guest wing, to begin the wedding preparations her mother had insisted upon. It did not matter that this ceremony was for naught but appearance sake. It had to *seem* real, her mother had reasoned, and so Alissende had been bathed and scented, her long, dark hair brushed until it had shone before being artfully arranged with jeweled pins interwoven with flowers.

Then, without complaint, she had donned the lush, rose-hued gown her mother had produced from a dressing trunk, adding a delicate golden girdle fastened low on her hips. It was encrusted with gems to match the circlet on her brow, and the finished ensemble was as fine as what any noble lady might choose for her wedding day.

A grand deception, played to perfection.

But it would not happen at all if Damien did not deign to show himself here soon.

"Try to stop pacing, Alissende," Lady Blanche murmured from behind her. "If you do not wear a path in the rushes, you will at the least attract unwanted attention— and perhaps unwelcome talk as well."

Though Alissende stilled her movements, a bloom of resentment flared in her breast. It was not directed toward her mother, however. As always, Lady Blanche was a gentle support in times of trouble and a source of unreserved love. Nay, it was bitterness at everything else, at the gossip she had to take such care not to provoke, that irked her so. She had spent her entire life under the spell of such worries, and it had cost her much.

"Ah, my sweet one," her mother continued, stepping close enough to gaze into her eyes and stroke her gentle fingers along her cheek. "I know this is difficult, but you must try to concentrate on the good of it all. On the protection you will be gaining by proceeding with this formality."

Alissende could not speak past the knot in her throat, though she tried to nod her head; Lady Blanche looked stricken at just how much her daughter was struggling, and she made a small sound of sympathy before she added in a choked whisper, "Never fear, *ma fille*. It is for but a short time, and then we will find means to ensure your safety once and for all, I swear it."

Heat did flood Alissende's eyes, then, her throat seeming to close even tighter against the overwhelming emotions those innocent words called forth. Her mother took such care of her. But she could not know . . . oh, God, she did not know the full truth—not about Damien those many years ago, or what had followed with Godfrey, or even what she was feeling right now . . . because Alissende had never told her. What Lady Blanche had discerned on her own had been wrenching enough for her to bear, and Alissende had never wanted to add to her dear mother's burden. But that did not mean she couldn't appreciate the love being given to her so freely.

Reaching out, she grasped her mother's hands and pulled her close in an embrace, kissing her cheek and trying to keep the tears behind a smile.

"It is all right, *Mère*. Please do not worry for me. What will be, will be, and I promise that I will remain strong and will not give anyone cause to think there is aught amiss with me or this union that I am about to undertake."

Alissende felt her mother nod, sighing against her cheek, and she reveled in the comfort of her arms, warm and secure around her. Closing her eyes, she released her breath fully, glad for this moment's peace to bolster her for the coming events. But in the next moment Alissende felt her mother stiffen. Alissende pulled back to study her face, concerned at the sudden change.

"*Mère,* what is it?" she asked, frowning.

The normally composed Lady Blanche wore a look of mild amazement. Alissende twisted to see what she was staring at, and her insides lurched at the sight greeting her.

It was Damien, approaching them from across the hall—but not the same Damien who had stood in the solar but a few hours since in traveling clothes, and with the dust of the road settled over him. Nay, the man who had just emerged from the stairway took her breath away. As always, he was stunning perfection in face and form, but above that, the garments he wore now appeared to have been made for him alone. They were of such a fine styling and costly fabric that they would be worthy of any of the highest-ranking lords at court.

She'd warrant his embroidered tunic had cost the equivalent of several months' wages of a simple knight, no less a former Templar who had been constrained by vows of poverty and had suffered in captivity for most of the past nine months. How he'd come by such elegant and expensive attire was an enigma to be sure, and one she was eager to solve.

She was still suffering the effects of his striking appearance when he finally reached her, his hitherto stoic expression shifting subtly to a frown.

"Is aught amiss?" he murmured, looking so serious that had he been anyone else, she might have made an effort to reassure him. As it stood, it was all she could do to subdue the strange twisting sensation his arrival had set off inside her, and settle for a jerky shake of her head.

"Nay. I simply did not expect you to have brought such finery with you."

"I did not. They are courtesy of your mother." The intensity of his gaze slid from her to Lady Blanche for an instant. "Is that not correct, lady?"

Her mother had far too much experience navigating the difficult social waters at court to be flustered by such a challenge, Alissende knew, and so she watched as Lady Blanche coolly accepted this one with her usual grace and style. "It is, sir. Further, you may consider it and the entirety of the wardrobe crafted for you, with Fra Benedictus's help in advance of your arrival, as my gift, given in gratitude for championing my daughter. I trust you do not object, considering that it reveals my assumption of your aid before you gave it."

Damien paused, so stiff in his aspect that Alissende could not help wondering if her hand might not encounter stone rather than warm flesh were she to touch him right now. But in the next breath he nodded and offered her mother a slight bow, his expression still tight but slightly less pained. "Considering my current situation, I would say that far from objection, I owe you my appreciation for your foresight. Thank you."

Lady Blanche did flush then, perhaps in response to the sincerity in Damien's voice, and Alissende knew the echo of something similar in herself. She remembered this about him—this way he had of disarming others with his forthright honesty. He hadn't lost the touch of that, it seemed, and she couldn't quite suppress her pleasurable shiver at that thought.

Her musings ended abruptly as he held out his arm to her. "Shall we proceed with what must be done, then, lady?"

Mutely she nodded, slipping her hand into the crook of his arm and trying to think of anything but the play of hard muscle beneath her palm. They set off for the chapel, making their way through the great hall and out the door, to leave the castle grounds and go to the larger church in the village.

As they went, the activity around them slowed; servants, serfs, and freeborn, men, women, and children alike, all seemed to pause in what they were doing, many of them straightening and swiveling to face them, watching as they proceeded through the village. Others joined the growing mass of people gathering behind and forming a wedding procession of sorts. Alissende had to call upon all of her strength to keep her face impassive . . . to hold her chin high through the painful charade of it.

Damien spoke not a word, and when she hazarded a glance at him, she saw that he wore much the same expression she was struggling to maintain: a look of controlled restraint. But she couldn't help wondering if beneath the surface, he felt the same wild tumbling of emotion as she did.

In a few moments she decided that if he *was* suffering any pangs, he was far better at masking it; twice along the way she stumbled as a result of her nervousness, and he was compelled to reach out his other hand to keep her from falling. Each time, he remained silent while he steadied her, though she saw the lean rope of muscle in his jaw twitch, as if he was clenching his teeth to subdue something at work inside him.

It was likely naught but his continued animosity at having been coerced into this bargain with her, she told herself. He was no longer the same man she'd once loved; nay, this stranger beside her was but a hard, dark shadow of that golden knight. That thought helped her to be strong the rest of the way, and she clung to her own resentments, pushing aside the old yearnings and regrets in order to gain a measure of peace that she prayed would aid her in getting through the remainder of this excruciating farce.

After what seemed an eternity, they arrived at the church door, along with the throng of villagers and servants who had amassed in their wake. Damien half-turned, and with barely a nod of acknowledgment to their sporadic cheers, he led her through the arched doors. She took three steps inside before pausing in the dim light. Looking straight ahead, she saw Michael waiting for them at the altar, with Fra Benedictus at his side.

Both men wore serious expressions, and she felt as if she stood apart, detached in some way from what was happening. She breathed in the smoky, sweet scent coming from the incense burners and beeswax tapers on the altar, and felt the cooler air inside the church wrap around her like gossamer.

But in the next instant Damien touched her elbow again. His grip was firm, leading her inexorably forward. And then the doors swung shut behind them, separating them from the crowd. . . .

Leaving them to carry out this first part of their great deception in the secret, holy silence.

Damien didn't know how much more of this he could take.

It had begun with the afternoon's feigned exchange of vows and had not let up since. After he'd led Alissende to the altar inside the village church, he had stepped aside, unable to do aught but watch in painful silence as she'd knelt in prayer—realizing too late that every moment he spent inside that holy place would only serve to prick and scrape at the raw place of lost faith inside of him.

Ben had tried to offer quiet support, but it hadn't mitigated the difficult truth. When Father Michael had cast him a somber look, Damien's mouth had tightened with bitterness, as he'd known that the priest expected him to go through the motions of praying, at least. He had refused. There would be time enough for such pretense in the countless days to come, when he would be living under the weight of strange eyes, watching his every move.

And yet even that had not been the worst of it.

The time they'd spent within those sheltering stone walls had also drawn into sharp contrast the reality between the farce of this mock wedding and what he had hoped for with Alissende five years ago. It had stung more deeply than he would have imagined possible. He had found himself watching her with a burning sensation in his chest, until she'd finally stood from her prayers and moved to the sanctuary with him at the Gospel side of the altar.

Father Michael had joined them there, using the remaining time to remind them both of the need to be convincing in their efforts to show the world that theirs was a love match and not one undertaken in an act of selfish disobedience to the king. Of immediate concern was the fact that there had been some grumbling and rumor within the ranks of the castle guard, who were now under Damien's command. It was imperative that they continue their efforts to quell any lingering talk here at Glenheim before they traveled to court.

The news had been unwelcome, though not unexpected. Damien had absorbed the import of it in silence. Alissende had as well, though her face had grown paler than it had been before, if such a thing were possible.

And then had come the wedding feast.

They had been trapped next to each other in the great hall, constrained to try to behave for the world as a happy, newly married pair. Damien had thought he might go mad from it. It had been a kind of agony, being forced to sit so closely beside this woman who had once comprised his most secret yearnings and deepest desires. A lady believed by all to be his wife, but who in all truth and honor he could not touch in the ways a man was meant to touch a woman. Ways that he had touched her before, many times in the days before she had ripped out his heart with her betrayal.

He swallowed hard at the bitterness that filled him with the recollection and turned to his recently filled cup of wine, draining it in one gulp before gesturing for the serving lad who bore the pitcher of drink to approach again. Everything had intensified over the course of the past three hours. It was as if against his will he'd become attuned to every nuance of Alissende's body—to each breath she'd taken, to the feather-light brush of her sleeve against his arm while they'd eaten, and the slight movement of her head as she'd inclined it toward any with whom she spoke.

To the gentle perfume he knew, from tormenting memory, that she always applied to the soft skin inside her elbow and the tiny hollow at the base of her throat . . . and to other more hidden places, as well.

That thought had teased him, maddened him, her scent wafting over him like a spell every time she'd raised her goblet in acknowledgment of yet another wedding toast. It had been all he could do not to drag her to him and force her to acknowledge the passion she called up in him in a manner that would dispel all doubt in the matter.

He'd been left feeling raw, his very flesh charged by constant stimulation that had had no release. If fate had not intervened in the form of external distractions, he would not have been able to keep himself from shoving away from the table and striding out into the cooling dark outside to restore his sanity. As it stood, he had been saved, after a fashion, by mundane necessity. A short while ago, the introductions had begun with nary a rest between them, except to choke down bites of food at irregular intervals from the astonishing array of delicacies that had been provided for the celebration.

He had met Sir Reynald Fitzgibbon, captain of Glenheim's castle guard, along with another threescore of the men now under his command. None had shown any outward sign of disrespect or suspicion, for which he had been silently thankful. He had been greeted with cautious good spirits by tradesmen and various other folk from the village: a seamstress and her daughter, a carter, the miller who served both Glenheim's people and those of the next village, a weaver, a master carpenter, the blacksmith, and an alewife.

The flurry of it all had helped to distract him, as had Alissende's decision, a few moments ago, to arise from their table and walk amongst the people, greeting them with thanks for attending the celebration.

Aye, he thought ruefully, their physical separation helped . . . as long as he could manage to keep himself from tracking her with his gaze, following her every graceful movement like a predator marking his prey. It seemed a near impossible task. Shaking his head, he forced himself to stare into the ruby red depths of his wine, willing his mind to less dangerous paths.

Another pointless exercise. Nay, nothing would assuage the ripening urge he felt building inside of him, and he was angry at himself for it. It was not as if he was a green lad, untested by desire. But he could not deny that he had never known a sense of want this intense. This demanding of his focus even to keep it at bay. He was failing miserably in that effort, which made Ben's timing as he approached from the opposite side of the hall all the more unfortunate.

"Damien—?"

"What?" Damien snapped, swinging his gaze for just an instant to Ben before he turned back to his

half-empty cup, lifting it to his mouth to down the remainder of it in one desperate swallow.

His friend made a huffing sound. "There is no call to
be so bad-tempered, man. This is not my doing."

Damien simply glared at him in response.

Impervious to the danger burning in that gaze, Ben
squatted down next to Damien's chair, so that he might
speak more softly and for his hearing only. "I came to
remind you that the feast will likely come to a close
within the hour, and yet there has been little evidence
of your interest in Lady Alissende as your newly wedded wife, beyond the act of sitting next to her at table.
Some of the men are beginning to take notice and talk
among themselves, only with the vehemence lent them
by the drink they've consumed this night."

"They can be hanged," Damien muttered, wishing
the warmth that was beginning to fill him in response
to his own swift downing of drink would hurry along
and ease him from his misery a bit. "Alissende is *not*
my wife. Not in truth. And the idea of a public display
of attention to her as such is more than I can bear right
now." He gestured to a serving lad to refill his goblet
once more.

"That is unfortunate," Ben answered, his mouth
smiling even as the words came through clenched
teeth, "and also irrelevant, I'm afraid. You would be
wise to set down your cup for a while, call on that
steadfast resolve for which you are so famed, and begin
behaving like the besotted groom you are supposed to
be, else all of your plans for these six months will
prove for naught."

Damien bit back a growl that he was certain would
have sounded more wolf than man had he allowed it

full release. He directed his stare toward the table of men-at-arms—*his* men-at-arms now, he reminded himself—noting several sideways glances, a few frowns, and what seemed to be murmured comments that were mostly hidden behind lifted cups. Ben was right, damn him. There was something brewing there. And if it was suspicion over the authenticity of his union with Alissende, then his duty demanded that he put it to rest with some kind of action.

The thought sat like a lead weight on his chest. It meant he would have to embrace her in front of these people. He would have to make them believe that he loved her. And that meant he'd have to—

Blast it all to hell.

His jaw tightened for a moment before he stiffly turned his head to meet Ben's gaze again and muttered, "If I do this, I will need to leave immediately afterward for the privacy of my chamber. My control hangs by a thread as it is."

Ben looked somehow sanguine as he nodded his acquiescence. "Aye, but just remember that it is your wedding chamber to which you retreat—and that you must needs bring Lady Alissende with you."

Damien did utter a curse aloud then, closing his eyes and tipping his head back as his entire body stiffened in reaction to that overlooked reality. This was going to call upon every ounce of his strength, and still he did not know how he was going to survive it. He opened his eyes, his gaze seeking her out in the chamber almost against his will, feeling that pang of need, hurt, and unadulterated desire sweep through him at the sight of her as she leaned over to speak to the miller's wife.

The bejeweled, glossy plaits of her dark hair caught

the same flickering torchlight that lent a warm blush of color to her throat and cheeks, while the silk of her gown clung to her elegant form, caressing slender spans and voluptuous curves in a way that begged him to sweep his hands along the same sweet paths.

By all that was holy, he did not know how he was going to get through this. And yet he had no choice. He had made a promise to protect her, and he had never taken lightly any vow he'd made.

He breathed in, willing his body to relax, to make his mind as blank as he could, save for the task ahead of him. He would think of this in the same way he did an entrance to a battle. Aye, that was what he would do. For this *was* a battle of sorts, only one with his heart and soul at the stake.

"All right, let's get on with it, then," he murmured, exhaling as he pushed himself to stand, all the while keeping his sights fixed on the woman who waited with such innocent allure across the chamber . . . the lady who was about to become his partner in the deed ahead, whether she realized it or nay.

Alissende first noticed that something had changed, subtly perhaps, but changed nonetheless, while she was speaking with Matilda, the miller's wife. A kind of hush seemed to spread over the gathering of villagers, men-at-arms, and other guests in the main hall, and by instinct, she straightened to see if she could discern the cause.

It took but an instant to realize that the blanket of quiet was in response to Damien. He had unfolded his lean and powerful body to stand in his place at the head table. And he was staring at her.

A jolt of heat unfurled inside. *What was this about?*

He remained silent, simply gazing at her, and she flushed. She felt warmth fill her cheeks, but she was powerless to prevent it. Oh, but he was handsome. There was no mistaking how he had earned the name Archangel those years ago at court; he was chiseled to muscular perfection, a breathtaking warrior who exuded at once an aura of dangerous sensuality and unwavering resolve that was nothing less than mesmerizing.

He continued to fix her with his stare, and the effect of those eyes upon her—icy blue and yet burning with such a delicious and sinful promise of pleasure—nearly caused her knees to buckle. Vaguely, she heard the scattered sighs and murmurs of adoration that swept through the female portion of this gathering. But she could not look away from Damien. And he would not relinquish his stare upon her, either.

The realization came with a sharp pang; it was the same look he'd given her time and again, before. The one that caressed her as if his hands were playing over her body, unlocking all of her secrets with his touch . . . that turned her insides to warm honey and caused her heart to beat faster with anticipation of what was to come.

The look that said without a doubt to any who saw it that she was his. His alone.

Sweet Jesu . . .

"It is time to bid this gathering a fond *adieu*," Damien suddenly called out, his voice husky, though still fully audible throughout the chamber. He stepped away from the table, moving deliberately, all the while keeping his gaze locked with hers as he crossed the distance between them. "For while I thank all of you here for your presence in celebration of this blessed day," he continued, coming closer, and closer, "I find that I can wait no longer to complete the vows I made to your lady. Vows best undertaken . . . in private."

If the floor had dropped away beneath her, Alissende would not have been more surprised than she found herself at this moment. She was rendered speechless—but the chamber around her was not. The room erupted with cheers and masculine calls of encouragement, intermingled with feminine gasps, murmurs, and sighs of envy.

She felt like she'd been swept into another world, to a place that existed only in the tormented shadows of her dreams. In sleep she had surrendered to this very fantasy, had imagined how wonderful this moment might feel. Now that she faced it in truth, she was brought to a shocked standstill.

But there was no time to think on it. Damien had crossed the chamber and was now standing directly in front of her. Alissende blinked, but he did not fade away as he would have in her dream. Nay, he stood close enough that she could have touched him if she wished. Still overwhelmed with all she was feeling, she could not bring herself to undertake that temptation. Not yet.

Damien seemed to possess no similar reluctance.

Before she could even consider protesting, he slid his arm around her waist, tugging her full against him, and the sudden rush of sensation made her gasp aloud. But when he raised his other hand to sweep up along her cheek, burying his fingers in her hair to cup the back of her head, everything seemed to go still inside her.

"Play along with me, Alissende—please," he murmured to her, even as he tipped her back the slightest bit and slanted his mouth over hers for a kiss of such passion that it stole what little breath remained to her.

Sweet angels in heaven . . .

Damien's tender assault broke the spell that had held her in thrall, and her instincts surged to life. Arching up, she kissed him back, tasting him fully and reveling in the sweet, hot demand of his mouth on hers. It felt so good . . . so good to kiss him again, and one hand grasped at the front of his tunic while her other slid up to the nape of his neck, tangling in the thick waves there.

She heard the low sound of pleasure from deep in his throat as he came back for more, and then more again, until she felt light-headed with the need that rushed through her like licking flames. Her arm tightened over his shoulders lest she sink to the floor in a boneless heap, the barrage of exquisite sensation almost too much to bear.

At last, with a feral-sounding growl, he pulled away, though just enough to reach one arm down behind her knees and sweep her up into his embrace. He cradled her against him, and the cheers grew deafening as he carried her toward the doorway that led to the upper floor . . . *to the private chamber they were to share as man and wife.*

That realization, coupled with what had just happened, stabbed deep, startling her from her sensual languor.

"Damien—?" she uttered in a hoarse whisper, seeking his gaze, struggling for purchase in a world that seemed to have gone whirling madly around her.

His glance sliced into her, sharp and filled with bittersweet agony. It silenced her, and she understood in that sinking moment that what had just passed between them had been for naught but show. That his kisses had been actions put on for the benefit of those gathered to witness their marriage feast.

Many of the more boisterous members of the crowd clamored behind them, forming the party of witnesses traditional to a couple's first bedding. Those most into their cups called out suggestive comments for conjugal bliss, while the women batted at their drunken mates, laughing and giving advice of their own, as they followed along on the journey to the lord's chamber.

At last they reached the door, and Damien paused, turning to face those gathered in the expectation of some sport. He cleared his throat, and the small crowd grew silent, eager to hear what he would say.

"As no audience is required for the consummation of a second marriage, I would ask that you leave us here to our privacy. For as warm as it is in the great hall this summer's eve, I warrant that this chamber will prove dangerously *hot* before long—pleasurable for us, perhaps, but for you? . . ."

He let his voice trail off, shaking his head and grinning at the hoots of the menfolk in response to his suggestive claim. Only Alissende knew how much the moment cost him, for it felt as if every muscle in his chest and arms tightened as he held her, and she saw the rigid clench of his jaw from the side.

The women reacted most swiftly to his request. Many of them winked and blew kisses to Alissende as they tugged their men away, enticing them with promises of more wine and some dancing. It did not take long for their efforts to bear fruit. With some final calls of naughty teasing, the crowd began to clear.

When the last few were turning to meander back to the great hall, and Damien had waved away her lady's maid and the servants who had come to light the tapers inside the wedding chamber, he nudged the door open with his shoulder and carried her across the threshold. For an instant, the light from the corridor spilled into the room on a slant from behind them, throwing into garish relief the milky leaded windows, the table and chair near the hearth, and the large, curtained bed.

And then the heavy wooden slab swung in behind them.

It shut with a muted thud, muffling the revelry of the final stragglers on their way back to the wedding feast, and leaving the two of them alone in the heady, silent darkness.

Chapter 5

With deliberate care, Damien released Alissende, easing her to her feet before stepping back and away from her as swiftly as he could. His insides were a jumble. His mind—and other parts of him—flamed with desires that had been stimulated almost beyond bearing in the act of kissing her. In hearing those soft sounds she'd made as his mouth had captured hers, tasting her again after so long . . .

In feeling her body pressed against him and breathing in her tantalizing scent until his body had pulsed with the need to take her in all the ways they'd once known so well together.

Heaven help him . . .

He had to stop this, damn it. Right now.

Glad for the shielding dark of the chamber, he stalked over to one of the few windows not filled with leaded glass and pushed open the shutter, letting in the

fragrant summer breeze. And then he simply stood
there, looking out and taking in deep, even breaths,
trying to recapture his self-control. Behind him, he
could hear Alissende's faint movements; she had shifted
from their spot in the doorway to approach the hearth.
Soon he realized that she was completing the task
the servants would have done had he not sent them
away.

She lit several of the beeswax tapers scattered about
in as much abundance here as they had been in every
other chamber he'd seen in the castle. Behind him, a
muted glow flickered to life, dispelling the darkness; it
created a shadow of her movements, a graceful display
against the lush blue and gold designs painted on the
wall next to the window where he stood.

But still he could not bring himself to turn and face
her directly. Not yet.

The room fell quiet. He concentrated on looking out
and heard naught but the sound of the summer breeze
whispering around the crenellations . . . until a tiny
clicking noise at last drew his attention. Instinctively,
he hazarded a glance toward the source of the sound
and immediately regretted the decision.

Alissende was loosening her hair from its pins and
circlet. Freeing those fragrant, glorious tresses in preparation for bed. *Hellfire and damnation . . .*

He tried to pull his gaze away but could not. To his
gratitude, she was sitting with her back to him, on a
bench at one of the large wooden trunks that served as
a table between travels. Her arms were lifted as she
removed the delicate jeweled pins, setting each one
down carefully as she pulled it loose of the arrangement. The final pin came free, releasing the spill of

dark, wavy silk down her back, and Damien felt his gut clench, felt his breath seize up in his chest. He was forced to fist his hands in response to the sudden, powerful memory that swept through him of another time and place . . . of burying his hands in that soft bounty to tip her head back as he lavished kisses along the tender, exposed column of her throat and lower, ah, sweet heaven, yes, much lower . . .

He choked back a groan, but not swiftly enough. Alissende stiffened; he saw her breathe in and heard her gentle, full exhalation before she twisted around to face him.

She met his gaze, and he saw that her vulnerable expression of earlier had been replaced by a look of seeming composure. Only one thing marred her controlled aspect. As had been the case since the day he'd met her, her eyes revealed all the inner workings of her heart, no matter how she tried to mask it. And right now she was not feeling as calm as she pretended.

"Do you wish to retire to the bed, then?" she asked.

Surprise and a sharp, unwelcome jolt of heat shot through him. Suppressing it by force of pure will, he raised his brow at her in challenge.

Her cheeks tinted a delicate pink, and he saw her struggle not to glance away. "I refer only to our arrangements for sleep, Damien. As lord of Glenheim, use of the bed is your right."

"And what of you?"

"That depends upon your wishes," she replied evenly, and he could not help but admire the way she kept her gaze steadfast upon him; if this moment was proving half as difficult for her as it was for him, then she was a veritable pillar of strength.

"Wishes and necessity often travel two separate paths, Alissende," he murmured, gratified to see a tiny crack appear in her armor, when the hands she'd folded so placidly in her lap clenched in response.

But still she kept her gaze constant, and he realized that he would not—could not—continue this sparring with her. Too much had happened today already, and he was feeling far too raw.

"The bed seems wide enough to accommodate us both in such a way that our agreement can be honored without fear," he settled for saying in a low voice. "However, tonight, I think it is safe to say that any restful sleep will elude me. You may retire to the bed alone."

"As you wish."

Damien felt a tiny jab of warning at her nonchalant tone. What—no argument? But it was too much for his tormented mind to unravel right now, so he pushed it aside and finished somewhat awkwardly, "You may prepare for sleep in privacy; I will turn around until you are within the enclosure of the bed curtains."

"Then you will be waiting for a very long time."

"Why?" Damien frowned, wanting nothing more but to have this already painful day over.

"Because I cannot disrobe by myself," Alissende replied matter-of-factly. She half twisted to show him the laces and a few very expensive buttons along the slender length of her back.

"How do you usually accomplish it?" he demanded.

"My lady's maid assists me. But you sent her away. Remember?" She blinked once at him, and if he wasn't so tired, he might have sworn that her gaze bore a glint of stung pride and—and the light of *battle,* by all that was holy.

"You will have to call her back, then." Damien's mind refused to consider the alternative. Nay, he could not venture there.

Alissende gazed at him, not speaking. But those eyes . . . blast it, as always she spoke volumes with them, only this time the message he read there pricked at his masculine honor.

"What?" he growled.

She paused, seeming as if she might answer, but then that horribly placid expression swept over her face again, and she gave a tiny shrug. "As you wish."

"Stop saying that."

Her lips pursed, but she remained silent.

"Tell me what you intended to say," he demanded, not the least bit mollified by her seeming cooperation.

"I cannot." She gave him a look of pure innocence. "You've forbidden me speaking it again."

Damien restrained another growl, clenching his teeth to mutter, "Not the cursed 'as you wish.' Tell me what you were going to say in response to my suggestion that you call your lady's maid back to this chamber."

"Oh."

"Well?" he demanded after another pause.

"I thought you might wish to reconsider how it would look."

He glared at her in exasperation. "Explain."

She pinned him with her gaze, clearly relishing the opportunity he had opened with his command for her to speak. "It is supposed to be our wedding night, and yet after sending everyone away, it will appear that you are not up to the challenge of removing your bride's garments for what would usually follow the retreat to the marriage chamber."

Her tone held an edge that belied her continued calm expression as she continued, "When word of that spreads, the people of Glenheim will either think you unskilled in a way most unflattering—or else anything you may have accomplished with your zealous display of kissing me in the great hall will have been for naught, as the gossip over the honesty of our union will erupt anew."

Damnation.

Damien scowled, unable to refute her. He met her gaze, hoping to intimidate her with his own, to make her realize that she was playing with fire in this, logic be damned.

She did not flinch.

Very well. No one could ever say he was the kind of man to back down willingly from a challenge. He fisted his hands, his jaw tightening.

"Turn around."

Her eyes widened a bit, but she did as he commanded; however, he noted how stiffly she held herself. Ah, could it be that this woman, who seemed to have turned into a creature of veritable stone since they'd entered this room, *was* capable of feeling, then, and perhaps fires similar to those which were burning him from the inside out at the thought of this?

The idea filled him with a sense of grim satisfaction that helped bolster him for what was to come. It still took him what seemed a full minute to steady himself before he reached out to touch her hair, pushing it forward over her shoulder to reveal the laces. The lustrous weight felt silken against his palm, and a hint of fragrance wafted up, teasing his senses with unmerciful power.

His hand began to shake, and he was forced to clench it into a fist and then release it again before he could trust himself to begin with the laces and three buttons that would need loosening.

"Is aught amiss?"

She spoke quietly and half-turned her head toward him, the movement exposing the graceful length of her neck more fully to his gaze.

In response, something deep inside him twisted in painful pleasure; he felt an overwhelming urge to brush his lips over that smooth skin, and it was all he could do to hold himself back from it. She had loved that, once, to have him kiss a sweet path along the side of her neck as he embraced her from behind. Lavishing gentle kisses that became more compelling caresses when she'd arch into him, murmuring and then making soft sounds of need before she twisted around to lift her mouth to his for a fiercer kind of loving . . .

Sweet mercy.

"Just keep still," he choked out, swallowing hard. He squeezed his eyes shut and tried to think of anything—the blood and sweat of battle, the monotony of swinging his blade in training, the dismal effort of trudging in full armor through the heat of a summer's day—anything to distract himself from what he was about to undertake.

Gritting his teeth for what seemed like the fiftieth time during the course of this unbearable day, he directed his focus to her back once more and attacked the laces, his fingers fumbling sometimes, both from lack of practice and from the edge of awareness that crept in, despite his best efforts, of just what exactly he was doing and with whom. He finished with the three delicate buttons, in his haste nearly popping them free of the threads that held them.

When at last he finished, he jerked back as if he'd been burned, muttering, "There. It is done."

For a moment Alissende remained still. Then she tilted her face back toward him once more and murmured, "Thank you."

Damien didn't trust his voice and so he gave a sharp nod in answer, before turning on his heel and stalking toward the windows again. He kept his back to Alissende, trying not to pay attention to the faint rustling sounds she made as she disrobed. Trying not to think about what would be revealed with each layer of clothing she peeled away.

It was almost unbearable. Not unbearable enough, however, to keep him from obsessively watching the movements of her shadow again. He grimaced with self-loathing. He should want nothing to do with the woman. She had deceived him and nearly destroyed him, and now she was using him for her own selfish gain as protection against Hugh de Valles. But he couldn't seem to stop himself from wanting her, damn it.

His gaze burned as that slender shadow raised its arms. She pulled up her smock—that final barrier between garment and skin—lifting it over her head to leave her as bare as Eve had been before the first taste of apple. When her shadow shifted, turning slightly sideways, he caught a glimpse of sweet curves, the delicious, tipped outline of her naked breasts, and his mouth went dry. Cursing silently, he forced himself to look away, back to the window.

What a fool he was not to have considered this prospect. Of course she would sleep naked. Everyone slept without clothing, especially in the warm summer months; it had been one of the freedoms he had come to miss when he'd served as a Templar, for the Brotherhood required garments to be worn at all times, even during bathing and sleep.

If only such precepts applied here and now, and with Alissende.

Though he refused to look directly at her shadow again, he saw from the side of his vision when she got into bed. She slipped wordlessly between the curtains that hung all around, suspended by golden hooks from the ceiling. He could turn around now without fear of seeing her, he knew, but he remained as he was. Otherwise, with the dangerous mix of lust and anger pounding through him, he didn't know what he might do, all vows and bargains be damned.

Stifling another groan, Damien leaned his forehead against the smooth wood of the window ledge, praying that night would pass more swiftly than it ever had—but knowing that the opposite was far more likely, and that he was doomed to wait like this, unsettled and unsatisfied, until the light of dawn.

Alissende lay very still in the bed, on her side, facing away from the place across the chamber where Damien sat at the window. Her heart pounded, but for the first time in the many months since Michael had come to her with his outrageous proposition of the proxy, it seemed to beat in a different cadence. With a kind of awareness that had been absent before.

The embers of something hot and dangerous still burned between her and Damien.

She had sensed it in his kiss and his touch, and she had seen it in his eyes when she'd used his pride against him in forcing him to help her disrobe. Oh, he'd resisted it mightily, aye, but it was there nonetheless. The possibility of it had at first bewildered her, sending a burning ache through her as he'd carried her to their bedchamber. But that had been replaced soon enough by vexation, an emotion far more welcome after he'd set her on her feet and run to the other side of the chamber as if he'd been on fire.

He had been on fire, she had realized with stunning clarity . . . on fire for *her.* He would not admit it, of course—perhaps he could not—and as she'd understood that truth, it had granted her a sense of control she had not known for a very long time.

What she would do with this newfound power, she did not yet know. She did not know, even, how *she* felt about it. Part of her still longed for the peace of the abbey, away from all men and their moods, intrigues, and desires . . . but another part of her yearned to tease and provoke—to stoke the flames between them until they were both consumed in a passion Damien could not deny.

It was too soon for such musings, though. The realization that she held some kind of sway over him, should she wish to wield it, was enough.

Aye, it was enough for now.

With that steadying thought, Alissende closed her eyes. This night was certain to be a long one, so she tried to relax as much as she could under the circumstances, doing her best to drift into peaceful, dreamless slumber.

Sometime between the dark of true night and the gray of early morn, Alissende stirred to a strange noise in the chamber. Still half-asleep, she struggled to open her eyes, noticing that the single candle she had left burning on the table when she'd crawled into bed had gone out. She sat up, trying to peer through the bed curtains. She could see nothing, but she heard the sound again—a strange, guttural noise, almost like a growl. She had never heard anything like it before, and it sent a chill up her spine.

Though the bed curtains were not sheer, they were of thin enough material that she could tell the chamber seemed brighter on one side. Tamping down her fear, she rolled in that direction and parted the fabric just slightly, to see what might be visible. The unshuttered window where Damien had been sitting at bedtime was still open, and the source of light she had noticed had come from that. It was apparently the waning moon, its milky glow spilling across the edge of the window and washing in muted tones what part of the chamber its weak force could reach.

And then she saw him. Damien was curled on the floor beneath the window, lying on his side with his knees drawn up and his fists clenched. Another growling noise came from him, then, and in concert with it he seemed to be tensing, restless in his sleep. Suddenly one arm flailed out, his fist slamming into the wooden floor with a crack that might have woken the dead.

But he did not rouse. He only continued to twist about restlessly, the growls interspersed with moans, now—the sounds he was making causing the hair on the back of Alissende's neck to prickle and making her throat tighten.

What in heaven's name was wrong with him—was he ill?

She paused for only a moment before worry outweighed reticence, and she slipped out of bed, pulling the sheet with her and wrapping it around herself to cover her nakedness. In a few steps, she reached Damien, her sheet making a faint whispering sound as the tail of it dragged along the floor in her wake, and she squinted as she neared him, trying to make out the details of his form and face in the dim light.

Though his eyes were closed, he shifted violently again just as she readied to kneel next to him, and she jerked back at the unexpected movement.

"Don't!"

The word burst from him in a fierce, sharp growl, though it was clear that he was still tangled in the depths of some terrible dream; his eyes remained closed and he was obviously unaware of her presence next to him.

Perhaps he had taken ill on his journey to Glenheim. Travelers often fell sick thanks to the rigors of the road, and those illnesses could turn deadly, especially if they were accompanied by fever that was not treated with the proper herbs and remedies.

There was only one way to find out if Damien was suffering in that way.

Taking a step closer again, Alissende dropped to her knees beside him; she kept one arm tight across her breasts to hold the sheet in place as she reached her other hand toward his brow. He had rolled onto his back, now, arms rigidly at his sides, so it shouldn't have been too difficult to accomplish—but he was clearly still gripped by distress, twisting and shifting in sleep, and his breath came in panting gasps.

She could not delay. Mouth tight with worry, she pushed forward and somehow managed to rest her palm on his brow. It was . . .

Cool.

His forehead was damp, but he had no fever.

She sat back on her heels as relief swept through her, along with a sense of surprise. He wasn't ill, then. So, what was it?

Just then one of Damien's arms lifted to crook over his face, as if to shield it from some unseen attack.

"Nay . . . no more . . . will not speak, will not . . ."

Different words this time, and a more urgent tone in his voice, hoarse and guttural, as if it was being wrenched from his throat. Heat welled behind Alissende's eyes to hear it, at the same time that her gaze happened upon something that had only just been revealed with Damien's movement and the ever-increasing light of approaching dawn.

Her hand flew to her mouth, stifling a gasp at the sight. He had taken off his elegant over-tunic before he'd fallen asleep, unlacing the linen shirt beneath as well, as the evening had been warm. When he'd lifted his arm it had fallen open, exposing scars on his torso that could only have come from painful lacerations or burns. They spread upward in an almost methodical pattern—along his ribs and across his chest until they were hidden from her sight. He moved again, his arm coming back down as he rolled completely on his side, facing her, and the edge of his shirt fell to conceal the marks once more.

Sweet Mother of God. When had this happened—and from what cause?

The Inquisition. His torture.

The voice echoed its dark message through Alissende's mind, and her throat felt as if it was closing. She reached out once more, gently stroking his brow and murmuring words of comfort to try to ease the throes of his nightmare. It was difficult enough to consider such horrible suffering when the injury was from accident or even the results of battle. But to think of being restrained and helpless while others purposely inflicted the kinds of wounds that had left these scars . . .

She could not think on it without becoming sick.

Damien made another sound, less anguished this time. It pulled her, thankfully, from her tormented thoughts, and she slowed the gentle stroking of her hand on his brow and hair, though she continued to speak softly to him. In response he quieted even more until the tension seemed to ebb from him, and he stopped twitching and shifting altogether, looking peaceful, except for the way his brow furrowed. Suddenly, he breathed in sharply—once, then again—before exhaling on a long and deep sigh.

"Alissende . . ."

She stiffened in surprise.

Her name had been released on that breath, laced with a note of longing that made her go still, made sweet warmth unfurl inside of her before she was able to fortify herself against it.

"My Alissende . . ."

At the same time that he murmured those words, he reached out, gripping the hand that had been stroking his brow, and she gasped—loudly—her own surprise throwing her off-balance as she tried to push herself up from her knees to back away. It was too late. Anchored by his grasp, she toppled forward onto him.

Before she could draw in her breath, he'd tugged her halfway up his prostrate form, his hands cupping her buttocks to ease her into a position that caused her legs to slide open, her knees touching the floor on either side of his hips. It was a decadent pose, bringing her into direct and stunning contact with the heat of his masculine length, covered by naught but a thin piece of cloth.

He shifted against her, and her moan came out as a half gasp. But the sound was lost to a muffled sigh as he threaded his fingers into the hair at her nape, curling himself up toward her and guiding her mouth to his in a kiss that seemed to sear her from the inside out. The sheet she had wrapped around herself upon leaving bed had long since come undone, and she felt the muscles of his abdomen contract against her naked belly with the movement . . . felt the hard contours of his chest press into her breasts in a way that was startlingly erotic, even as he began to rock his hips up, rubbing against her.

Oh, God . . .

It felt so good . . . so good that she couldn't bring herself to stop him, though it was surely wrong to enjoy such sinful pleasure with a man who was both half-asleep and bound to forswear her by reason of the darkness that had taken up residence in his soul.

She should stop this. Sweet heaven, she should.

She must, lest he awake to find her compliant—nay, yearning—to complete the intimate teasing he had provoked with his position.

With supreme effort, Alissende planted her hands on his chest and pushed, trying to lift herself up and break off their kiss. She made a sound in her throat as she managed to pull free, almost regretting her action as she uttered his name in a hoarse, demanding whisper.

The combined movement and noise was at last enough, apparently, to rouse him. His eyes snapped open, and he moved so suddenly that she fell in a rather ungraceful heap next to him.

"What are you doing?" he snapped, and she looked up from her awkward position on the floor to see that he was scowling down at her.

"I?" she echoed, her still-pulsing desire, the edge of panic, and pure exasperation all battling for supremacy in her voice. She struggled to sit up, scrambling to cover herself with the sheet again. "*I* am doing nothing, sir. It is *you* who caused this circumstance, I can assure you!"

He did not speak again right away, but rather sat up as well before leaning back against the wall, rubbing his hand over his eyes and brow as if attempting to bring himself to full awareness and regain his bearings.

When he looked at her again, it was clear that his body retained a clear memory of what they had just been doing, even if his mind did not. His gaze burned over her, lighting on her bare feet, the contours of her legs, hips, and breasts outlined by the thin sheet, her naked arms half-covered by long tendrils of her dark hair, before making its way up again to her face. She felt another tiny thrill at his expression, at the flaming heat in his eyes. But then he scowled even more deeply, looking like a thundercloud readying to burst.

"Why did you get out of bed?"

"I thought you were ill," she heard herself explaining. "I got up to see if you had a fever, but I . . . I . . . stumbled, and I lost my balance just as I realized that you were only suffering a nightmare."

Her cheeks burned with the falsehood, but she would not give him the satisfaction of knowing she had yearned to comfort him in his troubled sleep; she was his estranged lover, not his wife in any real sense. Yet even now, though she tried not to stare, she could not help glancing again at the scars that were visible once more through his open shirt.

She wasn't quick enough. He caught her glance and looked down to where it had strayed, terrible awareness spreading over his expression as the full import of what she had seen sank in. He did not move for the space of several breaths, except for the muscle that jumped at the side of his jaw, but when he raised his face again, his eyes burned with a depth of remembered pain that tore at her heart.

A swell of sympathy and anger over all he'd endured rose up in her, and she found herself murmuring, "I am sorry, Damien, that you suffered so."

He remained silent, his barren expression revealing that what had happened to him was too much to think on, much less speak about. At last he pushed himself to his feet, being careful to hold the edges of his shirt together as he did. Half-turning away, he refastened it.

It wasn't until he completed that action that he responded quietly, "Aye, well, it is over and done with now." He stared out the window, dragging one hand through his hair as he added, "And thanks be to heaven, it is almost dawn. Late enough that none should find cause to think it suspicious that I've left the wedding chamber."

"Morning mass will be in little more than an hour," she reminded him softly as she stood also. "Will you not wait until then?"

"Nay." He looked back to her, his expression still careful and composed, and it sent a twinge through her.

She studied him for a moment in silence, deciding that if the next six months were to pass in any kind of acceptable manner, it would be in her best interest to know all she could about this stranger who had once held her heart in his hands.

"I could not help noticing yesterday that you did not genuflect when we entered the chapel," she said evenly. "Or kneel in prayer at any point during our time there."

He met her stare with his own, unyielding. "You are correct; I did not."

"Why?"

The directness of her question seemed to startle him. Some dark emotion shadowed his face before he mastered himself again in an impressive show of strength—making her feel almost intrusive to have asked at all. But it was too important to let pass without knowing the answer.

"In our time together, I never knew you to enter a church without praying," she persisted. "Did you refuse to do so yestereve because you did not wish to appear to sanction our agreement, even in that way?"

A bitter smile glanced across his mouth. "Nay—though that seems as good a reason as any, if it suits you."

Alissende flushed, irritated that he was making light of her question. "I would not find it so strange had you not also been living previous to this under the rule of an order that observed strict hours of prayer numerous times a day."

When he did not speak, she paused for a beat, giving him a look that, along with what she was about to say, could not help but goad him into responding. "Of course, perhaps I am mistaken, and what I have heard about the decline of Templar morality is true."

Damien glowered at her then, his jaw set in a mutinous line.

"Templar laws never altered," he answered at last, his voice harsh and his tone deliberate. "The order is a noble one, and I acknowledged all precepts upon my initiation, striving to obey every rule without fault, even that which commanded me to give my life in protection of the Brotherhood if called upon to do so."

He paused, glancing away, and when he looked back at her, her breath caught at the stark pain in his eyes, even more wrenching than what she had seen there before.

"You remember my brother Alexander, do you not?" he asked.

There was no possibility that she could have forgotten. Her memory of Damien's brother and of the time they had all lived together at court—of the scandal involving Alexander and the Earl of Welton's daughter, Lady Margaret, and what had come afterward, which had cost herself and Damien so much—still burned after all this time. But she did not let Damien see it. She could not.

Instead, she settled for nodding and answering softly,

"Of course I remember. He was sent away to become a Templar shortly before you left for the same purpose."

"Aye. We served together for five years, until the night of the arrests, when we were both taken in France. After a time, I was separated from Alex in our imprisonment, and part of my torment came in not knowing how he fared. My captors used it against me. In their efforts to make me refute the Brotherhood, they were only too eager to tell me of the agonies my brother suffered. And eventually, they took great pleasure in relating how and when he paid the ultimate price of our Templar vows."

Damien's voice was hollow when he finished, "He died alone, Alissende. *Abandoned,* as was every Templar in captivity, cast away to hell by the very people for whom we had fought and bled."

Alissende blinked back the stinging in her eyes, and a swell of emotion filled her so that she could not speak.

"Alex died for a cause I once believed was God's will made evident on earth," Damien continued. "I survived, only with a bone-deep realization that the Templar Order is lost to me forever, as is—"

He stopped himself short, seeming to reconsider how he wished to phrase the rest; he was frowning, grief still masking his expression. "As is much else." He looked away for an instant before meeting her gaze again. "That is why I did not pray yestereve."

"I see."

"Nay, you do not," he countered quietly. "Not the full of it. And yet what you have heard is all I can offer right now. Or perhaps ever."

He exhaled, jabbing his fingers through his hair again, as if in a visible effort to redirect his thoughts. "However, you need not fear for my actions in public. I will keep proper appearances during these six months and attend mass with you each morning, following all the rites of worship as would be expected, with the exception of partaking in Communion."

That brought her up short. His captivity and torture had scarred him in many ways, it was true, and yet for a man with his history, even the hint of dissent against the governing power of the Holy Mother Church could prove dangerous.

"Such an omission is sure to be noticed, Damien," she chided gently. "How will you explain it?"

His eyes glittered in the dull gray light of morn that seeped through the window. "I will not explain it," he said. "If necessary, your cousin can ensure that those who must know are told it is tied to a penance assessed when I received the Writ of Absolution from the Church that you were so considerate to obtain for me."

Before she could say anything further, he shook his head and jerked into motion, leaning down to pick up his embroidered over-tunic, then crossing to the tall chestnut wardrobe that took up half the wall near the door. As he opened it and retrieved fresh garments, he said, "I am going to bathe and then make my way to the stables, where I will check my mount and meet with more of the men who are under my command. And in an hour, I will take my place at your side in the chapel."

Finding herself unable to respond in any meaningful way, she simply nodded.

After another moment of silence, Damien gave her a curt nod as well, took up a leather satchel of some sort that he had brought with him to Glenheim, and turned to the door.

And then he was gone, leaving her standing alone in the stillness of their bedchamber to contemplate all that had transpired . . . trying to make sense of what she was discovering about this enigmatic, tormented man who had once been as familiar to her as her own soul.

Chapter 6

The pain of training for seventy times seventy hours in the baking sun of Cyprus would have been preferable, Damien had decided, to the experience he had endured these past two weeks as lord of Glenheim Castle. Frustration had become as familiar to him as breathing, and he had been pushed to his limit in ways he'd felt woefully unprepared to face.

He could not deny, however, that some of what he had accomplished had been of worth. He had settled into a semblance of daily routine and had begun trying to forge a working relationship with Fitzgibbon, the captain of the castle guard. He had met with more of the men under his command, the rest of the servants, and many of the remaining tradesmen and women from the village. And after putting it off for as long as he could in all good conscience, he had finally sat down with Edgar Charmand, the quiet, educated man who served as the castle steward.

Damien had dreaded that meeting almost most of all, aware that it would require him to look over the holding's accounts . . . knowing that, as acting lord, he would be called upon to make assessments and give direction for what was to be bought and sold, not to mention the role he would be taking, soon, in listening to disputes between people of this demesne and dispensing rulings of justice at the manorial court.

But while his years as a high-ranking Templar Knight had ensured that he could take charge and make important decisions if called upon to do so, the same could not be said of some of the finer skills that would have made working with the knowledgeable steward more tolerable. They were skills reserved, generally, for titled noblemen and senior clergy—because as was true of most men from the knightly class, Damien had never learned to read or write.

Edgar had been patient, however, and Damien was stronger in his aptitude for numbers, managing to redeem himself in that area; but in all, his first real encounter with the steward had been humbling, to say the least.

And yet that had not been the most challenging aspect of this past fortnight. Nay, not by far. That distinction belonged to Alissende.

It had taken less than a day to realize that being so near to her was going to be a sensual torment the likes of which he'd never known. Her very presence in the chamber could drive him to distraction. Her graceful movements and her delicate scent—even the gentle resonance of her voice when she spoke—set him ablaze with desire.

And nighttime was even worse.

Aye, night brought with it its own special tests and trials. Evening had always been more difficult, even when he'd served with the Brotherhood; the veil of dark had somehow invited hidden thoughts he'd been able to control better in the light of day. But what he was enduring now at Glenheim surpassed by a thousandfold anything he'd known back then.

He had conceded to sharing the bed with Alissende once he'd realized that resting on the hard floor would prove far more likely to encourage the violent nightmares and memories of the Inquisition that often tormented his sleep. Yet when he was stretched out beside her he was like a man parched with thirst, denied all but the merest drop of water on his lips—a man who felt the licking heat of flame but who could not pull away from the fire. He felt consumed by longings and yearnings that teased him, with images that would not let him rest. His cursed body played the fool, even when his logical mind knew better than to soften in any way toward the very same woman who had cast him away so bluntly five years ago.

Always, it would begin innocently enough. He would keep very still and quiet, trying to avoid touching Alissende as she slept, when suddenly a vision would slip into his mind . . . a fragment of dream, almost, of stroking his palm down the smooth, naked expanse of her back. He would feel a twinge of delicious wanting in the imagining of it, but like the besotted fool he was, he would not heed the warning.

Nay, he would allow his mind to drift further into

the fantasy, to think of slipping his fingers through her soft hair, of tasting the delicate place just beneath the lobe of her ear. Of kissing the fullness of her mouth. He would imagine brushing his hand along the smooth path of her arm and then across her belly . . . and further still, up to her pink-tipped breasts, before sweeping down to the sweet apex of her thighs . . .

And then he would be lost, swept up in heated, tortured memories that consumed him and left him lying there in aching, rigid need.

His only saving grace had been his refusal to sleep unclothed, regardless of custom or the warmth in the chamber. He did not trust himself to do so. Nay, at least when wearing garments, he could sometimes force his mind away from the seductive images and half-convince himself that he was sleeping alone.

But at best it was a temporary delusion.

The truth was that none of his former methods of pushing thoughts of Alissende from his mind, practiced so oft during his time with the Brotherhood—prayer, fasting, the shock of icy cold water, or immersing himself in weapons training until he ran with sweat—seemed to be working any longer. He was certain that he was slowly driving himself to the brink of insanity with his constant, unsatisfied yearning for her.

It was a desire for her body he reminded himself, nothing more. Nay, she was not to be trusted with anything more meaningful than that. He had learned that lesson too well. But the fierce and sharp need for physical completion with her bit at him nonetheless.

Desperate to find some distraction from it, he had decided to convene his first group training session in the yard today, calling upon Fitzgibbon to assemble a score of his best men to participate. Ben had agreed to assist at the beginning, at least, to run through some of the exercises they had perfected together during the months spent training while Damien had healed; Damien hoped that the example they could provide together would speed the men's process of mastering the techniques, which would allow them all to delve into the kind of hot and sweaty weapons-work that could not help but keep him focused on something other than the woman who seemed to occupy his every waking thought and sinful dream.

First, however, he had to gain the men's trust. It was the primary rule of command: Earn the respect of your men, and all else would follow. But somehow he sensed that task was not going to be easy. He'd felt a vague animosity simmering beneath the surface whenever he'd made visit to the quarters of the castle guard, and he knew he'd have to put that to rest before anything else could happen.

"I cannot believe that I let you talk me into this."

Damien turned to the sound of the voice, grinning at its owner, who strode toward him from across the yard. Ben had exchanged his Franciscan habit for the same kind of sturdy, serviceable leggings and shirt he'd made use of during their exercises in Dover—all except for the new sword he had buckled at his waist. The *enormous* new sword.

Ah, yes. Ben was opening himself up to some good-natured jesting with this one, Damien thought, and his grin deepened. He gave a half nod in the direction of the new blade, waiting until Ben reached him before he spoke.

"I'm thinking that's quite a weapon you have there,

my friend. Especially for a man of your calling. It's rather . . . *large,* wouldn't you say?"

It only took an instant for Ben to react to the ribald nature of the comment, his razor-sharp glance taking in the lesser contours of Damien's own sheathed weapon before he raised his brow. "You are wise to note it," he retorted, "and to remember whose is bigger, be I a holy man or nay."

Damien let go a laugh. Ben chuckled as well, and they gripped each other by the forearm for a greeting, slapping each other's backs in affection. But there was no time to continue the exchange further, because at that moment Fitzgibbon emerged from the guardhouse across the yard with a dozen or so men behind him. All were fully equipped for a training session, it seemed, though by the expressions on many of their faces, they were anything but pleased at the thought.

Whether their irritation stemmed from being made to engage in training at all this day, or whether it was the result of that underlying hostility he had been thinking about earlier, Damien did not know. Likely, it was a bit of both. A few seconds later, Fitzgibbon reached him, and Damien nodded in greeting. The captain stood at attention for a moment before tipping his chin.

"I have assembled an even score of my top guard, my lord, as directed. We await your order to commence this training session."

"Good," Damien said brusquely, letting his gaze drift over the men standing behind Fitzgibbon. "Let's get started, then. For the first exercise, we will need two groups. Ben will lead one set and I the other. When each group has mastered its own set, we'll work them together."

The men began to shift into two parts at his command, reluctant and slow. As they moved, Damien heard grumbling coming from the back of the group, and he stiffened, the muscles in his back tightening in response to the parts of the complaint he could hear in detail.

Swiveling his head toward the source of the mutterings, he grated, "If any of you have aught to say before we begin, I pray you speak it for all to hear. Unless, of course, what I've feared is true, and I've been given leadership over a clutch of gibbering hens, rather than well-trained fighting men."

His pronouncement had the very effect he had hoped for. All movement stopped, and though none of the men spoke, several of them cast baleful glares his way.

Ben sighed, his expression a combination of long-suffering and acceptance, and Damien almost smiled. He knew his friend didn't relish confrontation, but there was no help for it right now. Shifting his gaze, Damien saw Fitzgibbon glance warily toward the back of the group, where one of the men seemed about to speak; Fitzgibbon cast him a silent look of warning.

"Nay, let him have his say," Damien called to the captain. "Better to bring it all out in the open now than to let it continue brewing beneath the surface while we swing blades at each other." He did allow himself a kind of smile, then, though it was a tight, bitter look he had perfected over several years . . . an expression he knew was far more feral than friendly.

"I have something to say, then, if you want to know."

The hostile statement came from the back of the group, and as the men shifted out of the way, Damien at last saw the speaker clearly. He was a man of about Damien's own age, he'd guess, well built for fighting, as were all of these soldiers Fitzgibbon had chosen for the training—but possessed of a cocky manner that had no doubt forced him to use his fists in defense on more than one occasion.

Several of the other men seemed uncomfortable, a few shuffling their feet and looking down, while the one who had taken up Damien's challenge stood with an insolent posture, his muscular arms folded across his chest as he continued to gaze at Damien.

"Your name?" Damien called in a voice that was deceptively calm.

"I am Sir Gareth de Burton, second in command of Lord Denton's garrison," the man drawled.

Damien didn't respond at first, letting the insult wash over him before he tilted his head in barest acknowledgment, countering in a voice thick with sarcasm, "I hate to be the bearer of bad tidings, but Lord Denton has left this world and is no longer in charge of this garrison. I am."

"By right of a hasty marriage, perhaps, naught else."

"The status of my marriage does not concern you. And as for my right to lead you, I can promise that my military experience gives me far more claim to command you in training and battle than I possess in many of the other areas of duty required of me as the new lord of Glenheim Castle."

Damien looked around the group of men, meeting Sir Gareth's gaze again as he added, "Fighting and winning are what I know best. If you will follow me, I will provide you with instruction in all that I have learned in seven years of skirmishing, tournaments, and actual combat, both here and abroad."

"Sir Damien is one of the finest knights I have ever seen, and I know of what I speak," Ben interjected from where he stood, leaning against his sword just behind Damien. "Though I am a Franciscan now, as a young man, before I took my vows, I fought in the Holy Land—"

Damien's gaze snapped to him.

"—and I was at Acre when it fell to the Saracens." Ben looked serious, his usually ruddy complexion seeming paler with what he apparently was recalling from that time. At last he nodded and finished, "I saw some of the most impressive fighting skills a man may see in his lifetime there—and more barbarity than I would ever hope to see again. It was my reason for turning my life over to God. But I can tell you without qualm that Sir Damien possesses greater skill with blade, arrow, and spear, in hand combat and upon horseback, than any I witnessed during my own fighting days."

The group fell completely quiet as Ben spoke, and Damien gazed at his friend now in stunned silence. He'd known Ben had learned to wield a sword at some point in his life, simply based upon his level of skill when they'd begun sparring together as he'd helped Damien regain his fighting abilities. But he'd never known the whole story behind it. Ben met his gaze with that wise, calm expression in his eyes that Damien had come to know so well during his time of painful healing, nodding to him in support.

The tension seemed to have dissipated somewhat with Damien's answer to Gareth and Ben's startling testimonial, but it was clear that something still simmered, so Damien remained quiet to see what else would come out into the open.

It took only another moment before he got his answer.

"My lord, I also have a question for you, if we may still speak freely."

The man who spoke this time, and in a far more courteous manner than Gareth had, stood to the right of Fitzgibbon; he appeared to be several years younger than most of the other men—a new knight of perhaps only eighteen or so, which was the age Damien had been upon his first arrival to court.

"Aye," Damien answered. "You may ask without fear, and I will answer, if I can, though as with your comrade, I would ask your name first."

The young man nodded. "I am Sir Reginald Sinclair, my lord, and I wish to know if it is true, as we have heard, that you were a Templar Knight of the inner circle—and that you were arrested by the Inquisition in France, under the charge of heresy."

Damien had known this would likely come up, but it nevertheless unleashed a fierce aching, as the vivid and painful memories suddenly reared up from the abyss inside him. Reginald seemed sincere in his asking, however, so Damien resolved to do his best to address the lad's question.

He nodded. "What you have heard about my service with the Templars is true." His jaw clenched tight. "And in answer to your second question—yes, I was brought into captivity and interrogated by the Inquisition in France late last year, during the mass arrests."

"We are not fools, *my lord*," Gareth broke in again in

a scoffing tone, clearly still not mollified in any way. "Word has reached us that thousands of Templar Brethren arrested in France have already confessed to heretical practices under the very questioning you mentioned. If you were indeed a Templar in that place at that time, how is it that your outcome was so different?"

A charged hush spread over the yard in the wake of Gareth's thinly veiled accusation of deceit on the part of their new lord, the area ringing with the silence of all that had not been said. Damien felt his fists clench and found himself needing to call on his inner resolve to keep from striding over to the wretch here and now and rewarding his insolence in a way he would have no difficulty understanding.

"I did not confess under interrogation, Sir Gareth," Damien finally ground out, "because I was not guilty of heresy."

"So you say," the knight muttered. His eyes flashed with righteous fire, and Damien was reminded of himself, those many years ago, when the world had been cast in shades of black and white, with little, if any, gray.

"The fact that Sir Damien is standing here before you should provide some assurance to his innocence in the matter," Ben offered smoothly, attempting to diffuse the rising tensions, and again, Damien found himself glancing to his friend in surprise. Ben's own morals would not allow him to lie outright, Damien knew, but he wasn't exactly being truthful about the way things had transpired with Damien's rescue from the Inquisition, either.

"That proves only that he takes breath upon the earth like the rest of us," Gareth countered, shifting that fiery gaze to Ben. "We have naught but your saying so to convince us of anything. It is common knowledge that every Templar in France was taken into custody in October of last year, to be questioned by a branch of the Inquisition notorious for the severity of its interrogations—yet here Sir Damien stands before us, hale and hearty."

Gareth's face tightened as if he knew how closely he was treading on the edge of disaster, but apparently he found himself unable to cease, by reason of his own pride. Lifting his chin in defiance, he swallowed hard and added in a quiet, but damning, blow, "I say I am not alone among the men of this garrison in thinking we have been fed a great lie. We do not believe that Sir Damien was *ever* a knight of the Brotherhood's inner circle—or that he was interrogated in France. Nay, more like he is a common soldier as any of us are, only one who somehow managed to coerce our lady into a union, with the sole purpose of gaining control of her vast wealth and estates."

There it was. The accusation that was behind all of the sidelong looks, grumbling, and antagonism he had felt in various forms since his arrival here.

All the muscles in Damien's body tightened. He had hoped to avoid the kind of visceral, violent confrontation this was going to require, but it was clear now that it had to be done if he had any hope of leading these men and commanding their respect and loyalty for the six months he would need to count on them, while he served out the agreement he had made with Alissende.

Gesturing for the men to widen their positions into a

half circle, Damien began to loosen his shirt, taking a few steps back away from the group, though never altering the steeliness of his gaze on Gareth as he said, "If you think that I will sully Lady Alissende by discussing any aspect of my union with her, then you are sadly mistaken. However, I possess no similar qualm in addressing your complaint about the truth of my *experience* with the Inquisition"—he felt his mouth twist in bitterness with the utterance—"or my service as a Templar Knight of the inner circle."

By this time he had freed his shirt from his breeches and unlaced it at the neck as well. Now he pulled it over his head and tossed it aside, standing before them all with his entire upper body revealed to their gazes. They could not help but see the scars—of burns, lash marks, and other wounds—that spread across his torso, ribs, and back.

It was not easy to look upon. He knew that and had come to terms with the difficult reality, accepting the fact that the fair-haired warrior, the physically imposing, flawless youth he had been once, was gone forever. He was still undeniably tall and strong, as skilled and powerful of muscle and bone as ever before. Clothed, none would know the difference between the man he had been then and what he had become after living through that hell.

But he knew—and now these men did as well.

"This," he said, still without breaking his gaze on Gareth, "should allay any doubt that I was in the hands of the French Inquisition. As you can see, I was *questioned* by them most thoroughly."

"And this"—he unsheathed his sword with a hissing, metallic sound—"should help to resolve any remaining doubt about the position I held as a Templar Knight, or my ability to lead this garrison." He gave Gareth a tight half smile, cocking his brow as he inclined his head and added, "That is, if you're willing to test the fact in a one-to-one sparring match with me. Here and now."

Gareth paused for a long moment, the cracking in his voice when he spoke belying the outward composure he was plainly trying so hard to sustain. "What then—do you intend to fight without any armor or even mail for protection?"

"I need none. My sword and shield will suffice."

Damien saw Gareth's sudden paleness, took in his astonished expression, and added in a mocking lilt, "Come man, and let us begin. I vow before your captain and the rest of these men that I absolve you of any injury you may be fortunate enough to inflict upon me, if that is the worry holding you up from engaging your blade with mine."

"Have a care, Damien," Ben murmured from behind, as they waited for Gareth's answer. "I would not take pleasure in stitching you again, when an injury could so easily be avoided with a bit less flair and a bit more caution."

"Never fear, friend. I know my limits," Damien muttered in return, low enough that none other could hear the exchange between himself and Ben.

More loudly he called again toward the group of men, "Well, Sir Gareth, what say you? I give my word to make this an exhibition only, for though your impudence has earned far worse, I am not of that ilk of castle lords who demand vengeance through the blood of their minions."

He nodded, giving Gareth a sarcastic smile again,

doing his best to prick at the man's pride in the hopes of eliciting some action from him. "Nay, indeed, it is to your good fortune this day that I *am* born of common stock, else I might decide to make a greater mockery of you than you have made of yourself already, with your cowardly hesitation."

That was enough, finally, to shake Gareth from his indecision. With a growl he strode up the impromptu path of men, toward Damien, unsheathing his weapon as he came.

Damien was ready for him.

He met the first, overhead blow easily enough, countering with a hard, swinging strike from the side. Gareth fended him off for a moment, but he wasn't practiced enough to see the next strike coming—a quick feint to the opposite side that shifted at the last moment to a jabbing thrust. The move slid Damien's blade along Gareth's until they clanked to a stop, hilts interlocked. Damien stood chest-to-chest with his opponent, the old, familiar battle heat filling him to make the effort to hold firm against him seem almost insignificant. Only another two moves and he would be able to hook Gareth's blade and hurl it from his grip.

He stepped forward, putting his foot between Gareth's own and shifting his weight in preparation. Just one more move, now . . .

Suddenly, a flash of deep, blood red against black drew Damien's attention to the edge of the yard. A shock went through him. It was Alissende. She had come outside, accompanied by Father Michael, and it was the priest's long, dark robes that had accentuated her ruby-hued gown so dramatically. Standing in silence, she watched their sparring match with an expression of combined surprise and worry shadowing her beautiful eyes.

Damien let his gaze linger on her for but an instant—and yet an instant was all it took.

Gareth used the moment of his distraction to slam his forearm hard against Damien's chest, knocking the wind out of him and forcing him to step back enough to allow Gareth to effectively disengage from their locked position. Scowling in disgust at himself, Damien scrambled to regroup, forced to seek another angle now, in order to approach and disarm his foe.

It did not take long, but it required more effort than he had intended to expend, and his back and arms had begun to ache by the time he'd managed to send Gareth's sword spinning from his grip. Then, just because he was irritated, he kept his blade raised to Gareth's throat, keeping him immobile at the point of that glittering death a few moments longer than he might have otherwise . . . until he saw some of the men around them begin to shift uneasily, clearly worried that he might renege on his earlier claim to make this naught but an exhibition and instead slice their comrade where he stood.

At last Damien pulled away, and Gareth collapsed to one knee, bent double as he gasped for air, while Damien stalked back toward Ben.

"A bit overzealous there at the end, don't you think?" Ben waited until Damien had sheathed his blade again and unfastened the sword belt before handing him his shirt.

"He deserved it."

"Perhaps." Ben glanced toward the group of men who had clustered around Gareth. "But I'd say you made your point in a way none of them will soon forget."

"That was my intent." Damien fastened his shirt and tucked it into his breeches again. "And yet now it is just as important that I give them and Gareth a way to follow me in honor."

After rebuckling his sword belt, Damien strode back toward the group, taking Gareth's weapon from the knight who'd retrieved it off the ground. As he approached the man he'd bested, he reached out his hand. "Come, Sir Gareth, and accept my offer of peace. You displayed fine skill and good instincts, and I would be proud to know you serve willingly in my garrison."

Gareth looked up at Damien, his expression unreadable for a moment. He was still breathing heavily. At last he reached up and allowed Damien to help pull him to his feet. Damien handed him his sword. After sheathing it, Gareth stood still and quiet, staring at the ground before finally glancing over to Damien again. "I thank you, my lord, and I hope you will pardon me for the doubts I harbored—and so rudely offered you this day."

"I consent on all counts," Damien said, "and consider it a fair price to have paid for the privilege of having such a fine sword-arm at my beck and call from now on." The second part was added half in jest, in an effort to put him at ease.

As Damien had hoped, Gareth looked pleased with the compliment, and in a moment he looked past Damien to the other men and Fitzgibbon. "If I am not mistaken, we will all be reconsidering the false judgment we placed upon you, my lord, and will follow you in honor from this time forward."

In response, a few of the men let go a chorus of "Aye!" and "You have our allegiance, my lord!" which was soon picked up by the rest.

Damien shook hands with Gareth, Fitzgibbon, and several of the men closest, and when the cheers died down, he said, "I am glad to have your backing; however, it might be best if you reserve some of your enthusiasm for the training still ahead of us."

A few groans, good-natured ones now, echoed from the group, and Damien nodded, smiling. "I know, I know . . . but we've much to accomplish, and the sooner we begin the sooner we will be done as well."

As the men turned to do as he bid, Damien allowed himself to glance back to the edge of the yard for the first time since the distraction of seeing Alissende, which had cost him in his sparring match with Gareth.

She was gone.

Ben caught his glance as he approached Damien to stand by him again, and he raised his brow, offering a comment that struck Damien as being less innocent than it seemed. "I noticed your wife watching you at the edge of the yard earlier as well. She seemed worried for your safety."

"So worried that she chose to leave with her cousin before she could speak with me." Damien leaned over to pick up his shield, slipping his arm into the straps and trying to subdue his ever-turbulent emotions where Alissende was concerned.

Ben shrugged. "It looked to me as if she and Michael were carrying baskets of some kind. Perhaps they were on an errand. Though her hasty departure might well have had more to do with her worry over the possibility of seeing you wounded."

"More like she was simply dismayed at the contrast between the man she once used to watch battle in tournaments and what she saw before her today."

Making a clicking noise of chastisement, Ben shook his head. "Methinks you know less about the workings of the female mind than I do, Damien—and I am the one who has taken vows of celibacy."

Ah, but I took such vows too once upon a time. . . .

The thought swept through Damien with startling virulence, catching him unawares. But he had no chance to say anything out loud, for at that moment he noticed a squire approaching them at a near run from the direction of the main hall. The young man had been trained well; when he reached the limits of the group of men, he stopped, breathing heavily and looking nervous as he waited for Damien's permission to come further.

"I wonder what this is about?" Damien murmured to Ben, at the same time gesturing the lad to him.

Some of the guard had taken notice as well, several of them turning and watching as the squire strode up to Damien and bowed in deference before he straightened to murmur, "My lord—pardon the interruption, but I come bearing news of approaching knights. A contingent of two dozen or more, fully outfitted for battle, bearing the arms of young Hugh de Valles, fourth Earl of Harwick—and led by Lord Harwick himself."

Damien felt all his muscles clench for the second time in the past hour. *Damn.* It was not that he hadn't expected Alissende's pursuer to appear in another defiant attempt to make claim to her, regardless of the proxy marriage she'd declared at court; after all, Alissende's own mother and Father Michael had warned him of the likelihood of Hugh's continued aggression.

He had just hoped he'd have more time to gain his bearings before Hugh showed himself.

Frowning, he swung his gaze to Ben. "We'd better ready the men for the possibility of a confrontation, then," he said in a low voice. "I must send word to Alissende and caution her of his approach, then go to the guardhouse and alert those still on duty there. In the meantime, if you will address the matter with the men here, I would—"

"Pardon, milord, but I must tell you that . . . that is, I think you should know that Lord Harwick—that he is . . . and that . . . that the Lady Alissende is—"

The squire stumbled over his words, pale of face and obviously worried about the harmful ramifications of interrupting his master not only once this morn but now twice, and the second time most rudely, in mid-sentence.

Damien tried to school his face into a less threatening glower, looking back to the youth and saying evenly, "Slow down, lad. You will earn no rebuke for speaking the news you have come to convey. Is there more to it than what you have already told me?"

"Aye, my lord," the squire said, his throat working as he swallowed several times, and his brown eyes troubled. "It is this: Lord Harwick approaches from the west. Lady Alissende, several of her maids, and their escorts departed the castle gates but a quarter hour past to go a-berrying in the woodland that borders the western portion of Glenheim."

Damien felt as if he'd been impaled through the gut

as the import of what he'd just heard sank home, even before the squire uttered the final damning words . . .

"Lord Harwick will come upon the Lady Alissende while she is protected by naught but a handful of men, Sir Damien. And if his actions in the past hold true, then she is in grave danger. Very grave danger indeed."

Chapter 7

The forest was a welcome refuge from the heat of the sun; Alissende relished it as she searched for the patches of thick-leaved strawberry plants that usually grew here in abundance. *Mère* had been craving one of their favorite summer sweets: ripe berries washed in red wine, then simmered in almond milk, thickened with flour and stirred with raisins, saffron, sugar, ginger, and cinnamon. The pudding would take the rest of the day to make, and so setting out this morn on a hunt for the berries seemed as good a reason as any to take to the peace of the woodland for a while.

Damien would likely be angry when he found out she had left the castle proper without notifying him, but she hadn't been able to bear the possibility that he would refuse her request. She needed to get away, even if only for a short while.

Thank heaven Michael seemed to understand; he

had happened upon her just as she'd been readying to leave with four of her lady's maids, and at first, he had been concerned by her plan—concerned enough to interrupt Damien's training session in the yard, even, in an effort to make her stay within the gates. But somehow, she had managed to convince him that would be unnecessary. It had taken some cajoling on her part, along with her agreement to allow four castle guardsmen to accompany her into the wood, but she had gained his support, eventually.

Now she was here, in the peacefulness of the forest, and allowing any heavy musings to cloud her mind only wasted this brief reprieve that had been granted to her. As if in reminder of that truth, Alissende saw brighter sun ahead, glinting through the trees in wide slants that danced with dust motes. It beckoned her forward, and in a few more steps, she'd entered a sizeable glade that seemed to fairly dazzle with light in comparison to the shade of the woodland. Spread across nearly the entire expanse of the clearing, lovely crimson strawberries peeped from beneath low-growing, dark green leaves.

It was perfect; just what she had been seeking.

Calling out to the two of her ladies in nearest proximity, Jeanette and Edmee, to join her, Alissende readied several baskets they'd brought along and prepared to pick.

"Ah, this is a fine patch indeed, milady," Edmee said, her rosy face alight with pleasure when she stepped into the glade with Jeanette. "Catherine and Marguerite will be jealous, for they have not yet found anything nearly as good. Shall we send one of the guards to bring them here as well?" She was a sweet girl, rounded and fair, with the soft blue eyes for which her family was known, and she made a striking contrast with the more slender, dark-haired Jeanette.

"Aye," Alissende agreed. "If they have not wandered too far, it would be best, I think."

"I will see to it, my lady," Jeannette murmured, curtseying briefly before turning back to speak with the guards, who lingered in the forest only a few paces behind them.

In a short while, Jeanette returned to the glade and fell to picking in earnest alongside Alissende. However, Alissende could not miss how Jeanette and Edmee kept exchanging whispered comments, giggling and sneaking glances at the remaining three quite attractive guardsmen who had taken up posts along the edge of the glade. The soldiers looked awkward, though intent upon fulfilling their duty, and Alissende smiled at her ladies' flirtatious chatter.

How young they all were. How innocent to the sharp edges that love could carry, along with its sweetness. When she watched them, it seemed so simple and uncomplicated. Not at all like her own feelings for Damien.

It was becoming unbearable, this rising push and pull of her emotions. With every moment she spent in Damien's company, she felt the tug of longing. With each brush of his hand against hers in public, or the touch of his palm to the small of her back as they walked through the main hall or from the chapel back to the castle proper, she experienced that sweet melting sensation inside. That yearning to fold herself into his embrace in the way that had once been as natural to them as breathing.

And yet she could not forget that he was a reluctant participant in their painful charade. He was not the same man he'd been then. Any tenderness he offered her now was all for show, and his protectiveness was for the sake of duty. It would end in a little less than six months, and he would walk away without turning back.

Just as he had five years ago, after she'd broken his heart.

In a way, she could not blame him. But another part of her raged at the horrible irony of it all, even as she cursed herself for continuing to harbor softer feelings for him. They were feelings that couldn't be trusted, she reminded herself, given for a man who no longer existed. That she had caused the initial rift between them did not alter the fact that the Damien who had reentered her life was harsh and angry from much more than just her long-ago rejection. He had even turned his back on God, and such abandonment of faith could not be so easily overlooked. It weighed upon her and—

Alissende suddenly heard a squeal of delight from Edmee, and she looked up again to see the young woman leap to her feet. Edmee turned to hold out a strawberry nearly the size of her palm, her face alight with excitement as she exclaimed, "My lady, look at this one!"

Sitting back on her heels, Alissende was readying to say something encouraging when she saw the color drain from Edmee's cheeks and heard her gasp, even as the three guardsmen suddenly cleared their weapons and a familiar voice rang out behind her.

"Ah, yes—will you look at that one, indeed."

Breathing in sharply, Alissende spun to face the one

who had spoken, her heart hammering as she met the sardonic gaze of her second cousin, Hugh de Valles, fourth Earl of Harwick. He stood less then ten paces from her, a tall and powerful man who had trained to wield a sword from the time he was a six-year's-child.

None had ever thought he would inherit the earldom; he was the second son, after all. Michael, as the third, had been promised at birth to the priesthood. But when their father and then their eldest brother had died in quick succession of each other, Hugh had found himself cast into the role of new earl, with all the power and potential corruption that went with the title. All that he lacked was the excessive wealth that he craved, and taking her for his wife would remedy that.

"Hugh," Alissende finally murmured, struggling to find her voice. "I—I did not realize you were . . . that I would—"

The rush of fear she was feeling choked off the rest of her words. The last time she had seen him, almost seven months ago, he had attempted to take her by force from one of her mother's holdings. He had made his intentions for her very clear, then, and though she had fought against him, she had been no match for his undeniable strength and size. All would have been lost, she knew, had Michael not arrived, bringing with him several other clergy, including a bishop, who had managed to convince Hugh that any further action taken by him under such duress would never be recognized as a sanctioned union by the Holy Mother Church.

The memory of that horrible day washed over her, and Alissende swallowed against her rising nausea. Hugh only smiled. Though he had donned armor for traveling, he wore no helm, and his dark hair looked well-groomed as always, accentuating a lean face with a strong jaw and straight nose that most women found pleasing to look upon. He would have been very attractive, Alissende had thought more than once, if not for the shadow of malice in his green-gray eyes and the hint of cruelty in the lines of his sensual mouth.

"My lovely cousin," he finally murmured, his tone setting the hairs at her nape on end. "Is that the best greeting you can offer me?" As he spoke, he stepped closer to her, not seeming affected in the least by her own guardsmen, who had also moved in toward her from behind, holding their weapons pointed at him.

"Lord Harwick," the most senior of her guardsmen called, "stay back, else we shall be constrained to defend Lady Alissende against you."

Hugh made a noise in his throat, waving his hand in dismissal as he continued to approach, and at the signal, a dozen or more of his men burst from the forest behind her. Her men had no chance, and within moments they were under the control of Hugh's soldiers.

Edmee shrieked and Jeanette cried out as well, dropping the basket of berries she was holding, as two of the soldiers seized them too, even as Hugh reached Alissende and gripped her upper arm with one hand and her chin more painfully with the other, forcing her to look up at him.

Her body went rigid and her hands felt icy, her fear not only for herself now but for her ladies and the men as well. And though her eyes stung from both the pain of his grip and her sense of panic, she clenched her jaw and tried to blink back the heat, determined not to show him any weakness.

"Still a fighter, I see," Hugh murmured, using the

hand on her chin to jerk her closer. She could not keep back a tiny moan, then, though her discomfort was followed swiftly by revulsion, as Hugh's movement compelled her to press along the length of his body.

When she was where he wanted her, he looked down, his face inches from her own, as he said, "Back to what I was saying a moment ago, then. I am certain that your greeting was far from the best you could offer me, dear Alissende. It has been so long, and you have been so . . . difficult. I think I deserve some kind of recompense for my patience and impressive restraint thus far, don't you?"

"I do not know what you expect," she said quietly, holding herself very still. "My proxy union was declared at court. I am a married woman."

"That proxy was naught but another of my brother's irritating ploys, Alissende, and we both know it," Hugh said, his voice a dangerous purr. "The sooner you accept that your place is with me, the easier it will prove for all of us. Now come, love, and greet me properly."

Holding her chin immobile in his grip, he tilted his face toward her and kissed her hard, taking his time, trying to thrust his tongue past her clenched teeth, as if her feelings about it mattered not at all. She beat on his chest, struggling to push away from him, and he pulled back finally, laughing at her.

"You're a fiery one, that none can deny. Do you not realize, Alissende, that if you stopped resisting so much, you might enjoy my attentions? God knows your husband complained enough to me about his failure to stir your passions in the bedchamber, although in truth I think that poor Godfrey simply wasn't man enough for the task," he finished mockingly.

"Cease this, Hugh—release me!" she muttered, the words sounding choked as she struggled to hold back her dread. Though it hurt to do so, she tried to wrench her chin from his grip, at the same time pushing against his chest once more with her palms.

He might as well have been made of stone.

He smiled again, at last releasing her face, though not her arm, from his grasp. However, the tightness of his expression made clear the fact that he was rapidly losing patience with her.

"Come, come, love. If you continue to refuse me on all sides, then I shall be compelled to try other, less pleasant means of gaining your cooperation."

He glanced over to her lady's maids and her men. Three of her guards still shifted against their bonds; Seamus, her senior man, lay senseless on the ground, having been clubbed down when he'd wrestled against his captors as they'd attempted to bind him.

Her ladies stood off to the side of that group. Catherine and Marguerite had been taken, along with the fourth guard, as they'd approached the clearing shortly after Hugh's appearance, and now the four women wept softly, kept from aiding her by the circle of stony-faced soldiers surrounding them.

Hugh flicked his gaze to Alissende again, keeping it fixed to her face as he called out, "Armand!"

"Aye, my lord?"

Alissende's heart pounded in her chest as she stole a glance to the man who had answered. It appeared to be the one in charge of all the others—Hugh's captain of the guard. Panicked, she looked back to Hugh, and he issued his order, all the while watching her to see her reaction to it.

"Choose one of Lady Alissende's men and run him through for his impudence in daring to thwart me this day."

She gasped in disbelief, her shock finally releasing a swell of tears. "Nay!" she cried out, trying to pull away from him, and looking frantically over to Armand. The captain appeared pale and his face was rigid, but after a moment, he tipped his head in a sharp bow, lowering his gaze and murmuring, "As you wish, my lord."

"You cannot order a man killed for such a thing! My guards were doing naught but obeying their orders to protect me."

"Orders issued by what authority, Alissende?" Hugh scoffed, his temper finally snapping. "You are a woman alone, under the pathetic protection of a foolish priest and your termagant of a mother. So either produce this husband that you and my brother crafted from thin air, or else concede to a marriage with me, sanctioned already by King Edward."

The glade echoed with that command, the area falling into silence for but an instant before an equally strong and masculine voice called out a scathing answer.

"Accustom yourself to disappointment, then, Lord Harwick, for there will be no wedding between you and Lady Alissende. Now or ever."

Hugh twisted to face the man who had spoken, and Alissende's heart leaped with relief, joy, and worry all at once. Her gaze locked with Damien's; he stood at the opposite edge of the glade, backed by twoscore of Glenheim's guardsmen, who filtered through the trees to rim that side of the clearing, glinting weapons drawn. Damien was a sight to behold, every powerful inch of him thrumming with rage, the predatory light in his eyes promising to do irrevocable damage to the man who had earned his ire this day.

"Who the hell are you?" Hugh growled, sounding only slightly less certain.

"I am Sir Damien de Ashby, former Templar Knight and swordsman to the late king." Damien pierced Hugh with the cutting ice of his gaze, raising one brow and giving him a mocking nod. "Ah yes—and I am also the man named in the marriage proxy you claim does not exist. So, either you will release Lady Alissende and step away from her right now, or else you will be making your *second* grave error of this day."

Damien smiled then, a slow, dangerous expression that sent a chill straight up Alissende's spine.

"Go ahead, my lord," he finished, in a voice that was low and yet frighteningly clear. "Make your decision. For if you do not, then I will do it for you . . . and I promise you that the dealing of it will be brief, as painful as possible, and will result in nothing less than your soul departing without delay from the miserable confines of your body."

Chapter 8

It took all of Damien's self-control not to lunge at Lord Harwick. He still gripped Alissende by the arm—and he was hurting her, by God, if the look on her face was any indication.

Harwick did not move, and Damien was readying to plant his dagger in the earl's throat with one well-aimed throw when Hugh suddenly let go of Alissende and took two steps toward his own guard. Alissende stumbled toward Damien at his nod, though his rage flared hotter when she came close enough that he could see the beginnings of a bruise forming along her jaw and cheek. Apparently the bastard had placed his hands on her there as well.

His gaze stabbed into Hugh again.

"Now Alissende's maids and my guards."

He heard the edge of tension in his own voice, barely controlled, so he took in a lungful of air in an effort to calm himself, lest he do something to the earl that he might regret later.

Hugh did not respond at first. Instead he stood where he had moved after releasing Alissende, gazing at Damien as if taking his measure.

At last he smiled, though Damien noticed that the expression did not reach his eyes, and he gestured to his men to release Glenheim's ladies and guards. Seamus was still senseless, so the other three guards carried him to Damien's side of the clearing, accepting help from some of the others to take him back to the castle where he could have his wound examined and treated.

Then all went silent. Damien wondered what tack Hugh would take, now that he had been thwarted. Would he launch a new assault? Try to engage him alone? Retreat? It seemed that neither Lady Blanche nor Michael had exaggerated when they'd termed Hugh de Valles a tenacious and dangerous opponent. Unpredictable men oft proved to be most challenging, and Hugh, with his ability to seemingly shift his demeanor from one moment to the next, appeared more volatile than the majority Damien had known.

Without warning, Hugh gestured for his men to sheathe their weapons, effectively breaking the stand-off. Damien echoed the order to his own men, and as he did, Hugh strode toward him, crossing half the distance between them and then coming to a halt, as if daring Damien to meet him in kind.

There was no question of it.

Clasping Alissende's hand warmly in his own, Damien walked forward with her, until they reached a distance from Hugh that was comfortable for conversation; then Damien pulled her close to his side, wrapping his arm around her protectively.

It was a clear sign, and one that could not be missed. Not by anyone, but most especially not by the Earl of Harwick.

Hugh's gaze glanced off that embrace for but an instant, his expression sour. But then the set of his face shifted, and his brows raised in what might have passed for self-deprecating surprise, had it not been for the antagonism still glinting in his eyes.

"So . . ." he drawled softly. "At long last I meet Sir Damien de Ashby—at one time known as an invincible opponent on the tournament field, later as a famously jilted suitor, and, most recently, as a disgraced Templar Knight. I confess that I had believed you dead, eased into eternity under the gentle tutelage of your inquisitors from France."

Damien tensed, but he refused to be goaded into a brawl by the man. Not here or now, anyway.

Hugh paused, as if to weigh the effect of his jab. The look he gave Damien was sharp enough to draw blood, for all the benignancy of his overall expression. "Of course you'll forgive me for assuming news of Alissende's sudden proxy with you to be false. After what I'd heard concerning the mass arrests and what followed, the timing of it all seemed a bit too . . . *convenient,* shall we say."

"Assumption often results in dangerous errors of judgment," Damien countered smoothly, still only just restraining himself from slamming his fist into the man's smug face.

"Right you are." Hugh gave him a tight smile. "But rest assured, I make it a point never to repeat my errors, whether of judgment or otherwise."

"The mark of an intelligent man."

The mockery in Damien's tone made Hugh flush, then go pale. His jaw tightened. When he'd apparently regained some semblance of self-control, he clipped, "While the warm welcome I have received here overwhelms, my visit to Glenheim is not the sole purpose of my journey. I am passing through on my way to Odiham Castle, where the tournament season gets underway a sennight hence. Dare I ask if you will be joining the events there?"

"It is my intent."

Hugh raised his brows in an insincere display of surprise and admiration. "Courageous of you. I can only imagine how difficult it will be. The mantle of shame can be a heavy burden to bear. One hopes for time to bury such things, naturally, but in this case . . ."

His voice drifted off and he shook his head, at the same time crossing his arms as he clearly built to something more malicious. "It is how I first learned of you, you know, since I was abroad when it actually happened. The court gossips have a horrible habit of reviving the account, every now and again, of what ensued during your last tournament five years ago, when before hundreds of spectators, you were publicly humiliated, rejected out of hand as an inadequate suitor for—"

Making a show of catching himself midsentence, he placed his finger to his lips and then feigned shock as he finished, "—why, for my cousin Alissende, strangely enough. The very same woman who now suddenly and without warning has embraced you—a man who fled

England in disgrace, entered a celibate Brotherhood, and was eventually arrested and charged with *heresy,* by God—as her lawfully wedded husband."

He seemed to take a kind of perverse pleasure in the sarcasm, though the look in his eyes at that moment might have made a lesser man question the wisdom in continuing to oppose him. "It is truly miraculous, I say. Astonishing."

Damien did not reply at first, instead willing himself to absorb the blow of Hugh's words. They were nothing more than that, he reminded himself. Sounds upon the air. The events themselves were long past. Though the memories might burn like fire, this bastard could go to hell before Damien would reveal that damning truth to him.

Never moving his gaze from Hugh's arrogant face, Damien kept his emotions tightly reined in so that he could answer with a sense of calm that surprised even him. "It *is* remarkable, my lord. And because of it, I am feeling magnanimous. Therefore, bearing in mind your obvious disappointment at having lost the right to pursue Alissende ever again, or to even consider speaking with her in the way I observed when I came upon you in this glade a short time ago, I will restrain myself from dealing with you as my instincts prompt me, and forgo driving my sword through your chest where you stand."

He felt Alissende go rigid against him, and he gently squeezed her shoulder in comfort, adding with a cold smile, "But I will see you at Odiham, never fear."

Hugh grinned, a predatory look sharpening his features. Taking one step back, he barked a laugh and retorted, "Ah, Sir Damien, in other circumstances,

I might have actually found reason to like you. But at the least, I shall enjoy facing you on the field—and besting you."

Turning away from them now, Hugh stalked back toward his men, one of whom brought Hugh's gelding to the edge of the clearing. After mounting, he twisted to face them once more, calling, "We will resume this at Odiham, then. I await the moment with bated breath, so do not disappoint me."

Then he wheeled the horse around and led his men from the glade, in the direction of the roadway that would lead them toward Hampshire and Odiham Castle.

"On the contrary, my lord," Damien murmured, his gaze never leaving the earl's back as he watched them go. "I would not miss it for all the gold in England."

Alissende sat in the solar an hour later, waiting for Damien to return from conferring with the physician about the injury Seamus had sustained during the scuffle this morning. He had requested that she meet him here when he was finished, and she felt a vague sense of apprehension, wondering what he wished to discuss.

There was much that needed to be resolved, she knew—details of their upcoming journey to Odiham Castle, for one. But there was more to it than that, she was sure, and she could not help wondering if it was tied, somehow, to the mocking comments Hugh had made during their confrontation.

In her mind's eye, she saw again the way Damien's jaw had tightened, felt the tensing of his body next to hers, when Hugh had dredged up the painful account of her rejection of him those years ago. Sweet heaven, she would have done anything to have been able to refute it, to make Hugh swallow his taunts. But she had been forced to keep silent, because all of it was true. Every ugly insinuation Hugh had made, every awful description he had offered, had been kinder than the reality of it by a hundredfold.

She *had* turned away from Damien that day. She had rejected him publicly, leaving him to gather the tattered vestiges of his pride under the gawking stares of nearly two hundred members of King Edward's court. It had been awful and heart-wrenching, and even now, her mind resisted the images that had been unlocked by allowing herself to think on it at all this day.

But it was necessary. She needed to remember everything again, to call up all those feelings if she was to be prepared for what she and Damien might face when they made their appearance at court next week. Closing her eyes, she tipped her head against the back of the chair and let the memories unfold, as clear and vivid as if they had happened in the past hour, instead of five years ago. . . .

Damien had won the tournament that day, the final and most important *pas d'armes* of the season. In a startling display of prowess, he had been the sole victor of more than twoscore competitors in half a dozen events, and he had thundered across the field to claim the first part of his prize—a favor from the lady he would choose to accompany him to the tournament feasting that night. The roars of the crowd had grown deafening as he'd reined his steed to a halt in front of the stands, dismounted, and approached.

He had been young, powerful, and incredibly handsome; the sun had cloaked him in golden light, as if affirming him the Archangel of court lore, and many of the ladies around her had been calling out his name. They had murmured in adoration, sighing as they'd offered him their fluttering tokens. They had been his for the taking. But he had had eyes only for her.

He had come closer, reaching out to her alone . . .

And it was then that she had done it.

It had been the most agonizing deed she had committed in all of her life, but she had felt as if she'd had no other choice. Even though they had planned this moment for weeks, even though they had decided together that he must win this tournament so that they might use this aspect of the prize to let the world know of their desire to be wed, she had turned away from him, acting as if she thought herself too far above him ever to consider his attentions.

The silence in the stands had been deafening. For a moment, everyone had seemed stunned. And then the whispers had begun, and she'd scrambled down from her seat, fleeing the field with the buzz of it ringing in her ears, and with the image of Damien's devastated expression etched into her mind.

To the members of the court, the incident had been scandalously exciting. Delicious fodder for the kind of talk that could go on for years.

Her action had not been altogether frowned upon, however. For all his breathtaking skill on the field, Sir Damien de Ashby was naught but a simple knight, the second son from an impoverished family, while she was the only child of a blooded earl. None at court had known the full truth of their hidden love—nay, not even her own mother—though it had been clear to everyone that she and Damien had engaged in a dalliance, developed over the course of the season.

Still, few had blamed her for rebuffing him outright at the tournament. Many had even approved, noting that her intelligent response had saved her sire from a potentially thorny scandal, as had happened only a few weeks before when the knight's elder brother, Sir Alexander de Ashby, had been caught trifling with Lady Margaret Newcomb, the daughter of another high-ranking nobleman.

But Alissende had suffered untold agony.

She had spoken with Damien only once after that public rejection, in her father's arms tent an hour later, where he had found her hiding, shaking, sick to her stomach in the aftermath. He had been anguished, too, his voice cracking and his face pale and disbelieving. It had been the only time she could ever recall him showing any sign of weakness or vulnerability, other than those private times, in the moments of wild abandon that had come with the powerful force of their love-making.

But she had brought him to his knees that day. She had watched his heart break and felt her own tearing along with it, telling herself that she was doing the right thing. The only thing she could do, for both their sakes.

Oh, God . . .

She had been so foolish. So naive about life and about love.

So afraid, and so very young.

And so she had told him more awful lies to get him to leave, and when he did, she had known that she would never see him again.

It had remained thus for five long years. It would have stayed so forever had Hugh not intervened, with his greed and his grasping. But now Damien was here. He had returned, for a short time, at least, a compelling, irate, and awesome force of nature. Still so much the man she had once known, and yet a stranger to her in so many ways. His nearness tempted her and tested her resolve, at the same time that it reminded her of the danger to be had in allowing herself to love again.

Opening her eyes once more, Alissende pushed herself up from her chair and strode over to one of the solar's leaded windows. Looking out, she tried to lock the memories back into the depths of her mind, troubled by them anew. It was done; the past could not be changed. She knew it, and yet it didn't seem to help her in managing the disarray of her emotions.

She had suffered for her youthful folly many times over, trying to make peace with herself the best that she could. But with Damien's return she was helpless to stop the flood of feelings that constantly barraged her. They confused her, tormented her, angered her. They gave her no rest.

She still wanted him, still felt deeply for him. But she was no longer the innocent, carefree maiden she had been when she had first loved him, any more than he was the same golden, noble knight of their youth. The intervening years had brought much that made her wish for nothing more than to be away from Damien and every man for the rest of her days, and she did not know how to reconcile her conflicting emotions. Perhaps she never would.

"See anything interesting?"

Alissende twisted at the sound of Damien's voice,

her heart seeming to skip a beat, so flustered did his presence make her, especially now, after allowing herself such intimate memories involving him.

When she did not respond right away, he gestured to the window as he reached her, adding, "You seemed so intent when I entered the chamber that I wondered if something in particular had caught your attention."

Only you.

The answer bloomed in her mind, sending a rush of warmth to her cheeks, though thank heavens she was vigilant enough not to have spoken the words aloud. To cover her agitation, she shook her head and tried to smile.

"Nay, there is nothing to see. I was simply lost in thought."

He nodded, and though his expression was pleasant, he appeared slightly ill at ease, as he always did whenever they were constrained to be alone together.

"Seamus has awakened," he said at last, coming closer and leaning back against the wall, next to the window where she stood. He crossed his arms loosely over his chest. "The physician says he will recover, given time."

"I am relieved," Alissende responded quietly. And she was. Seamus was a good man, loyal and true, and he, his wife, and four children were much loved in the village for their willingness to share what was theirs with those in need.

Damien nodded, falling silent again. Now it was he who seemed lost in thought, and she was just readying to ask him what it was that he'd wanted to discuss with her when he looked up, meeting her gaze with the warmth of his own; the gentle look of concern in his eyes sent a shock straight through her.

"How is your arm?"

"It is fine," she murmured. Another flush spread up her neck to warm her ears. Now he was staring at the bruise along the bottom edge of her cheek—the one Hugh had made when he'd gripped her chin so cruelly in the glade.

Embarrassed, she touched her fingers briefly to the spot and looked away. "It is nothing, truly. The tenderness will pass in a day or two, and all will be as before."

"I regret that I did not find you sooner, Alissende," he said quietly. "I would have prevented his touch upon you altogether, if I could have."

He sounded so serious, so filled with self-reproach that her gaze was drawn to him again.

"There was no way you could have known Hugh would come to Glenheim on this day of all," she said. "None of us did, else I would have never chanced a journey beyond the castle walls."

"Why did you leave, then?" He held her captive with the intensity of his gaze, and it was clear that his question referred to far more than the meaning of the simple words comprising it.

He caught her by surprise with it, and she stammered the half-truth, "I—we went to find strawberries, to make a pudding."

"Ah . . ."

The heat in her face deepened. In an effort to distract him from a discussion of her motivations or her feelings, she said, "I, too, am sorry that your initial meeting with Hugh was made so much more difficult because of me."

"In what way?"

"The woodland could not have been the most favorable setting for coming face-to-face with my cousin for the first time, and I regret the added danger it caused you."

"It is of no matter." His handsome face tightened, the expression reminiscent of that feral look he'd worn when he'd confronted Hugh. "What is important now is that he knows of me—and I something of him. The gathering at Odiham in a sennight promises to be interesting at the least."

Aye, interesting and likely uncomfortable as well.

Damien must have read something in her expression, for he frowned. "What—you have other concerns about it?"

"Perhaps," she answered, not wanting to hurt him but needing to remind him of the ugly truth that he would surely find in returning to court for the first time since their last painful appearance together. "It is just that going to Odiham is bound to be difficult in a number of ways, is it not? For you especially."

She braced herself as raw awareness swept across his face; his formerly relaxed posture faded, and he took his time before he responded.

"When I accepted the charge of your protection, Alissende, I knew that it would include the need to return to court . . . with all that entails for me."

The last part was spoken with a darker edge, as if it left a bitter taste in his mouth, and Alissende's heart twisted. Damien paused again, looking away, and her agony intensified. Naught could be gained by revisiting the sordid details of that awful day, she reminded herself. Naught but more misery and regret. It would change nothing, and—

"The past is over, Alissende," he continued quietly, breaking into her troubled thoughts, "and only the present need concern us. I can manage the old shadows as well as the impending dangers, as long as I can trust that you will not act as an adversary to me for these months we are constrained to live together."

The subtle shift of tension in his voice startled her, and she met his gaze, feeling breathless at the piercing look in his blue eyes.

"It is one of the subjects about which I desired to speak with you when I asked you to meet me here in the solar," he went on. "Now that the first confrontation with Hugh is past, I believe we should try to approach what is to come from a position of strength. Of one mind, if such is possible."

"I do not consider you an adversary, Damien," she admitted softly.

Far from it, in truth.

Those additional words echoed in her heart, but she forbore speaking them aloud.

"That is good," he murmured. He seemed as if he would say something further, but instead he silently reached out to brush his thumb over her cheek with a gentle touch, startling her enough by his action that it was all she could do not to tip her head into the caress of his palm.

In the next instant his fingers swept back, cupping her face and taking, in effect, the very action that she had longed to commit herself. This could come to naught, a voice inside her whispered. Sweet heaven, it couldn't, but his touch upon her felt exquisite, sending a tingle of sensation from the back of her head down to her toes.

Of their own volition, it seemed, her hands lifted, one of them coming up to rest lightly against his ribs and the other moving up his arm to his shoulder, as she slid by memory into the familiar contours of his embrace. They both paused, then, holding very still, and Alissende wondered if Damien was as surprised as she was at how easily they had fallen into this pose again. He had not lowered his hand from her cheek, and though it filled her with guilty pleasure to do so, she closed her eyes, soaking in the feeling and not daring to look at him for fear that she would be lost completely if she did.

For a long moment neither spoke; they just stood there, with no sounds audible other than their gentle breathing. When she could bear it no longer, she at last opened her eyes, only to feel the heat inside her bloom anew with the realization that he was staring down at her with that same expression she had seen in his gaze on the night of their feigned wedding feast.

Heaven save me from a certain fall . . .

"As long as the terms of our temporary union require us to spend this time together," Damien finally said, "behaving by all appearances as a newly married pair, perhaps we should endeavor to try to . . . enjoy each other's company more fully than we have been doing."

"As a newly wedded pair," she echoed, mesmerized by the delicious tension winding ever tighter between them.

"Aye, that is what we are supposed to be."

He ceased speaking then, but his head lowered a bit, and then a bit further, his chin tipping down as if he was readying to kiss her, by all the angels and saints . . .

Through the flood of sweet confusion that knowledge unleashed inside of her, Alissende somehow retained sufficient awareness—and spirit—to slow his progress by whispering, "We are supposed to appear as such to others, is that not correct?"

"That is the idea," he murmured, his mouth hovering so close to hers, now, that she felt the teasing warmth of his breath on her lips as he spoke.

"But there is no one in the chamber now, Damien. Except for us."

That made him stop altogether. Frozen to a halt, with his lips so close to hers that she could almost taste his kiss.

Ah, but she yearned to press forward, to accept without question that tempting caress. But her doubts and bruised emotions begged her to be strong, to resist him if she could. Her heart was pounding so that she thought it might leap from her chest as he pulled back just enough to look at her.

Another bolt of heat shot through her at the frustrated passion smoldering in his gaze. Yet in the space of another few breaths, amusement softened his expression, followed hard upon by reluctant acquiescence.

He would not pursue this further. For now, at least.

The phrase echoed in her mind, reminding her that Sir Damien de Ashby had never been the type of man to give up anything without a fight. And she knew that she would need the aid of more than heaven's angels or saints should he decide to make her the focus of his attentions in this way.

"I concede your point, my lady," Damien said at last, though his husky words sounded like anything but surrender. His mouth quirked into that sensual half smile that never failed to make her stomach feel as if it were dropping to her toes. "Instead, I will raise the second topic I wished to discuss with you here today."

Alissende found that she needed to swallow before she could speak, to ease the dryness in her throat. "Is it tied, perchance, to what you were saying just a moment ago?" she asked a bit croakily. "For if it is, I must ask you to release me before we continue—lest I be unable to continue," she added under her breath.

"In a way it is connected, aye."

He still looked as if he was up to something, though he stepped away from her after a few more delicious moments and moved back toward the window. She waited for him to expand on this second topic he'd mentioned, studying him through slightly narrowed eyes as she attempted to determine where he was going with this and why.

"It involves the two of us working together toward the common goal of thwarting Lord Harwick. However, our success will require you to undertake what many would consider an unorthodox pursuit."

Well, if that didn't sound like something she should avoid as if her life depended upon it. Knowing Damien, it likely was, and she couldn't quite prevent the flare of excitement that swept through her at the prospect of hearing his proposition.

"What is it?" she asked, with as much caution as she could muster.

"It is to engage in a special kind of instruction with me. The sort that will aid you in protecting yourself against Hugh's intimidation, should the need arise again. You and I will both rest easier knowing that you possess some means to defend yourself in the future."

After you are gone from my life again, only this time forever.

The words taunted Alissende, but she pushed them aside, focusing on her initial reaction to his suggestion.

"Such a thing is not possible, Damien. I do not possess the strength to oppose any man in a physical battle of wills, let alone Hugh, who is as well trained and nearly as powerfully built as you are."

"When I have finished with you, you will be able to use the skills you have learned against even me, should you wish it. Though of course you would only be successful if I was not prepared for your attempt . . . which, I must confess, will never be the case. It is only proper to give you fair warning."

His eyes twinkled as he spoke, and she was caught in a rush of sweet emotion at being offered this glimpse of Damien's playful side again after so long. Smiling with him, she shook her head, impressed at his seeming ease in shifting her mood away from her earlier pensiveness, while at the same time unable to subdue her skepticism concerning his idea.

"What?" he asked in response to her dubious expression. He placed his hand over his heart in mock injury. "I am wounded to know that you doubt me, lady. Truly."

Now she did laugh. "Ah, Damien, you cannot honestly believe that you can teach a woman to free herself from the grasp of a warrior who has been trained almost from the cradle to capture, fight, and kill. I have heard of women leading garrisons in defense of their lands in their husbands' absence, but I never knew of one who boasted the ability to meet a man successfully in an individual confrontation. Where did you get such a notion?"

"In Egypt, when I and a score of other Templar Knights passed through the Beni Hasan region."

"What?"

"In that place, there are those who practice an ancient form of defense that includes several hundred forms of holds, strikes, and escapes. The techniques are fundamental and very useful, and the men there have taught many of those skills to their women, for their protection in times of war."

Alissende looked at him in disbelief. "You are in earnest about this, aren't you?"

"I am, for I know it can be done."

She did not answer again right away. But the idea he was proposing had begun to work its influence on her, as he'd likely known it would. She had abandoned anything that had even hinted at impetuousness in the past five years, but Damien no doubt remembered well how she used to relish spontaneous and sometimes outrageous actions when she was younger. And this would have a pragmatic use, at least, if it proved as fruitful as Damien seemed to think.

"So, Alissende, what say you—will you agree to let me instruct you in this?" he asked. "It will require a daily commitment at first, as you become accustomed to the movements and positions."

In that moment she knew that she would do it, though it would look more than strange to any who might happen to stumble upon them in the process. However, that could be addressed easily enough.

She met his gaze. "If you wish it, Damien, then I

will attempt to learn these unusual skills you are advocating. However, I think it would be best if we undertook the training somewhere private, away from curious eyes and meddling tongues."

"I am relieved, lady," he said liltingly, "and pleased as well, to have your accord in this, though I am afraid I cannot comply with your request for privacy." Damien shook his head in a show of regret as he spoke the last, though the effect of it was ruined when he grinned at her.

She was still coping with her astonishment at his response when he turned and began to leave the chamber.

"Wait! Where are you going?" she sputtered, managing to pull herself together enough to glare at him and call more loudly to his retreating back, "and why in heaven's name are you unable to comply with my request?"

He paused, half-twisting to face her when he was near the door. "To answer your first question, I am going to ready what we will need to commence your training. And in answer to your second question—I am not *unable* to comply with your request for privacy during the activity . . . I simply refuse to."

Once again, Alissende was left speechless, choking out little more than a gasp, when he concluded his rude comment with an additional statement that, to her horror, made that first bit seem harmless by comparison.

"I intend to undertake your training quite out in the open, Alissende. Directly before the gazes of those 'others' for whom we are supposed to appear as a newly married pair, in fact." He winked and grinned again. "I'll leave you to make your own judgment as to why."

And then he turned and strode out the door . . . leaving her standing in the solar with her mouth agape, her pulse hammering wildly, and her ears echoing with the faint yet unmistakable sound of his whistling, drifting back through the stunned silence he had left behind.

Chapter 9

"I told you, I do not know what to make of it, *Mère*."

Alissende frowned as she yanked her hand from beneath the fine linen lavabo towel onto which she was attempting to embroider a lily; she sucked the fingertip she'd just pricked again with her needle, wishing she were not a lady so that she might curse aloud. Her uncharacteristic clumsiness annoyed her nearly as much as Damien had managed to do these past few days, with the undeniable relish he seemed to be taking in her daily instruction in defense.

In public.

"Perhaps he is concerned about his departure to court two days hence. Hugh is a formidable opponent, after all. Do you recall Damien as the kind of man who seeks solace during times of anxiety by pursuing matters of *amour*?"

Alissende's frown deepened to a scowl. "Damien de Ashby is far more likely to savor the idea of an upcoming battle than he is to feel apprehensive about it. In truth I believe he feels a sense of anticipation regarding his next meeting with Hugh."

Jabbing her needle, threaded with pristine, white silk into the linen square, Alissende jumped with a hissed intake of breath, yanking back another finger she'd just inadvertently stabbed.

"*Prendre garde,* Alissende," Lady Blanche murmured, suppressing what Alissende was shocked to realize looked suspiciously like a smile. "No matter how beautiful the embroidery, the priest will not be able to use a bloodstained cloth for drying his hands during the consecration of gifts."

For a long moment, Alissende stared at her mother, doing her best to determine if the expression she thought she'd seen was real or only a figment of her overwrought imagination. But except for a slight flush—and that could be attributed to the warmth in the chamber as much as anything else—her mother's face was serene.

"Is aught amiss, *amie?*" Lady Blanche asked at last, looking up in innocence from her stitching. "I hope my cautioning did not offend."

"Nay. You are correct as always, *Mère,*" Alissende sighed at last, looking away. "It seems that I am simply in no mood to be doing aught that demands my concentration this morn."

Or any time, since Damien de Ashby swept back into my life with his tempting caresses, sweetly whispered words, and ardent stares.

Feeling even more peevish with that awareness,

Alissende set the towel aside. Lady Blanche put down as well the credence cloth onto which she was stitching a delicate cross to say, "Come, *ma fille*. We can return to this work later, after we have gone out into the sunshine for a while to gather some sage for this evening's meat."

"That would be a welcome diversion," Alissende agreed, adding more softly as she stood and stretched her back, "though I should gather some stinging nettles as well, so that I might affix a few leaves inside Damien's braies and give him something more pressing to think about than dallying with me."

When she paused to brush some thread from her skirt, however, she glanced at her mother and caught her actually laughing this time.

"*Mère,* I assure you, it is not humorous in the least!"

"Ah, *chérie,* I know, I know," Lady Blanche said, still chuckling as she stood and slipped her arm around her. "Men can be maddening, obstinate creatures. The key, I have found, is to do what they are doing to exasperate you, only with even greater fervency. Meeting such challenges with confidence can do wonders for shifting the power into your own hands."

"What are you suggesting?" Alissende stiffened. "That I should behave as he has to me . . . to take the same kinds of liberties toward him in turn?"

"Perhaps." Her mother gazed at her evenly, pausing before adding, "It would help me to answer that if I knew exactly what Sir Damien is doing that has made you so out of sorts lately."

Alissende bit her lip and shook her head, stepping away toward the window. Her mother's question had unleashed a flood of heat at the memory of some of those moments with Damien, along with the unsettling awareness that she wasn't unhappy about his attentions. Nay, in fact she was enjoying every touch, every caress . . . every teasing whisper they shared as they were locked into the intimate embraces required for her training. Truth be known, she had begun to anticipate her daily session with Damien so fervently that it was her own daydreams distracting her, naught else.

Trying to seem disdainful of it, she lifted her chin a fraction, turning her head to look back into the chamber at her mother. "It is just that he behaves knavishly, stealing all manner of kisses and caresses while we are engaged in the lessons he has insisted I undertake with him in skills of defense."

"Ah," her mother nodded, "I have heard some talk amongst the servants about this new activity. I consider it a fine idea any time a woman gains a skill to her benefit, but naturally, the servants believe Sir Damien a bit"—her voice trailed off as she searched for the term—*"peculiar."*

"He is that and more," Alissende muttered. "What provokes me most is that I am helpless to prevent his advances, trapped as I am before the gazes of those who believe us truly married."

Liar.

The mocking voice inside her made its accusation. She felt her face grow warm, knowing full well that she wasn't being fair—or honest. She knew she could stop Damien from what he was doing at any time with only a single word of entreaty, but thus far she hadn't, because she didn't want him to stop.

Aye, her helpless feeling had far less to do with Damien's actions than it did with her own irrepressible desires for him, but that was too difficult to admit, especially to her mother. Pressing onward with what she hoped was a game front, she added in a mumble, "He knows this, and he uses it against me."

"I see."

Alissende stared at her mother in surprise. *I see?* That was all she intended to say? But Lady Blanche remained silent, looking thoughtful.

Ever more flustered, Alissende bridged the quiet by asserting, "Do not mistake me, *Mère*. I know that none of these attentions would be considered unusual for a newly married man to show his bride. But considering our arrangement . . ."

Lady Blanche tilted her head at last in a gesture of agreement. "Yet by treating him in kind, you may teach him a valuable lesson about such trifling."

"More like it will only encourage him in it."

Her mother shrugged. "That is a risk one takes in commencing this kind of rebellion."

She looked directly at Alissende, then, her gaze upon her suddenly very intent, in that way it had always been when she had questioned Alissende as a child, to see if she was telling a falsehood. "How would you feel if Sir Damien *did* respond to any actions you took by becoming even more attentive to you?"

Alissende knew all was lost, then. Whether or not she managed to utter a word would not matter. The expression on her face in that single, unguarded instant, along with the fact that she could not bear to meet her mother's gaze, would deliver her answer far more glibly than any protest she could have hoped to make.

After a telling pause, her mother nodded. "You do care for him, then. More than you are willing to admit."

Lady Blanche offered the comment matter-of-factly, as if she was discussing the state of the herb garden or ordering up bathwater. As she spoke, she bent to fold up the fine linens they'd been stitching earlier, placing them carefully in the basket, and then turned to Alissende with an expectant air, as if she was surprised that no answering comment had been offered yet.

"What do you wish me to say?"

"You need not try to refute it, *amie*. The answer is clear in your eyes. But as your mother I am interested to know how deeply this feeling runs—and what you propose to do about it."

"I—I, well, that is, I—" Alissende sounded incoherent, she knew, though it shouldn't have surprised her, as her very thoughts about Damien seemed to be incoherent most of the time.

"It is worse, even, than I supposed," Lady Blanche said.

"What do you mean?" Alissende asked in a cautious tone.

Her mother's fingers were laced demurely in front of her slim waist, and her expression was serious, but there was a definite glint in her eyes that Alissende could not remember having seen there before.

"You are in love with him."

Alissende's mouth opened—gaped, actually—but before she could speak, Lady Blanche shook her head and held up her hand to indicate that Alissende needn't struggle with trying to respond. Giving her daughter an affectionate smile, she came closer and brushed a stray tendril from her cheek.

"Do not fret, *amie*. Grown woman or not, you are still my child, and I have been watching you and Sir Damien carefully these past weeks. I watched you those many years ago as well, but I kept silent, thinking the decision you made then was necessary at that time. I can see what is happening without words needing to be spoken."

"But I do not know how I feel about him. Not truly," Alissende finished weakly.

"Of course you do not," Lady Blanche said in commiseration. "Even at its most sublime, love can inspire confusion." Patting Alissende's hand, she leaned in and kissed her cheek, and Alissende breathed in her sweet lily-of-the-valley scent, letting it soothe her for just a moment, though she pulled back as her mother said, "But now I have another question for you."

"What is it?"

"Why do you believe Sir Damien does not feel the same affections for you, *ma chérie?*"

Alissende shook her head, backing away from her mother with a laugh that edged on bitterness. "He does not; you must believe me in that. Aye, he is a man as any other, with a man's needs, perhaps, but we talked of the past only recently. What he lived through and the cruelty he endured when he was interrogated by the Inquisition—"

She rubbed her fingers over her brow, trying not to think about it overmuch, as she knew by experience that it would do naught but make her feel worse. It was the same wall of unalterable, cold truth that thrust itself before her every time she attempted to see her way around it, and it hurt too much to keep confronting it. "Nay, he has been too much changed by his experiences to go back to any of the feelings we may have shared before."

"You might be surprised, *ma fille.* What is in a man's heart is not always apparent on the surface—or sometimes even fully known to himself."

Alissende sank back again into her chair in response, and Lady Blanche crossed her arms with a sense of determination that sent a tingle of warning up Alissende's neck.

"Ah, well," her mother murmured, looking down in thought. "That part of it is neither here nor there. We must deal with what we know to be true right now." She met Alissende's gaze again. "You care for this man who has taken on the temporary role of your husband. Above and beyond the terms he himself set for your behavior in front of others as a married pair, he has begun to dally with you in ways that you are finding . . . unsettling, yes?"

Mute in her misery, Alissende simply nodded, but Lady Blanche was not content to let her get by with only that.

Covering the space between them in a few steps, she sat and took her daughter's hand in a grip of feminine encouragement and alliance. "Nay, Alissende," she chided gently, "that is not the strong and capable daughter I raised. It is time to show some spirit, *amie,* for a woman gains naught in this world by sitting and wringing her hands when confronted by a difficult problem or a stubborn male. The question that begs answering now is the same one I asked you but a few moments ago. Sir Damien has issued you a challenge, of sorts, in the liberties he is taking during these training sessions he has instigated with you."

Her kind eyes glinted as she smiled, raising her brow in an expression that was both fierce and mischievously wicked. "Now what do you intend to do about it?"

He had been playing with fire, and he knew it.

Damien brooded on that truth as he slipped into the cool darkness of the village chapel, grateful for the chance to be alone for a few moments as he tried to pull himself into some semblance of self-control. His estrangement from God notwithstanding, this was the most peaceful and private place that he had been able to think of when the urge to retreat had come upon him. Between masses it was generally deserted, and so he sat at the front, in one of the pews that stretched beneath the Madonna statue on the Epistle side of the altar.

And then he tried to think.

He was rapidly losing command of the situation with Alissende. For four days now the raw, erotic heat had been building between them until it had reached an almost unbearable pitch, tormenting him whenever he was in her company—and still he kept stoking the flames with a touch here, a whispered word there, a stolen kiss . . .

By God, he'd been able to think of little else these last days, it seemed, except for lavishing such caresses upon her body.

Her naked body.

He almost groaned aloud now as the thoughts, the sweet, hot images, swept over him anew, giving him no rest. In a short time he was due to meet with her again for another of the infernal training sessions he'd so foolishly initiated with her, and he knew without a doubt that no matter how much he told himself he would behave and maintain a certain distance as they worked together, he would end up abandoning all noble intentions when presented with the first good opportunity to taste her lips or to brush his hand over her delicate curves.

Curves normally reserved for true husbands or lovers.

That she seemed to respond in such delightful ways when he stole those caresses only added to the thrill of them for him. Her cheeks would flush, or the sweep of his palm across her breast would cause her nipple to tighten into a tantalizing bud beneath the fabric of her gown.

And just yesterday, before she'd caught herself and pulled away, blushing more deeply than he had seen her do before, she'd instinctively pressed back against him, molding her body to his in that way he remembered from long ago. He'd almost carried her from the yard and into their bedchamber at that moment, to bring their teasing to sweet, satisfying completion.

But of course he hadn't. He couldn't, no matter how badly he wanted her. She was a forbidden fruit to him, not only by right of the agreement they had struck or the trust broken between them long before that but also because he had nothing meaningful to offer her. Not anymore. He could give her less now as a man than he might have five years ago, for now he was but a shell of his former self, forsaken by God, the scars on his body only a hint of the damaged soul that slept within. He could not forget that.

Ah, but you need not restrict your passion to only customary practice, a sly voice inside him asserted. *There are other ways of appeasing desire. Ways that would allow you to touch Alissende . . . to taste and enjoy her and she you, without actual consummation. Ways that you once both delighted in with each other . . .*

Growling in frustration, Damien curled forward, burying his head in his hands and trying to force the thoughts from his mind. Sweet mercy, this wasn't helping. He was supposed to be strengthening his self-control, damn it, not giving in to all kinds of fantasies about the woman who tempted him beyond all imagining.

"Is the act of praying still so painful for you, then?"

The kind voice drifted to Damien from across the sanctuary, and he looked up to see Ben—good, steadfast Ben—approaching him.

"That is not the dilemma I struggle with this day, friend," Damien admitted as Ben came close enough to ease down beside him in the pew with a groaning sigh, "though, aye, the peace of it still eludes me."

Nodding with a half smile at the grimace Ben made while stretching back against the rigid wood of the pew, Damien added, "And what is this? Working so late illuminating a text for Father Michael again that you fell asleep on the table and earned a stiff neck?"

"Nay, Damien, this discomfort is your fault."

"How so?"

"It is the result of that infernal training you have had me assist you in giving the men." Ben rubbed at his neck, softening his criticism with a smile as he added,

"I am not the youth I once was, I'll grant you. But I am also no warrior, and the repetition of those blade sequences is going to do me in long before an enemy's weapon, I think. As a man of the cloth, I'm far more suited to tasks involving vellum and ink than sword and shield."

"I don't know about that," Damien said in a sly tone that pulled Ben's gaze to him, just in time for him to crown his comment with its intended jest. "You do quite well, I'd say, for an old man."

That earned him a response that was half shove and half punch, and he laughingly fended Ben off before sitting forward with a sigh to rest his forearms on his knees. His smile lessened, and he gazed up at the altar, not really focusing on anything, as he said, "In truth, friend, you should count your blessings that the men are all you need concern yourself with in the area of training."

A beat of silence passed.

"You refer to the rather unusual instruction you have been providing to Lady Alissende, I take it?" Ben asked, in a tone that should have warned Damien then and there to let this drop. But he was too wrapped in his own misery to heed his instincts.

"Aye," he replied, still staring into the sanctuary. "Curse my eyes for having conceived the practice to begin with."

Another pause ensued, though it was charged with a kind of tension that was impossible to ignore—a feeling strong enough to make Damien swing his head to the side to look at Ben. He caught his friend studying him, as if trying to discern something of importance.

"What?" Damien asked.

Ben shrugged, trying to look innocent. "I was only going to say that I happened to be passing by the courtyard yestermorn when you were engaged in Lady Alissende's instruction, and what I saw seemed very . . . interesting."

"Is that so?"

"Aye."

Damien's lips tightened, and he knew that he should simply change the topic. Or come right out and tell Ben he wasn't going to talk about it. Or leave.

But he suddenly realized that perhaps he'd come to the chapel for a reason. Perhaps he *needed* to talk about what was happening, to someone who might listen without judging him too harshly. The way Alex used to do.

A wash of grief swept over him unawares, and his breath caught. Though he and his brother had not always seen eye to eye on many issues, they had always shared an understanding and a sense of solidarity that Damien hadn't realized he'd been missing so strongly until just now.

Keeping his gaze steady on Ben, Damien decided to give it a try. "Would you care to expound upon what you deemed so interesting?"

"I thought you would never ask." His friend leaned back, clearly making himself comfortable. "But now that you have—"

Damien shot him a look that warned him to get on with it before he changed his mind.

"—I must say that the first impression I took from what I saw was that I was watching two people very adept at putting on a performance. Either that, or I was witnessing the amorous sport between a man and woman truly in love with each other."

The silence was so thick in the moments following that unbelievable comment that Damien felt choked by it . . . though the thought crossed his mind that his inability to draw in breath likely had more to do with the statement Ben had made than suffocating quiet.

"Well . . ." Ben amended gruffly, waving his hand in response to Damien's horrified expression. "Perhaps 'in love' is too strong a term. I should have said you appeared to be two people who are *falling* in love. That would be more apt, I think."

"It's hardly better," Damien managed to say.

"It is what I discerned," Ben said frankly, shrugging again. "You asked, and I told you. You cannot fault me for that."

"I do not fault you," Damien retorted, recovered from his shock enough to scowl. "But that does not mean I don't think you've gone a bit daft on me."

Ben snapped his gaze to him in a movement that was suspiciously agile for one who was supposed to be suffering stiff limbs and neck. "I have my wits about me as strongly as ever, Damien; that you know. However, after watching you these past days, I would hazard a guess that you cannot say the same about yourself, *hmm?*"

Unable to refute the jab, Damien held motionless for a moment, mulling it over. Coming to no satisfying conclusion, he breathed in deeply, and when he exhaled, he tipped his face to look at the floor as he clasped his hands together loosely, still balancing his forearms along his thighs.

"I cannot love Alissende, or any woman for that matter, Ben," he murmured, closing his eyes for a moment. "What I am feeling for her is something much less noble, I am sure."

"What in heaven's name makes you believe *that?*"

"The awareness that I am no longer capable of the softer emotion that love requires."

Ben didn't answer right away, though from the edge of his vision, Damien saw him nodding in thoughtful reverie, as if weighing what he'd heard. At last Ben said, "Aye, perhaps you are right . . ."

His voice trailed off as if judiciousness had stopped him before he'd finished with what he wanted to say.

This was no time for discretion, Damien decided.

Looking at Ben again, he demanded, "But? . . ."

"But if you are right," Ben finished, after flicking his gaze to Damien in confirmation that he wished him to continue, "then I would warrant what is ruining your peacefulness this day are the pangs of your conscience, telling you that you ought not to be dallying with Lady Alissende as you have been if you do not intend to follow through in all honor."

Damien flinched. Ah, that smarted. Yet it was the truth, like it or not. He'd done his best not to think too deeply or too long about the inevitable day in a few months when he would need to leave Alissende for the last time—not only because he knew it wouldn't be honorable to undertake a dalliance with her in the meantime but also because he realized more and more with every hour that passed how painful that break would be to him. It couldn't be helped, but that wasn't going to make the moment any easier. Sighing again, he sat up so that his back was flush against the pew once more.

"I have one last bit of advice, my friend," Ben said quietly.

"What is it?" Damien asked, through the unaccountable misery that was swelling within him at the thought of what he was going to have to do from now on; at the knowledge that he must cease without compunction all the teasing and pleasurable dalliances he had been enjoying with Alissende.

"It is this," Ben said, so seriously that it drew Damien's gaze to him again. "If you find yourself unable to continue resisting Lady Alissende's charms, then you must consider the possibility that there is something nobler than lust driving you into her arms. Lust may be eased with any available female—and conversely, a man may control base desire with his will, if he so chooses. You know this well, having served as a Templar Knight. But it is not so with love."

That made Damien pause. The hope of it slipped in, testing the waters of desolation within him, only to come up against the same barrier of darkness as always. He felt his mouth twist with bitterness. "What you are saying has merit, friend, there is no doubt, but it does not apply to me. Heaven help me, for I wish it could be true, but it isn't."

Damien gritted his teeth in determination, combating the seductive voice inside him that tempted otherwise, calling upon every ounce of his strength to follow through with what he knew would need to be done.

Ben went silent again, and Damien sensed that his

friend had shifted his thoughts to something else, something no less serious. In the next breath Damien discovered what it was.

"You know, heaven *will* help you with such dilemmas, if you will only ask," Ben offered gently, and Damien felt that strange punching sensation in his gut, realizing not only that he had indeed called upon heaven a moment ago out of long-standing habit but also that it still ached so much to remember that such solace was not his to claim any more.

"God hears all, Damien," Ben continued. "And He welcomes home any who seek entry, forgiving all sins and sinners—even those who turned away from Him out of grief or anger."

The aching stabbed too deep for Damien to speak at first, and so he simply pushed himself up from the pew, tamping down the hurt by force of sheer will, trying to assuage his ever-present longing for the very comfort Ben was advocating.

"God may forgive me, Ben, when and if I find means to ask Him for it," Damien said at last, his voice husky. "But first I must forgive myself—for many things. And I do not see that happening anytime soon."

Forcing himself to pull off a smile of sorts, he reached out and clasped Ben's hand, trying not to dwell on the troubled look in his friend's eyes, and grateful for the bond they shared in a way that went deeper than words. "Thank you for your counsel this day, Ben," he murmured. "All will be right in time, you will see."

At Ben's silent nod, Damien turned to go, making his way down the center aisle, toward the double doors at the back. But as he stepped through them, he thought he heard Ben say, "I pray it will, Damien. Aye, for your sake, as well as the Lady Alissende's, I pray it will."

Chapter 10

Damien was as ready as he was ever going to be. He stood in the portion of the yard designated for training, eyeing the small refreshment table he'd ordered set in the shade near the castle wall. For each of the past four days, he'd asked the kitchen servants to provide a light repast to be consumed during the brief respites he and Alissende took from the rigors of her instruction.

However, the sad truth was that most of the food they had set out in previous days had been left untouched, because he had been too eager to use his time with Alissende in more entertaining pursuits. He'd decided that he'd much rather practice the positions and holds of her defense instruction, since they had allowed him to take the sweet liberties that had brought him to the desperate state he suffered now.

But today, he promised himself, they *would* take

numerous rests—positioned at opposite sides of the table—eating and drinking until the bounty here was depleted.

Aye, he would maintain his control in this today, he vowed, even if it killed him. Ever since he'd left the chapel, he had forced himself to play out in his mind as many possible scenarios as he could bear to imagine, and all the tripping points along the way that were likely to make him forget his oath to behave properly with Alissende. He'd even come as close to praying as he'd ever managed to since his months of desperation with the Inquisition.

All that remained now was to see if he was up to the task of resisting what his own instincts demanded that he do with her, whenever she was near. To find out if he could bear the temptation of having her so close . . . captive in his arms . . . with his hands on her body . . . with her knee-weakening fragrance invading his senses with such seductive power . . .

Sweet mercy.

He could do this, he groused in silence as he stalked over to the table, and in an effort to distract himself he wolfed down one of the pastries there, following it with a cupful of cider, quaffed without pause. Then, setting down the empty vessel, he stretched out his back and arms in preparation for the instruction to come, keeping his mind occupied with the helpful thought that Alissende's own reluctance about these public appearances would likely serve him well in what he needed to do.

He was just beginning to feel a sense of confidence in his ability to remain composed about all this when he happened to turn away from the table and saw Alissende coming into the yard.

It took but one look, and all his hopes fled straight on a path to hell.

She moved with easy grace toward him, sending a prickle of warning up his spine. Something was different about her. Something he could not pin to any one aspect. But there was no mistaking it.

By all the angels and saints . . .

It was in her movements, in the gentle swaying of her hips and the tilt of her head, with that lustrous hair of hers pulled up to the crown. And that gown she was wearing. Good God, it seemed to slip along her curves, accenting every sweet nuance of her body.

And then she came close enough that he could see the look in her eyes, and he was left trying to swallow in a futile attempt to moisten a throat gone bone dry.

"I trust I have not kept you waiting too long, Damien," she murmured, lowering her gaze and giving him a moment's relief from the desire that was ripping through him.

"Nay," he mumbled. He coughed, trying to rid himself of his hoarseness. "I was just planning the sequence of moves I intend to hold—I mean show—you."

"That is good. If you have no objection, however, I would partake of some refreshment before we begin." She smiled contritely. "I became engrossed in a conversation with *Mère* as we were sewing, and I had no time to sup."

At his silent nod, she stepped past him, moving to take a fruit tart and a cup from the table. The sensual fragrance of ambergris and sweet woodruff she wore wafted over him, making his gut clench with fierce pleasure. He closed his eyes and almost against his will breathed in deeply, tormenting himself with the burning thoughts and tender memories that scent unleashed inside of him.

Not a very auspicious start.

Determined to distract himself from such dangerous musings, he opened his eyes again, only to realize that Alissende stood directly in front of him and that she had turned to face him again as she ate. Though he knew he should not do it, he watched her take a bite of the tart and sip at her cup of cider, mesmerized by the glimpses he caught of her mouth.

Those soft, rosy-hued lips were just visible at the cup's golden rim as she drank, until without warning, her tongue darted out, catching a drop of the sweet liquid. An answering jolt of pure heat stabbed through him, forcing him to shift uncomfortably with the predictable swelling of that portion of him that always seemed to have a mind of its own, no matter what his better intentions.

Damien tore his gaze away, reminding himself to concentrate on the work ahead and nothing else. There was naught to be gained and much to be lost in continuing with such indulgences, innocent though they might seem. He should have remembered that he did not need to touch Alissende to become aroused by her; he never had needed to. She tempted him just by being.

When he had finally mastered his thoughts enough to make movement comfortable again, Alissende suddenly stepped toward him, lifting her hand to his face. His gaze snapped to hers as she brushed her thumb in a silken, sensual stroke across his cheek.

That unexpected action and the sensation that accompanied it made him stop breathing so abruptly that he made a slight choking sound.

"Are you unwell, Damien?" she asked, with a kind of amused lilt to her voice. And those violet-blue eyes . . . ah, they held laughter as well, along with something more . . .

Pressing the cup into his hand, she murmured, "Here, drink something, for goodness' sake. I did not mean to startle you. It was only a crumb—see?" She held out her finger with the flake of tart pastry perched atop it.

He could not speak a word. Nay, for the first time that he could remember, he was utterly and wholly mute. And so he simply jerked two steps back, raised the cup she'd handed him, and drained it in one draught, wishing with a fervor quite unlike him that he had ordered the servants to set out goblets of something more potent than cider.

"I know you wish to embark upon our lesson soon," Alissende continued, her dulcet tones washing over him like honey, "but before we begin in earnest, I would like to ask your honest opinion."

"About what?" Damien managed to croak.

"About my progress these past few days."

If Damien hadn't begun to doubt his own senses by this point, he might have thought that Alissende's eyes were growing a bit heavy-lidded, and that she'd taken a step—nay, two steps again—closer to him as she'd spoken. Her brow curved in slight, wicked conjunction with one corner of her lush mouth.

"What say you, then?" She'd finished the tart she'd taken from the table, and as she waited for him to answer she lifted the tip of one finger to her mouth, gently sucking from it a dab of the sticky, sweet berry filling. When she pulled it from between her lips, the action was slow and smooth, leaving that gently rounded tip glistening with just a hint of wetness. "Have my skills . . . improved?"

In that moment, if Damien's legs hadn't felt like they had become rooted by lead weights to the ground, he would have needed to sit down. Right there.

As it turned out, he managed to recover enough not only to remain standing but also to utter what could pass for a reply, husky as it was.

"I would say that you're doing quite well, Alissende." He coughed, determined to see this through without cracking. "Quite well indeed."

Her smile washed over him, brilliant and, by all appearances, ingenuous.

"I am relieved to hear it," she said, slipping her hand beneath the crook of his elbow and pulling him into the center of the training area, "and I am also eager to get started, to see what clever positions you intend to teach me today."

Damien resisted the urge to look at her again, though the seeming double meaning in her words played havoc with his senses. He steeled himself to begin the lesson, preparing, as always, to review what she had learned during the previous session.

The previous session . . . oh sweet heaven, he had taught her a sequence of moves to free oneself from attacks that come from behind. That meant he'd taken great pleasure, yesterday, in directing her to stand facing away from him, with the sweetly rounded curves of her bottom fitted to his groin and her shoulders resting against his chest. His left arm had been wrapped around her waist, while his right had snaked around her chest . . . across the tops of her delectable breasts, good God . . .

"Shall we begin?" Alissende called cheerfully, and he realized that she'd taken a few steps away from him to stand, back to him and arms slightly raised, inviting him to take hold of her in the pose they'd left off with.

Damien bit back a groan, gritting his teeth and moving into position. This was ridiculous; he was a seasoned warrior, by God, tested through bloody battles, stifling desert sun, and the tortures of the Inquisition. He could manage this—this *need* she incited in him— without falling to pieces over it.

Slipping his arms around her, he tugged, pulling her back into him somewhat more forcefully than he might have under normal circumstances . . . enough that he heard her breath leave her in one swift rush.

Now his own irritation was getting the better of him, he thought in disgust. In this position, his lips were close to her ear, and he deemed it only proper to murmur an apology for his overzealous action, though just as he did, he could have sworn he caught a glimpse of her smile.

But when he looked more closely, she seemed composed, merely nodding in acceptance of his contrition. If anything, at that moment he thought she looked serious and ready to get to work.

Taking care not to breathe in too deeply, for fear of being captivated anew by her delicious scent, Damien stared straight ahead and set his jaw. "Do you remember what you must needs do first, lady, should anyone come upon you like this?" he asked gruffly.

"I believe so," she answered.

But she did not follow that statement with movement, and in another moment he almost growled, "Is something amiss, then, that you do not begin?"

"Nay." She sounded cool and unperturbed, despite the fact that they were locked in a close and quite sensual embrace. He did not know how she remained so steady in the face of it, for the feeling of her pressed against him like this was sending molten fire undulating to his core.

"I am not quite ready to begin yet, for I was just thinking," she continued. "Once we leave for court, day after next, we will no longer be able to pursue this kind of training in public. It would be more awkward there, even, than it has been here—yet I believe we should proceed with it, as I have not mastered enough in these few days to warrant ceasing my instruction."

As she spoke the last bit, she turned her head against his chest to look up at him, her eyes wide open and innocent. "What do you think?"

For the second time in this quarter hour, Damien choked. Gazing down at her, his lips mere inches from her own, he took in a shallow breath, then exhaled just as gradually, not making any other kind of movement or sound. At last, he blinked and somehow marshaled enough strength to murmur, "I think you are likely correct."

She gave a slight nod, seemingly unaware of the chaos she was unleashing inside him, a state that only worsened when she added, "I am glad, for I have been musing a good deal about this, and I must tell you that, despite my initial reluctance, I now realize how *grateful* I should be for the opportunity you have provided me. And because of it, I wish to repay you in kind."

She smiled again, sweetly, and Damien could not help but stare at her. His trepidation rose with every second, as he knew by instinct that whatever she was leading up to, with such a complete and unexpected turnabout in her demeanor, could not be good.

"What, exactly, did you have in mind?"

He spoke because she seemed to be expecting him to say something, though he groaned inwardly as soon as the words were out, well aware that it was likely the most ill-advised thing he could have asked her at that moment.

Alissende, however, seemed thrilled with the question; she smiled more brightly.

"I thought we could undertake an activity that you might find as stimulating as I have found my instruction. Though it, as well, would need to be undertaken in private, I think."

She tipped her head as if considering, and Damien struggled to hold still. It went against every masculine instinct to do so when her words stirred the fires inside him anew, sending heated jolts along familiar paths.

"Aye, privacy would be best," she added at last, looking up to cast him a glance of pure dalliance, "for I find it difficult to believe that you would want anyone watching us at the activity I have in mind."

Disbelief rocked through Damien at the immediate, erotic images that sprang into his mind. She could not be contemplating what he thought she was. Nay, it couldn't be. He was insane even to consider it . . .

"Actually, I suppose we need not wait until we arrive at court to begin," she continued in that cheery voice, while the implication of her words pounded into his stunned brain like iron nails. "In fact, I do not see why we cannot start as early as tonight, in our own chamber here at Glenheim."

Through the shock that kept rising higher and higher inside him, Damien somehow heard her say just after that, "There. Now that that's settled, shall we commence our lesson?" He even managed to grunt out a kind of response that seemed appropriate . . .

A reaction he immediately regretted, when she did exactly as he had bid her do during her instruction yesterday, taking hold of the smallest finger of his right hand and yanking painfully back on it, causing him to involuntarily loosen his grip on her, while at the same time using that opening to drive her elbow directly into his midsection.

Hard.

Damien's breath left him, for good, it seemed, just as was supposed to happen with this move, and he staggered back, bent over double and gasping in his effort to regain his wind.

Through the haze that covered his vision, he saw Alissende turn around, her startled expression quickly shifting to one of triumph. She dug her fists into her hips, and just before he dropped to his knee, having been defeated this afternoon, he realized, in more ways than one, he heard her gentle laughter. The sound of it washed over him, impish and merry all at once.

"It seems you were mistaken about one thing, in regards to my training, Damien," she teased, still laughing. "I did manage to catch you unawares. However, I must admit that you were quite correct about another."

"Oh, yes? And what was that?" he rasped after another moment spent catching his breath; in spite of his discomfort, he found himself unable to keep from smiling up at her obvious glee.

"That move does work, just as you said it would." She grinned even wider. "Far better than I ever might have imagined."

Evening couldn't come soon enough.

Alissende could not remember the last time she had so looked forward to something. She burned with a sense of purpose. Of course, that her purpose this day had been to sweetly torment Damien, exciting him to the same feelings of desperation he'd subjected her to for nearly the week prior, was likely wicked. It was sure to earn her the penance of completing a slew of novenas and good deeds were she to admit it to her confessor.

In the meantime, she was enjoying every moment of it.

When she had suggested that she return the favor of Damien's training instruction tonight, and in the privacy of their bedchamber, the look on his face had been beyond price. And seeing him react to every little nuance of her movements, her breathing, even the way she ate and drank . . . well, it had all gone a long way toward assuaging the feelings that had been bruised with his public sporting at her expense. She was beginning to understand why he'd enjoyed dallying with her so much. Aye, almost to the point that she'd considered forgiving him and letting up on her cruel torment of him. But that would have been far too easy.

"You seem in high spirits this evening, Cousin," Michael said, calling her thoughts back to the here and now. He was standing in the door to her bedchamber with his arms stretched around a large basket full of used vellum, some inkhorns, quills, and other writing implements, smiling in response to the outlandish grin she herself was sporting. His eyes crinkled at the corners as he added, "Surely it cannot be at the prospect of copying letters."

When she shrugged, he shook his head, laughing as he set down his burden. "I am well aware that your beauty is more than matched by your wits, *amie,*" he chided, "and I am happy to oblige you in any way I can, but even I cannot fathom why you asked for these things. In my mind there are few prospects less stimulating than an evening spent hunched over a table, getting a crick in your neck and ink stains on your fingers."

"Oh, I don't know," she murmured, picking up one of the quills he'd brought and twirling it in her fingers. "I fully expect it to prove quite stimulating tonight. Far more than ever before, in fact."

Michael just shook his head again, chuckling and mumbling something about the whims of females. Alissende schooled her answering smile long enough to help him set up the things he'd brought. When they were done, she turned to give him a quick, fierce hug.

"Thank you, Michael," she said, kissing his cheek and ruffling his hair. "I know how very dear these items are, and I will make good on my promise to send to the parchmenters and procure a dozen pieces of fresh vellum to replace these castoffs from the monastery."

"I do not doubt it, Cousin. The brothers will not miss these pieces in the meantime, and the scribes will be greatly enthused to have unmarked vellum upon which to work, once it arrives." He gave her a wink. "In truth, they are the only others I know who become even more inspired than you do at the prospect of working at their letters."

Laughing in response to his gentle gibe, Alissende linked her arm with his and began to walk back toward the door with him. "Ah, Michael, I am going to miss you so. Are you certain that you must remain here at Glenheim when we leave for court? Can you not come with us?"

"Nay, Cousin." He paused in their progress to cup her cheek in his palm affectionately. "Someone must stay to keep watch over your mother. And besides, there is naught for me there except for Hugh, and he would as like drive daggers through his eyes as be forced to acknowledge our kinship. More so now that he realizes my part in keeping you from him."

Alissende frowned. "Aye, he was none too pleased. He may turn against you because of it, Michael. You must be prepared. Your brother has never reacted well to being thwarted, and I fear blood will have no bearing for him."

Michael pulled back, gazing down at her in mock dismay. "What is this? Are you worried for me, Alissende?"

"I would not put anything past Hugh."

Pausing, Michael took her shoulders in his hands before leaning forward to press a kiss to her brow. "Do not fear, *amie*. I will try to remain vigilant."

She nodded, walking with him toward the door.

"Take good care of *Mère* while I am gone, Michael; if aught goes amiss, send word to me quickly. Odiham is but two days' ride away, do not forget."

"I will remember, Alissende. Godspeed to you as well." His gaze fixed on her, and he raised his brows to accentuate his words as he added, "And tell Sir Damien that I will be praying he proves the victor in the upcoming tournament. Perhaps he may finally teach that brother of mine a lesson in humility."

Flashing another grin, Michael waved and ducked through the door. Alissende waved back, watching him go with a mixture of fondness and anxiety. She had always considered Michael more a sibling than a cousin, and though she was pleased that he had found peace and contentment in the priesthood, she could not help worrying about him. It distressed her that he had none to turn to, truly, except for other holy men, her mother, and herself.

For all of his jesting, Michael knew as well as she that his brother could not be trusted; Hugh had made no secret of the vague contempt he felt for his more sensitive and physically weaker sibling. Alissende did not doubt for an instant that Hugh would use any means at his disposal to get what he wanted. Even Michael.

But Hugh would be dealt with soon enough, in an arena that he would not find easy to sway to his own liking with intimidation or even brute force. Nay, the tournament results were determined by only one thing: finely honed battle skills. If Damien's talents in that regard were anywhere near what they had been when she had known him before—and she had cause to think if naught else that they had improved—then Hugh would be fortunate to leave the field unscathed.

And yet before that satisfying conclusion was reached, she had other satisfactions to gain . . . namely the one that would come to fruition tonight, when she offered Damien the surprise he had earned by tormenting her with his public seductions this week.

Alissende smiled to herself, walking over to the table upon which were arranged all the writing tools

Michael had been kind enough to provide for her. She ran her fingers along the smooth contours of the wood, thinking about what she had planned. Aye, this evening was sure to be a pleasurable one, for if all went as she hoped, then Damien would learn his lesson as well, in a way he had never imagined he would.

She was going to make sure of it.

Chapter 11

Just after dusk, Damien stood in the hallway upstairs, feeling a surge of dread that seemed ludicrous, considering the fact that it was his own bedchamber door looming in front of him. But that was just the problem. It might be his bedchamber, but he knew what—or, more precisely, *who*—waited for him inside.

If he hadn't sworn to appear here after dinner, with a promise wrung out of him at the moment of what had been his greatest vulnerability this afternoon, he'd have put no less than ten miles between himself and this door by this time.

But he had made an oath to show himself, and so here he was.

He did not plan on staying long.

Nay, he would make his appearance, keeping as controlled and reserved as possible in the face of what he suspected would be temptation greater than any he had experienced thus far. And then he would flee.

He was not ashamed to admit it. It was what he had to do. Either that or he would end up giving in to the wicked thoughts that had been winding through his mind for the past four days . . . ideas for all the tantalizing forms of love-play that he could engage in with Alissende, without breaking their agreement to leave their union unconsummated.

What made all of this even more difficult to swallow was the knowledge that what he faced right now was his own fault. He'd realized it far too late of course, but he was not so daft that he couldn't see the truth. He had begun the wicked teasing that had made Alissende turn temptress on him, and now he could not change it back. That he had decided to swear off such conduct from here on out held no bearing, he knew; he had already unleashed the siren within her, coaxing her into the open with the lure of his own blasted desires.

Unfortunately, standing here in the hallway like a dolt for the rest of the evening wasn't going to accomplish anything.

Clenching his jaw and offering up a silent plea for the strength he needed to get through whatever seductive torment Alissende had planned for him on the other side of this portal, Damien took the remaining two steps to the door. He lifted the latch-string and pulled open the heavy wooden slab. Just a bit. Golden light spilled from the crack, but it was not wide enough for him to see aught inside the room.

With a final, longing glance back into the safer gloom of the hallway, Damien gripped the edge of the wood, yanked it open the rest of the way, and strode into the bedchamber. And then he came to a skidding halt. He heard the door thud shut behind him, but he could not seem to move forward, as his mind struggled to come to terms with the sight that greeted him.

Alissende was leaning over a sturdy-looking worktable that he had never noticed here before, wearing what in all kindness could only be called *serviceable* garments, with her beautiful hair completely concealed in a vast wimple of some dark fabric. Almost completely, he amended. One silky tendril had escaped the confines of the headdress to curl down her cheek in an artless, rather appealing manner.

Regardless, as a whole she looked as opposite the seductive enchantress she had appeared to be this afternoon as a sleek mare might look next to a peasant's workhorse. There were sheets of vellum, inkhorns, and quills spread across the entire tabletop, and she was shuffling a few of the pages aside, apparently to make room for something. She seemed not to notice him standing there. Or if she did, she did not seem particularly concerned about it.

"What the devil is all this?"

Damien finally found his voice, though he still did not move from his position.

She looked up at him for only an instant before she was back at whatever was engaging her attention so fully. "Why are you still standing near the door, Damien? Come over here and let us begin."

That set his jaw even tighter. He would not be ordered about, damn it. Nor would he be treated like an errant schoolboy . . . or at least what he imagined an errant schoolboy must feel like, having never actually been the pupil of any scholarly master in his life.

"Begin what?" he asked, when he was good and ready. He leaned back against the doorjamb, making sure to appear nonchalant, so that she would know he intended to stay there for just as long as he wished.

"Your instruction, of course," Alissende answered.

"Instruction?"

By the time he realized that he had just echoed her words again, surely not sounding very bright in the process, it was too late, and he had to make due with looking as indifferent as possible as he continued to lean against the door.

Gazing at him, nonplussed, Alissende finally ceased what she was doing for long enough to straighten up and plant her hands on her hips. "I told you I wished to repay you for the defensive training you have been providing me, and so that is what I've arranged to do. Beginning tonight, I am going to teach you to read and write."

"What?"

That got him moving. Shoving away from the door, he stalked toward her, coming to a stop on the side of the table opposite her. Then he simply glared, shifting his gaze from her unbearably serene face down to the pile of—of *writing* things, by God. This was unacceptable. It was damned disconcerting, in fact. Just looking at all those scholarly implements made him feel inept. He was built for war, damn it. For grasping sword hilts and spear grips, not quill pens.

Narrowing his eyes, he sliced his gaze up to her again. She continued to stare at him in cool tranquility, appearing not the least intimidated.

"What ever gave you the idea that I wished to learn to read and write?" he clipped at last, accentuating each word.

She folded her arms across what he assumed to be her chest. "What ever gave you the idea that I wished to learn the art of defending myself?"

"*That* was a necessity," he snapped. "For your own protection against Hugh or any other man who would try to overpower you."

"This is a necessity too. For you."

"It is not even remotely the same."

"It is, in that it is just as important, and what you learn will remain with you for the entire of your lifetime."

"I have managed for the whole of my life *without* the ability to read or write, and I see no reason to alter that now."

She graced him with a tolerant look. "Are you not the lord of this castle"—she paused for one pointed beat—"at least for these remaining months of our agreement?"

"Aye." He admitted that truth gruffly, crossing his own arms now, because he sensed where this was going, and he felt fairly certain that he was going to lose the argument.

"Need I expound upon the reasons it will be useful for you to learn at least the rudiments of letters, Damien?"

He would not answer. He scowled instead, feeling his hands tighten into fists. He did not want to do this. He *really* did not want to. It wasn't so much that he did not recognize the value of possessing such skills. They could be very useful, in fact. He had learned that firsthand, during his initial meeting with Edgar Charmand, Glenheim's steward.

But the truth was that never having been considered

important enough to be taught to read and write made Damien feel inferior. Deficient, somehow. It had not mattered as much in his youth, when he'd been naught but a simple knight battling to earn respect on the field and enough material reward to live comfortably. But from the moment he'd met Alissende, he had yearned for so much more. For things he could never have, by virtue of truths that were beyond his control.

His common blood and humble birth, for one.

But beyond all that, even, was a haunting fear that refused to let him give this idea of Alissende's any real consideration. He could not escape it, for it was inside himself, prodding and needling him: What if he could *not* learn properly, even if he tried? What if he was, as the gossips had insinuated, incapable of grasping this or any other art that belonged to the realm of true lords, being naught himself but a lowly, landless knight?

Nay, he would not open himself to that possibility. He felt unworthy enough already in his dealings with Alissende; there was no need to add dim-witted to the list of unflattering descriptions she could associate with him.

"Ah, Damien," Alissende said in a quiet voice, as if she somehow sensed the reason behind his obstinacy. "It will not be so difficult, you will see. There is naught to hold you back, if you will only take the chance. You must trust me and know that none other than we two will be privy to what happens here. No other will ever be privy to it, if you do not wish it."

Damien did not answer, still. He could not, though he lowered his arms to his sides in response to the jolt of awareness that shot through him with her heartfelt

words. His hands remained fisted, but something tight
and hard inside of him unwound a hair's breadth with
what she said. Perhaps it was only the way she'd said it.
It was clear that she was serious about this. Utterly and
completely serious, and somehow, he could not help
but feel that she would do everything in her power to
protect his sense of honor and his pride through what
would come, if only he would agree to it.

The feeling grew stronger, and then a little stronger
still.

"You, Alissende," he said huskily at last, breaking
off for a moment, lest he stumble over what he wished
to say, "you alone would instruct me in this, if I agreed
to it? None other . . . not Michael or even Ben, would be
privy to what we are undertaking here?"

"None other, Damien. I promise you."

She met his gaze with the even, kind force of her
own. Damien stared at her, really looking at her. She
was beautiful. That none could deny. Even swathed
in those ridiculous garments and head-cloth, she possessed a kind of luminous beauty that would outshine
the stars themselves.

But there was something more. Something that went
much deeper and was more enduring, and he suddenly
realized that it was that quality he had been yearning
for, that he had been missing, these five years, even
more so than the other desires that had been keeping
him awake at night. It was something that was unique
to Alissende and was in large part what had made him
fall in love with her the first time.

She possessed an uncanny sense of understanding
that went beyond simple concern. She seemed able to
feel what others felt and to see the world through their

eyes. Such ability was rare to begin with, but in that startling moment, he knew that he could spend the rest of his life looking, and he would never find the like of it again, from any other person, anywhere in the world.

"Why?" he asked her quietly, his throat tight with a thousand conflicting emotions. "Why would you want to do this?"

For me of all people, and now, especially . . .

Though he hadn't said that last bit aloud, they both knew what he meant. Alissende didn't have to be kind to him. After his teasing behavior to her during their public training sessions this past week, the maddeningly seductive way she'd handled herself earlier today with him had been far more in line with what he deserved.

She gave a little shrug, her mouth shifting into a half smile. "I opted to take the nobler path than what I might have, given the circumstances."

His mouth quirked, too. "How would you describe this afternoon's training session, then?"

"As but a hint of what is possible, should I choose a different way."

"Heaven preserve me."

Her eyes held a faint twinkle. "For now you may consider this a temporary truce. It would be best, I think, if we pursued your lessons when we retire to our chamber each evening at dusk. We will be able to work for an hour before sleep, and none will be the wiser, come morn."

"You are a clever woman." He smiled fully, unaccountable warmth filling him just to look on her.

Alissende returned the expression, and in that instant

he was overcome with a rush of . . . *happiness*, of all things. It took him by surprise, and he found that he needed to clear his throat again before he could speak.

"Thank you, Alissende," he murmured. "I do not know what kind of pupil I will be, but I—"

He glanced away and tightened his jaw, feeling the muscle there twitch, before looking at her again and finishing, "I think I would like to attempt this, if you are willing to instruct me."

"It would be my pleasure, Damien. Truly."

Her voice sounded as husky as his had, and at her beckoning, he left off the position he'd taken opposite her at the table to come around to her side. In the process, he could not suppress that strange warmth that continued to build in him. It rippled forth, the waves of it beating at the edges of darkness that had held dominion inside him for so long. As the feeling intensified, he realized that it was not the result of anticipation or even gratification at the thought of spending the hours in sweet and satisfying proximity with Alissende that would be required for this undertaking.

It was simply because he knew she had meant what she'd said. She had told him that it would be her pleasure to teach him—and because of that, he warranted, it would prove to be his pleasure as well.

In the cool dark of night, many hours later, Alissende lay on her side, sleepless within the gauzy curtains of their bed. She tried to keep from rolling onto her back to look at Damien, tried to pretend that he wasn't stretched out a mere arm's length behind her. If she imagined hard enough, she could almost sense his warmth soaking into the thin coverlet that was spread atop them. She could feel his strong hands slipping up her back in a gentle caress and then sliding forward at her waist to rest, palm splayed, warmly against her belly.

Almost . . .

Ah, but she ached to feel Damien, to hold him . . . to love him again.

She'd felt the sharpness of that yearning more than ever tonight, when he'd placed his pride in her hands and agreed to undertake lessons in reading and writing with her. She had not been certain he would do it. When she'd seen his expression upon entering the chamber, she'd wondered if he would simply turn around and leave again. But he had risen to her challenge—an offer she'd made him in a far different manner from what he'd tendered to her, with his erotic teasing—but perhaps for not so very different reasons.

Whether he wanted to admit it or nay, Damien still felt the pull of the bond they had once known with each other. She'd realized it from their first night together at Glenheim, and his latest teasing games with her had only revealed that truth more fully.

What she'd had to come to terms with herself, though, was how much the knowledge that she still wanted *him,* regardless of the painful stipulations he had placed upon the term of their agreement together or her determination to keep her heart her own, free from any man. Her desire for him tempted her, aching sweetly, even though she knew in all logic that emotion was futile. He was driven by darker demons than she would ever know, and he'd abandoned his faith in God, risking his immortal soul with such a blatant rejection.

To open herself up to him again in body or soul would be to blind herself to those immutable truths, would it not?

But she wanted him still, wrong as it was.

That overwhelming realization had struck her as she'd watched him struggle with the unfamiliar skills she'd begun teaching him tonight. His brow had been furrowed with concentration, his long, elegant fingers curved around the quill as he'd labored to scratch out the same loops and lines she'd demonstrated on the vellum. A lock of his dark gold hair had fallen onto his brow as he'd bent over the page, but his focus had been so strong that he had not appeared to notice.

She had. It had been all she'd been able to do not to reach out and brush it back. To proceed, then, with many other far more wanton things. She had wanted to touch him as badly as she'd ever wanted anything in her life. But she had forced herself to keep her hand clenched at her side.

In truth, when the lesson was complete, it had almost been a relief, and not because he had not been an apt student—just the opposite, in fact. Nay, it had been because at least in the shelter of their bed, she could turn to her side and avoid the temptation of looking at him. She could pretend to sleep and know that she need not torment herself with the erotically charged interplay of conversation they seemed to share whenever they were together.

It was driving her slowly mad.

She felt like she might jump out of her own skin, so fiercely did she desire him. Tonight, when her torment was making her feel more desperate than ever before, she was actually considering rising, dressing, and making her way in the dark to the chapel for some much needed prayer and reflection.

It must be close to dawn. Making her way to the village church this early might draw attention from a few meddlesome gossips, but it was not so strange that she might not be able to—

Alissende froze. For a moment she thought that she had finally lost her hold on reality. Either that or else she had somehow fallen asleep and was dreaming. There could be no other answer for it.

Damien was touching her.

His hand was beneath the coverlet and stroking up the length of her back. Her naked back, since as was customary, she wore naught to bed, even though in their years apart Damien had taken to wearing at least his braies and sometimes his shirt as well.

His caress was smooth and deliberate. His fingers paused just below her shoulders, the tips kneading and stroking in a pattern that eased all the stiffness from tension and the aching left behind from the demands of her training, in a way that felt so, so wonderful. She closed her eyes and instinctively stretched into his touch, too surprised and overwhelmed to do aught else. Tingles of pleasure swept over her back and down her arms, traveling to the front of her, and she felt her nipples tightening to aching buds in response.

Merciful heaven . . .

Was he asleep? If he was aware of what he was doing, then why was he doing it? Perhaps she should—

She made a sound deep in her throat, moaning softly, all rational thought fleeing as his palm swept forward to encircle her breast, his hand curving over her there with practiced ease. It was as if the intervening years had never come between them, and she was being swept back in time, to the countless, blissful moments of lovemaking they had shared together.

It was too much. Tears sprang to her eyes, and she started to roll to her back, to awaken him if indeed he was doing this to her in the throes of some passionate dream. But then with another sensual movement, he flicked his thumb expertly over her hardened nipple, making her gasp again and sending a rush of molten heat from that aching point down to the now lightly throbbing place between her legs.

Her mind was awhirl, her body consumed with the delicious sensations he unleashed in her. As if with uncanny awareness of what she needed, what she desired most of all, he took several tantalizing moments in stroking his palm in smooth descent down her ribs and over her belly . . . culminating that one, long caress by gently cupping the lightly-furred curve of her sex.

She gasped aloud, then, arching into his hand almost against her will as he slid one finger between the silky folds of flesh, rubbing over the swollen nub at the apex and making her see stars from the pleasure of it.

"Damien, please, you must awa—" she began to say, before breaking off into a sound that was a soft cry and a moan blended together, when he gave a gentle tug to roll her onto her back, and that probing finger found its mark more easily. Her legs parted almost against her will, as with a swiftness that stole her breath, he used the wider, blunt tips of two fingers to press and rub in perfect, slow circles over that most sensitive point of her arousal.

"Shhh, Alissende . . . only surrender to the feeling . . ."

He murmured that tempting command in her ear, before his lips nibbled a tingling path down her neck, toward the tightened tips of her breasts, even as his hand kept up its delicious torment between her legs.

"But we cannot," she managed to say on a gasping breath. Hot, sparkling jolts of sensations were building from the persistent stroking of his fingers, spreading upward into her belly, then to her aching nipples. "Our agreement, Damien—you said . . ."

"Aye, lady, I know," he said quietly. From deep within the fog of her own arousal she was aware that his voice sounded hoarse with the same, building need, still unsatisfied, that gripped her so tightly. Yet her thoughts seemed to come only in fragments, allowing her to grasp naught but pieces—not enough to make sense or to speak further in any meaningful way.

Damien slowed his tender ravishment of her throat and breasts and lifted his head. The intensity of his touch gentled, his pace slowing so that she nearly arched up into his hand again, using her body in a silent plea not to stop. Drawing in a deep, shuddering breath to aid her in keeping still, she tilted her head on the bolster to meet his gaze.

"We need not make love fully, Alissende," he said, his words a bit halting. He stared down at her through the dusky heat of pure and heady need that enveloped them. "I remember other ways," he whispered. "Other pleasures we can share, if only you are willing. But to go on alone, trying not to touch you and pretending to feel nothing . . ."

He paused for an instant, and a look that was a stunning blend of intensity, agony, and yearning swept across his handsome features. "We can abide by our agreement and keep from truly consummating our temporary union, but I am asking if you will allow me to love you in the ways that I can, right now . . . if only you desire it as much as I do."

In the dim light, she held Damien's gaze, his eyes so beautiful and earnest, and yet at the same time flaming with the very desires she felt scorching her from the inside out. Her body ached for him, it was true, but she could not deny feeling the gentle lurch of her heart as well then, as he spoke. A fluttering sensation that made her throat close and her eyes sting.

God help her, for it could come to naught. He could never commit to her—to them—by virtue of the damage done to him in the past and the wrenching events he had endured. Neither could she, for she knew the darker side of love now and feared she would never survive the loss if she allowed herself to be consumed so in him again. The unshakeable truth was that Damien would leave her in less than six months, and then she would be alone.

That realization cut too deeply to bear, and so she pushed it aside for now, subduing it in a burst of defiance and yearning for what *was* possible right now, for what she wanted more than anything, whether or not it was selfish or foolish or could not last. It would be enough, she told herself. She clung to that hope with a kind of desperation. In the long, empty years ahead, she would be able to remember this time with Damien and take comfort in it. Aye, she would . . .

Her hand trembling, Alissende reached up as she had a thousand times before with him in their other life together and stroked her fingers over his cheek. She endued that simple caress with all the emotion inside her, and he closed his eyes in response, leaning into her touch and taking in a long, slow breath, as if he wanted to soak in all the sweetness she was offering.

"I remember, too, Damien," she whispered at last, the words catching a little in her throat, "and I long to share them all with you again. But more than that, I want to make love with you. Truly make love, as we used to do."

Damien stiffened slightly, the intensity of his gaze filling with shades of what he could not seem to give breath to . . . hope, uncertainty, passion, and fierce need all apparent at once. His voice seemed lower as he finally murmured, "But what of the babe that might result, Alissende? I could not in all conscience—"

She shook her head, blinking back the sudden heat in her eyes as she said huskily, "You need not worry over that, Damien. There will be no babe."

His expression revealed his surprise and doubt, but she touched her fingers to his lips before he could speak. "The whys of it are best saved for another time and place, but in truth, there is naught you need fear in that matter."

He remained silent, then, his eyes closing and the muscle in his jaw twitching, before he seemed to regain his composure enough to look at her once more. And then she was stunned by the utter yearning she saw there, mingled with the shadows of something darker at work inside him.

"But beyond that, even, you understand, Alissende, don't you? . . ."

The aching, the vulnerability in his voice made her heart lurch anew, before he continued, "Naught can change what I have become or what must happen in the end . . . my leaving—"

He stopped, his voice suspiciously thick, his words laden with regret. "Do you understand?" he finished on a near whisper.

Unable to speak for the knot of tears blocking her own throat, Alissende simply nodded. She could say no more.

But then it did not seem to matter. She found herself closing her eyes, making a soft sound of combined need and pleasure as he pulled her into his arms, burying his face in her neck. He held her that way for a long time, close to him, and she reveled in the sensation of his powerful body pressed to hers, taking in his warmth and his tantalizing scent. Threading her fingers into the soft waves of hair at his nape, she held him close and kissed his brow, his temple and along his cheek, until she reached the temptation of his mouth . . .

And that unleashed the hunger that had been so long denied between them; their kiss tumbled them into the magnificent give and take of breath and passion.

Blindly, she slid her hands down his back, intending to free him of his braies, but Damien forestalled her in her effort. After another moment, he pulled back just enough to look at her, his gaze intense, his beautiful mouth quirking as he softly bid her wait just a little longer . . . that she would have her turn for that soon enough, after.

After what? she'd wanted to ask, but then all of her

conscious thought fled as he resumed his delicious, expert caressing of her body. His fingers slid a warm, tingling path along her side and over the curve of her buttocks before slipping forward to the throbbing place between her thighs. With a low groan, he cupped his entire palm over her sex once more before slowly sliding his longest finger in a tantalizing sweep, up and down the slick and engorged folds of her most intimate flesh, causing her to arch up into him.

"For so long I have thought of touching you again like this, Alissende," he said, his voice husky with emotion. "Sweet mercy, but I cannot stop—"

"Don't stop, Damien . . . please."

She wanted to make this last, to feel every moment and soak it in, like the parched earth taking in the first sweet drops of rain. But she felt the crest building in her with each sweetly tormenting stroke of his fingers. It had been so long . . . so long . . . yet he seemed to remember every nuance of her, his knowledge of her body and his magnificent touch upon her so right, so perfect.

"By all that is holy, Alissende, in my whole life, I have never known anything as beautiful as you are," he whispered. He feathered kisses around the shell of her ear as he spoke, the renewed tingling making her tilt her head back and to the side for more of his caresses down the exposed length of her throat. The sensation of his mouth nibbling, tasting that delicate skin, made her shudder with longing and sent molten fire spiraling along her limbs and through to her very core.

The knowledge that he wanted her too, fully as much as she wanted him, was intoxicating. She felt his hand trembling as he brushed the hair back from her brow and knew it was desire restrained for so long that caused it. He continued to stroke along her cheek, his lips traveling from her neck to the sensitive hollow at the base of her throat, and she instinctively twisted so he might in turn feast upon the bounty of her breasts.

And all the while the fingers of his other hand, buried between her legs, kept moving more swiftly, the tip of the longest teasing, slipping, and jabbing into her lightly, an erotic rhythm that made her almost sob aloud. Closing her eyes, Alissende began to move in concert with his touch, thrusting against his strong fingers. Her own hands tensed in her passion, one splayed out on the bedsheet, the other gripping at Damien's arm, feeling the delicious contractions of his muscles as he continued to work his fingers in and over her aroused sex.

"That's it . . . only a little more now," he breathed, as he eased another finger into her, at the same time continuing to rub in teasing circles the little pearl nestled just above, flicking and pressing with the pad of his thumb until she thought she might go senseless from the pleasure of it.

He coaxed her closer, closer to the edge of sweet oblivion—

Suddenly Alissende's vision exploded with sparks of light, and she cried out as her body took over, tipping into the bliss of completion. The shudders of her climax rippled through her, so intense that she almost lost her hold on awareness.

When she floated back to earth, her body still quaking gently, it was to find herself cradled against Damien's chest, the strength of his arms wound round her. Tipping her head up, she met his gaze for an instant before he slanted his mouth across hers again with a low growl of pleasure, and the sound of his desire set her own yearning blazing anew.

There was no denying his need for her; the jutting heat of him demanded attention, and Alissende reached down to his braies to untie them, finally, wanting him as naked as she, to see his magnificence again at long last. But he caught her hand, lacing her fingers with his and effectively stopping her from exposing the lower half of his body to her gaze.

"Nay, lady," he murmured, pulling back enough to look into her eyes. "Hold for one moment more, if you would."

"Why—is aught amiss?"

He smiled, the look slow and so powerfully sensual that her knees would have buckled beneath her had she been standing.

"Aye," he said quietly. "And the first is this—"

He kept his gaze locked with hers as he reached up to yank the heavy curtains closed around the bed, enveloping them in a heady cocoon of darkness that cast them both in shadow.

"Then this—" he continued on a huskier note, at last divesting himself of his braies in one fluid movement. In the next instant he startled her by pulling her up to straddle him, guiding her with the strong warmth of his hands so that her parted legs perched over his straining, hard length.

Then, taking in a deep breath and seeming to hold it, he finished on a low and utterly sensual rasp, "—and finally, this."

With that exhalation, he thrust up and slid with one,

smooth stroke deep inside her. She released a gasping cry that was echoed by his groan, arching back with the absolute bliss of the feeling. Lights danced before her vision, and she rocked instinctively against him after the first delicious shock had passed, overcome by the beauty of their joining, even as she realized in some distant part of her awareness that he had gone completely still.

"Ah, by all the angels and saints, Alissende," he said with a guttural sound, clutching at her hips and trying to halt her rocking movements, "you must wait, lady, or I'll not last. 'Tis why I pulled you atop me, hoping to withstand the pleasure a little longer, but . . ."

Alissende exhaled slowly, the wondrous feelings goading her to continue, so that she needed to exert all her effort in trying to fulfill his appeal for patience. She braced her hands on his chest and felt the warm play of muscles beneath her palms as they both struggled to remain still.

It was a futile effort.

He was buried deeply inside her, and it felt so good . . . so good that in another moment she realized that she could not comply with his request. Nay, not if the world commanded it—though she would not deny him the joy of the same kind of explosive completion as she had known, either, given freely in all its fierce, unstoppable glory.

And so, considering that the turnabout was fair play, she gripped his shoulders and suddenly rolled sideways, breaking their connection for what she hoped would be naught but a brief instant in order to bring him up, poised over her now. She cradled him between her legs, and his entire body shook slightly with the effort it took to maintain his control as she lifted her hips up, urging him inside her again.

"Wait no longer, Damien," she murmured softly. "Make love to me now, in the way we're both longing for. Fully and completely, right now . . ."

Even in the shadows of their bed enclosure, the delicious agony of his reaction to her command shone in his face. With a groan, he thrust forward, rocking deeply into her once more. And then they surrendered to the ecstasy of their lovemaking. Alissende clung to him, matching every exquisite thrust and feeling the bliss of it building again to an unbearable, exquisite pitch . . .

She curled forward to Damien with the glorious tension, closing her eyes and burying her face in his neck as she pressed her lips to his salty-warm skin. With one more perfect thrust he sent her tumbling into bliss again, and she gasped his name as she convulsed around him; a moment later she felt him stiffen and heard him cry out as he yielded to his own powerful release, filling her with the sweet warmth of his seed.

When the spasms had passed, Damien collapsed onto her. His weight was a welcome burden, and from some dimly lit place of awareness, she felt their hearts beating in rapid, pulsing tandem. She threaded her fingers with his and pressed a kiss to his brow, sated and complete in a way she had not felt in more than five years.

His eyes were closed, his expression peaceful, though in the next moment, he shifted away from her so as not to crush her. But his arm remained draped over her waist, his hand entwined with hers.

"I am sorry I could not make it last longer, lady," he murmured finally, his voice sounding gravelly. Spent. She smiled and raised his fingers to her lips, kissing them.

"There is no need to feel so, Damien," she said, brushing her lips over the back of his hand now before she conceded to release it, leaving his palm splayed, warm and strong, over her belly. "It was wonderful. And it has been a long time, for both of us."

"You have no idea."

She tipped her face to look at him.

With her movement, he tilted his head off the bolster, opening his eyes then and meeting her gaze. "My last time, Alissende, was with you."

"What?" The shock of hearing him say it pitched through her, making her feel wonderful and terrible all at once.

"After leaving you, I joined the Templar Brotherhood."

"Well, of course, I know that—but I'd heard that the strict precepts of the Templar Order had fallen by the wayside over the course of time." She gazed up now at the painted panels above the bed. "I suppose I assumed that in all this time . . . I just never imagined . . ."

Her voice trailed off, and she felt Damien shift to lie on his back as well, noticing that he took care to pull the sheet around himself as he did, to conceal the lower half of his body from her gaze. After a moment, he said quietly, "It is true that some did not live all their vows in good faith, my brother Alex among them. But I did, Alissende. One of the oaths I took was of celibacy." He paused before adding with a hint of awkwardness to his voice, "The precepts against self-pleasure were no less strict. I was a Templar until my arrest and interrogation by the Inquisition, and I have never taken any promise I have made lightly."

Alissende felt the power behind both that statement and the man who had uttered it. It took her breath away and left her feeling strangely shy. A gentle silence settled over them, and she resisted the urge to fidget. How should she act with him now, she wondered? Were they to go on as if naught had happened between them?

Sweet Mother Mary, *could* she go on as if naught had happened?

Damien solved her dilemma by extending his arm in silent invitation to nestle close to him so that he might wrap her in his embrace.

She hesitated only for an instant before she moved in gratefully, resting her head on the warm and powerfully muscled area between his shoulder and his chest. Once again she felt a twinge of surprise at how easily they had fallen into such a familiar position with each other again, and the bittersweet pang in realizing just how much she had missed it.

"Thank you, Alissende," he murmured after a deep sigh.

She thought she must be letting her imagination get the best of her, for she would have sworn he sounded as yearning, or perhaps even sorrowful, as he did content. Ridiculous, of course.

"You did far more than I, Damien," she settled on saying, closing her eyes and gently stroking her hand over the expanse of his chest. She could not help but feel the scars there, and she knew without second thought that they did naught to alter his magnificence in her eyes. "For what could I possibly deserve your thanks?"

"For accepting me as I am . . . and for letting me back in, in this way."

Ah, but you never left, Damien—not for me. Do you not know that?

That question echoed in Alissende's mind, but she was too exhausted after the astonishing progression of events these past few days to find means to voice it or anything else aloud.

Sighing in a softer echo of the sound Damien had made a few moments before, Alissende snuggled closer, listening to the slow, steady beating of his heart against her ear. She would *not* think beyond this moment and the sweetness of it, she resolved, lest she dissolve into some embarrassing display of emotion; for now this would be enough. This sense of belonging, of reconciliation with Damien, was too new, and it would be too cruel to remind herself that it would pass eventually, leaving her alone once more.

Damien tightened his powerful arm around her, his warmth comforting and wonderful. Even this simple embrace brought with it a kind of bliss, after so many years of fruitless dreaming and regret. And so, reveling in the beauty of it, she decided to do just what he had suggested earlier; she surrendered herself to the delicious feeling of being wrapped in his arms and eased into soft, dreamless slumber.

Damien knew the moment she yielded to sleep. He could tell by the heavier weight of her head against his shoulder, by the slower, deeper, even breaths she took.

It was almost beyond belief, what had just happened between them.

He hadn't planned it. He hadn't even allowed himself

to think on the possibility of it as they'd retired to bed. He had simply done it, which was as unlike him as aught he could conceive about himself—responding to the deep and instinctive longing to reach out and stroke his hand up the silken length of her back without thought, without care of the consequences.

And it had felt wonderful.

Closing his eyes, he settled back onto the bolster; her delicate scent filled his senses, and he allowed himself to believe, finally, that this was true and not just another of the hundreds of tantalizing dreams he'd known in the past. Alissende *was* tucked against him, cradled in his arms. He had pleasured her in one of many ways he had been hungering to do. They had made love, by all that was holy, and she had yearned for it as much as he had, pleading in sweet, whispered urgings for him not to stop.

The memory of it wound through him, sparking the embers of his spent passion anew. It had been like a glimpse of heaven. Too much to withstand without losing control. She had been unbearably beautiful, writhing with the pleasure of their joining. Ah, but he could have watched her like that for hours, had he only been able to keep them both at the edge of completion a little longer.

Her second climax, when it had come, had shaken him almost as much as it had her. It had toppled him into his own release, brought on so powerfully not only from the exquisite sensations of their lovemaking but also from watching her face during those moments of ecstasy . . . from hearing her gasp his name in her bliss.

It had been worth it. And though he did not know

what this would mean for them beyond now, he knew, at least, that it had been right. He did not regret it—he wouldn't—and it would be enough. It had to be, for he had nothing else to give.

He could provide her with his protection for these six months. He could give her all that he was capable of feeling, and he could offer the physical release they both hungered for. But he could not give her his heart. It was not his to give any longer, for it had been lost along the way, damaged and charred beyond recognition in the flames of bitterness, hatred, and spiritual abandonment.

He sensed in her a longing for more, though it had been she who had cast him off those years ago. But even if her feelings had changed, and even if somewhere deep inside him he had forgiven her—even if he could find some means to earn the wealth and standing that would allow them to have a true and lasting future together—it still wouldn't be enough. Nay, Alissende deserved a man who was whole, unspoiled, and accepted in the bosom of the Church. One who would not spend the rest of his life looking over his shoulder to avoid rearrest and interrogation by the Inquisition. Who could give her all those things that he was incapable of giving now.

So this bond, this understanding between them, would have to be enough for now and for the months remaining in the agreement he had made to serve as her counterfeit husband and her protector against the many kinds of darkness of the world.

The irony of it, that he, the world-damaged former Templar Knight, was being trusted to protect her against the very thing that had nearly destroyed him, almost choked him. But as he tried to settle into sleep, he repeated in his mind what he needed to remember, knowing that he had to convince himself of its truth, lest he lead them both into certain doom.

What they shared now would be enough.

Heaven help him, it had to be.

Chapter 12

Three nights later

I t was so quiet.

A cool breeze wafted through the shutter, awakening Alissende from the darkness of a dream. Opening her eyes, she tried to gain her bearings, realizing that she was in an unfamiliar place. *Kentley Abbey.* Aye, they had been on the road to Odiham Castle when darkness had fallen; she was in the chamber she and Damien had been given for the night. Her breathing felt shaky, and when she reached up she realized that her cheeks were wet. It had all seemed so real, the images still playing through her mind. Damien had left her, and she'd felt the heartbreak of it as if it had happened in truth, leaving her aching and bereft.

But it was only a dream, a voice inside soothed. *Only a dream . . .*

Tipping her head on the bolster, Alissende realized that dream or nay, Damien was not in their bed. She reached out and felt the sheets; they were cool to her touch. He had been gone for some time, then—but not before they had made love again, as they had each night since their first intimate reunion. Tonight, however, their joining had been slower, sweeter than ever before, and she'd felt like crying from the beauty of it as she'd shattered in his arms. He, too, had achieved bliss, but there had been a kind of darkness in his eyes . . . the shadow of something weighing on him.

Afterward he had held her close, propping himself up on one arm to look at her in silence, his gaze troubled, as he'd tenderly brushed his fingers along her cheek and tucked her hair behind her ear. Before she'd been able to ask him to speak of his thoughts, he had leaned down and kissed her. Then he'd rolled to his back, closed his eyes, and murmured a good night. After a time she had heard his breathing slow to what had seemed the deep, even cadence of sleep, and she too had allowed herself to drift into slumber.

Now he was gone.

Sitting up in bed, Alissende sought his form within the shadows of the abbey chamber. The moon was nearly full tonight, and it cast a muted glow through the modest room's single window. He was not here.

She slid off the pallet they'd been given use of as a bed and went to look out onto the garden adjacent to the building where they were housed; it was filled with medicinal flowers that every abbey and monastery in England cultivated, and the moon was so bright that it bathed the grounds in pearly elegance. Its glow blanketed glossy green leaves and spiky flowers, as if an artist's brush had stroked their surface with cool blues and silvery glimmers.

And then she saw him.

He was leaning against the stone wall at the corner, next to a wattle fence that had been propped there as an arbor. He'd pulled on his breeches, but he hadn't bothered to tie his shirt, and it gaped, showing his bare chest, even with his arms crossed as they were. Pulling on a wrapper, Alissende went out to him.

He glanced up as she approached, and her breath caught anew at how handsome he was. But he wore that pensive expression that made her yearn to take his face in her hands and kiss away the dark thoughts and memories that seemed to lurk in his eyes.

"I'm sorry if I disturbed your sleep by getting up," Damien murmured, when she reached his side.

"Nay, it was not you," she said. "I was awakened by a dream."

He looked away, giving a short nod. "The night and I have come to an uneasy truce on that score . . . sometimes she lets me sleep, and others I am forced to allow her full sway over my thoughts until daylight."

"She won the battle tonight, it seems," Alissende offered.

Damien's sensual mouth quirked into a half smile.

"Is the thought of the upcoming tournament making you restless, then?"

He glanced to her for an instant; the look carried a sharpness she had not seen there earlier, and his voice, when he answered after a pause, held an edge of bitterness. "Not so much the tournament itself, perhaps, but what will come with it. The people I will need face. And the talk . . ."

His words trailed off, but Alissende knew exactly what he meant, and it sent an arrow of guilt lancing through her. They'd both known that their return to court would be difficult, but she could not deny that Damien would bear the brunt of it. It was he who had served as fodder for the gossips more oft than not in the subsequent years, for it was he who had been rejected after proving himself champion of that long-ago tournament—he who had been a simple knight deemed not worthy of her love before all the lords and ladies of England's powerful nobility.

"I am sorry for what you may face at Odiham," she said quietly. *Because of me.* That added phrase lingered in her mind, but she gave it no voice.

"Do not be, for there is naught to be done about it. All will be well once I have my turn in the lists."

That hard edge still shaded his voice, and Alissende winced inwardly, knowing that what he'd said wasn't completely true. There *was* something she could do about this. Something she had resisted from the moment he'd walked back into her life. She could tell him the truth about why she had sown the seeds of their destruction five years ago. It would mean confessing what she had hoped would never come to light . . . something that was excruciating to admit even to herself. But she needed to do it now; it was unfair to let him continue to bear the additional burden of that falsehood atop all else.

Glancing at him, Alissende broke the quiet as she murmured, "Damien, I—there is something I wish to tell you. We only spoke once about what happened that day at the tournament those many years ago . . . and what I told you then was not the truth." Her words came out barely above a whisper, and her throat hurt, but she forced herself to go on. "It is to my own blame that I have not spoken to you of this sooner, but now for both our sakes I need to tell you the fullness of what really happened, and I am asking you to listen."

He did not move. He didn't even seem to breathe. The silence stretched between them, and she thought that perhaps when he stirred at last, it would be to step around her and go back inside without uttering a sound, leaving her to stand there alone.

But he didn't. He only lowered his arms and continued to look at her, his gaze wounded, as if he could not believe that she had said this to him—that she was daring to raise it again now, and after all this time.

"There is no need to explain anything, Alissende," he said finally. "It is in the past and there is naught to be gained from it."

"I know it cannot change anything, Damien. But I hope that it might make what is to come a little easier for you to bear."

She swallowed against the dryness, the aching in her throat, searching his face with her gaze. "Will you not listen? Please?"

His look of anguish was almost unbearable to see; the muscle in his jaw twitched, and she thought that he might say something more. But in the end he gave her only a single, curt nod, and with his willingness, a sense of calm filled her. It gave her strength to do what she should have done—to say what she should have said to him—five years ago.

"When I turned my back on you after the tournament that day, Damien, it had naught to do with your lower status or my feelings for you having changed in any way," she said quietly. "Those were the reasons I gave then, in my sire's arms tent, because I thought I could make you believe them. And because it was easier for me than admitting the truth of what was at work inside me."

Her fingers laced tightly into the fabric of her dressing gown, though she never moved her gaze from his as she continued, "In reality, I was simply too weak to do what my heart yearned for, out of fear of what could happen—because of what *had* happened already, in what seemed a terrible lesson and a warning to me."

Damien frowned. "I do not understand."

"My rejection stemmed not from you or my feelings for you but from something involving your brother, Alexander, and my friend, Lady Margaret."

He crossed his arms over his chest again, the gesture revealing his irritation. "That is difficult to accept, Alissende. Shortly after the scandal broke with Alex and Margaret, you and I spoke of it, several times. We planned the moment when I would claim you after the tournament for *that very reason,* lady, to ensure that none, including your sire, could fault us for lacking the courage to declare what we felt for each other, as my brother and Margaret had done."

"But there was more to it, Damien," Alissende countered, shaking her head. "You did not know all."

"What else could there be?" Damien asked harshly. "Alex fell in love with a woman above his birth, just as I did. He pursued their love in secret, just as we were constrained to do. Except that before my brother found bravery enough to declare his love in an honorable way, Lady Margaret's sire caught him with her, at which point Alex was given the choice of entering the Templar Brotherhood or remaining in England to face the kind of living hell only a blooded earl can bring down upon the head of a common knight who had ruined his daughter."

Damien's eyes flashed with that fire she remembered so well. "I would have been willing to risk that or any other trial for us, Alissende, no matter what the cost. My brother was not, and so he chose the easier path—as did you, when you turned away from me and pretended that we were naught to each other before the eyes of society. There is nothing else to know."

"There is more to why I acted as I did."

"Tell me, then," he demanded quietly, "for I cannot fathom it. We shared *everything,* then, Alissende. Do you not remember? Nothing was left unsaid between us. Ever."

"This was, Damien," she protested, "for there was no time to tell you. Lady Margaret was expecting a babe."

He stared at her in stunned silence. When he spoke at last, each word was uttered with careful distinction. "She carried my brother's child?"

Alissende nodded, her heart somber. "I learned of it on the morning of the tournament. Margaret sent a hasty and desperate message to me, begging me to come to her. She told me that her sire was sending her away, and when I found her in her rooms, her face was pale and tear-streaked. I was only able to speak with her in private for a few moments before the guard Lord Welton had assigned to her forced her out to the carriage. But she managed to tell me before she left."

Damien dragged his hand through his hair, still looking stunned. "Jesu, I cannot believe it. Alex never spoke of a child."

"Perhaps he did not know. Margaret had only known herself for a short time, and she shared it with me that morn out of desperation over her circumstances and our long-standing friendship."

Alissende looked down at her clasped hands, remembering, letting the difficult flashes of images wash through her mind once more. "I did not see Margaret again after that day, but I heard later that her child did not survive its birth, and she was left with naught but her disgrace, a broken heart, and several years of penance, served in an abbey away from all those she had loved."

Damien just shook his head, grief and shock still apparent in his face. He closed his eyes for a moment and tipped back against the wall.

When he looked at her again, she forced herself to meet his gaze, even though it was painful to acknowledge what she was about to say to him. He deserved not only to hear the truth of it in her words but also to see it in her eyes, after all that had passed between them.

"What I did to you that day, Damien, and to *us,*" she said, her voice quiet but resolute, "arose from selfish panic. I had lived until then as a pampered young woman, carefree and blithe through custom of my wealth and social standing. When I saw what happened to Margaret, I realized that it could have been me. *I* could have been the one sent off in disgrace, burgeoning with child. Even more unbearable to think on, you could have been sent off to exile or worse, for I knew you well and did not doubt that, unlike Alexander, you would have stayed to fight anyone who bid you leave me, no matter the cost, including that, even, of your life."

She glanced away for just an instant, fortifying herself against the grinding ache inside, so that she might say the rest of it. "I refuted you out of fear, Damien. I was young and foolish, afraid of what could happen, and I deemed it better to break our hearts quickly than to find ourselves suffering the drawn-out agonies Margaret and Alexander were enduring."

A tiny, choked sound came from her throat, and she looked at him through the building heat that made his face a watery blur before her. "I was wrong, of course. Horribly so. And yet being mistaken in something has never had the power to change it back to the way it was, has it?"

She held Damien's gaze, feeling that old connection between them flare up briefly again, as if they had never been wrenched apart . . . the understanding they had once shared that had gone deeper than words. He saw, now, the truth behind what she had done that day. It did not change aught between them—it could not— but at least he knew why.

His expression was drawn, as if the weight of this burden, lifted after all this time, had left him exhausted. He shook his head slowly, looking down. "Ah, Alissende, I wish that I had only . . . that we had—"

He stopped, the rest of the words too difficult to say. She knew it as well as he did; it was too late for words to mend the chasm between them. Too late to alter the path that they had taken, or to make the people they had become with time, suffering, and hardships transform back to the innocently passionate lovers they had once been.

Looking down, she closed her eyes, willing the tears back as she murmured, "I know, Damien. I wish it, too." But one tear slipped down her cheek as she raised her gaze again and forced what might have passed as a smile. "The final irony, of course, is that I needn't have feared suffering Margaret's fate, though I did not know it then."

That brought Damien's troubled stare up to hers once more.

She shook her head slightly, her fingers coming up to press against her lips, before she could rein in the grief that always bloomed inside of her with these bitter thoughts. Taking in a shaky breath, she admitted, "I told you three nights ago that there would be a better moment and place for me to speak of the reasons behind my certainty that a babe would not come of our joining; it is now. It has become apparent over the course of time that I am unable to bear children."

He frowned. "But when I first arrived, your mother . . . she worried about the possibility of it, did she not?"

"My mother has not accepted the truth. I can do no less, after four fruitless years of marriage with Godfrey. My inability to conceive caused much strife between us. And during that final year it led to many other kinds of suffering as well—"

Her voice broke, then, and she stopped speaking, closing her eyes and forcing the difficult memories back by sheer will, though the throbbing ache inside her refused to subside. And so it was that when she felt Damien's hand touch her own, it took her by surprise.

"I am sorry, Alissende. It seems that neither of us has found much in the way of peace these past years."

With his understanding, the aching inside her seemed to ease a little. But the same regret that shadowed every breath she took tinged his voice as well when he spoke, and she looked at him, knowing instinctively that there was more he wished to say.

He appeared to choose his words carefully. "I am grateful for your honesty, Alissende. But in turn, there is something I need you to understand. You must cease blaming yourself for not telling me the truth earlier. There is no way for either of us to know what might have turned out differently back then. But even now, had you told me it all when I first came back, I would not have—"

His mouth tightened, and he paused for an instant, his expression so earnest and filled with the same kindness and warmth he had shown her when they had loved each other that her heart felt like it was breaking all over again.

"I am trying to say that it would not have changed the decision I made upon my arrival at Glenheim," he continued. "I did not set the terms of our arrangement to wound you, Alissende. It is simply that I cannot go back. I am no longer the same man I was." His jaw tightened. "Aside from that, none who are close to me will be safe from interrogation if my Writ of Absolution is ever discovered to be false, and for those two reasons all must remain as it stands between us."

"I understand," Alissende murmured, knowing he was right and yet finding herself desperate to call up whatever remaining strength she could find to combat the fierce longing that had blossomed anew with the gift of his candor. "And I agree, for I too have changed in many ways."

He nodded, the movement jerky, as if he was trying to convince himself of the truth of what they'd both avowed. Alissende said nothing more.

He met her gaze again with the stunning warmth of his own, the shadows having ebbed, it seemed, for the time being. Raising his fingers to her cheek, he used his thumb to brush away the lingering wetness there.

When he spoke again, his voice was softer, but the emotion behind it was just as intense. "All that I can give, Alissende, I will. Our arrival at Odiham tomorrow will mark the beginning of what I can do to ensure your safety from Hugh or any man who thinks ever to claim you against your wishes; none will be eager to test the matter further when I am finished. This I promise you."

Alissende wanted to say so many things to him in response, but she found that she could not. Nay, the lump in her throat prevented her. So she settled for nodding in silence, determined to be strong in this . . . to remember the futility—the danger—in wanting anything more than what they had right now. To forget about the past and future and live only in the present, aware that all the wishing in the world would not change what had already been or what would be.

Damien held her gaze for another moment that was charged with all the emotion of what had been said . . . and what had not. Then, lifting his arm, he invited her into the warmth of his embrace, saying quietly, "Come, lady. It will be dawn in a few hours, and the morrow is certain to be eventful. We should try to get some sleep."

Chapter 13

Odiham Castle, Hampshire
Two mornings later

When Alissende stepped out of the large silk pavilion she and Damien would call home for the next week, she looked up at the sky. Lead-gray clouds gathered angrily at the horizon, promising rain. Not the most auspicious of beginnings, to be sure.

They'd arrived here yesterday, as planned, and had spent the day gaining their bearings as their servants had set up their temporary dwelling. The pageantry of the tournament would not get underway until this evening, with a grand gathering that would include food and dancing inside Odiham's unusual, octagonal keep. If the number of colorful silk tents and pavilions pitched across this field was any indication, the area within those stone walls would be crammed with revelers tonight.

The actual battle events would commence on the morrow, and she could not help but hope that the weather would have cleared enough by then to keep the tournament participants from being forced to slog through mud or engage their opponents under a blanket of uncomfortable drizzle or outright rain. Only time would tell.

Before that, however, they had to get through the opening ceremonies, complete with the call of introductions before the king, which promised to be as enjoyable for both her and Damien as having a physician lance a festering wound. But it had to be done.

"Are you ready to make our appearance, then?"

Damien spoke as he came out of the tent, looking up at the sky as she had done, before he directed his gaze to her. With that, the tension that had been apparent in him from the moment they'd ridden within view of Odiham's jutting towers eased to something softer.

"You look beautiful, lady."

"Thank you."

His murmured compliment drew forth the heat that always seemed to be lingering just below the surface of her cheeks whenever she was with him. It did not help that the memory of his most intimate touches upon her flashed to mind whenever she happened to look upon the mocking, sensual lines of his mouth, or his elegant hands with those strong, expert fingers.

"The hue you're wearing becomes you," he said, breaking into her heated thoughts with his teasing. "Perhaps because it serves to accent your blushes in a rather enticing way."

"You have cleaned up rather nicely yourself, sir," she somehow managed to quip in response.

"It is none of my doing, I confess, but rather courtesy once again of your mother's foresight."

He flashed a brilliant smile, meant to disarm.

It did.

Ah, she saw the way to handle Sir Damien de Ashby this day. "It is fortunate, then," she retorted, arching one brow, "that *Mère* possesses such a keen eye—able to make the most out of whatever she is given to work with."

For a moment she thought Damien's mouth might actually drop open. But he recovered swiftly enough to offer her an exaggerated, gallant nod. "You may tender my undying appreciation to her, when next you meet, for without her skills, I would surely be fit for naught but stable or scullery." He followed it with a sweeping bow and flourish of his hand, making her laugh, before he straightened up, tall and very fine indeed, to offer her his arm.

"Shall we proceed to the feast, then, milady, such as I am?"

"Aye, sir, I would be honored to appear beside you," she said, laughing again and slipping her hand into the bend at his elbow.

And that, she feared, would likely be the last lighter moment they would share for several hours, or perhaps even the rest of the week.

As they approached the main gate to the castle, she saw that it was wide open with the portcullis raised, as expected, and that what seemed to be several royal guards were manning the entrance, backed by scribes on either side. They were keeping a list of all who passed through the doors, for the purpose of notifying the tournament's appointed king-of-arms about each noble or knightly combatant scheduled to compete. That, as well as for providing King Edward's herald with the names for presentation upon commencement of the festivities.

They came a bit closer, within twenty paces of the gate . . . and it was then that Alissende noticed it.

"And so it begins."

She heard Damien murmur that cryptic-sounding assessment at the same time that she felt the weight of the stares begin to shift toward them. Some of the lords and their ladies were better at masking their surprise or curiosity, only glancing and then lowering their gazes, while others seemed to feel no scruple in outright gawking at them as they neared the table to the right of the gate.

They came to a halt before the scribe, who, aside from appearing bedraggled in the damp weather, looked up expectantly, an affable expression on his face. Alissende tried to smile in return, though she knew that the man's pleasant demeanor was likely not sincere but rather a way for him to buffer himself until he learned the identity of the person whose name he would need add next to the list, be he a high-ranking noble or a simple knight.

In the event that it was someone important, he would be able to move smoothly from that genial look to the appropriate scrapings and fawning expected of him. And if it was naught but a scrapper-knight, here seeking fame and a chance at one of the golden prizes, then he could cast off his obsequious demeanor, perhaps even becoming snappish, as more likely suited his true outlook on this busy, busy day.

This scribe's expression shifted from affable to awed even before Damien uttered his name.

"Sir Damien de Ashby, with Lady Alissende of Surrey." Though Damien spoke low, the sound seemed to reverberate from the castle walls, in the sudden silence that surrounded them.

"I—well, yes, of course," the scribe sputtered, going a bit pale, Alissende thought, before he flushed red, shuffling his parchments as if he was searching for something.

"Is aught amiss?" Damien asked in a quiet, clipped voice, leaning into the scribe with a scowl.

"Nay, of course not. It is just that I—" The scribe's voice broke off as he glanced to the other scribe positioned at the opposite side of the gate; the two exchanged a pointed look before the first scribe fumbled once more for his quill.

"All right, then," he murmured, as if to himself, "let us notate this correctly . . ."

Alissende frowned at the man's strange reaction, though Damien remained stony-faced.

"Sir Damien de Ashby, of the house of Ashby," the scribe intoned, scratching away at the vellum as he did. He glanced up. "Do you still bear the same coat of arms as previously, sir, or have you taken on another in the time you were . . . *away?*" he finished lamely.

Realization struck Alissende with stunning force. This strange reception did not stem simply from the scandal attached to Damien's last attendance at court, or even to the ties he might be perceived to bear, still, to the beleaguered Brotherhood of Templar Knights. She had expected that. But more so, it seemed that this man—this low-ranking servant in the king's household—somehow knew about Damien's brush with the Inquisition in France. To most humble folk, speaking with a person like Damien was tantamount to standing face-to-face with a ghost. Or a soul damned to hell.

Either way, she knew they had Hugh to thank for this uncomfortable welcome.

"I carry the Ashby coat of arms, as always," Damien affirmed tightly.

"Very good, sir. I will convey as much to the tourney's king-of-arms and to King Edward's herald."

The scribe seemed to have regained much of his composure, and he added the remaining information to the parchment before looking up and motioning them through the gate. "His Majesty's official welcome will begin within the hour. In the meantime, there are trestles set around the courtyard laden with refreshments for your pleasure."

Nodding, Damien escorted Alissende through the gates, though neither of them missed the second pointed look and nod that the scribe directed to his cohort across the way. They had hardly taken ten paces into the courtyard before a young squire darted past them, disappearing after he crossed the yard, into one of the many ornate, arched doorways of the keep.

"Hugh demanded notice of our arrival," Damien murmured, still leading her on with seeming nonchalance.

"So it would seem."

Alissende felt the muscles of Damien's arm tighten, and she glanced up at his face, seeing that the bitter, strained expression from earlier had returned.

"We do not need to continue with this, you know,"

she said quietly, after looking to ensure that none were within earshot of her words. "It would be little trouble to withdraw your name from the lists. We could be back at Glenheim in less than two days."

Damien glanced down at her in surprise, the tightness of his expression shifting to a smile that somehow seemed at odds with the sharp and feral light still glowing from his eyes. "Nay, lady; that would be the very worst thing we could do. None must doubt the fullness of your protection. I am up to the task of facing Hugh de Valles or any other, never fear."

She did not answer. Still, the knot in her stomach twisted more tightly, and she resisted the urge to wipe her suddenly clammy hands against her skirt. Hugh was a master of manipulation, and who knew what other plots he was brewing for them in his devious mind?

But Damien was aware of that now as well as she was, and so she kept silent, instead following him toward one of the refreshment tables laden with cups of wine. As she did, she sent up a silent prayer, asking that she might find some way to help calm her anxieties enough to get through the rest of this day and the meeting with the king that lay ahead.

Damien watched Alissende sipping—nay, gulping— her third cup of spiced wine in the quarter hour they had been within the sturdy confines of Odiham's curtain wall. Her gaze darted nervously around the groups of people who stood at a respectful distance from them, while still managing to surreptitiously stare to their hearts' content.

Many of these nobles looked familiar to Damien from

his time at court those years ago, but none apparently wished to be the first to make an approach. Nay, it was too risky, from a social standpoint. He was a pariah of sorts, not only a publicly disgraced former champion but also a recent member of the suspect Brotherhood of Templars, fresh from interrogation by the Inquisition. Add to that the perception that Alissende had seemingly thumbed her nose at the king himself by taking a low-born husband without royal permission, and it was little surprise that many of these lords and ladies wished to avoid them.

However, as little as that circumstance bothered Damien, he could not deny that it was affecting Alissende adversely. Her nerves were on edge, by all appearances, winding tighter and tighter, regardless of the wine she consumed. It was up to him to do something to try to ease her tension.

"Come with me, lady."

He took her hand gently but firmly, and she was forced to set down her cup as he tugged her away from the table. Locking her hand and wrist in the crook of his arm, he began to walk toward the castle keep, giving her no choice but to follow him.

"Where are we going?" she whispered, still casting nervous looks about her as they strode on.

"Inside."

"But—why?"

Fortunately for him, the drink she had consumed was making her less intractable than usual in the face of his insistence; her hand gripped his arm as they strode on, but she stumbled once, and he felt compelled to slow their pace as he ducked down several narrow passageways in search of the perfect spot. They passed a few servants and at least one noble lady along the way, but they kept moving onward . . .

And then he found it. *Ah, yes . . .*

Easing to a stop, Damien paused almost at the end of a wider stone corridor that had led away from the hub-bub of the main courtyard. It was cooler here, and it overlooked a smaller and thankfully empty court, the center of which boasted a nicely carved stone cross, surrounded by a rectangular garden of herbs.

One arched and stone-latticed window-hole was cut into the wall, so that passersby within the castle could look out, if they chose, and see the peaceful sight of the little garden. That window in turn provided the only light for the dim passageway, and Damien pulled Alissende to a stop at the edge of it, turning to face her as he did.

"Here, now," he murmured, taking in a deep breath and noting with pleasure the faintly spicy scent of the air here. "I want you to take a few moments and do nothing. Try to remove all else from your thoughts but the quiet of this place."

"What?"

Alissende's face was slightly flushed, from the wine as much as from the afternoon's heat, he warranted, and she was gazing at him right now as if he'd grown a second head.

"Do as I ask, lady, before you fret yourself into a faint." He smiled. "And in the process, remind yourself that it is the opening ceremony of a tournament we attend this day, not an execution."

"I am well aware of that." Her flare of indignation deepened those unusual eyes of hers almost to sapphire, and she dug her fisted hands into her hips. "I cannot believe you pulled me away from the main courtyard for—for—" Stuttering now, she gestured out the stone window in the direction of the herb patch, managing to finish with the very eloquent, "—for *this!*"

Damien resisted the urge to laugh, however, deeming it likely dangerous to tease her in her current state. Instead, he reached out his right hand and cupped her chin, an action that made her fall silent immediately. Before she had time to formulate another question in regards to it, he murmured, "What—do you not find it beautiful, lady?

She appeared nonplussed. "Well . . ."

Unable to look again at the garden because of his grip upon her chin, she simply gave a short nod, her wide-open gaze locked with his. "I suppose it is." That maddening and yet somehow lovely flare of irritation lit in her eyes again, and she countered, "And what of you, sir? Do *you* find it pleasing?"

Damien let another slow smile lift just the corners of his mouth, and the fact that he was staring at her alone when he spoke made quite clear the fact that it was not the garden he referred to at all. "Aye, lady, what I see is undeniably lovely."

He felt, rather than heard, her hastily drawn-in breath in response to that, and it gave him unaccountable pleasure to know that he had succeeded, at least for this moment, in getting her thoughts off the endless intrigues and forthcoming tensions of their court appearance.

"That is not the reason I brought you here, however."

"It's not?" She sounded far less certain of herself

this time, and again Damien resisted the urge to grin at her.

"Nay. Having been to Odiham only once before, I confess to not even knowing this garden existed. Last I was here, this courtyard held little more than two benches and some weeds."

"Why did we come here, then?" she asked, looking even more adorable for the hint of confusion that appeared in the slight crinkling of her nose.

"For this . . ."

As he spoke, he tipped his head forward for the kiss he had been longing to give her all day, his lips nibbling, teasing hers, brushing with gentle tenderness across her mouth before coming back for a deeper taste.

Alissende made a sound that shifted to a soft sigh. In the instant after his mouth touched hers, she tensed slightly, but then she seemed to melt into his arms, her hands slipping up his shoulders as she stretched into his embrace.

She returned his kiss with a vigor that surprised even him. He wondered if it was the effect of the wine that made her amorous so quickly. It was certainly possible. Through the warm waves of sensation lapping at him as they kissed, he made a mental note that wherever they were living in the future, be it Glenheim or another of her dower estates, he would be sure to keep the place well stocked with a hearty vintage.

After a long, delicious moment the kiss ended, and Alissende teetered back a little, swaying, so that he reached out and grabbed at her waist, steadying her.

"Careful." Unable to keep from smiling fully now, he continued, jesting, "I'm flattered, however. I'd always hoped my kisses would be powerful enough to make a woman swoon."

"I am not swooning." Alissende sounded peevish that he had managed to take her by surprise. "I am simply a bit unsteady." She frowned. "Perhaps I indulged too heartily in the spiced wine."

"What a pity that is the cause and not my wondrous skill." He gave an exaggerated sigh. "I suppose I shall have to keep working on it, then."

That made her laugh. "You do very well already, if you must know. But you'll be getting no more kisses until I am in full possession of my senses."

"When will that be?" he asked, raising his brows hopefully.

"You are incorrigible," she retorted, but the scolding lost its effect for the dreamy look in her eyes.

"I am simply eager to learn when I might know the pleasure of your lips again."

"I cannot tell you, though I can give you assurance about something else."

"Pray, do not keep me in suspense," he murmured, never expecting her somewhat pert response, delivered with a soft smile of her own.

"I am indeed more relaxed now, if that was your intent."

A darkly familiar male voice echoed from behind him, "How touching . . . I am almost sorry to interrupt such a tender little moment."

Turning, and in the same, smooth movement tucking Alissende behind him for safety, Damien faced Hugh. He met his rival's gaze, his own cold and steely, his immediate assessment telling him that though Hugh was in the frame of mind to stir trouble, he was not planning any kind of aggressive behavior at the moment.

"Lord Harwick," Damien intoned, giving him just enough of a nod, and shifting so that Alissende could slip into place at his side if she wished. She did, looping her arm around his waist in a way that, even in the tension of the moment, felt strangely gratifying.

"Ashby," Hugh echoed back with a similar tip of his chin. His green-gray eyes looked impassive and assessing as his gaze took in Alissende. "My darling cousin," he murmured. "You look fetching in that rosy hue. Ashby had best keep a close eye on you, lest you be deemed a better dessert than those set upon the king's tables. I could gobble you up myself."

He finished his crude comment with a smile that looked more lecherous than pleasant. Damien felt Alissende's faint shiver, and he gave her shoulder a gentle squeeze, staring at Hugh coldly. "Alissende will be well protected by my side, as always." He paused with deliberate insolence before adding, "My lord."

"We shall see."

Hugh's murmured response, along with the fact that he did not react to Damien's jab, sent an arrow of warning through Damien, but he had little time to consider it further, for Hugh's demeanor suddenly brightened, and he lifted both hands, rocking back on his heels as he said with false joviality, "But why are we dawdling in this dank hallway, when the festivities are elsewhere? I came seeking you for just this reason—to bid you come, for the introductions are getting underway." A sly look slid into his eyes, then, though there was no outward change in his expression. "I know you would not wish to miss that, after all your years away, Sir

Damien. And many of those in attendance are more than eager to have a glimpse of you as well, you can be certain."

Damien did not respond, well aware of the insinuation Hugh was casting with his carefully selected words. The bastard had been busy spreading gossip in preparation for Damien's arrival, likely reviving some of the old stories and rumors as well.

Hugh made a show of seeming surprised at Damien's silence. "What—do you not relish the chance to evaluate those you will be facing on the field tomorrow?"

Damien allowed his expression to alter, then, favoring Hugh with a chilling, wolfish grin that set Alissende to trembling again at his side when she caught sight of it. "It is of little matter to me. There is only one combatant who interests me, though for reasons that have naught to do with our imminent meeting on the lists." He lifted his brow in another gesture of pure and intentional disrespect. "I evaluated him prior to this day and find myself . . . unconcerned."

It was apparent that Hugh had never mastered the ability to keep his emotions suppressed, or even hidden, when facing an adversary. A sense of affront fairly billowed from him, and his face contorted with anger, but he managed to bring himself under control enough to clip off another tightly muttered, "We shall see, Ashby."

"Aye, we shall," Damien answered, not the least bit perturbed. He could tell that he'd startled his rival with the pleasantry of his tone, and he gestured down the corridor, adding, "However, in the meantime . . . shall we make our way to the great hall?"

Hugh jerked into motion, striding ahead without

another word, and Damien followed behind, releasing Alissende's shoulder to grip her hand warmly in his, and glancing down at her to give her a look of encouragement. Her eyes were wide, and she seemed pale and more than a little tense again. Damien cursed Hugh for having undone all the good they'd gained in getting away from the crowds to pause near the herb garden for a while.

But in the end, he supposed it couldn't be helped. Alissende would have become nervous again anyway upon their necessary return to the festivities getting underway. Hugh had only cut short their brief interlude by a bit.

Damien kept his gaze fixed on Hugh's powerful back as he followed him, knowing that for all his insults to the contrary, Hugh de Valles, Lord Harwick would likely prove a formidable opponent on the field. Whether or not he would conduct their combat fairly remained to be seen; regardless, Damien intended to keep up his guard where the man was concerned. The king would be another matter altogether.

Aye, it promised to be an unpleasant evening any way Damien looked at it, and as they neared the great hall, he thought longingly of that moment's interlude he and Alissende had shared near the little garden. He half-wished they could have remained there and avoided all that was to come.

But that was sentimental foolishness, he knew. Time had run out for such fancies. He needed to cloak himself once more with the cold, hard aura of the battle-hardened warrior he had been if he hoped to traverse these next few days—these next few *hours*—successfully.

The time was now, he thought, clenching his jaw and

slipping Alissende's hand into the crook of his arm again as they paused before the great doors at the portal of the reception chamber. He watched them swing open at Hugh's command; the sounds of the revelers billowed out, along with a wave of jumbled scents from the milieu of bodies, perfumes, and food and drink inside.

Aye, the time was now indeed.

And he was ready for it.

Chapter 14

⟨separator ornament⟩

Alissende gazed around the great hall, everything about the royal court gathering bringing back a flood of sharp memories. The last time she had attended such an event had been when King Edward's sire had still sat on the throne. That had been only two summers ago. Godfrey had insisted they make an appearance, for Hugh had convinced him it was in his best interests to show his face before the king more often if he wished to be the recipient of royal favor.

Two years ago.

It did not seem possible. In some ways that time was as fresh in her mind as yesterday, and in others—many others—it seemed a lifetime ago.

"Come, lady. The king and queen are already seated, and the tourney's combatants and their ladies are gathering for presentation," Damien said, breaking into her thoughts. "We should join them to await our turn."

He sounded tense when he spoke to her, and she glanced over at him. She was not used to seeing him so ill at ease, though she could hardly blame him; they were about to face the king himself and receive judgment for the marriage she had coerced him into undertaking. At best it would be uncomfortable; at worst it could prove disastrous.

Nodding wordlessly, Alissende moved along with Damien through the crowd, forcing herself to look around and see whom she might recognize. There were several ladies with whom she had spent hours sewing at court the last time she'd been here; though she caught two of them blatantly staring at her as she passed, both looked away when she attempted to smile in greeting.

It was to be expected, she supposed, but she felt the twinge of it nonetheless. They were snubbing her. She had been an earl's daughter from birth, and then with her marriage to Godfrey, an earl's wife as well, always deemed worthy of conversation by society dames and maidens alike. But they were turning their noses up at her now.

Her decision to marry a simple knight in defiance of the king seemed to have diminished the value of appearing in her company. She'd always listened to complaints about the fickle nature of society without possessing much real understanding of it. Even those years ago, when Damien had quietly seethed over the slights dealt him due to his common blood, she had tried to ease his anger without truly comprehending it.

Now she understood, at least a little, what he must have felt. This kind of rejection stung—the more so in realizing she had been duped into thinking these people were her friends.

She realized her fingers had clenched onto Damien's arm, for he looked away from what was happening in the main part of the court, where he had been watching, as best he could, the process of the royal reception of combatants. Gazing down at her in concern, he murmured, "Is aught amiss, Alissende?"

"Nay, I—" She shook her head, then looked up into his stunning eyes and face, which were so dear to her. "It is just that I never realized how difficult it was. And I—"

She stuttered to a stop, and Damien wrinkled his brow in consternation.

Taking a deep breath, she began anew. "I am trying to say that I wish to thank you once more, for walking with me into the lion's den like this."

He surprised her—and several other people, if the reactions around them were any indication—by throwing his head back and laughing aloud.

"I suppose that is as apt a description of a royal court as any I have heard, Alissende." His eyes twinkled. "You are very welcome. It helps me that I have you on my arm as well, you know."

For some reason his honest and, in its own way, tender admission made her eyes well with tears, and he looked at her in confusion again.

"By the rood, woman, I did not mean to make you cry," he said, his voice sounding hushed with disbelief. "I was not laughing at you, you know."

She could not help but grin through that watery haze, pulling on his arm and half-laughing herself as she shook her head. "Nay, it's not that."

"What is it, then?"

"It is your sweetness that caught me off guard so. Your kindness and understanding."

He continued to appear completely bewildered at what she was saying—and none too pleased that she had termed him, the fierce warrior of countless tourneys and battlefields, "sweet."

"It is naught, Damien," she said, laughing again as she tried to smooth over the moment. "Just attribute my reaction to my anxiety about this evening. Think no more on it."

That was not a total falsehood, she decided. She *was* feeling nervous about what was still to come.

Shaking his head, Damien murmured something about never truly understanding the workings of a woman's mind, to which she retorted that it was just as well, for such was beyond any man's ken, just as God had intended it. She was readying another pertinent comment on the matter when she felt him tense, at the same moment that she heard the herald's call.

"Sir Damien de Ashby, with his wife, Lady Alissende of Surrey."

Her stomach felt like it rose into her throat, and the room was a blur as they made their way down the impromptu path of spectators, toward their audience with the king of all Britain. In contrast to the low hum of conversation and the restless movements of the crowd prior to this moment, a kind of heavy silence spread over the chamber with the announcement of their names. At the same time, everyone seemed to cease what they were doing, craning to hear what the sovereign would say to his two so recently disobedient subjects.

Alissende's nausea was not helped by the fact that in addition to Edward's new queen, Isabel of France, and the king's favorite, Piers Gaveston, Hugh also stood on the dais, behind the royals. He appeared quite serious in demeanor, but she knew she had not mistaken the flash of a less proper expression—a lecherous wink directed at her—when she felt all the muscles in Damien's powerful arm tense to rock under her fingers.

But then they reached the dais, and Alissende was constrained to dip into a low curtsey, while Damien offered a deep bow to their king and queen.

"Rise and receive your greeting."

King Edward issued that command in a voice that was at once filled with authority and at the same time somehow less awe-inducing than she remembered his sire's having been. Daring to glance at the young sovereign and his queen, married only seven months prior, Alissende noted that the king was still handsome and athletic in appearance, as he had been the few times she had been granted a glimpse of him at prior courts. But he bore that softer look about the eyes and mouth that Michael had foretold when he had first predicted that her proxy union with Damien would be accepted at court.

Isabel was fair as well, though not in the manner of delicate English ladies. She appeared bold and dramatic, and rumors had run rampant, reaching even Alissende's ears, concerning the resentment she bore Piers Gaveston, or at least her husband's involvement with the man. At this very moment, in fact, she looked none too pleased that she sat on one side of the king while Piers lounged on the other, in a chair set only slightly back from the monarchs' and of just as opulent a design.

The silence continued for what had to have been a full minute, as King Edward gazed at Damien then turned his stare to Alissende, and then looked back to Damien without uttering a sound. His brows frowned slightly, and his mouth looked tight, but other than that, he showed little expression.

Damien stood at attention after having been bid to do so by his king; he remained in that position, unmoving, a knight of unmistakable discipline. She, however, was having difficulty keeping herself from fidgeting under the weight of the royal gaze. At last, when she thought she could bear it no longer, King Edward swung his stare to her again and spoke. And then that was almost as terrible, for he revealed his displeasure in a voice tinged with royal annoyance, delivered in such a way that the words seemed to echo from the very walls.

"Lady Alissende, you are of noble birth, and We wish to make note before this assembly that you have disparaged the honor of your ranking by seeking marriage to a man so far beneath you in title—especially considering the fact that such was undertaken against Our express desire to see you wed to Our dear Hugh de Valles, Lord Harwick. It is to Our offense, lady, that you completed such an impetuous and ill-advised action."

Alissende felt her stomach drop to her knees, the effect making her nausea swell anew and causing her to wish she was not required to remain still, with her hands by her sides, while facing the king.

But the sovereign was not finished, for he frowned at her, adding in a clipped voice, "You knew of Our desire in this, did you not?"

She had no choice but to answer and trust that in the process she would not be sick. Lowering her gaze with what she hoped was a demure and repentant-looking bow of her head, she murmured the very phrase she had practiced so oft with Michael, secure in the knowledge that it was the truth, at least. "Aye, sire. I beg your forgiveness and throw myself to your great mercy, beseeching you to consider that mine was a waywardness inspired by the heart and not the will. Never was there intent to show insolence to Your Highness or to deny the ultimate power you wield over us, your unworthy subjects."

Damien's head snapped sideways to look at Alissende, shock flooding him in hearing that smooth apology to the king. Where had that come from? He realized he was almost gaping at her, and shamed at his lapse of discipline, he snapped his gaze forward again, standing at attention once more.

King Edward appeared almost as surprised as Damien had been, the scowl he'd worn thus far replaced by something much more open and assessing. The queen seemed to be biting back a smile, and Piers looked interested, while Hugh's expression was so black that Damien was surprised not to see thunderbolts shooting from his eyes.

"Is that so, lady?" King Edward said at last, though he spoke in a much less commanding tone.

"Aye, sire," Alissende said gently, her head still bowed.

"Are you willing to affirm to Us, God's appointed on earth, that you are with this man you have taken to husband for a reason *other* than that of attempting to avoid Our choice of Lord Harwick for your new lord and master?"

That question rang out over the assembly, and Damien felt himself tense. Would Alissende be able to lie successfully? Self-preservation hoped she would, and yet the part of him that still remained of the principled and unbending sword-arm of God decried the practice, knowing that falsehoods almost always led to something destructive.

"I do affirm that, sire."

Alissende's voice sounded far more steady and *sincere,* if that was possible, than that which she'd used before, and Damien once again could not resist a slight shift of his head so that he might glimpse her from the side of his gaze.

It was fortunate that he had trained from childhood to master his outward reactions, for though he had thought Alissende finished with what had proved to be a very convincing deceit, she still had more to say, it seemed—and when he heard it, it might have otherwise made him sink to his knees.

"As many in this chamber are aware, Sir Damien de Ashby and I first loved each other long ago, when I was but a maid and he a new knight. It is true that we parted badly, but our reunion has brought me great joy, and it is for such reason I am with him now, within the bonds of this marriage begun in proxy four months ago. Once more I beseech you to forgive the seeming impetuous action that has caused us to fall into your disfavor, for it was committed out of love and not disrespect to Your Highness."

A hum of reaction sounded behind them in the great hall now, dispelling the silence, and through his own surprise Damien saw King Edward glance back at Hugh, who looked down at the floor of the dais in response, as if bowing his head. However, rage crackled from every inch of him, making it clear that this was not over for him. Not in the least.

"And what have you to say about all of this, sir?" the king called out to Damien, once he faced the assembly again. "We have heard something of you and wish to know if you have aught to add, after having taken such a fine prize into your possession, without a by-your-leave?"

"Nay, sire," Damien responded in a low but firm voice. His jaw clenched tightly for a moment as he resisted the urge to glare at Hugh, reminding himself not to rise to any challenge but to simply say what must be said to remove himself and Alissende from the tip of the dagger. "What my lady has said covers all. We both humbly ask your pardon for our hasty union, undertaken in so much . . . emotion."

King Edward's mouth tightened and then relaxed. He waved his hand in exasperation, saying quietly, for them and those within their immediate vicinity, "Very well—though We will remind you both to tread very carefully in future. Our good humor in this is at an end."

More loudly, for the sake of the entire assembly, he added, "While We were astounded and dismayed to receive word of your union, unsanctioned by Us, We have no choice but to show Our obedience in yielding to the only authority greater than Ours—that of God and His bride, the Holy Mother Church in the form of the sanctioned and legal proxy taken up between you. Go in peace with your king's reluctant blessing."

Alissende curtseyed again as Damien bowed, and then they moved from the reception area before the dais to the main portion of the chamber, hearing the herald call out the name of the next tourney combatant and his lady for their greeting by the king.

It was over. It did not seem possible, but they had made it through without catastrophe.

Damien led Alissende forward, looking for a quiet spot along the wall. He was surprised that it wasn't very difficult, given the number of people in the chamber. Coming to a stop near one of the long trestle tables that had been placed around the room to hold various delicacies, he released Alissende's hand and faced her.

"You did well."

"Thank you."

She sounded subdued, and he studied her for any sign of how she felt about the interview they'd just endured. She looked strained, perhaps, but that was no doubt from the obvious reason of having felt the sting of the king's wrath.

"You were very convincing," he continued, still fixing her with his gaze and wondering if she would reveal anything of her motivation in speaking as she had. Wondering how he would feel about it if she did. But she remained silent, glancing down to her clasped hands.

"I was impressed, lady," he said after a moment's

pause. "You have either become a very fine liar, or else you—"

Her gaze snapped to his again then, cutting off the rest of his words an instant before the shield of her lashes came down; but he had seen her beautiful eyes for long enough that he could swear that he had seen the answer to his question there, and he felt the sweet impact of it down to his toes.

By all the saints . . .

"We say what we must, Damien, when it is expected of us," Alissende murmured at last, so low that he almost couldn't hear her, with the sounds of conversation and music that had resumed in the chamber.

"That is all it was, then? You said only what you felt compelled to say?" he asked, unrelenting. He drew her gaze to his again, holding it and feeling somehow irritable and relieved all at once by her answer.

A softer, troubled look slipped across her features. "Damien, I—"

"Pardon, sir."

Damien and Alissende both turned to look at the serving lad who had approached them unnoticed. He wore the king's livery, but Damien did not remember having seen the youth before. That was not unexpected, of course, considering the number of attendants the royal entourage contained, but even more than his sudden appearance, the lad seemed nervous, glancing back and forth between Damien and Alissende, his Adam's apple bobbing as he swallowed several times in quick succession.

"You are Sir Damien de Ashby?"

"Aye. What do you seek with me?" Damien asked, frowning.

"I come bearing a message, sir, from one of your men-at-arms, Sir Reginald. Your tourney mount suffers an ailment, and your man entreats you to come posthaste to the stables, lest the steed be unfit to carry you through tomorrow's events."

"What kind of ailment?" Damien scowled at him, and the lad went pale. Concern and doubt warred within Damien as he waited for the boy's answer. His gelding had served well in training these four months, and when he had left the horse only a few hours earlier, he had seemed as fit as he had ever been.

"He said not, sir," the lad said, swallowing convulsively again. "He offered only that he would not interrupt your evening but for the dire need of the moment."

Cursing under his breath, Damien looked at Alissende, seeing his own concern reflected in her serious gaze.

"Go," she said before he could say aught. "I will return to our pavilion to await news."

He scowled more deeply, liking this less and less. It was not far from the main keep to the tilting grounds and the field where all the combatants' silken tents were pitched. The path would likely be well lit with torches and far from deserted, with the number of ranking combatants in attendance here this week. But he still hated for Alissende to go anywhere without escort.

The serving lad looked as if he was ready to jump from his skin in his eagerness to be gone, now that his message had been delivered, but Damien forestalled him a moment longer.

"What is your name, lad?"

"Simon, sir." The boy crushed his soft cap between his fingers and seemed to be shifting his weight back and forth.

"Here, Simon," Damien said, reaching into his leather side-pouch to retrieve a coin. "Escort my lady back to our pavilion, whilst I attend to the problem in the stable."

"It is not necessary, Damien," Alissende protested softly. "None will hinder my progress in returning to our tent."

"Nonetheless, I will see you protected at all times."

In case this is a trap, set by Hugh in an effort to separate you from me.

That part of the statement, left unspoken, echoed between them, prompting Alissende to nod her head at last in wordless concession.

"Go swiftly, Simon, and do not diverge from the path to the pavilion field, lest you earn far different recompense from me than the coin I have given you just now."

"Aye, sir—I mean, nay, sir, I will see your lady nowhere but straight to your tent and the attendants that await her there."

Damien nodded, touching his finger briefly to Alissende's cheek, only breaking his gaze with her reluctantly. He did not like this, but he had little choice. He could not compete in the tourney tomorrow without a mount.

Wanting to get this settled so that he could return to Alissende's side as swiftly as possible, Damien turned and strode through the clusters of people in the chamber, earning more of their stares as he made his way out into the dark of the yard that led to the stables.

The path was strangely empty, Damien thought as he tried to make his way by faded memory and the faint light of the moon. The stables and outbuildings at Odiham were set at the furthest edges of the retaining wall, thanks to the unusual, octagonal shape of the main keep, and Damien berated himself for not remembering this sooner so that he might have at least grabbed one of the hall torches on his way out here.

In truth, he'd never thought to find so few servants moving about. Then again, perhaps they were all occupied with duties inside, thanks to the opening celebration.

He would get there soon enough, though; he could see the flicker of light from the stables ahead in the gloom, and he could hear the soft nickering of horses. That Reginald had not sought him out along the way did not bode well, however, for it likely meant his mount was even worse than he'd thought, and that Reginald had needed to remain by his—

A rustling sound behind Damien gave him a breath of warning, allowing him to tense an instant before something long and hard cracked across his back, up near his shoulders. Whatever it was hurt like hell, and he realized that it would have caught him on the base of his skull had he not reacted with hard-won instinct to the whispering approach of the blow.

Twisting in the direction of his unseen assailant, Damien braced himself in a half crouch, wishing he had time to reach for his blade even as he tried to ready himself for the next strike. He'd been hit with a jousting lance, apparently, and he saw it come swinging in at his head again, wielded by a short and stocky man. As he ducked and rolled, Damien caught little more than a glimpse of red hair and glittering eyes in the wash of moonlight that broke from behind the clouds.

The blow missed him, but he collided with a second man, unseen before in the darkness. Damien felt him though, by God, when the bastard's fist cracked into his jaw as he tried to lurch to a standing position to face the two of them. The strike sent Damien back to the dirt, filling his mouth with the metallic taste of blood and setting off a dull ringing in his ears. He had no time to react, however, because at that moment a well-aimed kick drove deep into his belly from another direction, unleashing a wall of white-hot agony and stopping his breath on a choked grunt.

Damn, there were three of them.

As he rolled to his side, hunched over, that realization echoed dimly through the pain stunning his mind, while the blows began to rain down on him. To his good fortune, in the space of time it took to drag a tortured breath into his lungs, something flared to life inside him. The will to fight swelled, building to a fierce burning as it had when he'd been under the diabolical torments of his inquisitors—only this time, unlike then, he was restrained only by his own pain.

And that sure as hell wasn't going to stop him.

With a growl of pure rage, Damien curled upward and swung out with his fists, catching one of his assailants in the chest and knocking him back at the same time that he drove his heel into a second one's knee. He heard the man's strangled-sounding scream as the joint broke. The man fell back, but before Damien could do aught else but suck in another much-needed breath, the other two dimly outlined attackers converged upon him.

With battle-honed instinct, he struck out at them, catching the lance and yanking it free just before it could find its mark against his body again.

Ah—a weapon at last.

They did not know it yet, but even three to one, the wretches had just evened the field. He used the lance against them with relish, jabbing and cracking it into the shadowy targets with the precision borne of countless training sessions and numerous skirmishes over the past decade.

But then, almost as suddenly as he had turned the tide of the brawl to his own favor, it was over.

He heard a muffled grunt, followed by a low call to retreat uttered by one of the men he fought. The one whose knee he'd broken earlier seemed to have vanished, but both of the remaining assailants suddenly left off their attack. He caught the edge of one of the men's tunics as they turned to flee, wanting some answers about why they had set upon him. But the cur broke free, leaving Damien with naught but a fistful of cloth and empty air for his efforts.

As if from afar, Damien heard the thud of a door and some scrambling sounds, as if someone was climbing over a wall or gate. And then all fell silent.

His breath rasped and his chest felt tight; in the aftermath of the fight, the wrath that had helped him keep going ebbed away, leaving naught but throbbing pain and the deep aching of the injuries he'd sustained.

He hurt, by God. In too many places to count.

Sinking to his knees with a stifled groan, Damien tried to pull together his muddled thoughts. He didn't need a clear head to know that there was more to this attack than being at the wrong place at the wrong time. Hell, none of his assailants had even made the show of demanding his purse.

Just then, he looked down at the piece of cloth he still clutched in his hand; the clouds shifted again, letting the moonlight spill down and illuminating the edge of the garment he'd ripped when his assailant had first been attempting to flee. It was of gold-hued fabric, slashed with red.

Hugh's colors.

Christ, the bastard was more underhanded, even, than Damien had thought. He closed his eyes, taking even, panting breaths and reminding himself that any rage he allowed himself to feel now would be wasted. Better to save it for when he could put it to useful purpose. Against Hugh, for example, on the morrow.

Lifting one hand to his head, Damien winced when his fingertips encountered a gash above his brow. That explained why he'd had to keep blinking in order to see what little he had during the brawl, though at the time he'd thought it was sweat that was obscuring his vision. Spitting, he realized that the second cur's blow to his jaw had filled his mouth with blood as well.

He bit off a curse. Yet as much as his head hurt, the rest of his body felt worse. He'd need to wait an hour or so before he'd be able to assess the full extent of his injuries, but he knew with sickening certainty that he had at least one cracked rib. That much was clear, based upon the jagged pain he felt trying to take in a breath deep enough to yell for one of his men to come out from the stables, which still loomed a hundred or more paces away—too far for any of them to have heard the scuffle.

He attempted to breathe in fully again, only to feel a nauseating, piercing sensation that stopped the effort short and made him see stars. Obviously, summoning help that way wasn't going to work.

Nay, he would have to push himself to his feet again and walk the distance.

Gritting his teeth, he forced himself to stand, letting his own anger drive him on. He wrapped one arm around his aching ribs and headed toward the stables. Perhaps the attack against him had been in retaliation for the insults he had dealt Hugh in the hallway near the herb garden. Or perhaps it was simply Hugh's attempt to intimidate or disable him for the contest to come between them in the tournament tomorrow.

But he could not discount the possibility that this three-on-one beating had been a nasty ploy to keep him separated from Alissende long enough for Hugh to get to her, and it was that fear which gave him strength to go more quickly.

Aye, he would make it to the stables all right. He would find his men and send several of them ahead to his pavilion, knowing that they could reach it and Alissende far more swiftly than he could in his condition.

And then he would make Hugh pay.

By God, injured or not, on the morrow he would make Hugh de Valles, Lord Harwick, pay for the cowardly ambush he'd ordered this night.

And he would take pleasure in every moment of it.

Chapter 15

⁓ ◦◦◦ ⁓

Alissende paced the limited confines of the silk pavilion, breathing in the comforting scent of the beeswax candles she'd brought from home and attempting to distract herself by watching the shadows that twisted and stretched against the tent's silken walls as a result of the carefully placed, flickering tapers.

She glanced every now and again to Edmee, who seemed to be trying her best to remain busy with some needlework, though it was clear she was distracted as well. It had been more than a half hour with no word since Alissende had returned to the tent; she'd been delivered there by Simon, who had touched his fingertips to his brow and tipped his head in acknowledgment before racing off back toward the castle, looking as if the hounds of Hades might emerge from the darkness to pursue him.

It was unlike Damien to be so long without sending

word. The stables were less than a ten-minute walk from the training grounds and adjacent pavilion field, and she had thought he would at least dispatch a message with one of his men if what he'd found was so serious that he himself could not leave.

It did not bode well.

Edmee suddenly stiffened, letting her needlework fall to her lap. "Do you hear that, Lady Alissende?"

Going still herself, Alissende paused, straining to discern what her maid had noticed. She frowned, hearing naught but the usual sounds of the pavilion field: the rustling of breeze against the fabric of the tents, a few clattering of pots, and the low hum of conversation amongst the servants, who were all awaiting their masters' and mistresses' return from the royal reception.

"There—I heard it again, my lady . . . someone calling your name!"

This time Alissende recognized the sound herself. It was faint and in a voice unfamiliar to her, but it became clearer the next moment when it was repeated again, as if the speaker had come closer to the tent.

Springing to her feet, she ran to the tent flap and pushed it open, glad for the light of several torches that had been left burning along the path between the castle and the pavilion field to guide the noble guests back to their temporary quarters once the royal reception was finished.

"Lady Alissende—my lady!" the voice called, half-muted, in an effort to get her attention without attracting the undue notice of the servants in all the surrounding tents.

At that moment, Alissende caught sight of the figure

running down the path. Startled, she took a step back before she realized it was one of Glenheim's men, who had been given berth by the king-of-arms to sleep with the tournament mounts in the stables.

"What is the matter, Bernard—where is Sir Damien?" She searched his face with her gaze, desperate for some explanation of his strange approach.

"Are you well, my lady? Have you passed your time here in peace?" he asked through gasping breaths, not answering her question, she noticed, but rather looking around her as if for some intruder, his hand on his sword hilt in readiness.

"All is quiet, and it is only I and Edmee here, awaiting news." She took a step closer, forcing Bernard to meet her gaze. "Where is Sir Damien, Bernard? I demand to know without further delay."

"I am sorry, my lady. Under Sir Damien's orders, I could not pause to answer aught until I knew you were safe," Bernard murmured, having caught his breath now and appearing more confident that all was as it should be. "He was set upon in the darkness of the yard by three scoundrels who showed not their faces. He believes Lord Harwick behind the attack, and therefore feared for your safety as well, causing him to send me ahead to check upon you."

"Is he hurt, then?" Alissende asked, gripping the edge of Bernard's sleeve. "Sweet heavens, where is he—what injuries has he sustained?"

"He comes shortly behind me, lady, able to walk. In truth he refuses any assistance, though he will surely need tending once he reaches the pavilion," Bernard answered, frowning. "You had best ready your remedies, for it is possible that he suffers other hurts worse than the cuts and bruises that were apparent upon looking at him."

God have mercy . . .

After calling to Edmee to get out the casket of herbs and healing potions they always carried with them while traveling, Alissende started down the path into the darkness toward the castle, determined to seek out Damien herself and help him back to the tent, whether or not he stubbornly refused the assistance of his men. But she was pulled up short by Bernard's hand upon her arm.

"Nay, lady. I regret that I cannot allow you to leave this pavilion."

"You most certainly can!" she retorted, pulling her arm from his grip, turning her frustration on him in a blast of righteous anger. "I am your lady and bid you do it. There is naught else for you to consider."

"Your lord husband forbid me it and told me it was on penalty of my life that I let you leave. He is now head of your household, and by rights, I must obey his orders above all else, my lady."

That obstinate, mulish fool . . .

But before she could argue her point with Bernard further, a movement at the edge of the pavilion field caught her attention, and both she and Bernard turned to see three indistinct figures making their way down the path toward them. Alissende's heart seemed to rise up to choke her. It was two more of Glenheim's men, walking with Damien between them; they came very slowly, though as Bernard had said, Damien moved under his own power.

As they neared, she gasped and ran out to meet them, regardless of Damien's orders or how it might appear to any who happened to be watching. He sported a gash on his brow that was already bruising, as well as a cut lip, though the fierce light in his eyes cautioned her to restrain herself from tending to him in any way out here, any more than he had allowed his men to bodily support him along the way.

"Where are you hurt?" she asked quietly, holding aside the flap of the tent, only taking his arm, helping him to the raised pallet of their bed once they were inside the confines of the tent.

"Everywhere," he answered wryly, sitting with great care on the edge of the feather-stuffed mattress, then letting out his breath with a hissing sound when he released his arm from around his ribs.

"Here, let me help you disrobe, to get a better look at your injuries," Alissende murmured, beginning to pull gently at one of his sleeves.

Damien stiffened, though she knew, somehow, that it wasn't from pain.

"Perhaps it would be better if one of my men did the honors," he said quietly, giving her a sideways glance. "I would not wish to disturb you with what you might see."

"Nonsense. I learned to stitch wounds at the same time that I was taught to sew cloth, and I have treated scores of bruises as lady of the keep. You need not worry about offending my sensibilities in any way."

"It is not the new injuries I mean, Alissende."

The import of what Damien was saying—that he referred to those scars as yet unseen by her, the ones that affected the lower half of his body—finally sank in. He had never allowed her to see him completely naked in full light, she realized. Nay, even when they'd made love, he had always drawn the bed-curtains close to ensure that they were both cast in concealing shadow.

Remembering that now, she gave hardly a moment's pause.

"There is no one else I would have tend you, Damien, but me." She held his gaze as she spoke so that he would see the truth in what she said. Though it would surely disturb her to look upon any damage done to him, both old and new, it would be the result of anger at the cruelty of mankind, not disgust.

Apparently he was in too much pain to argue the point more, for he simply nodded once, giving her his permission to send the others away so that she might see to his needs.

It took but little time to ensure she had what she required by way of herbs, wine, and water, both for poultices and to give him to drink as medicine, as well as bandages for wrapping any broken bones he might have sustained. With a few murmured instructions to Edmee, Bernard, and the other two retainers not to disturb them until morning unless called upon, Alissende saw them ushered from the tent and tied the flap closed.

Then she faced Damien again, her hands upon her hips.

"Before aught else, you should take a draught of healing powders in wine. It will aid with the pain." As she spoke, she strode over to the chest of herbs Edmee had retrieved for her, measuring out some yarrow and comfrey for healing bruises and knitting broken bones, and stirring them into a cup of wine. "It would taste better warmed with honey, perhaps, but I do not think it would be wise for you to wait longer to drink it."

In answer, Damien held out his hand for the cup, grimacing after he quaffed its contents. "The cure may be worse than the injury, lady."

"You'd be wise to accustom yourself to it," she retorted, hiding her smile as she took the empty cup from him and turned to gather up the rest of what she would need to dress his wounds.

"Why?"

"Because you will be taking a dose of it twice each day until you have healed."

"We will revisit that later, when I am feeling stronger," he said, reaching up to touch the gash on his brow. "On the morrow, perhaps, when I am readying to pummel your cousin to within an inch of his miserable life."

"You cannot be serious!"

Damien glanced at her again, wincing at the quick movement before he answered, "And you cannot be harboring sympathies for him still, after all he's done, Alissende."

"Nay," she retorted hotly. "I would delight to see him humbled on the field or elsewhere. What I mean is that you cannot intend to still compete in the tournament tomorrow in your condition."

He made a scoffing sound. "Of course I can. There is naught else I can do, in all honor."

"But you will kill yourself trying to fight, wounded as you are!" She faced him fully now, placing the pots and bandages down on the table beside the bed and glaring down at him where he sat. "And then you will be giving Hugh exactly what he desires, which would accomplish a great deal of nothing, wouldn't you say?"

"I will be giving Hugh exactly what he *deserves* during the next week of tourney games, do not fear, lady."

Damien's voice sent a chill up her spine, and she realized that she was thankful she would never need to face him on the field of battle. She met his gaze, watching the intensity of it sharpen, if such was possible, even as an apparent wave of pain went through him, noticeable only by the slight catch she discerned in his breathing.

"As for my wounds," he continued, raising his brow, "you have yet to examine them to know how severe they may be. With the exception of this rib and the need for a few stitches, I'd warrant there is little to worry over."

"We shall see." She pursed her lips, shaking her head at his stubbornness. "Come, then, and let us get on with it."

First she cleaned the gash above his eye with a tincture of thyme oil and water, and though she knew it stung, he made nary a sound; he did not react, even, when she pressed bruised cloves onto his cut lip, both to cleanse it and to deaden the hurt. Even more so than the thyme oil, clove burned on open cuts; she knew it from experience. It was so painful that the last time she had needed to use some on her own cracked lips this past winter, it had made her eyes water for ten minutes. But he didn't even flinch.

Appreciative of his self-control, Alissende gestured for him to hold out his right arm—the one opposite the side he seemed to be favoring—to help him in disrobing. Easing him from his tunic, shirt, and breeches proved less difficult than she had thought it would be. Of course she suspected that had more to do with his stoic acceptance of pain than with any finesse on her part. She saw the tightness of his lips and heard the catch in his breathing again whenever he was forced to move in a particularly uncomfortable manner.

Soon he was unclothed completely but for the undergarment of his braies, and she saw once again the array of scars that were the awful reminders of his ordeal with the Inquisition, layered over with several fresh bruises and at least one other cut across his ribs. What she had not been privy to see before, however, was the sight of those that continued down from his torso, under his braies, visible again below, along his legs. Her eyes stung as she was forced to bite at the inside of her cheek to keep herself from becoming emotional rather than tending to him in the calm, methodical manner that she knew would be best.

"I am sorry to upset you, Alissende," he said quietly, and she glanced to him, realizing that he had been watching her to gauge her reaction.

"I am not upset in the way that you think. Truly."

She'd managed to speak, but even she realized how hoarse her voice had sounded. He would have further reason to think her a liar, just as he had when they'd stood before the king and she'd affirmed the reason for their marriage as one of love. It was just as well, she supposed. Better than him guessing the truth—that what she had said then hadn't been a lie at all for her.

"I had hoped to avoid the need for you to see the rest of it." He gave a tight-sounding laugh. "The contrast is great, I know, between the man I was before and what I am now. At least with these covered, it is easier for me to hide from myself . . . and from you." He shifted his gaze to hers, where she sat next to him on the bed, and she saw pained humor competing with the deep sense of shame apparent in his eyes. "I would be glad if you would work quickly, lady, so that you need not be burdened with the sight for longer than is necessary."

She paused, letting the fullness of what he had just said sink in before she decided that she could not let it pass. To speak with him of her thoughts on this would require that she expose a portion of her heart, perhaps, and that was always dangerous where Damien was concerned. But she realized that she could go no further without setting him straight on this point.

"You speak often of this different man you have become, Damien," she answered quietly at last, "and yet I must tell you that these outward changes—the scars of those many hurts that were inflicted upon you—mean naught to me in the way you think they do. When I look upon them I feel no revulsion or pity, even. Nay, I feel only anger over what you were made to endure. Do you not know that?"

She blinked, forcing herself to keep her gaze steady upon him while she shared the rest of this difficult truth. "I need you to understand something once and for all, Damien. My feelings for you have never been tied to your appearance. I will not deny that I have always thought you a handsome man, but that has not changed. I continue to find you very attractive, as I am sure you have noticed when we are alone of the evening in our bed."

She picked up the pot of liniment and a roll of bandage then, setting her jaw as she finished, "That is all I intend to say on the matter, Damien, but I wished you to be clear upon that point, if upon naught else."

He was staring at her as if she'd sprouted feathers

from the top of her head, though he remained silent in the face of her declaration. Surprisingly so, for someone who had never seemed to have difficulty voicing his opinion about anything before.

A bit uneasy at having shared such personal feelings with the very man who was the subject of them, Alissende tried to avoid meeting his gaze, though she felt his on her, warm and steady. Instead, she concentrated on dressing his remaining injuries, applying poultices to the bruises on his legs, stitching the cut on his ribs and wrapping it tightly with a bandage around his middle, after first placing another poultice-soaked pad atop the wound for protection.

He grunted once, when she pulled a bit too hard on the dressing as she tightened it, but other than that, she noticed precious little reaction from him in the minutes after she stopped speaking . . .

Until she helped ease him to his back, once all the bandaging was done, and she happened to glance down, toward his waist. Then she perceived a reaction all right, only it wasn't one in words. Nay, this was an entirely physical, very male response to her recent ministrations.

Alissende felt her cheeks heat with that seemingly ever-present blush as she struggled to look anywhere but at the stiff and enormous swelling that pushed up from beneath his braies. Damien had not allowed much in the way of her touch upon him these past few days, concentrating the time of their sensual interludes on his reexploration of her body. But she enjoyed this aspect of him. Ah, yes, she enjoyed it well. She would never forget her shock and amazement that first time, when as an innocent virgin she had seen this tangible and very impressive proof of his desire for her.

The yearning to touch him there right now nearly overwhelmed her, but she resisted, thinking that perhaps such an action might not be the most tactful or understanding one to take, considering that he was likely still in a good bit of pain from the effects of his wounds.

Desperate to resolve the problem in some way, she reached for the linen sheet and threw it over him up to his waist, preparing to stand and move away, to put away her pots of salve and tinctures. His strangled laugh made her go still, and she snapped her gaze to him again, feeling more than a little belligerent and ready to put him in his place, if such was needed.

His eyes twinkled in response to her glare, and she almost let loose a sharp comment, until she glanced down once more at her handiwork with the sheet. And then she saw that it wasn't *her* he was laughing at, at all.

The effect of the sheet over the rigid, protruding length of his erection appeared ludicrous, to say the least. The cloth meant to conceal him had done naught except to create the illusion of something that looked like a miniature tent, with fabric draped over a massive center pole.

"There's no covering him, methinks," Damien commented wryly. "As always, he seems to have a mind of his own where you are concerned."

"Oh, I . . . I suppose I could—that is, I—"

Alissende's cheeks felt like they might ignite to flames as she stuttered and tried to keep herself from dissolving into a fit of choked giggles.

"There is only one help for it," Damien sighed, still

with that humorous lilt in his voice. But keeping his
gaze locked to her face, he raised his brow and tilted his
head slightly in concession as he added, "Well, perhaps
two or three. But I assure you that the first is infinitely
more enjoyable than the others."

Alissende had caught her breath by this point, and
she boldly offered, "I believe I know of the first to
which you refer, but pray tell, what are the others?"

"An icy bath, for one." Damien's face was expres-
sionless, all but for that glint of fire in his eyes. "That
might prove difficult, however, as chilled water is in
short supply in midsummer, not to mention the fact
that it is rather messy to use upon an invalid. It soaks
the mattress along with the man, you see."

She arched her brow back at him, finding that she
was rather enjoying this. "You are an invalid now, are
you?"

"Aye, lady. I find my injuries have rendered me motionless." The heat in his eyes flared again, and the
edge of his mouth curved up wickedly. "I am completely at your mercy."

"Hmmmm . . ." she mused, placing her finger to her
lips in an exaggerated pose of deep thought, though in
truth the idea of being in control in this way was
strangely thrilling. "What to do with such powers? . . ."

She gave him a look meant to approximate a sudden
idea striking. "I know! I shall begin with this—"

She moved the sheet so that she might grasp the
string that kept the front of his braies closed, loosening
it and undoing the laces, while all the time being very
careful not to make contact with any part of Damien's
body, even through the fabric. She glanced up at him,
almost losing her nerve to continue when she saw the

searing look in his eyes. The muscles of his stomach tightened with a delicious ripple as she completed the task, but still he did not speak or make any sound other than the shallow, even breaths he took.

"Let me see," she murmured, "I believe that I should follow up that action with this—"

Her voice was husky with the desire building inside her as well, as she reached to the gaping edges of his braies and tugged them open further. Then she deftly pulled them down over his hips, allowing his erection to spring free, so that its hard, plum-capped length bobbed with the motion. Though she still did not touch him, she could not keep her eyes from widening at the glorious sight of him, denied her for so long, and her breath came out on an appreciative sigh.

In response, Damien's lips curved again, this time in a self-satisfied way, and she felt a flare of irritation for having revealed so much of her thoughts. Ah, well. She knew how to shift control back into her own hands. Quite literally, in fact.

"Now, then . . ." she said, letting her voice drift off with her own teasing lilt, "I wonder what would happen if I did *this*—"

At that she brushed her open palm gently but firmly up his straining, swollen length, feeling a burst of satisfaction when he closed his eyes and sucked in his breath at the pleasure of her touch upon him.

But it wasn't enough yet.

Resting her hand gently over the length of him, she did not move. Nay, not so much as a finger, until his eyes snapped open. Then she met his gaze and asked sweetly, "Am I doing well so far, Damien, in helping you?"

"Aye, lady." His expression looked almost pained. "Very well—though I do not think it would be amiss if you would deign to continue your . . . assistance."

If his voice had sounded strangled before, it now sounded positively choked.

Offering him a brilliant smile, she answered, "Oh. Do you mean, perhaps, that I should do this?" In saying so, she grasped his erection fully in her hand and stroked upward, repeating the motion with a sure, firm caress, and unleashing from him at last a low groan that was rife with combined agony and ecstasy. Music to her ears.

The sound, the sight, and delicious feel of him writhing in pleasure beneath her touch spurred Alissende on; she continued stroking him, loving him with her hands and murmuring soft endearments as she brought him closer and closer to the edge of completion.

"Ah, Alissende," he gasped after several delicious minutes of that sweet torment, "be careful, lady, for I cannot hold back much longer . . ."

"It is all right, Damien," she whispered. "Let go and do naught but feel."

With wordless acceptance, he reached down, gripping her wrist as she continued to stroke him, easing him toward a powerful orgasm. Her name was on his lips, a whisper that built to a groan of pure ecstasy at the moment that he came in a shuddering release.

The sheet she held ready caught most of the pulsing flow, and after the final, pleasurable spasm had passed, Alissende kissed his brow. They did not speak as she helped him back into his braies and saw him comfortably settled in the bed for the night; his eyes were closed, and she wondered if he had fallen asleep. A silly smile curved her lips at that idea that in her own way, she had made *him* swoon—at least into slumber.

Getting up, she undressed and pulled her hair from its arrangement, combing it out, then weaving it into a long, thick plait down her back. At last she blew out the burned-down tapers and crept into bed next to him, being careful not to press against any of his tender places or injuries as she did.

And so it was that when he moved, she was startled. Even more so when he pulled her close to cradle her against the length of his body and ease her head onto his shoulder.

"Is this not uncomfortable for you, Damien?" she whispered, wondering that the soreness he must surely be feeling from his wounds did not bring him to sudden and painful awareness.

"Nay," he murmured sleepily. "I am a swift healer, you know. And with your help—in more than one way this night," he murmured, and she could hear his smile, though she could not see it in the dark, "I will be fit as ever in no time."

But before she could make answer to that bold claim, he astonished her further by adding, "In truth, I am more comfortable than I have been since the last time I held you in our bed. Though perhaps I would like it even better if I was given leave to offer you the same kinds of caresses again, now, with which you have just gifted me? . . ."

Alissende bit back her own smile. "I do not think that would be wise in your condition, sir. Better that you rest and regain your strength."

He sighed. "I suppose you are right. Though I will not concede without striking fear into your heart with the promise that when I am able, I will extract a double—nay, perhaps even triple—payment from you for the tender torments you played upon me this night."

Pretending a shiver of terror that was really one of delicious anticipation, Alissende grinned, closing her eyes and nestling into his arms as she whispered dutifully, "I am trembling with the dread of it, my lord."

"Good."

He tucked her more closely against him, pressing a kiss to the top of her head and sighing again, this time with a sound of pure contentment. After a few more moments without further conversation, Alissende knew he had fallen asleep—so she decided to try to do the same, knowing that the challenges coming on the morrow would require all of her concentration if she was to navigate them successfully.

And she intended to be ready for them.

Chapter 16

The final day of the tournament at Odiham
One week later

The combat would be today.

Damien felt a surge of dark anticipation, knowing that at long last, this day he would face Hugh de Valles, the Earl of Harwick, for a one-on-one contest in the lists. Nodding to his squire to help him slip his mail coat over his head so that it would lie atop the protective, padded aketon he had already donned, Damien spent a few brief but satisfying moments considering all that had passed this week to bring him to this point.

One thing stood out most clearly above the rest: He had vastly underestimated Hugh de Valles' cunning and his ability to influence the circumstances of this tournament; for instance, as of this day, Damien had yet to face Hugh himself. Damien suffered no illusions that their lack of personal combat had been due to Hugh's cowardice or even by accident of timing. Nay, Hugh had made it clear, on the field as well as during each night's feasting, that he considered himself far above Damien, not only in title and birth, which was undeniable, but in fighting skill as well.

Because of this, as the lead tenant, holding the field with more than a score of his comrades in the king's name against all-comers to the tournament, Hugh had ensured that he would face Damien in single combat only if Damien proved to be the lead venant, or challenger, after the first six days. There had been no doubt in Damien's mind that he would do whatever it took to claim that position.

All that remained now was to bludgeon Hugh into the defeat he deserved.

"My lord, your plates are ready to be fastened. Will you hold out your arms for them?"

His squire's voice pulled Damien from his reverie, and he gave the lad a half smile. "Aye, Thomas. Thank you."

Damien waited while Thomas completed the task of buckling the individual pieces of plate armor to his back and shoulders, along with the pieces Damien had decided to add, for this tournament at least, at his sides. They would shield his ribs better from another strike that might come in the midst of the combat on foot that followed the joust on horseback. Knowing Hugh, and knowing that he would have been apprised of the damage inflicted during the cowardly attack in the yard a sennight ago, it would be considered a prime spot to deliver a blow.

The earl's chances at reinjuring the area were few, however, not only because of the armor plate but also because of the expert way Alissende had been wrapping his ribs each day in preparation for battle.

Alissende.

Damien had tried to keep himself from dwelling on her this morn, but he could not forestall the rush of sweet warmth that spilled through him at the thought of her. Since the evening of the ambush against him, they had not shared any intimacies, resolving that he needed to rest as much as possible to help him keep his edge and reserve his strength for the rigors of his combat each day. But it had not kept him from yearning for her anyway every night, and he had refused to forgo the pleasure of holding her until they fell asleep.

At his request, they had already said their farewells this morn so that he might ready himself in mind and body for the contest ahead; she'd left the tent for the spectator scaffolding that was designated for ladies of the combatants, presenting him with a parting gift— her token—before departing. The violet-blue ribbon, chosen, she'd said, because he had once noted that it was the same hue as her eyes, already dangled from the tip of his lance, where it would be seen by one and all as he thundered onto the field.

It was wrong to take pleasure in such trifles, he knew. Allowing softer emotions like those in which he was indulging today oft led to dangerous mistakes on the field. Still, he could not help but wonder if the work of keeping Alissende out of his thoughts was proving a greater disruption, and therefore a greater danger to his success.

The truth was that she occupied his mind almost

constantly, just as she had those years ago, when last he had fought with all his heart and soul to be champion of the tournament at which he was to claim her. Yet he wasn't the same man now that he had been then, despite what Alissende seemed to think. He could not forget it. The harsh reality replayed itself over and over in his mind like a cursed chant: This was entirely different—a battle that needed winning not to claim Alissende but to help protect her for the future she would need to lead without him in a few more months. The future she must live as someone else's wife.

Ignoring the sharp lance of agony that went through him at that thought, Damien gritted his teeth. He shifted to allow Thomas to fasten on the cuisse plates that would protect the top portion of his legs, reminding himself that the outcome with Alissende could be no otherwise. He was a former Templar Knight, an accused heretic who lived in freedom under naught but the flimsy protection of a false Writ of Absolution. That ruse would not hold forever, and when someone discovered the truth, disaster would follow. He would be hauled back into the foul keeping of the Inquisition, along with anyone intimately attached to him.

A wife would be as suspect as her husband in such an instance, for to be united in marriage was to be of one flesh, in the eyes of the Church. He could not imperil Alissende like that, even if she was willing to imperil herself.

In recent weeks he had allowed himself the fantasy of imagining something different. Of envisioning Alissende as his true wife, a woman who loved him enough that she would leave everything behind and go with him to the hills of Scotland, where those who had found themselves damned by the Church could find refuge. Scotland's king, Robert Bruce, had himself suffered papal excommunication, and so he had opened the doors of his kingdom wide to others in that same predicament, including any Templar who managed to evade arrest and make his way across the border.

But he knew he could not ask Alissende to sacrifice so much for him. He wouldn't. He did not think he could bear the pain of her refusing him again if he did.

So he had resolved to do what he could to keep her safe from Hugh. He would defeat her odious cousin on the lists today, stinging the man's pride and hopefully, in the process, ensuring that he would lose the stomach for pursuing Alissende again. It was what Damien did best, after all—fight and win. It was all he could offer her in good conscience, no matter what the growing need inside him desired.

"It is almost time, my lord," Thomas said quietly, stepping back, and Damien glanced up, jolted from his musings for a second time this morn by his squire's low voice. In the minutes he had been lost in thought, Thomas had seen him completely padded and armored for combat, all but for his helm, which would be donned just before the first pass of jousting on horseback.

Damien shook his head, wondering at the number of distracting thoughts he was allowing himself this day. By heaven, he'd better pull himself together and find his focus soon, or all of his plans for giving Hugh the drubbing he deserved would prove for naught, and *he* would be the one forced to withdraw in defeat.

"You have done well, Thomas," Damien said, meeting his squire's reverent gaze. "Your help, now, with my surcoat over all, and we shall be ready to go out and face the crowd that is gathered to witness a grand spectacle this day."

"Aye, my lord," Thomas answered, clearly struggling to contain his excitement.

The youth slipped the cloth garment over Damien's head, tugging and lacing it over his chain mail and armor so that the Ashby emblem hung straight and true. For all his humble beginnings, Damien wore it with pride. It was the same design that was emblazoned on his shield: azure, an ermine chevron between three golden leopard faces.

"Are my lances readied, Thomas?" Damien asked, adjusting the mail portion of the gauntlet on his sword hand one last time.

"Aye, master. They await you with Reginald and Bertram at the end of the lists—three softwood lances, blunted as is required, along with a second tourney sword, your favored destrier, and your shield."

"And the second mount I requested of you—the one not suited for combat but for riding. Is it readied near the field as well?"

"Aye, my lord."

Nodding, Damien ruffled the boy's hair, earning another grin, this one filled with all the exasperation that only youths who yearn more than all else to be full-grown men can show.

"All right then, Thomas," Damien said, smiling back and giving him a wink for good measure. "Gather the sacks of water and our other supplies. It is time to go and ensure that none in attendance today will ever forget the battle that is to come . . . most especially his lordship, Hugh de Valles, the Earl of Harwick."

* * *

Alissende sat in the first row of scaffolding facing the lists, granted that prime position by virtue of the fact that Damien had proven himself the most valiant and skillful venant of the entire tournament this week. She felt a combination of pride and dread in that fact. She should have known that even wounded as he was, Damien would defeat every opponent for the chance to battle with Hugh, but still she could not help worrying at the risk he was taking with himself.

Binding his ribs for him each morning had given her a small sense of comfort; at least she'd known it had been done properly. But it had not quelled her trepidation over what might come from a direct confrontation with her dangerous cousin.

Taking a deep breath, she tried to calm herself, knowing it would do no good to dwell on what she could not control. Instead, she tried to look around and distract herself from her worried thoughts. The scaffolding was nearly full in readiness for the start of this final match.

Yet there were three empty seats on every side around her.

She was becoming rather used to the feeling of being avoided, she decided, for though many of these noble ladies and lords felt no hesitation in cheering Damien's prowess in the lists, their goodwill did not extend to social acceptance of them as a married pair. Hugh's powerful influence at this court had rendered them undesirable in this sense, even with the king's reluctant acknowledgment of their union; none wanted to be the first to appear too friendly to them as a couple.

It was just as well. She'd preferred her solitude to the gossip about the king, the queen, and Piers Gaveston. The upstart Gascony knight had been handed the title to the rich earldom of Cornwall but a year ago, and most of the high-ranking members of court despised him. Further, his constant presence and unnatural closeness with Edward seemed to be causing much discord between the king and his bride, leading to no end of rumor and speculation.

As if in echo to her thoughts, at that moment the trumpet sounded, signaling the approach of King Edward and Queen Isabel; predictably, trailing only a step behind them, was Piers Gaveston. The crowd stood, and though Alissende could not see the royals very clearly from her position, she caught a glimpse or two of the richly robed monarchs before they took their seats and the king waved his hand in signal that the jousting could begin.

A flurry of activity erupted at the end of the field, and with a collective hum of reaction, the spectators fell silent in expectation of the combatants' appearance. The gate that blocked off the tilting lists from the groundlings was pulled open by three of the king's servants. Another trumpet sounded, this one of higher tone, signaling the entrance of the tenant champion, though he was preceded by a herald who stepped into the end of the arena and called out, "His Lordship Hugh de Valles, third Earl of Harwick, riding under the banner of the Valles household in honor of Her Royal Majesty, Queen Isabel!"

At that Hugh came through the gate atop his charger, resplendent in colors borne on both surcoat and shield: gold slashed with three red bars. The crest on his helm—a tiny golden crown draped in crimson ribbon—picked up the same hues, with two plumes, one in each color, waving back from the center of it.

From his lance fluttered a small banner, decorated with the fleur-de-lis of France, given him by the queen.

The crowd roared their approval as he rode by, and if Alissende had not known what a scoundrel he was, she, too, might have been swayed by the impressive sight of him. As it stood, she felt naught but dread and lingering disgust in looking upon him. Pray God that this battle would pass without harm to Damien and with enough shame to Hugh that he would leave off pursuit of her for good.

Then it was Damien's turn. Alissende looked toward the entry gate once more and saw him approach, walking next to his steed. Her heart beat harder at the sight of him. He held his helm, with its blue and gold plumes, in the crook of his arm, and as the sun glinted off his hair, her breath caught. He was incredibly, achingly handsome. A warrior of stunning power and deadly skill.

As he put on his helm and swung up onto his mount, his herald stepped forward into the arena and called out, "Sir Damien de Ashby, riding under the Ashby banner, for the honor of the Lady Alissende of Surrey!"

Damien thundered through the gates at the call, and the stands erupted in shouts of approval, some of the spectators who remembered him from tournaments years ago calling out, "Archangel! Archangel!" as he rode past. From his lance fluttered the violet-blue ribbon she had gifted him with this morn, and her heart seemed to skip a beat when he looked toward the stands and tipped it in her direction as he rode past.

Damien continued to the end of the list, pausing, as Hugh had done, to make homage to the king and queen before wheeling around his mount and riding back

down the lists to take up his position of readiness at the
end nearest the entrance gate.

And then, amidst more shouts and cheers, the herald
dropped his arm in signal, and it began.

Chapter 17

With the roar of the crowd undulating over the field, Damien slipped the end of his lance into the rest built into his armor, nudged his heels into his steed, and set off at a pounding pace toward Hugh. With naught but an open field before them, it was up to the combatants to aim their mounts at each other and be sure not to veer away, lest a point be taken from the one who faltered.

He would not falter.

The sound of the crowd faded as if in the far distance as he aimed his lance, his concentration focused upon the center of Hugh's breastplate. Unhorsing Hugh was the goal, but doing so would mean far less if Damien didn't shatter his lance against Hugh in the process.

They came together with a splintering crash, Damien expertly slowing his steed an instant after the impact and pulling around to judge the damage done to his opponent. Hugh remained seated, but the lance he held in his hand was still whole, having only grazed Damien's shoulder, while Damien's lance had shattered down near the grip from the force of collision against Hugh's chest.

He had won two points with this pass, he realized, feeling a surge of fierce elation as he lifted his hand to the cheering crowd and rode back to his position at the end of the lists. Lifting his visor, he accepted the skin of water Thomas offered, drinking while Bernard took the shattered lance from him and handed him a new one.

"You did well, my lord," Thomas said, rubbing Damien's mount with a dampened cloth. "Two more like that and the battle on foot will almost not matter."

"We shall see," Damien answered, glad to realize that his ribs did not ache as of yet. "That pass is sure to have enraged him, and Hugh is not accustomed to losing. I doubt he will allow it to go to the full three passes without using some means, be they honest or cunning, to try to sway the contest to his side."

Thomas looked so stricken at the suggestion that Damien smiled and said before locking his visor down again, "I will keep watch, Thomas, do not fear. Perhaps I can thwart him enough to make him show his true colors before the king and all the witnesses of court, so that none will be deceived longer about the kind of man he is."

"It is time for the second pass, Sir Damien."

The reminder came from Reginald, who gestured to the end of the list just beyond them. Far across the way, Hugh was coming into position on his mount, a new lance also clutched in his grip, though he had not broken the one before. Damien squinted, trying to see him more clearly. He thought he'd seen the glint of metal on the tip; knowing Hugh it was more than likely, even considering the tournament rule for using blunted weapons. But it was useless to ruminate on it, as the heat of the sun rippled over the field, obscuring the clarity of his sight.

He would know soon enough, he thought grimly, as he wheeled his horse into position again, setting his own lance in the rest and awaiting the signal.

It came in the space of another heartbeat. Digging his heels into his mount's sides, Damien found himself hurtling toward Hugh again, felt the crashing impact as his lance shattered once more against Hugh's shield . . .

And felt a stabbing sensation in his side before he felt himself suddenly hurtling through the air.

The force of his collision with the ground stole his breath, but he forced himself to roll and stand even through the burning pain flooding him, trained as he had been during countless battles in the Holy Land and Cyprus to continue fighting, lest your enemy use your moment of weakness as the opening needed to take your life.

Still, it took him a moment to regain his bearings. His helm had been knocked away with the fall, and in addition to the ringing in his ears, everything seemed to slow down to a strange, crawling pace. He saw his mount regain its feet and trot down the lists, and he watched Hugh, also helmless, struggling to stand. Damien had managed to unhorse him as well, he realized with a flash of dark pleasure, though by fair means, not foul, as had been done to him.

And foul it was, he realized, as he glanced down, aware in that moment that his side armor had been pierced by something sharp, right at the area of ribs he had fortuitously decided to protect this morn.

The bastard had used a sharpened lance against him, in violation of all the rules of a *pas d'armes*.

Another quick look and touch assured him that he'd sustained no real damage. If he had been wounded by the lance, it had been only slightly. In that regard Hugh had made a far graver error than he had in cheating to begin with, because now Damien wasn't only angry; he wanted blood.

With a growl, Damien strode the fifteen paces between them, deliberately alerting Hugh to his approach and giving the bastard time to draw his own blade before Damien sent his crashing down on Hugh's upraised shield. He kept the blows raining down on his opponent, hard and steady, knowing it would be all Hugh could do to defend himself from them. Hugh's expression, determined at first, soon shifted to a look of fear as it became apparent that he would not—that he could not—win against Damien.

Still, to try and cover his weakness, he offered taunts when he could, hoping to distract Damien and allow himself an opening to strike.

"Did you honestly think I would allow you to keep Alissende for yourself?" Hugh breathed heavily between sword strokes. "You aren't worth the dirt that will soak up your life's blood when I'm through with you, Ashby."

The insult needed no response from Damien. It would be far more useful to let his actions speak for him.

He took another three swings at Hugh with his blade, just to keep him off balance, and then circled him, waiting for the best moment to make his final strike. As he did he reminded himself to remain calm and focused, and not to allow his emotions to influence his movements. Discipline was nearly as important as skill in battle, and he could not forget it.

Vaguely, he noted the swirl of color behind Hugh. It was the royal pavilion, and Damien knew the king and queen sat in judgment of this combat. But the clouds of dust kicked up by the fight obscured much else. He heard naught but the pounding of blood in his ears and tasted the grit of the dirt, along with the metallic tang of blood in his mouth . . . saw naught but the pale and desperate face of his enemy across from him.

And then his opening came.

Hugh lifted his blade out to the side in preparation to throw himself at Damien, and in that instant, Damien stepped forward in a move practiced a thousand times with his Templar brethren but one that was almost unknown in this part of the world; shifting his sword smoothly from his right hand to his left, he jerked upward with it, slicing the underside of Hugh's forearm at the same time that he threw his weight forward and slammed his elbow with a satisfying crack right across Hugh's face.

Hugh went down like lead, flat on his back. His sword popped from his grip to thud uselessly onto the dirt. Blood poured from his nose and stained the sleeve of the fine white shirt he wore beneath his armor plates, as Damien shifted in one fluid motion to widen his stance and swing the tip of his blade to within an inch of his rival's exposed neck.

"Honor has been served, and this combat will cease!"

That sudden shout came from King Edward, Damien realized, when against every instinct he forced himself to lift his gaze away from the man pinned at the end of his blade. The king had leaped to his feet, and he appeared aghast at how near a death-combat this proclaimed joust of peace had become.

Damien's arm quivered with the desire to follow through with the last part of the sequence for this move, to drive the blade point straight into Hugh's throat and make an end of this. But the king had commanded that they cease the battle, and whether or not Hugh had cheated, this was supposed to be a *pas d'armes*. Damien could do no less than obey his sovereign's command.

Pulling his sword up and away from Hugh's throat, Damien turned to face the sovereign; he sheathed his blade and stood at attention, while Hugh scrambled up from the dirt, cursing, to stand next to him, holding his injured arm. Only then did Damien notice the silence that had spread over the lists and scaffolds, and for the first time he saw the looks of shock, worry, and blatant interest that were directed toward them.

"Honor has been served on both sides!" the king called out, "and as We have no desire to see any of Our subjects maim each other in a joust of peace, We will say that this tournament is concluded, with the prize to be divided equally between Lord Harwick and Sir Damien."

"Nay, sire!"

The call had come from Hugh, and Damien turned his head to look at his rival, thinking either that he had lost his mind, or Hugh was up to no good. Another moment more proved that Damien's mind was as sound as ever.

"I would beg Your Majesty's retraction of that decision, for I assert that Sir Damien used devilish trickery in attempting to best me in combat. In fact—"

"You lie!"

Damien swung around to face Hugh again, reaching his hand across to rest it on his sword hilt, in preparation for drawing it again and finishing the task his king had bid him leave off moments ago. "It is *you* who violated the rules of *pas d'armes* by using a sharpened lance during the joust!"

As Damien leveled that accusation, Hugh stumbled toward his blade, which still lay in the dust of the lists, taking it up and turning back to Damien with a look of bitterness on his face that Damien had seen before, in the expressions of men who could not accept defeat.

Such men usually ended up dead, he had found, and he could not say that he would be sorry to see that probability played out in such a way now.

"Put away your blades, gentlemen, lest you risk all, for We have forbid any further combat between you."

This time the king's voice rang out in royal ire, and a few of the ladies in the lists nearest the silk-draped scaffolding reacted to the thought that many were likely harboring at the moment, that one or both of the combatants might not comply and might therefore end this day with naught for his troubles but his head upon a pike at the city gates.

Hugh glared again at Damien before sheathing his sword, and though his arm itched to do otherwise, Damien also forced himself to release his grip on his hilt.

When they both faced the royal box once more, the king addressed them together.

"These are serious charges you have leveled. What proofs have either of you to offer in support of your claims?"

Hugh said nothing, having no evidence except that of his word, but Damien glanced to Thomas, who stood at the end of the lists. Well-trained squire that he was, Thomas had run onto the field after his master had been unhorsed to retrieve the steed and any lances that might have been dropped or broken in the combat. Clearly, he had been quicker than Hugh's man, for he now held up the sharpened lance that Hugh had used against Damien and grinned as he nodded affirmation of the booty.

"Your Majesty," Damien said, bowing his head to show his respect before meeting his sovereign's gaze again. "I have the sharpened lance Lord Harwick used against me to show as proof of my claim."

A ripple of gasps and murmuring erupted amongst the spectators as he finished by nodding to the end of the lists and saying, "My squire holds it, having retrieved it from the field during the combat. He awaits but your command to bring it forward in evidence."

As the rumble of gossip swelled anew, Damien's gaze caught on a movement in the scaffolding—a woman dressed in a flutter of deep blue trimmed in gold, her glossy, dark tresses swept up in waves intertwined with ribbon and flowers.

Alissende.

She was making her way closer to him, moving past other courtiers and excusing herself as she stepped by several earls and their wives, approaching the edge of the arena nearest to him. Her beautiful face was filled with worry, and he met her gaze for an instant, trying to offer her encouragement.

"What you claim proves nothing except the lengths to which you will go to play your trickeries on this court," Hugh grated, drawing Damien's gaze again even as Hugh gestured toward Thomas. "It is Ashby's own lance the boy holds, and none of mine."

"I am beginning to think that every word that comes from your mouth is a falsehood, my lord," Damien said in a voice that was quiet, yet deep enough to carry to the king and those around him.

"I would not deem it a falsehood were I you, Ashby, to hear me say that your hours are numbered. You dare much to insult me as you have, from the day I learned of your presence in England, a corrupt Templar Knight tainted by heresy, impudent enough to take my promised bride as your own, against all the precepts of the Brotherhood to which you professed to belong . . . against our king's command, and against God Himself!"

Damien heard the crowd react with a renewed surge of exclamations, but it faded to a blur of sound as he spun sideways and in one, blinding movement gripped Hugh by the throat for just long enough to mutter into his face, "But that my king has forbidden me use of a weapon against you right now, you would feel the cold steel of my blade between your ribs. Yet you will answer later, rest assured."

And then he thrust Hugh away with such force that Hugh stumbled backward, kept from launching at Damien again only by the grip of the guards the king had ordered dispatched to the arena. Another two guards took hold of Damien's arms, though unlike Hugh, he did not struggle against them and make a spectacle of himself.

"Not another word will be spoken by either one of you unless We command it, nor will you come within ten paces of each other until you are given leave to do so!" King Edward glared at them both, clearly pushed beyond his limits this day. "Though it is Our duty to see this quarrel honorably resolved, We admit to being sorely tempted to see you both clapped in irons and cast into the dungeons here at Odiham until you have regained some sense."

His regal glower passed from Hugh, to Damien, and then back to Hugh again. "Provided that neither of you breaks Our command in the next few moments, We are prepared to offer a solution to this dilemma." He directed the full force of the cold, Plantagenet stare upon them, asking in a voice dripping with sarcasm, "Have We your leave to continue?"

"Aye, sire," Damien said, bowing his head, the response and action echoed in turn by Hugh.

"Good." Directing his gaze around the assembled courtiers and combatants, the king called out loudly enough for one and all to hear, "Our proclamation, then, is this: You, Hugh de Valles, Earl of Harwick, and you, Sir Damien de Ashby, will meet on the lists at Guildford Castle in Surrey one fortnight from today, to duel under the watchful eyes of Our royal judges. The combat will be for the purpose of honor and the right to claim the gold and gemmy sparrow-hawk that was to be the prize for this, the first tournament of the season. The joust will be with sword, axe, and dagger, and will conclude in two rounds of each. Do you accept the terms?"

The ice in his gaze as he stared at them both made clear that their answer had better come swiftly and be in the affirmative. It did, and it was.

"We are relieved," he drawled. "Should either of you fail to appear at the appointed time, you will be deemed to have forfeited the combat and with it, all honor and prizes." He pursed his lips, saying more quietly, for them alone, "If you believe you can maintain control of yourselves, you may attend the closing feast We are hosting this eve. If not, then We suggest you take your meal elsewhere, to avoid spending the next fourteen days manacled and tucked away somewhere suitably dark, unpleasant, and away from Our sight."

After letting that bit of advice sink in for a moment, the king raised his hands and addressed the crowd again. "This combat is finished until a fortnight hence. You may all depart to prepare for the eve's festivities."

With the sounding of trumpets, a flurry of servants, and the flick of his royal robes, the king reached out his hand to the queen and escorted her from the silk pavilion and the tournament area altogether.

And then it fell quiet.

The guards still held onto Hugh and Damien, and the crowd seemed reluctant to disperse when some excitement might still be had. But Damien had had enough. He had proven his point with Hugh and made clear to all, noble or common, that he was not a man to be trifled with. Alissende would not need to fear that any knight or lord would mistake the kind of protection she would know with him as her husband. But Hugh's scheming had deprived Damien of one aspect of this day's combat that he had hoped to gain . . . one last moment that he had intended to take to dispel some of the nightmares that troubled him and Alissende still.

There was naught in the king's command to stop him from enjoying it now.

After a few murmured words to the guards, who promptly released him, Damien strode back toward the end of the lists, where Reginald, Bernard, and Thomas waited, taking from Bernard the lance he had used for the entrance ceremony—the one with Alissende's violet-blue ribbon attached. Carefully plucking the strip of silk free, he held it clasped in his palm and turned back toward the field. As if in benediction of his plan, the sun broke through the clouds once more at that instant, bathing him in golden light as he faced the scaffolding full of spectators.

Then Damien lifted his face to meet Alissende's gaze among all those who stood there, and giving her a slow, sensual smile, he began to cross the distance between them with determined strides.

Alissende watched Damien's approach, her entire body going hot and cold at the same time, tingles spreading from the top of her head down to her toes. *What was this about?* . . .

Heaven help her, but he looked exactly as he had on that day long ago, when he had won the tournament and come striding forth to claim her favor as his prize. And astoundingly, the people around her right now were reacting just as they had then; the men initiated the applause of stamping on the scaffold, while the women murmured at the magnificent sight of him striding across the field toward her.

But as before, he had eyes only for her. He was coming to exchange the token she had given him for a kiss, by his action showing everyone that he favored her above all other women. The import of that insight startled her, but on the heels of it came another equally staggering realization.

There was no reason for him to be doing this right now.

Even for the sake of appearances in their feigned union, it made no sense. In the eyes of those who had judged the tournament, he had not actually won, and there was no expectation that he—or Hugh, for that matter—would make claim to any lady in attendance, as the declared champion traditionally would.

Unless he was approaching her like this simply because he *wanted* to.

By all the saints . . .

"My lady."

Alissende almost jumped. Damien's voice echoed close to her, both affectionate and persistent, and she realized that he had attained her position on the raised scaffolding. He stood just below her on the ground of the lists, reaching up to her, her ribbon fluttering in his grip.

"This is yours, lady, returned in all honor." The hint of a shadow flickered through his eyes just before he added, "For the price of a kiss, and your acceptance of my devotion this day."

Her heart seemed to beat harder in her chest, and her throat tightened. Oh, God, this was the very moment when she had turned away from him five years ago. The moment that had haunted her for every day, every breath, it seemed, ever since. Her gaze locked with

Damien's, and she felt the enormity of it all washing over her. He was offering her another chance, placing his pride in her hands once more, to do with as she would.

This time, she vowed, she would not fail him.

Her lips trembled as she tried to return his gentle smile. Leaning forward, she reached to take the silk ribbon from him with fingers that seemed to have gone numb, though she felt a jolt of delicious sensation in the instant that his hand brushed against hers.

But before she could straighten up again, he caught her chin, and her own eyes widened to realize that the ice blue of his had deepened to sapphire.

"Not so quickly, lady. You have forgotten something."

"What?" she murmured.

"My kiss."

He drew her closer to him with the gentle pressure of his touch, taking her lips with such tender passion that she thought her knees might buckle beneath her. In blind panic, she reached out to clutch his shoulders, and the unexpected approval of the crowd grew louder as he lifted her at the waist, clearing the scaffolding with her to set her down beside him. When she looked up at him after righting herself, another shock coursed through her at the intensity she saw in his gaze.

"Now we've one last bit to cover," he said quietly. "Do you accept my devotion, Alissende?"

His eyes were fixed upon her, loving her with a look, if such was possible, and a very pleasurable shiver coursed through her. But she needed to keep her head; Damien had performed convincingly for audiences in the past with public kisses and shows of affection.

"Perhaps," she whispered, reaching up to brush the hair back from his temple with her fingers. "I suppose it depends."

"On what?" he demanded.

"On whether or not you truly mean it."

An enigmatic look swept over his face before it was replaced by a smile. "The answer to that is better shown, I think, than spoken."

Before she could say anything further, he took her hand and led her from the field, releasing her only long enough to approach his squire near the end of the lists and murmur something to him. Returning to her, he lifted her to sit upon another horse Bernard was holding in wait for them there. Then he swung astride behind her, wrapped his arm around her middle, and set their mount to a lively gallop . . .

Riding with her off the lists, away from the knowing stares of the stamping, cheering multitude that filled the scaffolding around the field.

Chapter 18

Alissende felt a lurch of surprise as Damien cantered with her down the path of silk pavilions leading to their own . . . and then rode by the gold-and-blue tent they shared. She twisted halfway in his arms as they passed it, glancing behind him for an instant before swiveling her gaze up to meet his.

"I hate to mention the obvious, Damien," she said, "but our pavilion is back there. And what is also peculiar, your squire Thomas is trailing us several lengths behind. Where are we going, pray tell, and why?"

He offered her naught but a smile, the expression sending a melting sensation through her at the same time that it made her want to kick her heel back into his shin.

"Patience, Alissende." He kissed the tip of her nose. "You shall see."

She made a disgruntled sound that seemed to only

make him smile more broadly before she faced forward again.

"I recall that you used to enjoy surprises," he murmured, and the warmth of his breath brushing over her ear sent a tingle through her.

"Perhaps." She squirmed, her hips shifting against his groin as she sought a more comfortable position in the saddle. Her unexpected movement made his breath catch, and his arm flexed against her belly, even as she added somewhat crossly, "But more oft than not that was because I was the one doing the surprising."

"You have not lost your touch in that, lady," he said on a laughing groan. "Pray take pity and cease wriggling like that. We're almost there."

They had left the main path a few moments earlier and passed through a wooded area before entering a cool, green glade bordered by a pond that sparkled in the sun.

"This is it," he announced, reining in their mount.

"What?"

"Our destination."

She waited for him to elaborate, but he remained silent, helping her dismount before he began to stride away. Frustration bloomed as she glanced back toward the wood and then glared at him again. "Just where are you going, Damien de Ashby—and where is Thomas?"

Damien did not seem to notice her irritation, glancing over his shoulder and telling her as he approached the water, "I am going to bathe away the dirt of battle. And Thomas is standing guard at my command, just beyond the copse of trees we passed through earlier, to ensure that we are not disturbed."

"Disturbed from *what?*" she demanded, putting her hands on her hips. This time her voice held enough of an edge, apparently, that Damien paused and turned around, smiling, though he was shaking his head.

"Ah, Alissende, try not to fret so. It is nothing disagreeable. I've arranged for us to share a light repast, away from prying eyes, if that meets with your approval. You'll find the basket and a large blanket right over there"—he pointed to a mossy area beneath a towering oak that spread its branches in a lush canopy above—"and if you'd consent to arrange the things while I clean up, I promise to show you my appreciation most thoroughly when I am through."

She just gaped at him. "You mean you planned this ahead of time? But how could you be certain of the battle's outcome today? Or that you—or that I would even—?"

He shrugged. "I did not doubt my ability to match Hugh on the lists. It was your reaction afterward that I was not certain about." He grinned. "I am glad I wagered correctly on that point."

His teeth flashed white, and the expression on his face was both playful and devastatingly handsome. But she had no time to form a reply, for at that moment he turned back toward the water and started pulling off pieces of his armor-plates and clothing, dropping them to the ground next to him. In the space of a few heartbeats he stood completely naked at the edge of the pond, the sunlight washing over him in a play of gold and shadows.

Then, reaching into the long fronds near the water for something—a chunk of soap, she guessed when he straightened—he stretched his arms up and dove in, the sight of his powerful body as he moved nothing less than breathtaking.

She had actually stopped breathing, she realized, as she'd watched him disrobe; now she was forced to take in a deep breath as he resurfaced, giving a shout and brushing the wetness from his face before shaking his head to release a spray of glittering drops.

"It's cold," he called up to her, laughing.

"Do not linger too long, then." She smiled back at him in spite of herself. Something fluttered to life inside her when she looked at him, and the tingling up her spine made her wish she could simply stand there and watch him all day. But he had asked her to ready the basket he had prepared, and she saw no reason not to comply with his request.

Trying to keep her thoughts focused on the task at hand, she made a quick task of spreading out the blanket before preparing to empty the contents of the basket. But when she opened the woven lid, she frowned. What in heaven's name . . .

Goose feathers?

A handful of long, silky plumes rested on top of what appeared to be a set of men's garments. A bag of ripe strawberries was nestled inside the basket as well, it was true, but there was no explaining the clump of mint leaves or the small pot of what seemed to be some kind of liniment she discovered at the very bottom of the basket. The only other consumable item she found was a sack of red wine. The rest was mystifying.

She'd knelt on the edge of the blanket and was readying to twist around and call to Damien for an explanation when he rushed up behind her in a laughing ambush, grabbing her and tumbling her onto the blanket before rolling half atop her. He had dried himself off, it seemed, but apart from the warm sheen of sunlight burnishing his body, he was wearing . . . nothing.

She gave a little yelping gasp as he began unfastening the laces of her gown. Pressing her palms flat against his chest, she pushed, managing to move away from him just far enough that she could scowl up into his face.

"I demand that you stop, Damien de Ashby, until you explain what all of *this* is"—she gestured wildly to the contents of the basket, scattered next to them—"and just what exactly you are doing."

Damien did stop for a moment then, taking in a steadying breath and realizing as he did so that he was enjoying this far more than he had a right to. But he couldn't help himself. She was so beautiful. Even indignant as she was—perhaps especially because of it—she entranced him. Her cheeks flushed a shade of rose no flower on earth could match for loveliness, and the delicate color highlighted the spark in her eyes and accented the glossy sweep of her dark hair.

Lifting his hand away from her back to stroke his fingertips along the side of her face, he smiled, experiencing a surge of unaccountable feeling as he looked upon her, something that welled up from a place he'd thought long dead and destroyed. But it was there, he realized in shock, pulsing in wonderful, glorious life. An emotion he'd thought never to feel again.

Sweet angels preserve him . . .

Doing his best to quell that sudden and astounding

awareness, he swallowed hard and tried to steer his attention back to the more lighthearted banter they had been enjoying before.

"What I am doing," he answered, his voice hoarse with all he was suppressing, "is attempting to disrobe you, Alissende. With your permission, of course. It will be difficult to do what else I have planned otherwise."

"But—out *here?*" she whispered, sounding somewhat choked. Her eyes, though, sparkled with that light he remembered well—the impetuous, fun-loving glint that had entranced him from the very first time he'd seen her.

Damien tried to grin again, only to discover that his mouth wasn't cooperating. The strange, wobbling sensation in his lips made the expression that resulted lopsided, he was sure, in a way that was most distressing. It took him a moment to pull himself together enough to speak again. He would concentrate only upon the pleasure to be had right now, he told himself. That and nothing more. He had to, God help him, for if he permitted himself to dwell on the inconceivable— that he had allowed himself to fall in love with Alissende all over again—it would drive him mad.

Clearing his throat, he made the effort to sound far more normal than he was feeling. "We used to meet for our trysts long ago in the meadow beyond Seton Castle, sheltered by naught but the canopy of sky, sun, and a few trees. I recall those moments . . . fondly to say the least." He managed to quirk his brow at her in what he hoped was a wicked way. "Aside from that, Thomas is on guard, and I have a vow to fulfill. You will remember that I promised to extract triple payment from you, once I was able, for the tender torments you played upon me in our tent seven nights ago."

She paused, smiling. "That you did."

"And you admitted to trembling with dread at the prospect of it."

"Aye, I do recall saying that." Dropping her gaze to his mouth, she brushed her thumb over his bottom lip, nearly undoing him with the innocent eroticism of the gesture.

"You are trembling now, are you not?" he asked huskily.

Alissende met his gaze once more, stealing his breath with the look in the violet-blue depths of her eyes. She swallowed. "Aye. But no more than you are, I think, my lord."

"If I am, it is with desire for you, Alissende," he whispered, abandoning all words, then, as he tipped his head to kiss her again.

Her mouth was soft. So soft and gentle beneath his. She tasted of honey and apples, and when she used the tip of her tongue to trace the outline of his lips, it unleashed a fierce wave of yearning that spilled through him and pooled in the heavy, demanding length of his erection.

He took her mouth more fully, wanting her to feel the need she stirred in him, even as he reached behind her to finish unlacing her gown. It slipped off her shoulders, and without breaking their kiss, he eased it down, hooking his thumbs under the straps of her chemise at the same time and pulling both garments down further, over her hips, until they slid off her completely.

She was as naked as he was, now. He watched her face, reveled in the sense of combined pleasure and shyness she seemed to feel in being freed of the constraints of her clothing. By all that was holy, she had no idea how beautiful she was, he thought, his heart lurching. Ah, but she was perfection to him, and his hand trembled with the desire to stroke his palm over her smooth skin, all pink and cream, warmed in the gentle gilding of the sunlight.

Yet he did not touch her yet. Nay, he withheld that pleasure from himself for the moment, instead leaning up on one elbow and cupping her face as he kissed her still. He lavished his attention on her mouth, tasting her, wanting her to feel the fullness of his desire for her. Breaking free of that sweet caress took almost all of his will, but at last he shifted to the side, nibbling more kisses along the edge of her jaw, toward the tender spot just beneath her ear, and reveling in her low moan of pleasure.

Forcing himself to pull back, to slow down and make this last, Damien reached for the bag of strawberries. He took one out, and with a kind of teasing nonchalance, half sat up and murmured, "I'm hungry—aren't you?" Without waiting for her answer, he took a bite of the plump fruit he held, grinning at the look of shock that swept over her beautiful face with his abrupt abandonment of their love-play.

She batted at him in the next breath, laughing and pushing herself up to her elbows. She reached for the bag as he eased back down beside her on the blanket, managing to quip at him as she did, "I think I would like to try a berry or two . . . though I fail to see why I needed to be divested of my clothing in order to do it."

"Your lack of clothing has nothing to do with the strawberries," he murmured, his gaze affixed to her, watching the sensuous display as she bit into the berry's juicy flesh.

"Nay?" She kept her gaze locked to his as well, clearly enjoying their erotically charged banter as much as he was, as she finished the first fruit and began another.

He shook his head. "The berries are for nourishment alone, to sustain you through what comes next . . . which is the part that required you to be unclothed."

As he finished speaking, he reached for the pot of cinnamon-infused liniment. "We will begin with this," he said, unfastening the lid and dipping one finger into the smooth, sweet-smelling unguent, "as it must come before the mint leaves or the feathers."

"And what *is* that?" she murmured playfully, nodding to the clay pot before tipping her head back and to the side with a breathy sigh as he lightly stroked his liniment-covered finger down her throat to the hollow between her breasts, following the trail with gentle kisses.

He dipped his finger again, this time lavishing his attention on her delightfully puckered, pink nipples before answering, "It is a balm I discovered when I traveled through the Holy Land, most often used for easing sore muscles and bringing a flow of blood to the surface of the skin to aid in healing. Until now, that is," he finished, smiling.

"Mmmmmm . . . it feels wonderful. And warm. Warmer than the sun," she said, lying back onto the blanket at his urging.

"That is from the cinnamon. It is a mild warmth, though, is it not?"

She nodded, clearly relaxing under his ministrations—which was just what he wanted . . . at this point, anyway.

"Close your eyes now, Alissende," he commanded softly, and as she did, he trailed his finger down her belly . . . closer, closer . . .

Her delighted gasp when his finger slid gently between the delicate folds of her most intimate flesh almost brought him to completion then and there. She was wet already, silken to the touch, and she writhed with sensuous abandon under his ministrations. His erection throbbed mercilessly. He swallowed hard and reminded himself to breathe, calling upon all of his self-control not to end this tender torment without further delay in the way that would be most fulfilling to both of them.

But not yet, he thought. Nay, not yet . . .

Setting the pot aside, he grabbed a few of the mint leaves and took one of the feathers—the longest and softest of the bunch. Crushing the mint between the fingers and thumb of his other hand, he retraced the path he had taken with the unguent; Alissende's gasp of pleasure, as the cooling mint offset the liniment's warmth, sent renewed surges of desire shooting from his tingling fingertips to settle in the raging, heavy ache of his groin. But still he waited, knowing there was more, wanting to love her in all the ways he'd envisioned for so long . . .

Her body rose into his touch shamelessly by the time he applied the silky edges of the feather, her nipples like sweet, ripe raspberries, tightening to points that begged to be kissed as he stroked the tip of the plume over them. But he held off a little longer, sweeping it slowly around the lush curve of each breast and down to the juncture of her thighs, until Alissende's breath came in a shallow rasp, and she arched her back, lifting herself toward him.

"Please, Damien," she moaned. "Do not make me wait longer. Touch me . . . make love to me, please . . ."

Her throaty plea broke the last threads of his control, and with a low growl of surrender he bent toward her, cupping his palms around the soft fullness of each breast in turn and taking her mouth in a soul-searing kiss. She threaded her fingers into his hair with another gasping moan, pulling him close to her as he trailed his lips down her throat to lavish his attention on her nipples, suckling at the delicate buds before shifting lower. His palms splayed over her smooth, sun-warmed skin as he traveled a path down the gentle curve of her belly, knowing that he never wanted to stop. That he could not stop. Nay, not if his life depended on it.

"You are so beautiful, Alissende," he murmured between kisses, breathing in her sweet scent, tasting the heat of her skin, along with the traces of mint and cinnamon. But as he reached the apex of her thighs, she stiffened slightly, murmuring his name as her hands tightened in his hair. He paused long enough to tip his face up to murmur, "Nay, lady, do not ask that I cease, for I long to pleasure you in this way as we did long ago. Will you let me?"

She had lifted her head from the blanket to look at him, and she was so stunning in her passion, in the need he had incited in her, that his breath caught as he waited for her answer. And so when she nodded hesitantly as she gazed into his eyes, he whispered his thanks through a throat tight with emotion. Then with a tender, firm touch, he slid his palms down to her thighs, easing them apart.

The beautiful sight made his erection throb anew, and he was forced to shift his lower body in order to maintain some level of comfort. The sheen of her arousal teased him from within the swollen, pink folds, and he tormented himself with the delicacy of her spread before his gaze, until he could resist no longer. Stroking his fingers up that sensitive flesh, he paused to caress the plump bud at its apex, and Alissende gasped, writhing against his hand. Her body rose to his touch and melted into him as he tasted her at last, lavishing tender kisses interspersed with gentle strokes of his tongue along her silken woman's flesh.

It was like a taste of heaven. Aching with the pleasure of it, Damien continued his tender ministrations until he felt her tensing, heard her breathing cease on a gasp, and then experienced the almost unbearable satisfaction of watching her crest and splinter into an orgasm so powerful he feared that she might have gone senseless from the force of it sweeping through her.

He paused for a moment in the aftermath, but she did not move. His heart pounded and his groin was demanding and heavy, as he finally lifted himself up, cradling her against him and stroking her face to murmur, "Alissende . . . lady, open your eyes, so that I know you are well."

A breath later she looked at him, her lashes half-closed and her mouth curved into a smile. "Oh, I am well, Damien. Splendid, in fact."

He smiled back at her. "I am glad."

"However, you cannot be feeling quite so wonderful, I'd warrant." As she spoke those words softly, Alissende rolled toward him, pressing her thigh with gentle persistence into his hard swelling and eliciting another groan that he could not keep back in time. She rubbed against him again, and he closed his eyes, this time rising to her touch as she whispered, "And I think we should remedy that as soon as possible."

She pressed her palm to his cheek and kissed him, then, the sweetness and absolute love in that gesture undoing him in a way he knew he'd never recover from. "Be one with me, Damien," she whispered, "as we were meant to be, before all else intervened."

It was that gentle entreaty that did it finally, delivering the blow that cracked the last of the armor he had welded around his heart. Something splintered wide open inside him, flooding him with warmth and tenderness and *need*, by heaven. Need like he had never known before, more than physical, to love Alissende, to cherish and worship her with everything he possessed. Murmuring her name, Damien capitulated to the emotions swelling through him, half-rolling atop her, slanting his mouth over hers, and letting all of what he was feeling spill into that kiss.

She pulled him closer, and he tasted her tears on her lips . . . heard her sweet cry of surrender as her thighs opened to cradle his hips and her body arched up, ready to accept him.

Damien's heart pounded in his chest as he pushed himself up to balance on his forearms. He stared down at Alissende, so beautiful, so precious to him. Her eyes were half-closed in passion as she met his gaze, loving him with her expression, and without waiting any longer, he buried himself deep within her. It was incredible, the sensation hot, wet, and magnificent beyond all imagining. He cupped her face in his palms, pressing kisses over her eyelids and cheeks before taking her mouth again, the delicious agony of thrusting into her slowly, again and again, sweeping through him in powerful, rising waves.

"My God, Alissende, you feel so wonderful, so perfect," he said hoarsely, feeling the swell of orgasm building to a knot of sensation at the base of his spine, driving him to thrust harder and faster.

In response, she arched up into him, gasping, "Ah . . . I cannot bear how good it is, Damien—the feel of you inside me . . ."

With another moan, this one of pure ecstasy, Alissende climaxed again, her slick heat clenching rhythmically around him, and the feeling of her release set off his own. Pulling back, Damien thrust once more, deeply and fully. The force of his climax ripped through him, making him cry out and blinding his vision; he felt as if his hold on his senses slipped, and all that remained was that flawless connection between himself and this astounding woman . . . the exquisite joining of his body, heart, and soul with Alissende, as it had been meant to be from the beginning.

Spent, he slumped over in exhaustion, trying to shift sideways enough not to crush her. His breath came in heaving gasps, and with what seemed his last ounce of strength, he rolled most of the way off her, freeing her from the bulk of his weight, though his legs remained entangled with hers, with the blanket wound around them. Aye, they were pinned together, like it or not, he realized as he slowly regained his normal awareness of the world around him. And it was marvelous.

He was facing Alissende, and after a few moments more he dared a peek from beneath his arm to look at her. She lay on her back still, eyes closed, looking replete and even more beautiful, if that was possible, than she had while they'd been making love. But as he gazed upon her, her mouth edged up into a mischievous smile, and he knew then that she was aware of his watching her.

"Vixen," he murmured, smiling at her even more impish expression when those lashes fluttered up. He reached out and brushed back a silky tendril of hair from her brow, searching out her gaze and feeling a pleasant lurching sensation in his chest when he found it and she smiled more deeply at him.

"Beware, lady," he said with mock gravity, "lest I be coaxed into taming your wayward nature with my own lascivious methods. It would only take a touch or two to begin bringing you into control again. Aye, a slight caress here, perhaps"—he brushed his fingers over the tip of one of her breasts—"or better yet, right here." This time he stroked his hand down her belly to tickle the soft curls between her legs, prompting her to squeal and twist away, laughing.

"You see? I already have you leaping to my commands," he teased, though the laughter ebbed from his voice as she caught his hand in her own, raising it to her lips to press a soft kiss to his fingers. A throb of emotion rocked through him then, choking off any further words as he met her gaze.

"I love you, Damien."

Alissende spoke softly, the sincerity of those words

clear in her expressive eyes as she lay next to him, so beautiful and trusting. His heart swelled, the longing to tell her how he felt rising up until he knew he could suppress it no more. That the world and fate seemed aligned against them did not mean he must keep silent about what was at work inside of him right now. About what she had wrought in him with the sweetness of her love . . .

"Alissende, there is something I need to—"

"My lord! I beg pardon, Sir Damien, but I must speak with you!"

The voice rang out from the edge of the clearing. It was Thomas, and there was a kind of urgency in his tone that set Damien's instincts on alert. He called for his squire to wait, even as he sat up and rolled swiftly off the blanket, murmuring to Alissende to dress quickly.

After donning the fresh breeches and shirt that he'd retrieved from the basket, Damien slipped on his boots, and after a glance back to ensure that Alissende had had time to pull her clothing back on in some semblance of order, he called out to Thomas to approach. The lad did, but he was accompanied by Reginald, who appeared distraught or, at the very least, nervous.

"Reginald—what is the matter, man?"

"Many pardons, my lord." Reginald looked ill at ease with his mission. "I came seeking you at the insistence of a visitor to court who demands to see you."

"A visitor?" Damien echoed, frowning. "Who is it?"

"A large man, my lord—a knight, near as broad and as tall as you. He approached me in stealth back at the stables, saying he did not wish to attract undue notice." Reginald made a sound of irritation. "Though he asked me several questions about you, he would not give me his name, but instead handed me this, telling me to bring it to you immediately, and saying you would meet with him when you saw what it held."

At that Reginald held out a small leather satchel, knotted at the top. Damien felt a twinge of some latent memory upon looking at it but nothing definite enough to give him an answer to this mystery. Taking the purse from his guardsman, he untied its top and eased it open, looking inside and seeing naught but what appeared to be a piece of white cloth, folded several times.

But as he pulled it out and unfolded it to look at the insignia displayed there, the faint jangling inside him rose to a clangor. He looked back at Alissende, and the strain of this unexpected development showed in her expression as well. Gritting his teeth, he clenched his fist and flicked his stare back to Reginald's suddenly pasty face before barking an order for him to return to the castle grounds, find the visitor, and meet them back at the tent without delay.

As Reginald and Thomas left to do as they were bid, Damien opened his hand once more, staring at the rectangle of cloth that had sent a less-than-pleasant sensation lurching through him. A breeze swept through the glade, then, stirring the leaves on the trees with a rustling sound, and lifting the edge of the fabric. On it was a design he had seen many, many times before—a symbol that over the course of years had become as familiar to him as his own hands, in fact.

For resting in his grip was a rectangle of white linen, its surface embroidered with a distinctive, eight-tipped *crosspattee*. It was the emblem of a Brotherhood under siege, of an Order decimated by the power of the French Inquisition . . .

It was the crimson cross of a Templar Knight.

Chapter 19

~~~⌒GG⌒~~~

Alissende waited with Damien in their tent for his visitor to be brought to them, trying to quell the confusion of her emotions in the tense silence that surrounded them. She had changed into a fresh gown and she sat as if composed, but every now and again she still experienced the rippling quakes deep inside that were the lingering effects of the powerful lovemaking she had shared with him.

Briefly she closed her eyes, reliving those beautiful moments in her memory. Reginald's interruption could not have come at a more difficult time, just when Damien had been about to tell her something important. Something about them, she was sure of it. How could it be otherwise, when they had just made love in a way so moving that it had made her nearly weep?

And heaven help her, but she had told him she loved him.

He had not answered her in kind. Nay, instead those old shadows had sifted back into his eyes, and that realization made the lump in her throat swell even tighter. Yet whatever they might have discussed would need to wait, now, until they'd dealt with this new crisis.

It promised danger for Damien, she feared, regardless of aught else, for the Templars in England had been placed under arrest eight months ago by order of King Edward; he had issued the mandate unwillingly, it was true, under pressure from his father-in-law, France's King Philip the Fair, as well as the directive of the pope, but it was in effect nonetheless.

Because of it, any Templar found within England's borders was to be arrested and confined for questioning. According to gossip, the interrogations were less brutal than those employed by the French Inquisition, but they could go on for years. If Damien's visitor was a Templar, he would need to possess one of the very rare Writs of Absolution like the one Michael had forged for Damien, or else risk capture with every moment spent in the open.

They would know soon enough.

As if in answer to her anxious thoughts, a commotion near the tent flap caused Damien to stride forward, and Alissende lurched to her feet. Soon a stranger ducked into the tent, and Alissende watched Damien stiffen in shock.

"Richard?"

The man looked equally startled—and relieved as well—to see Damien. He was just as Reginald had described: tall and strong, a few years older than Damien, perhaps, and with dark hair, but clearly a man built for battle. Aye, he seemed a powerful knight, and one whose expression shifted to a look of pure joy just before he crossed the remaining distance between them to grab Damien and pull him into a back-breaking hug.

"It *is* you, man! By all the angels and saints, I had feared you dead!" he said to Damien, his voice roughened with emotion.

When he pulled away again, Alissende stepped closer, not only to study him better but also to hear what he might have to say.

"Richard, my God . . . I cannot believe it. After that night in France—the inquisitors . . . they told me—" Damien's voice caught, and he had to swallow hard to continue, Alissende saw; she needed to restrain herself from going to him. "I believed you had died as well," Damien continued quietly, shaking his head. "How are you able to travel England freely? And how in hell did you find me?"

"I was granted a Writ of Absolution when I won a battle of justice late last year," Richard replied. "There is much to tell you of it—of many things, in fact. As to how I found you, it was through word of the tournament. I was traveling home from abroad and had stopped at a tavern not far from here. Your name was being bandied about as the leading venant on the lists, and I decided to see for myself if it was you." Richard shook his head. "It is a great boon to see you so hale and hearty. Twice now, I have been to France and back with John seeking word of you, and—"

"John survived as well?" Damien broke in, appearing incredulous at the news.

"Ayé. He was taken for a short while near Montivilliers that night, but he managed to escape before he was brought to a place of interrogation."

Damien nodded; a muscle in his jaw twitched, but he gestured for Richard to come and sit at the small table they kept in the pavilion for taking meals, seeming to realize as he did that he had not yet explained Alissende's presence. Richard had glanced at her upon entering, nodding in deference to her clear status as a noblewoman, based upon her style of dress, she supposed, but now Damien stopped and held out his hand for her to approach them.

"I am sorry, lady; I have been remiss. Before you stands Sir Richard de Cantor, one of my closest comrades within the circle of Templar Knights amongst whom I served in the Brotherhood. He, Alex, Sir John de Clifton, and I rode across France together on the night of the mass arrests." Glancing to Richard, he continued, "Richard, this is Lady Alissende of Surrey. It is through proxy marriage with her that I was brought out of captivity and restored to health earlier this year."

"You're *married?*"

Now it was Richard's turn to look incredulous. Quickly, though, his mouth snapped shut, and he looked to Alissende apologetically. "Pardon, lady. I meant no dishonor to you; it was surprise alone that prompted my comment."

"I understand, Sir Richard," she nodded, sitting with them and hoping she looked more serene than she was feeling in the wake of all the upheaval and changes this day had brought. "I am sure this is all a bit of a shock and a great deal to try to absorb so quickly."

"It is." He looked down for a moment before glancing back to Damien. "In my turn, I must share the sad news that my wife Eleanor, of whom I had spoken with you previously, died shortly after my return home last year."

"I am sorry, Richard," Damien said, and Alissende echoed the sentiment. "I know you had hoped for her return to health."

Richard nodded, and Alissende could see the weight of that memory in his gaze. But then he offered a small smile. "By God's grace, however, I have found joy again in marriage to a wonderful woman. There is much I need to tell you, but for now it will suffice to say that Meg and I were wed earlier this year; she is at Hawksley Manor even now, awaiting the birth of our first child."

"What?" Damien gripped Richard by the arm, truly smiling, Alissende noticed, for the first time since Richard's arrival here. Giving a short laugh, he slapped Richard's shoulder. "You're to be a father again? Congratulations, man! That is welcome news indeed."

Once more Richard nodded, still smiling. "It is strange how life turns so quickly, is it not?"

"Aye, it is." Damien glanced at Alissende, and her stomach did a pleasant flip.

In the next breath, Damien turned back to Richard. "We have much to discuss, about many things, I think. Far more than can be said here and now. If you would be willing to forestall your return home for a few more days, I would be glad for your company. The king has ordered me to travel to Guildford Castle within a fortnight to joust with an earl who engaged in unfair combat with me here." He gave Richard a rueful look. "Another long story, I am afraid. But we would be pleased to entertain you until we must depart."

Richard paused, something in his gaze setting off

warning bells inside Alissende. "I wish I could do that, Damien," he said, "but I am afraid that I bear more news, still, which will likely alter your plans of the next few days."

"What is it?"

"It concerns Alex."

Damien's face tightened, and Alissende sensed that same affect over his entire body. Though she could see only his profile, she knew his eyes would be flat with the grief that always came with thoughts of his brother's death.

"You do not need to tell me, Richard. I learned more than I wanted to know from the hell's spawn interrogating me. There is nothing left to say."

Richard seemed taken aback. "I know you were angry with Alex for breaking his Templar vows, Damien, but I cannot believe you would not wish to know where he is."

"What do you mean?" Damien scowled. "None know where the Inquisition buries the victims of their cruelty. Even could it be found, there are so many dead, 'twould be near impossible to find my brother's resting place."

As Damien spoke, Richard's face shifted through expressions of confusion, then shock, and finally a seemingly sudden awareness. "Buries their victims—?" he echoed. He jabbed his hand through his hair, tipping his head up and making a sound of disbelief before he met Damien's gaze again. And then he said quite clearly, "I do not know what those devils in France told you, Damien, but your brother is not dead."

"*What?*"

Richard nodded, his stare intense. "Alex is alive.

And he is in England right now, not three days' ride from here."

Damien wasn't sure he could continue breathing for the shock that seemed to spread through him with Richard's announcement. His lungs, his muscles, and his thoughts all froze on that one, unbelievable point: Alex was *alive*. It could not be, and yet Richard was sitting here in front of him, saying it was so.

"It is true, Damien," Richard said, seeming to know how impossible it would sound to him. "John and I found Alex in France but a month since, bribed his guards with some of the Templar treasure in our keeping, and brought him back to England with us."

From the side of his vision, Damien saw that Alissende had pressed her hand to her mouth, but he felt like a statue, so little did he move. He was not even certain his heart still pumped in his chest right now. "My God, I cannot believe it." He barely said the words aloud, but it felt like they had been ripped from his throat. "After all this time . . . he is alive?"

"Aye," Richard answered. "He was living when I left him in John's care less than a week ago."

Damien uttered a soft curse, finally leaning back in his chair, bewildered. "I must go to him." He raised his gaze, seeing that Alissende's eyes held a telltale sheen that he kept trying to blink back from his own; she nodded wordlessly to him, taking his hand and squeezing it in support.

"It would be wise to make it sooner rather than later, Damien," Richard said.

Damien looked at Richard sharply, a fist of worry dropping in his gut. "How bad?" he asked.

Richard tipped his head, clearly trying to ease him into it. "It isn't good."

Damien looked away, closing his eyes at the thought of what Alex must have been through. He remembered his own torture and how close to death he had come, and that had been nearly five months ago. To think that Alex had endured even more was unbearable to consider.

"I must leave as soon as possible, then," he said, almost as if to himself.

"That would be best," Richard said. "However, I am afraid I cannot accompany you there. I have been gone from Meg too long already, in her condition. But I will be sure that you know exactly where John is hiding with Alex, so that you and your men may find them easily. When your brother is stronger and able to travel, we can bring him to my home at Hawksley Manor, where he may heal more fully, God willing."

"Does John also possess a Writ of Absolution, then?" Damien asked.

Richard shook his head. "He hides, along with Alex. But what of you? You clearly move about freely through the country, and under your own name. How did you obtain one?"

Damien hesitated, and he felt Alissende's fingers clench on his before she interjected for him, "My cousin Michael is a priest. Along with the proxy documents he arranged for us before Damien was freed from France, he included that as well." She glanced down briefly. "However, it is likely not as binding as the one you bear, Sir Richard."

Richard paused. "I see." He shifted his gaze to Damien. "You must take extra care, then, Damien—and consider Scotland for a destination. Since the Bruce's excommunication for slaying Red Comyn on holy ground at Dumfries, he has found sympathy for others in similar plight. As long as he continues to open his borders to all Templars, Scotland will be the safest berth for any under papal ban without benefit of a standing writ."

"I intend to make my way there eventually, Richard, but for now, my work here is not yet done."

"Understood. In truth there are a handful of us who have remained in England by choice, working to free the pockets of brethren being interrogated by the French inquisitors who have made their way over here. Of us all, I am the only one thus far who may move about freely."

"You said the *French* Inquisition is interrogating men here, in England?" Damien asked, frowning.

"Aye, unbeknownst to King Edward. In our search for you and Alex, we learned of several places, generally near holdings where the Order had encountered resentment, that have secretly brought in the French, whose methods of questioning yield better results for those seeking to destroy the Brotherhood." Richard's expression was grim. "I am sure I don't need to tell you why."

Unable to answer, Damien simply jerked his head in response.

"Will I be accompanying you when you seek your brother, Damien?"

The softly spoken question came from Alissende. He looked at her, struck anew by her beauty, which shone as much from the inside as it was apparent in her outer form. She was clearly worried for him, and yet the true danger would be to her, if she came along. In addition to the usual risks of bandits or even accident, at the pace he would need to assume in order to reach Alex, was the fact that he traveled toward two men who were wanted by the Crown for questioning. Men considered heretics under law.

"Nay, lady," he answered gently. "I will take but my squire and one other man, if they will agree, so that I may travel with all haste. I would see you safely home with the rest of my guard and will join you there when my goal is met."

She looked distressed for a moment, but then she seemed to swallow her disappointment, and acceptance settled over her lovely face. As her lashes came down once more and she nodded, he felt a pang of emotion he could not speak of right now—not until this crisis was past and he was by her side at Glenheim again.

"It will be as you wish, Damien," she said finally. "I hope that you find Alexander recovering, and that you return home safely to me before long."

"Thank you, lady, for that and much more." Damien took Alissende's hand in his, calling that remarkable gaze to him again and holding it as he lifted her palm for a kiss, finishing on a low note of promise, "I will see you within a sennight, I swear it."

In the hours after Damien, Thomas, and Bernard left Odiham's grounds, they made good time, so Damien called a brief rest to give the horses some water. It felt good to stretch, but they could not delay too long. As soon as Thomas returned from deeper in the wood, where he'd gone to take care of necessities, they would be on their way again; then, if they stopped only once more for the night, they might indeed reach Alex and John before nightfall tomorrow.

"Sir Damien, riders approach."

Damien looked up from adjusting his mount's girth to follow Bernard's gaze down the road from the direction they'd just traveled. It looked to be a sizeable group—at least a dozen men—from the sound of the horses and the amount of dust they kicked up. Bandits would not travel thus, Damien reasoned. Likely, it was one of the lords and part of his entourage from Odiham, heading for home, now that the tournament was done.

"Should we remount to face them?" Bernard asked, apparently noting the number of soldiers as well.

Damien nodded his head in silence, swinging up onto his own steed as he did. Of course, if these were men looking for trouble, the disparity of numbers would make being mounted or not a moot point. That realization made him grateful all over again for Bernard's willingness to come on this journey. Both Bernard and Thomas had known that it might prove dangerous on many counts, and both had affirmed themselves ready to face any challenge if such was required in support of their lord.

Unfortunately, this developing situation might well be the first test of their mettle in that regard.

The first line of men came close enough to be seen clearly, and Damien understood at that moment that this might be far more than a coincidental meeting. These men wore the Earl of Harwick's colors . . . and Hugh himself rode with them.

Thank God he had had the foresight to send Alissende back to Glenheim with his full contingent of men, Damien thought. Hugh would not find her here, but that did not mean there wouldn't be trouble. Still, except for some sport, perhaps, there was little for Hugh to gain. Even he was not foolish enough to attempt to kill outright the very man King Edward had named as his opposite for the jousting two weeks hence. Doing so would risk the king's wrath and likely lead to being stripped of all title and lands, along with his honor.

Unless there was some other reason behind this newest aggression. . . .

"Ready yourself," Damien called out in a low voice to Bernard, unsheathing his sword and looking around the edge of the clearing for Thomas. He slapped the back of Thomas's mount, sending him into the cover of the forest. Where the hell was the lad? Though it went against every instinct, Damien knew they could probably outrun Hugh and his men, but he did not want to risk leaving Thomas behind to face them himself.

Pray God it would not come to that, though. He took comfort in knowing that he'd instructed Bernard and Thomas to seek Richard at Hawksley Manor should they become separated by accident or attack along the way. He'd not see trouble brought back to Alissende, and Richard would be more likely to find means of protecting her, should Damien be arrested again—or worse.

He glanced again to the approaching forces, noting that they had picked up speed and were barreling toward him and Bernard with blades drawn.

"Take my flank for protection," Damien called to Bernard, still keeping his gaze fixed on Hugh. "They will likely have little interest in you, and with any luck Thomas will be wise enough to remain in the shadow of the wood until the danger is past."

But to his surprise, as the soldiers neared, they veered around and away from a direct clash, instead surrounding him and Bernard in all directions, no matter which way Damien wheeled his mount. He kept his blade out and at the ready nonetheless, wondering if perhaps Hugh intended to challenge him one-on-one again, only this time with naught but his own corrupt rules to follow.

It did not take long to find out.

"Ashby, how fortuitous to find you," Hugh said in a mocking lilt, punctuating the comment with a smug smile as he approached. He reined his mount closer— though not close enough that Damien might be able to reach him with his blade. "But enough of these preliminaries. If you value the life of your man, you will order him to sheathe his sword, and you will do the same. Now."

Nodding in Bernard's direction, Hugh added, "I must tell you that one of my best archers has a bolt trained on him even now, under orders to let it fly if you do not comply with my directive by the count of ten." Raising his hand in signal and shifting his gaze to a spot far off Damien's shoulder, he began counting, "One, two . . ."

Damien twisted to follow Hugh's stare, seeing that this at least was no bluff. The sun glinted wickedly off the tip of the arrow notched back in the bow of the archer he'd mentioned, and Bernard had gone the color of milk, stiffening in his saddle as if he expected the piercing blow at any moment.

Snapping his gaze back to Hugh with a scowl, Damien slid his blade back into its sheath, and he heard Bernard follow suit. Hugh smiled. "Now throw the scabbard and belt to the ground." Damien was forced to scramble to comply in time, but Hugh nevertheless waited another heart-chilling count before calling off the death-watch.

The bastard.

"While I am duly impressed by your show of power, *my lord*," Damien said, echoing Hugh's sarcasm when the tense moment was past, "can you not simply tell me what you want without surrounding me with a score of soldiers first?"

Hugh paled in anger at the insult, jerking his mount closer to Damien. His hostility made the steed stamp and prance as he muttered, "You will not be so blithe when I have done with you, Ashby. The sound of your pleas for mercy will be music to my ears, I assure you." He flashed him a look of pure, gloating evil. "If I'm not too occupied in fucking Alissende to hear you, that is."

That was all it took.

Damien threw himself off his horse, tackling Hugh before the wretch had a chance to even raise his blade, and pulling him to the ground on the other side of his destrier's stamping hooves. Commotion erupted all around them, but before Hugh's men could drag Damien off their lord, Damien got off three good shots with his fist, reveling in cracking it against the cur's arrogant face.

Too soon he felt himself being yanked back, held at the arms by two men; Hugh lurched to his feet and swiped at the blood coming from the side of his mouth and his nose, his expression filled with rage as he lunged forward with a growl and planted a rock-hard fist into Damien's belly.

A wall of agony shot through Damien with the blow, seeming to arch up along the still unhealed rib on his left side. The pain of it choked off his breath and would have likely dropped him to the dirt but for the men still holding him up. Coughing, Damien forced himself to regain his own feet after a moment; he'd be damned if he'd even appear to cower before Hugh de Valles.

"Not so glib now, are you, Ashby?" Hugh asked tightly, flexing his fist and calling for one of his men to bring a cloth to clean the blood from his face.

Damien didn't bother trying to answer. Instead, he used the time while Hugh was occupied to try to regain his breath, letting his gaze slip surreptitiously around, checking the perimeter of the road—until he spotted a small movement behind the trees off to the right. A face peered out for an instant, looking overwhelmed and distraught.

Thomas.

Christ, the lad looked like he was preparing to come out in the open, probably to try to stage a rescue. It shouldn't have surprised Damien, knowing his squire's penchant for tales of valor and heroism. But he was too young to have learned the difference between courage and outright folly; if he emerged from the wood now, he'd be dead before he could take five paces.

He attempted to meet Thomas's gaze without being caught at it, feigning another attack of coughing. To his relief, it worked. Thomas's eyes were fixed to him, and Damien shook his head sharply, hoping he conveyed the message, even as Hugh walked up, blocking off his view by standing directly in front of him.

"Now let us get down to the meat of this enjoyable meeting, shall we?" Hugh grated. "You have taken something that is mine. While I would relish killing you because of it, I have decided there are other methods of ridding myself of you that would prove even more useful—and satisfying."

"This tired tune does not bear singing again, methinks," Damien said calmly, "but if you are entertained by it, then do go on."

"Don't pretend ignorance, Ashby. Your secret has been exposed," Hugh hissed. "The marriage proxy with my cousin? The Writ of Absolution from the Inquisition? Both as flimsy as the parchment upon which they are scribed."

Damien remained silent, though he could not suppress the feeling of dread that swept through him at the idea that Hugh might have indeed discovered the truth . . . not for his own sake, but for Alissende's.

He must not have been as successful as he'd hoped in concealing that flare of anxiety, for Hugh gloated, "Ah, at last a hint of reaction from the impervious Sir Damien. Aren't you going to ask me how I discovered your ploy to dupe us all? Are you not curious what I intend to do with this delightful information?"

Damien met his stare with the penetrating chill of his own, experiencing the satisfaction of watching Hugh shift back a step in response. "I do not need to ask anything, Harwick," he grated at last, abandoning all pretense of respectful address. "Men of your ilk cannot help but tell all eventually, with or without question." He nodded, mocking, "So why don't you just go ahead?"

"It matters little," Hugh said. "You're a dead man anyway. My dear brother Michael was as forthcoming with the truth about your falsified proxy and Writ of

Absolution as I'd hoped he would be—after the proper incentives were applied to him, of course."

Damien cursed under his breath, shocked into it by the sickening understanding of how far Hugh was willing to go—and struck with fear over what that could mean for Alissende.

Hugh appeared to be enjoying himself, and he made a show of looking impressed. "I must say that I never realized gentle Michael possessed such strength of will. I've been told he was barely clinging to life once they'd finished with him. But each man has his breaking point, doesn't he, Ashby?" Hugh's expression turned more sinister. "You hadn't quite reached yours when Alissende arranged your rescue from France, it seems. Thank heavens there is still time to revisit that . . . ah, yes, and perhaps to learn what Alissende's is as well, poor dear, depending upon the choice you make in the next few mome—"

"Leave her out of it," Damien growled, going for Hugh's throat as he threw himself forward against the grip of the men holding him. But they were ready this time, and they yanked him back, hauling him a few paces away from Hugh, who just stood there with his arms crossed, shaking his head.

Making a clicking sound with his tongue, Hugh approached Damien again. "Control, Ashby . . . what has happened to your legendary control, man? I am disappointed." He stopped then, all mockery vanishing as his gaze sharpened to ice, the force of it boring into Damien. "And as for leaving Alissende out of it—she *is* it, you insignificant, upstart mongrel. I have done more for the sake of claiming her than you could ever dream, and I am capable of far worse. You should consider that carefully when making the choice I am about to offer you."

"Say it then, and let us get on with this," Damien muttered.

Hugh smiled coldly. "Your first choice is to sign a parchment declaring your marriage to Alissende false. You will then go willingly to be confined in the dungeon of my lesser estate at Grantley Hall a few miles hence, to resume interrogation by the Inquisition as a Templar Knight—"

Hugh's sadistic pause forced Damien to bite off a clipped *"Or?"*

"Or you can decline signing the parchment and be taken into custody anyway, only with the added and rather distressing scenario of seeing Alissende arrested along with you, for aiding and abetting an accused heretic. Of course the rest of her household at Glenheim will face questioning as well, no doubt. And when one considers what happens to gentle-born women in such circumstances . . ." He made a sound feigning concern. "As I am sure you know, it is often less than savory."

"You bastard." Damien's voice was barely audible at the thought that Hugh would even consider exposing Alissende to that kind of hell.

"Just remember the choice is yours, Ashby. Sign the document, and I will ensure that Alissende is kept free of all taint in the matter."

"Free for your taking, you mean," Damien grated, aware of what this would mean for the woman he loved. Yet the alternative of her imprisonment and interrogation would be far worse, he knew.

Hugh shrugged, smiling lecherously. "The spoils of war, nothing more." In the next breath, however, his grin vanished, replaced by a menacing stare. Leaning in, Hugh fixed Damien with a look that made clear he would brook no further delay.

"Now choose."

Chapter 20

❦

Glenheim Castle
Five days later

Alissende paced the solar, agitated not only by her continued worry over how Damien fared but in distress now over Michael as well. Upon returning to Glenheim, she had been told that Michael was missing. Lady Blanche had been the last to see him, just before he'd set off on the journey to Chertsey Priory to deliver the new vellum Alissende had procured for repaying the scribes there. But he had not returned to Glenheim when expected, and a message sent to the monks at the priory revealed that he had never arrived.

Alarmed and fearing that he might have fallen ill along the way, Ben had set out in search of him amongst various groups of monks and priests and at holy houses, hoping that someone had seen or heard something. But thus far there had been no news.

"Alissende, try to eat something," Lady Blanche urged softly from her seat at the table they'd placed before the fire.

"I cannot, *Mère*. But please, do not wait for me. I will try again at supper, I promise," Alissende answered.

Her mother looked concerned, but she set down her knife as well, with a sigh. "I cannot manage much either, *ma chérie*. It is this waiting without word that is so difficult, no?"

Silent, Alissende nodded. They'd begun taking their meals here since her return from Odiham, preferring the sunny quiet of this chamber to the noisy gatherings in the main hall. But until Damien was back at her side and Michael was found, Alissende knew her appetite would continue to elude her.

A commotion down in the yard below drew her attention, and she moved closer to the glazed panes to look out. The sight set off a strange twisting in her belly. Something was wrong. It looked like Glenheim's guard was spilling out onto the green, coming in groups from the guardhouse, shouting and scrambling as they took positions at the walls and gate.

Had Damien returned? Was he hurt? Or was this about Michael?

The confusing thoughts swept through her, and she called her mother to the window, both of them glancing out before hurrying to make their way down to the hall. They had just reached the central hearth when Reginald burst through the side door, wearing an expression of grim resolve and carrying before him a sealed parchment.

"My lady," he said to Alissende, coming to a halt and bowing his head as he handed her the vellum, "this message has been sent through the gatehouse, for delivery to your hand alone. Lord Harwick waits outside the walls with troops some fivescore strong."

Alissende's hand trembled as she peeled open the wax seal stamped with the insignia of the Valles house. Her head felt light and her heart was in her throat by the time she finished skimming the contents; clasping her mother's hand as if she might find some means of anchoring herself from the wild surge of fear and dread roiling through her, she lifted her gaze.

"Hugh is demanding immediate entrance to Glenheim for a private interview with me," she murmured.

Alissende heard Lady Blanche's sharp intake of breath, but Reginald scowled and stood straighter. "Let him try to get past the gates, my lady," he grated. "Sir Damien may be absent at the moment, but we are well trained and will rout Lord Harwick and his men, making them scurry home like rats."

Unable to find the words at first for the horror seeping through her, Alissende simply shook her head, finally murmuring, "Nay, we cannot fight him, Reginald."

"Why on earth not?" Her mother frowned. "He must be witless to attempt to intimidate you so now. Your marriage has been recognized at court. It would be far better to resist until help arrives from Sir Damien."

"We have not the luxury of that time, I am afraid, *Mère*. Nor am I certain, after reading this parchment, that Damien will be able to help me, ever again—"

Her voice broke off in a sob, and she pressed her fingers to her lips, barely able to finish, "Hugh has made it clear that it is he who has taken Michael. My gentle cousin is near death by his own brother's command, and Hugh has promised that Michael will not see the dawn if we do not open our gates to him within this quarter hour."

As if from a faraway place, Alissende watched Hugh's mouth moving, saw his sickening smile, and heard her own emotionless answer before he turned and left the chamber.

The door slipped shut behind him, and she was left alone again.

Slowly, she sank to the floor, the fierce determination that had allowed her to remain upright for as long as her depraved cousin stood before her seeping away until naught was left but dark, cold emptiness. And grief. It lapped at her in waves, growing in strength and hurt until she bent over double from the agony of it, wrapping her arms around her stomach and rocking soundlessly, too raw for tears.

Damien was dead. The man she loved was dead.

It could be no otherwise, though she had allowed Hugh to think she believed his claims to the contrary. Aye, she had pretended to swallow his lies about Damien for Michael's sake. Poor Michael, who had been tortured by Hugh's men until he had finally revealed the truth about the incomplete marriage proxy, still undeclared in public by the parties involved, and so therefore still invalid. Worse yet, under the force of his torment, Michael had confessed about the Writ of Absolution, admitting he had penned it without Church sanction, to protect Damien from further interrogation by the Inquisition.

Yet even though tortured to within a breath of his life, Michael had not died, and so Alissende had pretended to accept Hugh's version of events to buy some time. She had feigned agreement to the marriage he'd proposed as if she'd lacked the will to deny him longer. And to her surprise, he had believed her. Nodding his approval, he had left to make the arrangements for the ceremony to take place the day after next.

It had been a hollow victory.

His lies still rang in her ears, each word cutting at her heart. Damien had fled to Scotland, Hugh had claimed, when given the choice between suffering rearrest and interrogation by the Inquisition or signing a parchment asserting that their marriage had been in name only. He had given Damien the option, he'd told her in a revoltingly false display of care, to protect her from the ugliness and danger a public scandal of this nature would incur. And he pretended grudging admiration in Damien's supposed decision to flee, calling it ultimately selfless—and making her glad she had not been able to eat earlier, else she would have lost the contents of her stomach at his feet.

With every wretched syllable he'd uttered, she had known Hugh lied. Even when he had shown her the parchment, signed in Damien's own unpracticed hand, she'd known. In truth, the sight of that wobbly signature had nearly broken her composure, flooding her with heartbreaking pain and loss, for it had done nothing but confirm her worst fears. She knew better than anyone that Damien never would willingly break a vow he made, even if he risked his life to complete it. He had promised to protect her from Hugh, and if he could no longer fulfill that oath, it was because he was no longer breathing, not because he had fled the country.

And so she was left with naught but stunning grief and her own resolution to stop Hugh from hurting anyone else, through whatever means were left open to her. She had looked him in the eye and told him that she saw the wisdom in finally yielding to his decision to wed her. Promised that she would stand in the chapel with him and pledge him her troth . . .

And then, after the wedding feast was over and he led her to their chamber to consummate their vows, she would ease into her palm the dagger she would hide in her sleeve, and she'd drive it straight into his black heart.

If she succeeded, she would be tried for his murder and no doubt hanged, since a woman—even a noblewoman—could not commit such a crime against a man of title and be absolved of it without forfeit of her own life. And of course there was always the possibility that she might falter at the necessary moment, perhaps miss the mark or become overpowered by Hugh's superior strength. He might in fact turn the dagger on her, instead.

It did not matter. Either way, she would be dead and released from the pain of this existence.

Resolve.

It was all Alissende had left, and she decided to hold onto it and nurture it like a bitter, shiny seed within her breast, keeping it safe until it bore the deadly fruit that would end Hugh's life and her own torment . . .

Once and for all.

The dungeons at Grantley Hall
That same day

It had been like stepping back into hell.

From the moment Damien had been tossed into this diabolical lair, the horrific sights, the cries of agony and pleas for mercy . . . the smells, oh God, the smells, of rot, waste, and burning flesh—had assaulted his senses with merciless brutality. He had not been able to breathe, his gorge rising up to choke him.

The fact that he knew what was still to come had been almost enough to drive him mad. His inquisitors had not begun his interrogation in earnest yet. They clung to the belief that they might yet free him from the grip of Satan through the cleansing purification of their questioning, and so they made sure not to take him down that path too quickly, lest they be deprived of their prize.

They would never have the chance to do more, if he had any say in it.

Pressing back against the wall of his fetid dungeon chamber, Damien concentrated on the thin line of light visible beneath the door. He focused on it, even as he heard the sounds of scraping and clanking that let him know the first group of Templars was being returned to their cells. Spent, tortured unto senselessness by their ordeal, they would be exchanged for fresh blood, as happened every day.

In a few minutes, Damien's door would open, the guards would stride in, and he would be dragged, squinting against the light, into one of the various interrogation rooms. His session of questioning would begin shortly thereafter, after they'd bound him to a table, or to a chair, or perhaps, as they had promised if he refused to cooperate today, to the rack.

His stomach clenched at the thought, and he willed his mind to slow and his panic to recede, lest he be unable to complete the steps needed to make sure that it turned out the way he intended this time.

For all was not lost. Nay, he had been shocked to realize, even through the threat of unspeakable agonies and the knowledge of the immense physical pain they could unleash on him if they chose, that something burned within him, giving him strength and a sense of hope he had not realized he possessed.

His love for Alissende.

Ah, sweet Jesu, but he loved her—and even more miraculously, she loved him too, having spoken those very words to him moments after they'd made love, following the tournament. He had not answered her then . . . he had not known how to, overwhelmed as he'd been by his own fears for their future. But the future had come. He was living the horror of it right now, and it had not changed anything about the feelings he cherished for her.

He needed to get to her, to break free of this confinement and tell her the truth of it. He needed to protect her from Hugh. And so through the torment of these last few days, Damien had formulated a plan.

He had been aided in it by the force of something else that had changed inside him. Aye, at the moment that he'd accepted his love for Alissende and hers for him, he had felt the understanding flood his heart, helping him fill the empty place that had been aching inside him for so long. Against all odds, against hope itself, he had been given another chance to love Alissende and be loved by her in return. And suddenly it had become crystal clear to him that no God who would abandon him in his greatest need would then grace him with such a life-sustaining treasure.

That awareness had freed him from the bitterness that had stifled him for so long. He was not alone in the hell of his imprisonment. He never had been, even in France. Nay, it was he who had turned his back on God, refusing to see. Now that his vision was clear, there was nothing that could stand in his way of getting back to Alissende. This day, he would put into motion the plan he had whispered to this tattered and weakened group of Templar brothers, liberating himself and them from their inquisitors at last.

Tapping lightly on the wall, Damien waited for an answering sound. They'd housed him alone because of his strength and size, but he'd found his means of communicating with the others anyway. Soon another scratch came, and he knew that the man there would spread the message, so that as much as they were able, those who could might be ready to offer a united burst of resistance when the opportunity came.

His heart pounded as he heard the guards approach his door. Though it disgusted him to do so, he positioned himself sideways on the rotted straw that covered the floor of his vermin-infested cell, pretending that he'd fallen senseless—from fear or illness, it did not matter. He only needed to appear unable to respond, talk or stand.

Certainly unable to fight back.

The door grated open, and the wash of light shone across his barely closed eyes. The same two guards who collected him each day strode through the door, one of them cursing at the sight of him.

"The bastard's out cold, and he hasn't even been questioned properly yet," the first man complained to his mate, leaning over to grab one of Damien's arms. He pulled, yelling, "Come and help me with 'im, why don't you, Eustace! Get 'is other arm and pull."

Eustace lumbered over and complied, and Damien forced himself to remain motionless in their grasp as they pulled him out into the open, into the hallway that connected all the cells. The corridor wound around further up, leading to the interrogation chambers, and Damien knew there would be precious little time, depending on how much noise Eustace and his mate made when he offered his counterattack, to begin opening the cell doors before other guards would come running.

He would simply have to make the most of it.

Eustace grunted, pausing as they dragged him over the filthy stones, with a mumbled call for a rest . . .

And it was then that Damien made his move. With a soundless burst of energy, he shot to his feet, taking the two guards so by surprise that Eustace fell back, hitting his head against the wall, and uttering one loud groan. He seemed dazed, but the other guard started to call out for help, so Damien dealt with him first, choking the sound off to a gurgle as he grabbed him by his throat and squeezed. The man's eyes bulged in fear, but Damien had no intention of killing him, much as the wretch likely deserved it. Nay, that would take too much time. Instead, Damien pulled back his fist and slammed it into the guard's temple, setting him down when he slumped over, senseless.

A good crack across Eustace's jaw put him in the same condition, and, breathing heavily, Damien scrambled to lift the bars on the four remaining cells on his side of the corridor. To his great relief, Bernard emerged from one of the filthy chambers, and Damien gripped his arm in solidarity before moving on to the doors at the other side of the corridor. The poor souls within them were unlikely to be able to move from where they'd been thrown after their latest interrogation sessions, but he could at least give them a fighting chance.

Tumult ensued when three more guards and two of the inquisitors came charging down the hallway toward Damien and the other prisoners. By force of pure will, it seemed, and perhaps a touch of good luck, the bedraggled lot of long-tortured Templar brethren, Bernard, and Damien managed to hold their own, using improvised weapons—and, in Damien's case, his bare fists.

By the time the commotion settled, two of the Templar prisoners were dead, as was one of the guards and an inquisitor. The remaining tyrants were locked into the filthy cells to which their captives had been consigned for so many months.

"We are free, brothers," the scrawny, bearded man from the cell next to Damien's rasped, sounding as if he was near to tears. He was slumped against the wall where the uprising had taken place, his wrinkled face tipped up to the ceiling. "Praise God, we are free!"

The sentiment was echoed in the laughing coughs and choked sobs of the other men who had survived. There were six in all, aside from Bernard and Damien. None of the brethren surrounding them right now had been Templar Knights; they were instead simple brothers in charge of farming or keeping accounts at the priory where they had all lived and worked. Four of the six were in their waning years, and they all looked like survivors of a pestilence, painfully thin, dirty, and covered in sores, cuts, and bruises. Damien's jaw clenched with the thought that, unlike those who had lived through a plague, however, these men had suffered at the hands of their own.

"It is not over yet, brothers," Damien said quietly. He motioned to them to gather behind him. "First we must find our way out of this damnable place without being caught by any of Lord Harwick's servants or guards above."

Two of the old men shuffled nervously, while the one who had been housed next to Damien pointed a bony finger down the hall. "Just past the devil's chambers yonder, there is a storeroom. I heard them speaking within it, once, when I was being questioned. They would come and go by that room."

Damien nodded. "Follow me. We shall see if this storeroom is to be the gate to our salvation this night."

The strange parade of old and injured men did as Damien requested. There was indeed a corridor leading out of the storage chamber. Even better, once they'd reached its limits—which opened into the kitchens, by the look of the goods stacked near that final door—there was also a covered, rough-hewn hole in the wall, quite large, that angled down toward the ground below. Naught could be seen at the bottom; it was night, apparently, and pitch dark, but anyone with a nose would know what this was.

They'd discovered a refuse chute, used by the kitchen

workers for throwing away scraps and garbage. The tunnel, hewn right into the stone wall, emptied into a pit dug outside the fortified manor house's barbican. It would be an unpleasant landing, perhaps, but at least they would be clear of Grantley Hall when they were through.

Damien went first, just in case there were any guards stationed outside. It seemed unlikely, but after all they had risked to escape, he wasn't about to chance it. To their good fortune, naught but an open field edged by woodland greeted them below. That and the reeking mound of garbage that broke their fall. Trying not to breathe in the stench, Damien moved as quickly as he could, getting clear of the pit and then helping the others do the same.

•None of them had smelled pleasant before, he could attest, but now they reeked of dead fish, rotted onions, and other unmentionables as well. As he moved the group carefully toward the wooded area a hundred paces away, he tightened his jaw, more grateful than he had ever been for the fresh, outdoor air.

They traveled on foot for another quarter hour through the cover of the trees, and Damien was just turning to murmur his next command when he heard a crackle of branches. In the dimmed light of a cloud-covered crescent moon, he made out the slowly approaching forms of what appeared to be several men, coming through the trees toward them. Mounted men.

This close to Grantley, and so comfortable traveling at night, they could only be Hugh's guard.

Biting back a curse, Damien stiffened. He gazed around blindly for something he could use to perhaps knock one of these soldiers from his steed. If he called attention to himself, at least one of them might charge him, and he could take the man's sword if he toppled him. With a weapon he'd have a chance at least—not much, but a chance nonetheless—to fend off the others so that his weakened brethren and Bernard could flee.

Twisting back to the men behind him, he murmured, "Move slowly away from me, divide up, and then run when I attract their attention."

"Whose attention?" the old Templar behind him rasped.

"Theirs."

Damien looked forward again, jerking his chin in the direction of the mounted knights thirty paces ahead, but he knew exactly when the men behind him spotted them as well, for he felt an almost palpable wall of tension sweep into his back. He did not blame them for their fear. Quite likely this would be a suicide effort for them all, trying to outrun mounted warriors—well-fed, well-rested, and almost certainly well-trained warriors.

And as for any man stupid enough to deliberately seek their notice . . .

Well, better to leave that thought unexplored, Damien decided.

Gripping tighter the hefty branch he'd scrounged from the ground, Damien waited only long enough to know those behind him had begun to shift away as he'd bid. Then he stood to his full height, widened his stance, and called out in an insolent voice, "All right, then. Which of you bastards wants to take a turn at me first?"

The sound of what had to be a dozen swords clearing their sheaths simultaneously filled the area with a metallic hiss. Damien breathed a prayer and gritted his teeth, waiting for the onslaught to begin.

But it did not come.

Instead, after a pause, one of the riders clicked his mount forward a few paces, and a voice rang through the wood, "Damien? Is that you, you reckless fool?"

A shock of surprise jabbed through Damien, and the stick fell from his grip. The clouds that had been hiding the moon's glow shifted away in that moment, illuminating twelve mounted warriors with Richard at the head. And for the first time since Hugh had taken him captive on the roadside, Damien felt a surge of gratitude.

"Thank God, Richard," he said quietly as his friend dismounted and strode over to clasp him, forearm to forearm. "How did you know?"

"Your squire found me and told me what happened." Richard looked him over. "I have to say, you look like hell, Damien—and that stench . . . by heaven, it is more than foul."

"Aye, well, a stay with the Inquisition and an escape through a refuse hatch will do that to a man," he jested, trying not to dwell on the week of torment he'd endured.

Richard seemed to realize what Damien was feeling, and his expression shifted. "I am sorry it took so long to reach you, my friend. We only slowed as we approached Grantley, knowing we might encounter Lord Harwick's troops. There are enough escaped Templars now that we need to be cautious in our travel."

He clasped Damien's arm again. "I am only thankful that you were not harmed overmuch, my friend, and that you have eluded danger for the time being. In the time you were held, you should know that I also received some good news from John. He believes Alex has passed the point of danger, and though the odds were all against him, your brother seems likely to return to full health, given time."

"Thank God," Damien murmured again, though his joy at that news was tempered by worry over the woman he loved. His heart was heavy, and fear gripped him as he added, "However, there is another who is still in jeopardy, Richard. Have you heard aught about Alissende?"

Before he answered, Richard nodded to his men to offer aid to those who had escaped with Damien. Then he pulled Damien aside. "Only that she arrived home to Glenheim by nightfall the day after we left Odiham."

"Hugh intends to take her as his own, that much I know," Damien murmured grimly. "He will likely go there if he has not already. I must reach her, Richard. God help me, but I must free her from his grasp. I *will* free her, even if it is at the cost of my own life."

Richard nodded. "I thought as much. Know that I and these men are ready to stand with you, Damien, whatever is needed."

For the third time that night, surprise jolted through Damien. "But what of your wife? And these men . . . do they realize the danger they ride into, to follow me on this?"

"Aye, they know, as do I. I cannot deny that Meg worries for me, but she was the first to bid me go when your squire arrived at Hawksley."

Overwhelmed with gratitude, Damien gripped Richard's shoulder, turning with him as they strode toward the horses. "Glenheim is a three-, perhaps a three-and-a-half-days' ride from here under normal circumstances," he said, reviewing the calculations in his mind.

"I must make it in two, Richard, pausing only long enough to eat, perhaps bathe away the stench of my confinement somewhere along the way, and obtain both a strong blade and a fast mount."

Richard nodded. "Until we can secure a horse and the rest of what you need, you will ride with me, stench and all."

His tone, offered half in jest with those words, shifted to something far more serious as he paused, meeting Damien's gaze in the milky light of the forest. "Never fear, my friend," Richard murmured. "As always, we will be in this together. Come what may."

"Aye, come what may," Damien echoed, realizing that that Templar maxim was no longer painful for him to utter; in fact, he drew strength from it, feeling its power wash through him, channeling it into the determination he would need for the challenge ahead.

"I promise you, Richard, whatever it is—I am ready for it."

Chapter 21

❦

It was almost over.

The priest's voice droned on, speaking the words that would make this a union sanctified by the Church. Alissende had never seen the man before; nay, he had been brought in by Hugh, under orders to see this ceremony completed swiftly, eschewing any nicety that might slow it down.

But it did not matter, she realized. Nothing did anymore, aside from getting through this day.

She stood near the altar next to Hugh, her spine stiff, her gaze slipping without real sight over the people of her castle and village, who filled the pews, as well as the score of armed soldiers he had ordered to stand along the outer aisles of the chapel. He claimed

361

that they were there to provide witness, since the public declaration of their vows would not be made before the people of his demesne until after this pledging ceremony. But everyone knew better. The guards were here for Hugh's protection, a reminder of the power he could wield against her and her people if she dared to refute him again, and a way to ensure that none could stop this now, should anyone be foolish enough to try.

She might have laughed at the stupidity of it had she been capable of feeling anything at the moment. Damien was the only one who could have challenged Hugh's audacious and contemptible action, and he was dead. Whether at Hugh's hands or by his command was beside the point; Damien was gone, and in that aching loss Alissende had grown numb.

The inability to feel was a blessing, she supposed—a means of getting through the next few hours without collapsing. She could only hope that the lassitude possessing her would persist through tonight, and that God would have mercy on her soul when the mortal sin she planned to commit was done.

"Come, Alissende, it is time."

Hugh's oily murmur slid into her thoughts. She shifted her gaze to him, staring blankly.

"The priest has finished, lady, and it is time to pledge our troth."

She continued to look at him without any reaction, though her gaze slipped away for a moment into the nave of the church, seeking her mother. *Mère*'s eyes were red-rimmed with anguish, and her fingers were clenched so tightly in her lap that Alissende could not contain the peculiar thought that her hands would crack like shards of glass if she did not stop squeezing them together so.

"*Alissende.*"

Hugh's suddenly much more irritated tone pulled her attention back to him. His expression was pinched, as it always was when he felt he was being thwarted in some way, and he shook her arm none too gently.

"Pay attention, woman. It is time to speak our—"

"By God, Harwick, I thought even you would know the difference between holy truth and blasphemy."

The voice rocked through the chapel, from the shadows at the back, and the gathered assembly broke out in gasps and exclamations. Alissende's heart rose into her throat, her vision blurring with tears and her senses flooding with sweet, life-giving love, as she twisted to face the powerful figure who stepped forward. He was an avenging angel, tall and imposing, whose icy blue eyes shone with the fires of justice and the need to wage bloody war for the wrongs done to him and those he loved.

Hugh's men had drawn their blades, but they did not move. Hugh himself seemed to be in shock, staring at Damien as if he were some kind of disembodied spirit, rather than a flesh-and-blood warrior who stood before him.

"You cannot marry Alissende no matter how many times—or ways—you try to make it happen," Damien called to Hugh before at last shifting his gaze to her. The fullness of love in his eyes stole her breath, and his next words made her want to cry anew, for she was one of the few in the chamber who recognized the real power and meaning behind them. "It is against the laws of God and man to marry one who is pledged to another, Harwick . . . and I stand here before you to claim in no uncertain terms that Alissende is *my wife*."

Damien could not look away from Alissende, the sense of relief and love so strong in him that he could hardly move. She was safe. Thank God she was safe, and he had gotten here in time, before Hugh could dishonor her any further. There were dark circles under her eyes, and her complexion was pale, but she seemed unharmed. Even more miraculously, her gaze was filled with love—for him, by heaven—and he thought her the most beautiful woman he had ever seen.

Hugh interrupted his brief moment of respite, however, calling Damien's attention back as he growled, "She isn't your wife, Ashby. Not in truth. The parchment you signed only a week ago proclaims that your proxy union was false from the start, arranged by my feeble brother in a last effort to keep Alissende from me by wedding her to a Templar heretic!"

The murmurs and sounds of shock rose anew in the chapel, with people twisting to stare from him to the altar, and the priest standing behind Alissende and Hugh. The cleric appeared stunned, and Damien wondered if Hugh had neglected to tell the man any of this history between them.

"The laws of proxy have not changed so far as I know, Harwick," Damien answered finally, letting the chill seep into his voice and his gaze as he looked upon the earl. "All three requirements were met: First, in the existence of official document. Second, in the act of consummating the union—"

Damien paused for just a beat, his brow arched

wickedly, and Hugh's look of outrage was underscored by the reactions that broke out in the crowd at that bold proclamation.

"—and third, in public declaration of vows," he continued, shifting a far warmer stare upon Alissende again. "My lady, do you claim me here, before all these witnesses, as your husband?"

She looked at him from where she stood, slightly apart from Hugh and the priest, her beautiful eyes glistening. "Aye, Sir Damien de Ashby, I do claim you as my husband."

"It is done, then, and we are a married pair," he replied in a voice clear and forceful. As he spoke, the feelings welled up from somewhere deep inside of him, and telling the world at long last what was in his heart was more perfect than he'd ever thought it could be.

Perhaps sensing that he was losing the battle, Hugh suddenly cursed under his breath and grabbed for Alissende, dragging her to him; his left arm snaked around her waist, while his right wrapped around her throat and shoulders, pinning her. Clearly shocked, the priest shouted his protests, while the assembly reacted with exclamations and gasps, even as Damien unsheathed both his sword and his dagger in one, smooth movement, steadying them for use against Hugh.

Then all movement ceased. Alissende looked terrified, and danger seemed to curl, hot and thick, through the chamber, until tension thrummed from the very walls, bouncing off every blade Hugh's men held at the ready. The silence stretched, unbroken, until Damien nodded to the bastard who so cruelly held the woman he loved.

"Your plan to rid yourself of me failed, Harwick, and you cannot refute the validity of my marriage to Alissende," he called in a tone that made deadly clear that his tolerance was at an end. "If you do not take your hands off of her right now and step away, I shall be constrained to see that you do so through my own means."

"I would like to see you try, Ashby," Hugh grated, "especially when I am holding the goods themselves before me."

Damien fixed a glare of ice on his rival again, and he nodded with dark promise. "As you mentioned earlier, I was a Templar Knight. I served in the inner circle, trained among the very best to wrest victory from impossible circumstances. Using a woman as your shield will not save you. I am fully capable of exacting the vengeance I seek, from you or anyone who chooses to stand in my way, without harm to her."

He focused on Hugh, reminding himself not to let himself think of Alissende's fear or her plight, lest he be weakened by worry for her. On a sinister note, he added, "What may be less clear, however, is how eager I am for the opportunity to do it."

A perceptible agitation wavered through the men of Hugh's guard at that; though they kept their swords at the ready, several of them eyed Damien nervously.

However, Hugh had recovered enough to bark a disbelieving laugh. He did not move back, but rather threw an enraged glance to the captain of his guard. "There are a score of you, and only one of him. I command you to take him into custody without delay, so that he may be confined and questioned, as is to be every Templar found in England, at our great king's behest."

"You might want to reconsider that order, Captain," Damien called in answer, and at that signal, he heard the movement behind him indicating that Richard and the other Templar Knights were stepping forward from the shadows near the door to show themselves. Damien tilted his head at the captain, never moving his gaze from the man's face. "As you can see, I am not the only Templar Knight here this day. You will need to arrest us all, if you decide to obey your lord's command."

Without turning to look, Damien knew the Templars were lining up in a position of defense behind him that would be awe-inspiring to behold, forming a wall of the most fierce and skillful warriors the world had ever known. They aligned with each other in a readiness borne of constant training, lethal focus, and unwavering discipline to the art of warfare. Aye, they were outlawed Templars, desperate under the weight of the persecution against their Order and the Brotherhood that had sustained them—but nevertheless prepared to dispense justice with the bite of their blades.

And Hugh's men knew it.

The soldiers could not help but react, their indecision turning to blatant fear in the face of the mighty Templar force only half their number. The priest looked more dismayed than ever, and he stepped back, as if standing too closely to Hugh might in some way taint him with sin. At the same time, Alissende struggled to pull away.

But Hugh was not ready to give up.

"You are going nowhere, sweet, until I say you are," he growled to her. Suddenly his arm moved, and he grasped something near his waist before his hand raised

again, with lightning speed, back to Alissende's throat.
Damien stiffened, bone-numbing fear surging through
him when he saw that a dagger glinted in Hugh's
grip.

In reaction, the Templars all cleared their swords,
and tumult ensued in the chamber, the assembled
people not knowing whether to shrink back from the
altar, or the aisles, or the doors at the back, hemmed
in as they were on all sides by men wielding deadly
weapons.

"Lord Harwick!" the priest called, compelled into
action at last by this second burst of violence. "This is
a house of God, and such threat of bloodshed is not
only unmanly but profane! You risk excommunication
in behaving so!"

"Then let it be, old man, for I will not give her up
now. The king will back me and see this escaped heretic returned to the custody of the Inquisition!"

Hugh gripped Alissende more tightly, the edge of
the blade digging into the tender skin beneath her jaw;
she lifted her chin with a choked whimper as he leaned
in to rasp in her ear, "Come along now, Alissende.
We've no more time to waste."

Then, yelling to his men nearest the door on the
Gospel side of the chapel to give him cover, he began
pulling her with him, slowly and painstakingly making
his way toward the escape he was preparing.

Richard rushed forward with his men, but Damien
lifted his hand to forestall them for a moment, not wanting any further distraction to hinder what he prayed
would happen next.

Desperate, he sought Alissende's frightened gaze,
trying to keep his own calm, in that instant nodding

and lifting his dagger in preparation, hoping she understood his unspoken message to her. He was encouraging her to take action, so that he might save her from the glittering doom at her throat.

And then everything seemed to slow, strung out in images that caused his blood to freeze, even as blind instinct and love took over.

Alissende took a deep breath, the panicked sensation inside her subsiding under the force of Damien's gaze. She felt Hugh pulling at her, felt the sting of the blade at her throat, but she concentrated, remembering, and fisted her hand as she brought it forward. Then in one burst of explosive movement, she drove her elbow into Hugh's belly with all the strength she possessed, at the same time gripping the smallest finger of the hand that held the dagger at her throat, and yanking back on it.

Damien and everything around her seemed to fade in a burst of white-hot light. She felt the blade bite sharply, felt the warm trickle of something—it had to be blood, her shock-dimmed mind supplied—slip down her neck.

I've failed. Oh, God, I've failed . . .

That horrible thought swept through her, the stunning realization overwhelming, sickening. But then suddenly, Hugh let go of her, and with a sudden rush everything that had been fettering her to him seemed to fall away. The world went topsy-turvy, and something hard slammed into her with a jolt that was none too heavenly. It felt like she'd hit the floor. The very hard floor. But she couldn't feel that if she was dead, could she? She frowned in confusion and tried to speak, but no words came out.

"Alissende—oh, God, Alissende. Open your eyes, lady. Answer me."

The low, penetrating voice filled her senses, and calm spread through her. It was Damien's voice, and the unbearable love echoing in it made her want to smile. So she did, opening her eyes at the same time and seeing him hovering over her, before he clasped her to him. Then he pulled back and cupped her cheek, anguish, relief, and laughter all battling for precedence in his expression, making her smile more fully as she murmured, "I am not dead, it seems."

"Nay, thanks be to God," Damien said hoarsely, smiling too as he helped her up. "The wound is slight and should heal without stitching," he murmured, brushing his thumb gently over the stinging cut at her throat. He gazed into her eyes for one long, beautiful moment, all the feelings inside of him apparent in his face, his love for her visibly driving out the fear that had dwelt there.

Then he leaned in and kissed her, gently and so sweetly that she knew she could not be dead, because she could not imagine feeling such sensations if she was no longer in flesh. In fact every inch of her felt the wonder of it, and hungry for more, she pressed her palms to his cheeks and pulled him closer, breaking their caress only when she was too breathless to continue.

But before they could speak aught else to each other, *Mère* came running up to them and pulled Alissende close to her, crying, the tears interspersed with kisses and murmured endearments in French. It was all quite dizzying. Damien apparently tried to move a little apart to give Lady Blanche room, but her mother would have none of it, pulling him closer again, and hugging him too, in gratitude and affection. In the next instant, though, she turned back to Alissende, examining the cut Hugh had given her, before she was gone again like a whirlwind, off to fetch her kit for healing ointment.

"My, but *Mère* moves quickly," Alissende said under her breath. Still feeling dizzy with all that had happened, she reached out to Damien, who supported her, holding her close as she struggled to bring the world around her into focus once more.

The sounds and sights of people—so many people—moving and talking finally broke through her dazed feeling. She looked around her, watching Richard and several others of the Templars moving around the church, containing Hugh's soldiers and trying to restore order among the people, many of whom still appeared distraught themselves. She saw the old priest, bent over near the sanctuary in prayer, his face ashen, likely thanking God for the blessing of living through the disaster that had almost come to pass.

And then she saw him.

Stiffening, Alissende clutched Damien's hand more tightly, unable to tear her gaze from the sight of Hugh, who was lying not ten paces from them, sprawled upon the altar. He was on his back, and his eyes were sightless; his mouth was opened slightly, as if in shock . . . and the hilt of Damien's dagger protruded from the center of his chest.

"You killed him, then," she said with the slightest catch in her voice.

"Aye, Alissende. I am sorry, for I know he was your kin, but I could not risk anything less. When he held that blade to your throat—"

Damien broke off, and Alissende finally tore her gaze away from the body to look at him again. The muscle in his jaw twitched, and a telltale sheen clouded his beautiful eyes, but he shook his head, pausing for a moment before he continued, "I would have done anything to save you, lady. Anything."

"Why?" she asked softly. A feeling similar to the one that had rocked through her when he'd burst into the chapel swept again from her toes to the top of her head, but after all that had happened, she wasn't going to content herself with it alone. She wanted to hear him say it. She needed to hear him say the words aloud to her, so that she would know they were real.

He smiled, the expression somehow gentle and yet wicked, tender but compelling, sending another icy-hot sensation up her spine—a feeling compounded by the delicious, shiver-inducing sweep of his fingers along her cheek as they threaded into her hair to cup the back of her head. He gazed intently into her eyes, murmuring, "I would do anything to keep you safe, Lady Alissende of Surrey, because I love you. More than any man has a right to love a woman, perhaps, but it is true, and I will fight it no longer."

Her eyes welled with tears, then, all that they'd been through together making her realize now more than ever the truth of what she felt inside for him. "I love you just as much, Damien. I will never stop loving you. I never have, through all these years."

He looked humbled by her words, but something was troubling him still, and she brushed her fingers over his brow, trying to smooth the lines of worry there as he glanced away. "What is it?" she asked quietly.

His eyes were dark with uncertainty when he met

her gaze again. "I will need to travel to Scotland, you know," he said, "to live there at least for a while, and perhaps for good. Can you still feel the same about me, knowing that, Alissende?"

Ah, this was an easy one. Her breath caught with the happy tears that kept threatening to overpower her, but she smiled tremulously up at him, lifting her face so that she might brush her lips over his in a kiss. Pressing her brow to his, then, she looked up at him from beneath her lashes, whispering, "My sweet Damien, do you not know that I love you past all boundary of place or time? It does not matter where we must go, as long as I am with you. Only you—for you alone are all that I need for perfect happiness."

"Truly, Alissende?"

"Aye, Damien, truly. With my whole heart and soul, I swear it."

He heaved a grateful sigh and tipped his head up for a moment, but when he looked at her his eyes twinkled mischievously. "You know when you take such a vow it is your sacred duty to see it through?"

"Aye, well, the last one you made to me cut too closely for my comfort."

"What?" He feigned dismay. "I promised to see you within a sennight, didn't I?" He looked up as if calculating. "And that was exactly—"

"—one sennight ago today," she finished for him, arching her brow at him in wicked response. "Almost to the hour."

"Well, I arrived in time, didn't I?"

"Just barely."

Reaching up, she wrapped her arms around his neck, pulling him close to whisper in his ear, "Pray don't ever make me worry so again, love, for there is naught that could harm me more swiftly than to be parted from you forever."

"You will never have to fear again, then, Alissende," he answered, the warmth of his breath tickling her ear, "for I will always find my way back to you, to love you and cherish you, from now until the end of eternity."

"But how can we know, Damien? There is so much darkness at work around us, and so many—"

He gently put his finger to her lips and pulled back enough to look at her, cupping her face again in the tender warmth of his hands. "I know, Alissende," he murmured, pausing, just before he kissed her thoroughly, passionately, and with a depth of feeling so great that it nearly swept her away, to smile as he gazed into her eyes, "because I swear it."

Epilogue

Musselburgh, Scotland
May 1309

When the time had come, it had come swiftly, and there had been no possibility of delay.

Margery Joan de Ashby had made her arrival into the world with a lusty wail, startling her father, who'd come bursting into the birthing chamber, convinced that something was amiss, and bringing her mother to happy, laughing tears with the thought that this little, squirming miracle possessed the voice of an angel, no matter how loud.

It had been the culmination of a series of miracles, Alissende had thought, beginning with their escape from England. The happiest of miracles, in the form of a child who was part of her and Damien together.

"Shall I take her for a while, *chérie?* Michael is

eager to see what she looks like when she is not crying." Lady Blanche said, at Alissende's nod, lifting the warm bundle from her daughter's arms.

"Aye, *Mère;* she has eaten—again," Alissende said, leaning back on her bolster with a relieved sigh. "She should be peaceful for another hour or so, at least," she added, smiling. "But if she begins to fuss, bring her back to me, for I never tire of looking into her tiny face, even if she is howling in demand."

Smiling, too, Lady Blanche started to leave the room, but she looked back over her shoulder at the last moment to say, "Ah, I almost forgot. You should know that your husband has just returned home."

Alissende made a sound of bemused exasperation at the idea that her mother could have kept such news from her for even an instant, but before she could say aught, Damien swept into the room, looking windblown, and so very, very handsome; Alissende's eyes welled with love for him, and she reached out as he came to her side and pulled her into his warm embrace.

"Ah, how I have missed you, my Alissende," he murmured into her hair, pressing soft kisses along her brow and temple before taking her mouth in a hungry kiss. "How fared you and our sweet babe while I was away this time?"

"It was for only three days, Damien," Alissende said, laughing. "You talk as if it has been several months."

"It felt like years."

His expression made her smile again, and she tugged him closer, inviting him to stretch out beside her on the bed. He slid into the position easily, tucking her against him, and she sighed in perfect contentment. She could almost go to sleep. But before she did, she needed to ask about his trip.

"Did you learn any news of Alex, then, in Edinburgh?" Tipping her head up, she met his gaze, basking in the love there, even as she added, "Were you able to confirm that he is in Scotland, even?"

Damien shook his head, leaning back on the pillow himself, now, with a sigh. "Knowing my brother, he could be anywhere, doing just about anything. The ghosts of the past torment him too much, still, for him to rest anywhere for long, I think. And as for the Templar treasure he took with him when he left . . ."

His voice trailed off, and he shook his head again. "I can only pray that he will protect it rather than sell it."

"You think he would exchange something so valuable as that for money?" she asked.

"I cannot say. Reverence has never been his strongest point. But Alex has surprised me before. Perhaps he will find peace and make his way back home to us. God willing, it will be so, though I will keep searching for him in the meantime."

Silently, Alissende nodded; then she closed her eyes and snuggled into her husband once more. *Her husband.* It still felt so wonderful to think that and know it was true. Damien was her husband in truth, and naught in this world could change it.

"I love you, Alissende," Damien said, his lips close to her hair. "I need you to know that."

"And I you, Damien. I will be grateful for every moment we are granted together, every day for the rest of my life."

"Nay, lady, even longer than that," he murmured, and she heard the smile in his voice, even as she began to drift off to sleep.

"How long, then?" she managed to whisper.

The beat of his strong heart was steady beneath her ear, and though her eyes were closed and slumber was swiftly overtaking her, she smiled too, when he answered at last.

"Forever, Alissende . . . forever."

Author's Note

While there are numerous historical tidbits I'd love to share with you about some of the events and people described within the pages of this book, I think it would be best to begin by mentioning one aspect that I found difficult to portray realistically if I was to hold true to the conventions of the romance genre: the depiction of Damien's torture by the French Inquisition.

In actuality, few men, Templar or otherwise, escaped from the Inquisition (except through death) during the years following the mass arrests in France—and the kinds of torture applied to those questioned were far more brutal than what I was free to show in describing what Damien suffered. Rather than go into disturbing detail here, however, I can recommend several texts that not only examine the darker aspects of the interrogations but also elucidate the Templars' rise and fall, as well as elements of the actual trials in various countries, along with commentary on public response to the Order as a whole. These include: *The Knights Templar in Britain,* by Evelyn Lord, *The Templars,* by Piers Paul Read, and *The Trial of the Templars,* by Malcolm Barber. I found all invaluable during my research for this book and for my entire Templar Knights series.

As an interesting aside, I based the final scene of *Sinful Pleasures* on an incident depicted in Barber's book. It seems that in the years following the arrests in France, several provincial councils were called in the Rhineland to consider the case of the Templars. During one of these councils in 1310, which was headed by the Archbishop of Mainz, a group of twenty fully armed Templar Knights burst into the chamber, led by Hugh of Salm, Preceptor at Grumbach. The knights decried the charges that had been leveled against the Brotherhood and essentially used their stunning military prowess to intimidate the council and put an end to the proceedings. In *Sinful Pleasures,* I tried to depict Hugh's men and their reaction to the "human wall" of armed and dangerous Templar Knights in a way similar to what I imagined the Rhineland council must have felt in acknowledging the awe-inspiring sight of the Templars surrounding them.

Speaking further of military skills, the scene wherein Damien teaches Alissende holds of defense is also grounded in real history. During my research I learned that in the Beni Hasan region of Egypt, there are four separate tombs with hundreds of wall paintings depicting an ancient form of grappling and self-defense, dating from 700 BC. Travelers through the region would have almost certainly marveled at such a display, and so it allowed me to provide that element of interest as I wove the plot of my story.

And now a bit about some details involving Damien and Alissende's relationship, as portrayed in this book . . .

I had great fun writing the tournament scene at Odiham—and actually included in the first version of the manuscript quite a bit more detail about the crowd, the vendors, and some of the interactions that might have happened just prior to the entrance of the combatants. Tourneys were a fact of life in the Middle Ages and one of the few chances for men of lower birth to earn social respect. This worked out perfectly in Damien's case, since as a commoner, his level of knightly skill and its successful application on the field would have been one of the few aspects of social status within his control.

Regarding the marriage proxy laws mentioned throughout the book, I stretched common practice a bit. During this period, church weddings were not all that common, whether on the steps, inside the nave, or otherwise. That aspect of marital unions seems to have developed over the course of the next century or so. It was indeed enough for most couples to declare they were wed and consummate the union for it to be considered binding by society—though of course a woman who brought land and/or wealth into a union, as did Alissende, would be more likely to endure an arranged match, or at the least close scrutiny by those who bore an interest in the pairing she made (like the royal family), and this I tried to depict.

To close, I have to say that Damien and Alissende were one of the most enjoyable couples I've written to date. I think it has something to do with the "reunited lovers" aspect (I had a similar kind of fun writing *The Maiden Warrior*), but I also enjoyed each character's personality in the making as well. I'd had Damien, in particular, in mind from the very first moment I conceived the Templar Knights series, and writing about this tormented, deadly angel-warrior who had been scorned in love and toppled from a place of high faith and social acceptance before regaining all he'd lost (and then some) made my writer's heart beat at a swifter pace. In Alissende, I tried to create a woman who could match Damien in mood, sensuality, passion, and depth of feeling. The heartbreak and secrets she herself bore made my efforts to bring these two together both challenging and immensely satisfying at the same time.

I can only hope I succeeded, at least a little bit, in providing that same enjoyable outcome for you as well, the reader of my tale. As always, thanks for coming along on the journey. . . .

MRM

Next month, don't miss these exciting
new love stories only from
Avon Books

The Duke in Disguise by Gayle Callen

An Avon Romantic Treasure

A dashing duke is hiding a dangerous secret, and loving him might be the most daring thing governess Meriel has ever done. But what will happen to their passionate union once she learns the truth?

Silence the Whispers by Cait London

An Avon Contemporary Romance

Cameron's life has been marred by tragedy, but when hunky Hayden Olson moves in next door things begin looking up...if only she'd accept his brazen overtures. But can she find the way to silence the whispers of her past . . . and end the nightmares of her present . . . in his strong arms?

Sins of Midnight by Kimberly Logan

An Avon Romance

Lady Jillian Daventry promises to behave—at least until her sister's coming out! But how can she resist solving a mystery, especially when it brings her into daily contact with handsome Bow Street Runner Connor Monroe.

Be Mine Tonight by Kathryn Smith

An Avon Romance

For nearly six centuries he has roamed the earth . . . a mortal man no longer. But when Prudence Ryland touches his heart, he knows that he must sacrifice everything to save her body . . . and her soul.

Avon Romances

the best in

exceptional authors and unforgettable novels!

DARING THE DUKE
by Anne Mallory
0-06-076223-3/ $5.99 US/ $7.99 Can

COURTING CLAUDIA
by Robyn DeHart
0-06-078215-3/ $5.99 US/ $7.99 Can

STILL IN MY HEART
by Kathryn Smith
0-06-074074-4/ $5.99 US/ $7.99 Can

**A MATCH MADE
IN SCANDAL**
by Melody Thomas
0-06-074231-3/ $5.99 US/ $7.99 Can

SCANDALOUS
by Jenna Petersen
0-06-079859-9/ $5.99 US/ $7.99 Can

RULES OF PASSION
by Sara Bennett
0-06-079648-0/ $5.99 US/ $7.99 Can

KEEPING KATE
by Sarah Gabriel
0-06-073610-0/ $5.99 US/ $7.99 Can

GYPSY LOVER
by Edith Layton
0-06-075784-1/ $5.99 US/ $7.99 Can

SCANDALOUS MIRANDA
by Susan Sizemore
0-06-008290-9/ $5.99 US/ $7.99 Can

A KISS BEFORE DAWN
by Kimberly Logan
0-06-079246-9/ $5.99 US/ $7.99 Can

THE BRIDE HUNT
by Margo Maguire
0-06-083714-4/ $5.99 US/ $7.99 Can

A FORBIDDEN LOVE
by Alexandra Benedict
0-06-084793-X/ $5.99 US/ $7.99 Can

Avon Romantic Treasures

Unforgettable, enthralling love stories, sparkling with passion and adventure from Romance's bestselling authors